Pr

Her

"A lovely installment in a consistently entertaining series."
—*Locus*

"Good entertainment in the romantic fantasy subgenre . . .
Heroes Adrift is well paced, never bogging down . . . a
pleasant way to spend the time." —*Grasping for the Wind*

Resenting the Hero

"This incredible romantic fantasy will appeal equally to
fans of both genres. The sexual tension between the two
protagonists is so strong that readers will feel sparks fly
off the pages." —*The Best Reviews*

"An enchanting fantasy that introduces two interesting
and complex protagonists and a fascinating world . . . The
tale has everything—magic, mayhem, a hint of romance
and a thread of wry humor." —*Romance Reviews Today*

"[A] fast-paced plot . . . The various threads come together
in a satisfying way." —*SFRevu*

"A wry twist on classic fantasy . . . *Resenting the Hero* is
a funny book with occasional dramatic spans . . . a good
choice for a rainy afternoon." —*Infinity Plus*

"An entertaining read . . . sure to be a hit with romance as
well as fantasy readers." —*Fresh Fiction*

Heroes
Return

Moira J. Moore

ACE BOOKS, NEW YORK

THE BERKLEY PUBLISHING GROUP
Published by the Penguin Group
Penguin Group (USA) Inc.
375 Hudson Street, New York, New York 10014, USA
Penguin Group (Canada), 90 Eglinton Avenue East, Suite 700, Toronto, Ontario M4P 2Y3, Canada
(a division of Pearson Penguin Canada Inc.)
Penguin Books Ltd., 80 Strand, London WC2R 0RL, England
Penguin Group Ireland, 25 St. Stephen's Green, Dublin 2, Ireland (a division of Penguin Books Ltd.)
Penguin Group (Australia), 250 Camberwell Road, Camberwell, Victoria 3124, Australia
(a division of Pearson Australia Group Pty. Ltd.)
Penguin Books India Pvt. Ltd., 11 Community Centre, Panchsheel Park, New Delhi—110 017, India
Penguin Group (NZ), 67 Apollo Drive, Rosedale, North Shore 0632, New Zealand
(a division of Pearson New Zealand Ltd.)
Penguin Books (South Africa) (Pty.) Ltd., 24 Sturdee Avenue, Rosebank, Johannesburg 2196,
South Africa

Penguin Books Ltd., Registered Offices: 80 Strand, London WC2R 0RL, England

This is a work of fiction. Names, characters, places, and incidents either are the product of the author's imagination or are used fictitiously, and any resemblance to actual persons, living or dead, business establishments, events, or locales is entirely coincidental. The publisher does not have any control over and does not assume any responsibility for author or third-party websites or their content.

HEROES RETURN

An Ace Book / published by arrangement with the author

PRINTING HISTORY
Ace mass-market edition / August 2010

Copyright © 2010 by Moira J. Moore.
Cover art by Eric Williams.
Cover design by Annette Fiore DeFex.

ISBN: 978-0-441-01952-6

ACE
Ace Books are published by The Berkley Publishing Group,
a division of Penguin Group (USA) Inc.,
375 Hudson Street, New York, New York 10014.
ACE and the "A" design are trademarks of Penguin Group (USA) Inc.

PRINTED IN THE UNITED STATES OF AMERICA

10 9 8 7 6 5 4 3 2 1

To Lucy Maud Montgomery,
whose books I still read occasionally.
A scene in Anne of Green Gables
influenced one of the scenes in this book.

Acknowledgments

Many readers have sent me comments filled with questions, constructive criticism and quips. They have made me think and made me smile. One reader agreed to let me use her lovely name for one of my characters. She will know it when she sees it. And, of course, I am grateful to Jack Byrne, my agent, and Anne Sowards, my editor.

Chapter One

"Seriously," I muttered. "You would think someone would have figured out by now how to build a carriage that didn't cause the passenger to feel every rock and hole." All the jostling about had given me a blistering headache.

"Are you getting old?" Taro asked. "You've been complaining a lot."

I had not. I had merely been making accurate observations. "And you've been unusually quiet," I responded. "Do you think we've switched personalities?"

"Lee, I never complain," he claimed loftily.

"Never?" I snickered.

"Almost never."

"Ha."

All kidding aside, Taro had been uncharacteristically silent for much of our journey. No doubt because we were heading for Flown Raven, Taro's place of birth, and not by choice. If Taro had had his way, we would have never stepped foot in Flown Raven.

But we didn't have a choice. Emperor Gifford, assuming an authority he didn't have, had sent us there, for reasons neither of us could determine. And Taro hadn't been quite himself since we'd gotten the news.

I wasn't thrilled with the transfer, either, for a lot of reasons. There was the fact that we shouldn't have ever been transferred by the Emperor, of course. That just alarmed me. We could have reasonably expected a few more years in High Scape, where we worked with six other Pairs, and where everything we could possibly want was close to hand. Most important, in my own mind, at least, Taro's mother, the Dowager Duchess, didn't live in High Scape. She did live in Flown Raven. In my opinion, that made Flown Raven the worst of all possible posts for us.

I despised that woman.

The carriage drew to a stop. I looked around the edge of one of the curtains. We hadn't reached Flown Raven itself, so I assumed we were taking another break to allow the horses to rest. Our driver seemed unusually careful of his horses. I didn't mind. I'd hate to be stuck out here with an injured animal, but it did seem to lengthen the trip immeasurably.

The door to the carriage was pulled open. "Source Karish," the driver said to Taro. "Shield Mallorough," he greeted me. As he did every time we stopped. He was oddly formal. "You might wish to work your legs."

I did, actually. I preferred riding to sitting in a carriage for days, but the last livery in our path, once learning of our destination, had refused to lend us riding horses, preferring to send a driver and a carriage with us. Technically, we could have insisted on the riding horses, but I didn't like making that kind of fuss. I could understand why a livery wouldn't want to trust us to borrow the horses and arrange for them to be returned when we were going as far as Flown Raven.

So we stepped out, and I spent a few moments enjoying the fresh air and stretching the kinks out of my knees.

Taro lingered by the carriage, though, his gaze a little blank, his mind obviously leagues away. I wished there were a way to make him feel better, but the only handy method I could think of was sex, and I wasn't prepared to do that in a confined space with the driver listening in.

The sky, which had been dark all day, rumbled, and it began to hail. Only little stones, they didn't hurt, but all three of us scrambled back into the carriage. I'd heard of hail that got as big as teacups and I had no interest in risking something like that landing on my head.

I was worried about the horses being unattended. What if they spooked?

The driver looked at Taro. "Can't you fix this?" he demanded.

Taro's eyebrows rose in surprise. "This is just the weather, my dear boy," he told the driver. "Not our bag, I'm afraid."

I glanced at him with concern. I hadn't heard him use that kind of airy tone for a while. It was one he used when he wanted people to assume he was an idiot, when he was feeling uncomfortable.

"Thought you two were supposed to deal with the weather," the driver insisted. "That's what you're paid for."

Well, no, members of the Source and Shield Service, or the Triple S, weren't actually paid. We were supported. We could commandeer rooms in boardinghouses, as fine as we liked, and requisition clothing and food and services. But we could never demand money.

"Ah, if only we could," said Taro. "Hail and rain are so annoying, and snow should be made illegal. It would be delightful if we could just will"—he waved a languid hand—"it all away."

Well, I could affect the weather. Sort of. I just wasn't any good at it. And we weren't telling anyone that, because it wasn't part of a Shield's regular bag of tricks.

"So what do you do?" the driver asked with asperity.

I was surprised to meet someone so ignorant of Sources and Shields and their roles. I wasn't aware that there were people who didn't know what we did. On the other hand, our new post hadn't had a Pair in recorded history, having only recently been afflicted with earthquakes. Perhaps people in this area honestly never thought about Sources and Shields.

"When there is an earthquake, or a tornado, or an erupting volcano, or other natural disaster, I gather up all the forces of these events and channel them"—and this time Taro used both hands to make a sort of waving motion— "away."

"And what does she do?" The driver indicated me with a thrust of his jaw.

"The forces are powerful things, my good man. She makes sure my skull doesn't fly apart while I channel."

Actually, I made sure the forces he wasn't handling didn't rush into the vacuum created by his channeling and crush him, at the same time making sure his brain and heart didn't tear apart under the strain of doing something that was unnatural for the human body to do. But I had a feeling Taro was, for some reason, going for maximum dramatic effect as opposed to accuracy.

The driver sniffed. "Seems to me a man who really knew his stuff wouldn't need some kind of assistant to help him do his job."

Pompous little moron. And I wasn't an assistant.

"Why don't you do something about the hail, then?" Taro suggested in the friendliest of tones. "Show us how it's done."

And the driver surprised me by snorting and saying, "Fine." He left the carriage momentarily and returned carrying a small leather bag. He pulled from it the smallest knife and scabbard I'd ever seen, a small pouch, and what looked like a bleached finger bone of the human variety.

I knew what those trappings meant. He was going to try to cast a spell. He sliced the palm of his hand with the little knife, just a small cut to bring up just a dot of blood. He poured yellow powder from the pouch right onto the blood, and I wondered if that stung. The greenish yellow powder looked like something that would sting. He spat on the same area, and that was just disgusting. I noticed a strange acrid scent rising up from the man's palm. Finally, he crossed the bone through the mess. "Forces of earth, forces of air, clear of the water, skies be more fair. I offer my blood, I offer my will, I seek clear skies, for better or ill."

Ooh, bad poetry. I wondered if I could make up a bunch of rhymes and sell them as a book of spells. I had written some ghastly stuff when I was fifteen or so.

That seemed to be it, but the hail continued. We looked at the driver. "It takes a while to work," he said.

Ah. So whether it took an hour or whether it took all day, he could claim it was his spell that had cleared the skies and Taro and I, in theory, wouldn't know any better.

But I would know. I could feel it when a spell was being cast. I'd felt nothing from him.

Of course, I couldn't tell the difference between when a spell was being cast ineffectively or when it was actually working. That, I thought, would be a nifty skill to have.

At least the carriage hadn't exploded. I had witnessed attempts to cast spells that had destructive results.

And despite my former exposure, it was still something of a shock to see someone so openly attempting to cast a spell. I had spent most of my life happily not thinking about spells, except for the odd time they showed up in novels and plays. I certainly hadn't thought they could actually be real, nor had I known anyone who believed in them.

And then the depth of my ignorance had been revealed. Spells were real. I had seen them work, though I had denied what I'd seen until someone used a spell to save my life. I knew my flaws; I could be hard to persuade of things I didn't want to believe in. But when someone cleans away poison in my blood with a few words and some multicolored fire, even I had to admit there was something to the belief in spells.

Pretending to cast spells was against the law. Actually casting a spell was not, because the official story supported by the law was that spells were nothing more than performances put on by swindlers. The official story was bunk. And the Emperor knew it. He had used a spell during the coronation. I had felt it. I still didn't know what the spell was supposed to accomplish, but I had no doubt one had been cast.

So why were the lawmakers so sure spells were just poetry and ritual with no real effect? Or was that something they were just pretending to believe for some reason?

The driver didn't seem to care who saw him perform—or pretend to perform—his spell. That was interesting. Did he not know that the Emperor had made the sanctions against the performance of spells much more brutal, or did he just not care?

There was no way to measure the passage of time with the sky clouded over, but it seemed to take a while for the hail to stop. That didn't prevent the driver from giving us a look of triumph as he left the carriage once the air was clear again. I wondered if he really thought he could affect the weather, or if he was merely pretending he did.

The driver got the carriage moving. I knew this was the last leg of our trip. I hated the thought of the trip ending. It would mean we were actually in Flown Raven, and there was no getting out of it.

"It won't be that bad," Taro said suddenly.

I looked at him. "I know."

"You're braiding your fingers."

I looked down at my lap, where my fingers were all locked and twisted together. I pulled them apart. Taro was tense enough without my contributing to his unease with my behavior.

"Fiona seemed nice," Taro said to reassure me, naming the cousin whom he'd assisted in acquiring the title of Duchess of Westsea. We'd met her briefly at the Emperor's coronation.

"Aye, she did." Not what I'd expected of a relative of Taro's, she'd had a warm manner and an easy smile.

I heard a strange thud, closely followed by a second. The carriage jerked into a faster speed, and I heard the driver shouting at the horses. Three more thuds sounded against the side of the carriage.

What the hell was going on?

The carriage continued to speed along. It tilted as it took a corner and I slid on my seat. "What's happening?" I shouted.

I received no answer.

Was someone chasing us? It was the only reason I could think of for the speed, but who would be chasing us? Why?

I pulled the curtain away from the window and took a look outside. All I could see were trees racing by.

Taro and I were bounced and jolted within the carriage. I felt helpless. There was nothing I could do to control what was happening. There was nothing Taro could do, either. He had one hand propped against the wall of the carriage, the other on the seat, as he tried to stay centered.

There was another hard jolt as a wheel clearly hit a hole in the road. I was sure the wheel must have been broken by the abuse, but we kept rattling along, just as quickly as before.

I held on to Taro's arm. I didn't know why that made me feel infinitesimally better. It just did.

The carriage took another turn. It tilted, hard. Time seemed to slow as the carriage held askew, as if it were deciding what to do next. Then it completed its fall, landing Taro and me in a heap on the side of the carriage.

Taro could be heavy.

A few moments later, the door was yanked open. "Out, now," a gruff voice ordered.

It was difficult to get out of a carriage on its side. It took some time to accomplish it. The carriage had fallen into a ditch, and the mud on the sides covered our trousers as we climbed out.

Our driver was sitting on the ground, blood pouring from his right temple. There were arrows sticking out of the side of the carriage. I guessed they were the source of the thuds.

Two men held four horses. A third had a bow with an arrow aimed in our general direction. The fourth person stood beside the carriage. "I'll be taking your earrings," she ordered. Taro and I took out our earrings and put them in her palm. "The harmony bobs, too."

I didn't mind losing the earrings, but my harmony bob was special to me. It was a sign of affection from Taro. And it had helped save my life.

"Get your bags."

The trunks hadn't been shaken from their bindings. That meant they were hard to untie.

"Hurry up!" the woman snapped.

I couldn't believe we were being robbed. We had the worst luck in the world.

Once the trunks were free and open, the woman picked through our belongings. She was apparently disappointed with what she found. "You're Triple S," she muttered. "You're supposed to be rich."

It always amazed me, the rumors that were out there about Sources and Shields. We owned very little, though I didn't doubt there were some Triple S members who used their right to requisition goods to acquire fabulous jewels. That might make them appear rich in the eyes of regulars.

She didn't fail to find the little jewelry Taro and I did have, or the small stash of coins Taro kept for gambling. Everything else we owned ended up on the muddy bottom of the ditch. I was too cowardly to object. The idea of being speared by an arrow horrified me.

"Don't tell anyone about this," the woman said. "Or we'll come back for you."

The hell with that. I would be telling everyone we met.

The four thieves rode away, leaving us in a mess.

"How are you doing?" Taro asked the driver. "Can you see all right?"

"Aye, I'm not hurt bad," said the driver.

"Lee?"

"I'm fine." I was sure I would have an array of bruises soon, but that wasn't worth mentioning.

"Do you think we could push the carriage back over?" Taro asked the driver.

The driver laughed.

Under the driver's instructions, we freed the horses from the carriage and gave them to the driver to lead. What could be packed on the horses was, but Taro and I each ended up dragging a trunk behind us. The ache that created between my shoulder blades was brutal.

This probably wouldn't have happened if the livery had given us horses to ride. We would have been able to outrun the thieves.

On the other hand, they might have fired the arrows directly at us. That would have been messy. And it would have hurt.

It was twilight when we first saw the wall of thick, dark gray stone that was ominous in its solidity. It was an unnecessary remnant of a time when titleholders battled each other for land and power. We passed through an iron gate being held open by two servants. There was an emblem high on the gate that I recognized as the family's crest. Taro used to wear a ring with that emblem.

The grounds beyond the gate were lush and green,

with small bushes huddled against the base of the house.
I supposed it was a house. I thought it looked more like
a castle would look, though it lacked the size and gran-
deur of Erstwhile, the seat of the Emperor. It was made of
stone, proof of a people who didn't worry about natural
disasters. It looked long, and it appeared to be four stories
high. There were two towers, one at either end, with only
slits for windows. The rest of the windows in the structure
were wide, and I thought I saw some kind of iron inlaid in
a diamond pattern. All of those windows had shutters, odd
single and heavy-looking slats that were propped up over
the windows and meant to be lowered to cover the windows at night. I'd never seen that arrangement before.

The front door was huge, three men high and four men
wide, arching to a point at the top. It looked solid. Impen-
etrable. Like it would make an ominous clanging sound
when it closed and one might feel trapped within. Like a
prison.

Beyond the house, I could see, in the distance, a significantly smaller house in the same style. The dowager house, I guessed, where Taro's mother lived. She was
going to be our far-too-close neighbor, as we would be
Fiona's guests for as long as we were stationed in Flown
Raven. That meant we were likely to see the Dowager
Duchess on a weekly and possibly daily basis. Cold, ma-
nipulative, evil wench of a woman.

There was a third building that looked like a stable.

Beyond the buildings was what looked like some kind
of mountain range, but smaller. More like a rocky hill
range. It looked kind of vicious and dark. I knew that beyond that, at some point, was the West Sea, and that Fiona
controlled the waters of that sea for several leagues. As
she controlled hundreds and hundreds of acres of farm-
land all around us.

What did it feel like, I wondered, to control so much?
To be so important to the people who lived on and worked
that land and those waters? It was a staggering amount of

responsibility. I certainly wouldn't want it. I could understand why Taro hadn't wanted it, either.

Two people ran out from the back of the house as we approached the steps leading to the front door. "Sir, ma'am," the blond servant said. "What has happened?"

"We were robbed," Taro answered grimly. "The driver is injured."

"I'm not," the driver protested. "I don't have the coin for a healer. Especially now. Don't call one."

"We had to leave the carriage in the ditch," Taro added.

"I'll have someone fetch it," said the blond servant. "You, there," he said to the driver. "Come with us and you'll be seen to for the night. Sir, madam, if you would approach the main entrance. We'll see to your trunks."

Couldn't I slip around to the back, too? My hair was half falling down and I was a sweaty mess. Not at all the image I'd hoped to present to the Duchess of Westsea and her family.

We climbed the steps toward the front door. The door seemed even larger when I stood right in front of it. Really, who needed a door so large? What purpose did it serve, other than the attempt to intimidate people?

I was intimidated by a door. That was sad.

Taro knocked on the door.

This was it.

Chapter Two

The door was opened by a tall, slim man of middle years, his silver hair cut short. He wore a dark tunic and trousers and a belt with a lot of keys. "Source Shintaro Karish and Shield Dunleavy Mallorough?" he asked.

Taro wore a black braid on his left shoulder that identified him as a Source. I wore a white braid that identified me as a Shield. Everyone would know who we were as soon as they saw us.

"Yes. We're reporting to Her Grace to assume our post," Taro answered formally.

Not that we had to report to Fiona. She had nothing to do with the Triple S beyond offering us a place to stay. But it was her house, and presenting ourselves to her first thing was the polite thing to do.

"Of course." The man bowed. If he noticed anything odd about our appearance, he was too polite to say so. "Please come in." He closed the door behind us, and the sound of it wasn't at all ominous. "I am called Bailey, and it is my pleasure to show you to Her Grace. It is also one of my responsibilities to see to any of your needs, so please don't hesitate to ask me for anything." The man seemed to pause a bit, and then he looked at Taro. "I was a footman here when sir was a boy here. If it is not too presumptuous of me to say so, it is a pleasure to see how well you've done, and to see you back home."

I'd never considered the possibility of some of the staff still being the same as when Taro lived here. That was twenty years ago. This was horrible. It was enough that we had to live in the house that was the source of so many bad memories for Taro, but to have to deal with the people who were here while it was happening? That had to be a nightmare.

I looked at Taro. His face was blank. "Thank you, Bailey," he said.

I wondered if he remembered Bailey.

"My pleasure. Please come this way."

The foyer was gorgeous. A large rectangle of space with the ceiling stretched high to the fourth floor, each floor decorated by a long dark balcony allowing people to look over and down to the foyer. The walls were mostly a pale cream color, but were painted with beautiful landscapes of light green and blue. Our feet clattered against white marble floors. It was an airy, peaceful room, uncluttered and tasteful. I liked it.

Opposite the entrance was another door. Bailey, with a slow, smooth gait, headed toward it. Before we reached it, he gestured toward the door to our right. "That way lies the court room, where the Landed and others give their requests to Her Grace." He gestured to the door on the left end of the foyer. "The ballroom is through there. Our Grace will be holding a ball to announce your arrival to the community."

Oh. I had to nip that immediately. "That's really not necessary." Nor wanted. At least, not by me.

"It has already been planned, ma'am. In Flown Raven it is considered crucial to have new members of the community properly introduced. It is merely common etiquette."

I sighed, feeling chastised. I would have preferred to keep my head down, stay unnoticed, so I could explore and meet people on my own terms. Instead, I was going to be put on display. I never performed well in front of an audience.

Bailey led us through the door, letting us into a wide corridor of dark paneled wood. "The library is through there," Bailey said, indicating a door on our right. "And the music room is there"—gesturing at a door on our left. "I believe a more thorough tour is planned for tomorrow. Of course, sir might remember a great deal."

"Not as much as you might expect," Taro muttered. He'd spent most of his childhood locked in his bedroom. He wouldn't feel familiar with most of the rest of the house.

"That is the dining room," Bailey said, pointing at another door. "Cook will prepare trays for you tonight, to enjoy while you are meeting with the family. We will be preparing baths for you later." He opened a door and stepped through into some sort of sitting room, a spacious room scattered with seats and settees, filled with windows and candlelight.

"Your Grace, Your Grace, Source Shintaro Karish and Shield Dunleavy Mallorough."

There were four people in the room, three of them sitting on the floor. There was Fiona Keplar, Taro's cousin on his father's side and the Duchess of Westsea. She was a tall, slim woman with wispy blond hair. There was a man I assumed to be Fiona's husband, Dane, who as he stood showed himself to be a tall, stocky man with dark eyes and hair. The blond toddler at their feet was no doubt their son, Stacin. I couldn't even guess the identity of the slim, blond, bored young man sprawled out on one of the settees.

"She knows who we are, Bailey," Taro teased the man I had already figured was probably too serious all the time.

"Things should be done the way they are supposed to be done, sir," Bailey chided. I was pretty sure he wasn't supposed to do that—correct Taro—but I liked him the better for it.

Fiona stood, picking up her son with her. "What in the world happened to you?" she asked abruptly.

"We were robbed," Taro told her, leaning forward to kiss her on the cheek.

Fiona drew back. "My gods, are you all right?"

"Just some bumps and bruises."

"What did you lose?"

"Our jewelry."

"Where did this happen?"

"Just up the road."

Fiona looked angry. "I do apologize. It is my responsibility to keep order."

"I don't know how you can prevent crime within your borders," said Taro. "These things happen."

"People are supposed to respect me so much that they wouldn't dare attack my people."

I'd been keeping my mouth shut, feeling it was Taro's place to do the talking, but I couldn't let that slide. "I think part of the definition of a criminal is a lack of respect for authority."

"What did they look like?" Fiona asked.

I let Taro give her the descriptions. He had a better eye and memory for that kind of detail.

"We'll ask around to see if anyone recognizes these people, or if there have been any other robberies," Fiona said. "I think our guests could use some tea, Bailey. Or would either of you prefer brandy?"

Taro and I both agreed to tea. Bailey left. Then we all stood about awkwardly. This was Taro's family. All the other members of his family, those I had met or heard about, were complete prats. I suspected Fiona was different, but I didn't know what to say to her.

I didn't know what Taro's excuse was.

"I never expected to have the title," Fiona blurted. "Never in my whole life."

"Neither did I." Taro grinned, and there was something sharp about the expression. "Better you than me."

"Thanks," Dane said sourly.

His tone made me curious. Was he not happy about being married to a duchess and having to move to Flown Raven? It was hard to tell; he looked calm enough. I hadn't officially met Dane yet, as he hadn't been in Erstwhile when I met Fiona. "Good evening," I said, holding out my hand. "I'm Dunleavy."

Dane smiled sheepishly. "I'm Dane. It's good to finally meet you." We shook, and so did Dane and Taro.

"Stand up, Tarce," Fiona ordered the young man, who raised an eyebrow in response but otherwise didn't move. "Where are your manners?"

"You claim I've never had any, my dear sister," he drawled.

"Gods forbid you ever prove me wrong."

"But you are never wrong, Fiona, my love." Despite his words, he did stand and offer me his hand. He was very tall, and before I met Taro I would have thought Tarce impossibly handsome. "Welcome to the middle of nowhere."

"You didn't have to come with us, Tarce."

"Where would I live but with my beloved sister?" He offered his hand to Taro, who shook it silently, and then he went back to his seat.

"And this," said Fiona, cuddling her son close to her, "is Stacin."

Stacin wasn't interested in meeting us, if the way he buried his face in his mother's neck was any indication. He was cute, though, all rumpled blond hair and, when I saw them, big blue eyes. "Good evening, Stacin," I said, feeling foolish using formality on such a young child, but unaware of what else I could do.

"Greetings, little man," Taro said, lightly rubbing a little fist with the tip of his finger.

Stacin chanced a quick peek at him and then buried his face again.

"Isn't this sweet," a sour voice said from the main doorway. We all turned to see a woman lounging against the side of the door at the end of the room, a tall, slim woman with blond hair and blue eyes. She was scowling. "Thank you so much for letting me know they'd arrived." She pushed herself away from the door and headed for the liquor sidebar.

"I'd hoped to give them a chance to relax before dealing with you," Fiona snapped, her change in manner surprising me. "Shintaro, Dunleavy. This is my sister, Daris Keplar."

"Your older sister, Daris Keplar," she corrected. She looked at Taro. "The one you decided not to give the title to." She filled a tumbler to the rim with brandy. "Despite the fact that I'm older."

Wonderful. An instant enemy. Taro didn't need that; he already had his mother. And it looked like Daris could really hold a grudge. It had been more than two years since Fiona had taken the title, and Daris was still bitter.

Zaire, that was a lot of brandy to be gulping down like water on a hot day.

Everyone knew that the titles didn't have to go to the oldest sibling. They went to whomever the original titleholder gave the hereditary code or password to before death, in most cases. Or in Taro's case, whomever the potential titleholder—that being Taro—gave the code to in order to avoid taking the title himself. Anyone could be chosen to receive the code. I didn't know why he'd picked Fiona; he never talked about it much. But clearly his choice, of the family members I'd met so far, was the best one.

Two maids came into the room using the same door Daris had used. They were carrying trays. "I hope you don't mind," Fiona said, "but we usually eat in here. The dining room is a cold and forbidding place. We don't use it unless the numbers demand it."

The trays were placed on a small round table, possibly used as a card table, and when we sat the maids laid a serviette on each of our laps. "Thank you," I said. "I really appreciate it." Actually, it made me uncomfortable.

"Yes, it's very kind," Taro added.

"Oh, aren't we all polite," Daris sneered. She was more than halfway through her brandy. "Treating the servants like you think they're real people. I'm not going to let you ignore me, you know."

What an unpleasant person.

"Believe me, Daris." Fiona sighed. "No one could ignore you."

"He could." Daris pointed at Taro. "He ignored me right out of a title. This should have been mine."

How very presumptuous of her. It wasn't as though she had been born expecting to inherit Westsea. She'd had no expectation of anything until Taro handed the whole lot over to Fiona.

"Well, it isn't," said Fiona. "And it never will be, for I have already chosen my heir and you're not it. Now, you've humiliated yourself enough for tonight, so I suggest you remove yourself to your suite."

Daris snorted. "You can't send me to my room like a child."

"I can and I will. I will have two of the footmen escort you to your suite, if necessary, and have one stand there as a guard all night, if you force me to."

That seemed an overreaction.

Daris rolled her eyes, slammed her glass of brandy on the sidebar with a splash, and stormed out of the room via the staircase at the back.

This room had so many entrances to it.

"I apologize for my sister," said Fiona. "As you can see, she is quite bitter about how things turned out."

Then why was she here? Why didn't she stay in Centerfield?

I looked at Tarce, who noticed and looked right back at me. Was he bitter, too?

Then he smirked at me. That confused me, so I stopped looking at him.

"I never thought about what difficulties you might encounter when I chose you," said Taro.

"There was no reason why you should have," Fiona assured him. "And it's not your fault. I didn't have to take the title, and Daris's reaction isn't entirely unexpected. Please don't let her disturb you. And please treat this as your home, for it is." She hitched her son up higher into her arms. "It's time this one was in bed. Enjoy your meal. I'll be back down momentarily." She took Stacin up the staircase.

Feeling a little awkward to be eating in front of people who were not, I looked down at the table. Each tray had a small bowl of cold, savory soup, a chunk of heavy dark bread, a few slices of pale green cheese, and flakes of some kind of fish I'd never encountered before. It was a light meal but tasty and filling, perfect after a day of travel.

"The house seems in sound shape," Taro commented to Dane. "Did you suffer much damage in the earthquakes?"

"The house didn't," said Dane. "But some of the tenants' homes were destroyed, and the tremors wreaked havoc on the stages and the flakes."

"Stages and flakes?" I asked.

"Structures built along the shorelines. They're used in preparing the fish for transport and market. You'll see them in a day or so." Dane smiled. "You'll be learning a fair bit about fishing and whaling, I expect."

Two things I'd never particularly wanted to learn anything about.

"Was anyone hurt?"

"Two wee ones died when their cottages collapsed."

That was grim. And it was my fault. Taro had been able to feel the earthquakes in Flown Raven while we were still in High Scape. At the time, we hadn't known the events were taking place in Flown Raven. We had only known that Taro had barely been able to control his channeling, and I had barely been able to keep my Shields up. I'd made Taro stop.

Those deaths were my fault.

"That won't be happening again," Taro promised.

That, I thought, was optimistic. We had no reason to believe we'd have an easier time channeling in Flown Raven itself than we had in High Scape. But that was none of Dane's concern, and it was time to change the subject. "Were you involved in fishing and whaling in Centerfield?" I asked Dane.

"Whaling, yes. Though I didn't always do much of the hard work. I mostly ran the books for estate production. That's what I do here, too. Fiona hates working with numbers. Not that she really has time to do it herself. This estate is a complex operation, with both farming and fishing tenants. Everything you're eating was caught or made on our grounds."

"It's delicious," I said.

"We'll show you around tomorrow, if you like, to meet some of the tenants and see if there's anything you'd like to take your hands to."

That was an interesting idea. I'd always wanted to be able to do something with my hands.

"And you needn't worry about looking for company. There are dozens of families within a day's ride, and there is always something going on."

Hm. Within a day's ride. That wasn't quite the easy access to company that Taro was used to. In fact, now that I thought of it, there probably wasn't easy access to any of the things—the horse racing, the gambling halls, the

variety of taverns—that Taro was used to. He was going
to go out of his mind with boredom.

All right. I would just have to make sure he didn't get
bored. I had no idea how I was going to accomplish that,
but lack of competence had never stopped me before.

There was a short shout from the stairway, followed by
the unmistakable thuds and bumps of someone falling
down the stairs. My heart in my throat, I joined Taro,
Dane and Tarce in rushing to the bottom of the stairs.

Fiona was sprawled halfway down them, bent in an
odd and painful-looking angle. We all froze, unsure how
best to help, and I worried that Fiona's stillness meant
she'd snapped her neck.

Then she blinked and said, "Please."

Dane stepped forward. "Where are you hurt?"

"Everywhere."

"Anyplace more than others?"

"I can't tell."

"Maybe we shouldn't move her until a healer can get
here," I suggested.

"Get me up," Fiona ordered.

Dane climbed up the stairs and slowly picked Fiona up
in an impressive show of precise strength. He carried her
to a settee, and the way she moved to make herself comfortable assured me that she didn't have a dangerous injury. She was, however, favoring her left knee.

"What happened?" Dane asked as he yanked on a
bellpull.

Fiona accepted a glass of brandy from Tarce. "I don't
know. My foot just flew out from under me."

"Were you light-headed or distracted?"

"No. Nothing like that. I just slipped."

Fiona was looking a little pale, and I watched Taro to
see if he was going to do anything about her pain. He had
the ability to ease it, which was not a regular skill for
Sources. It was a badly kept secret. He didn't want the
Triple S council to know about it, but he had helped

enough people in High Scape that it seemed everyone in that city had heard the rumors about him.

Taro made no move toward his cousin. Perhaps he thought the pain was not great enough for him to expose himself, for Fiona was very composed. I thought any hope of his hiding his gift was overly optimistic. We were going to be living here for a while, and eventually something would come up compelling him to help someone.

I chose one of the lighter lamps and carried it to the bottom of the stairs. I saw a flash of someone in the darkness at the top. "Hey there," I called. They didn't come back.

"What are you doing, Lee?" Taro asked.

"Looking for something on the stairs to slip on."

"Well?"

"I don't see anything. But there was someone up there."

"Probably someone heard Fiona's fall," said Dane.

"Then why didn't they come down?"

"It wouldn't be appropriate for them to come down and gawk at her. They need to wait to be called."

I supposed that made sense.

"I can't believe this," Fiona muttered, embarrassment bringing a blush to her cheeks. "Your first night here."

I almost told her I was used to it.

Chapter Three

When I woke up the next morning, it was still dark, and I could hear Taro breathing quietly beside me. That meant it was much too early for me to be getting up. I wondered what woke me, for in general I was the sort to sleep in until something forced me out of bed. I lay and listened, wondering if it was a noise that had woken me up, but I heard nothing strange.

I was hungry, though. Starving, in fact, my stomach curling into a knot in its protest of the lack of sustenance. I lay still awhile longer and watched the air lighten a little, but I really didn't think I could wait until whenever the house served breakfast. I was that hungry.

When this had happened in the Triple S residence in High Scape, I'd simply gone down to the kitchen for some bread and cheese.

Fiona had told me to treat this place as my home.

But I didn't like the idea of taking advantage of that invitation so soon.

Who would it bother if I went down to the kitchen and nibbled on something?

Damn it.

I slipped out of the biggest bed I'd ever slept in, wrapped myself in my dressing gown and made my way through the maze of chairs, settees and tables sprinkled throughout our bedchamber and sitting room. Once I was out in the hall, I couldn't remember which direction took me to which set of steps, so I went right, because I was fairly sure I would hit stairs eventually. And I did.

I saw some candlelight curving around the walls, and a few moments later I heard sounds. Odd, grunting sounds. Frowning, I moved a little faster, and I came off the stairs onto a large, wide balcony. I was looking down into a large, long room. It was lit up with candles and Fiona and Dane were standing in it. It took a few moments for me to figure out what they were doing, it was so bizarre.

I saw Fiona strike out at Dane with her fist. I saw Dane block her blow and slap her on the face. Hard.

For a few moments, I was too stunned to do anything. Then I shouted, "Hey!" and the two of them broke apart and looked up at me. "What the hell is going on?" I ran down the next flight of stairs and jumped the last couple of steps to the floor.

"Don't worry," Dane said, stepping forward with his hands out. "It's all right."

"I wasn't asking you," I snapped. "Fiona?"

"It's fine, Dunleavy," she said. "I walked into it."

"What the hell does that mean?"

"We're just training."

"Training for what?"

"So I can protect myself."

"By him slapping you? That hard?"

"Just watch. Dane?"

Dane stood before her. She was the first to throw a punch, which he dodged before striking back. She evaded his fist and reached out with her foot, hooking it behind his knee. He crumpled to his knees and she punched him in the nose. He rolled away and Fiona pressed forward, kicking and striking at him. He stopped suddenly, grabbing the leg on which Fiona's weight was resting and yanking her off her feet. She landed flat on her back on the hard floor.

I covered my eyes with my hands. "Are you crazy?" I demanded.

"It's wise for the titleholder to be able to fight," Dane answered breathlessly.

I uncovered my eyes. Fiona was still on the floor, the breath clearly knocked out of her, while Dane sat on the floor beside her, unconcerned. "This is insane. What if you really hurt each other?"

"Then we stop, though, of course, we wouldn't have that luxury in a real fight."

Fiona was finally able to breathe, and after a few more moments she sat up. "I'm fine."

"You're demented."

She grimaced. "Is there something I can do for you, Dunleavy?"

I suddenly felt embarrassed. I was presuming on a familiarity that didn't exist. "I'm sorry. I just got turned around. I'll go back up to my room." I ran back up the stairs, ignoring dignity. What a horrible nearly first impression.

Daylight was much stronger when I found my way up to the suite I shared with Taro. And I smelled coffee.

I saw Taro, dressed for the day, standing at a window and staring out. His posture wasn't quite as correct as it usually was. His shoulders seemed a little slumped.

I wondered just how hard it was for him to be here.

"Where have you been?" he asked.

"I was looking for something to eat."

"The girl brought something for us."

"Which girl?"

"She said her name is Lila. Apparently Fiona just hired her to see to us."

"She didn't need to do that." In fact, I wished she hadn't. We didn't need a personal servant.

He shrugged. "It is done."

I looked for and found the source of the wonderful coffee aroma. It was a large silver pot of coffee on a tray that held also a pot of tea, plates of pastry, cheese and fruit, and a letter with the Triple S emblem addressed to me.

"Lila said that came for you over a week ago."

I poured myself a cup of coffee and grabbed a pastry, then settled at a table. After a few sips of coffee and mouthfuls of the delightfully light pastry that tasted of almonds, I cracked open the letter.

To Shield Dunleavy Mallorough:

I trust this missive finds you and your Source in good health and meeting your obligations with competence.

As you are aware, it is the honor and duty only of the council of the Source and Shield Service to assign the posts of our Pairs. Be not alarmed. It can be understood why you and your Source accepted your transfer, but we trust you understand why we need to remind His Imperial Majesty that assigning the posts of our Pairs is not one of his responsibilities. It is for this reason that we ask for a complete account of the circumstances leading up to the oath of fealty given by your Source and the transfer made by His Majesty.

You may or may not be aware of the Source and Shield Service policy, which dictates that Sources are not to be posted at the places of their birth. Sources have been known to experience difficulties channeling in such circumstances. We require from you careful

*observation of your Source's performance and a report
describing such.*

*For the same reason, we request from you a report
of the circumstances surrounding your temporary re-
moval from the roster of High Scape by Her Imperial
Majesty Empress Constia.*

*Finally, you resumed your post at High Scape only
a few months ago after being absent from that post for
over a year. We are aware that this absence was due to
an order of the Empress Constia. Again, this is an action the Crown lacks the authority to take. Despite several requests, you have not yet informed us of the
nature of the reason behind your absence, and where
the relevant activity took place. We expect a thorough
explanation of this matter in your next report.*

*Yours very truly,
Shield Kayan Lucitani
Source and Shield Service Council*

Wonderful. What an annoying letter. I couldn't really
explain why the Emperor had done what he did, because
I couldn't figure out what the man was thinking. There
was no logical reason for the Emperor to send Taro to
Flown Raven. The man didn't like Taro. Unless the Emperor knew being sent to Flown Raven would be a punishment for Taro, not a reward, but how would he?

I couldn't tell the council what had been going on with
the Empress, because we had been sworn to secrecy. The
Empress was dead and could no longer hold us accountable for keeping that secret, but I still didn't think it was
wise to tell anyone that she had chosen us to look for the
descendants of the collateral line to the throne, and that
she had sent us to the remote southern island of Flatwell
to do so. I didn't know what the repercussions would be
if we told anyone, but I was sure they would be nasty.

So that was going to be a short couple of paragraphs.

As to Taro experiencing difficulties, we already knew that. "They want me to tell them how well we channel here."

Taro frowned. "We'll channel well enough."

"You know we've had difficulties before."

"You were ill. We'll do better now."

"I'm not so confident."

"We're here now. We weren't meant to channel from so far away. Now that we're here, it will be better."

Could that be true? "The Triple S must have forbidden Sources being posted at their birth places for a reason."

"I think we can agree that the Triple S doesn't know everything."

That was true. "But if we tell the Triple S we're having trouble, they might transfer us." If they could. Sure, the Triple S was supposed to be independent, but its expenses were paid with money set aside by the Crown. Practically speaking, the Triple S couldn't afford to try to discipline the Emperor. They simply lacked the power.

Taro stiffened. "I was born here," he said. "These people have supported my family for generations. I won't desert them."

I was shocked. Taro had never shown any kind of loyalty to Flown Raven. "They won't be deserted. Another Pair will be sent here."

"That won't be the same as me looking after them."

No. It would be better, because it would not be a Source from Flown Raven. But Taro clearly wasn't in the mood to be sensible, and he might be right. Channeling might be easier for us now that we were in Flown Raven.

A maid walked into the room. I was surprised that she didn't knock, and I was uncomfortable at being seen by her in my nightgown. She didn't appear to feel there was anything unusual in her behavior. "His Lordship"—that was Dane—"asks to speak with Source Karish and Shield Mallorough. Are you receiving?"

"We are, my dear girl," Taro announced in a complete change of tone. "I'll see him in the sitting room so my lovely Shield can fortify herself against the demands of the day."

"Of course, sir," the maid murmured as Taro wafted by her. She curtsied to me, which just looked wrong, and closed the door behind her.

I wolfed down another pastry and gulped down the rest of my cup of coffee. In my dressing room, some invisible person had hung up all of my clothes. I had no idea what we were going to be doing that day, but a tour had been mentioned, so I put on trousers and a shirt.

I entered the sitting room at the tail end of some comment Taro was making. Dane was frowning at him. Not in anger, I thought. More like confusion.

Dane had changed his clothes. His nose was very red. I wondered if he and Fiona had continued fighting after I'd left.

He smiled when he saw me. "Ah, Shield Mallorough, you're looking lovely this morning."

I was not. I was looking as plain as I possibly could, with loose clothing that did nothing to help my unremarkable figure, not a scrap of cosmetics to disguise my pale skin, and my red hair tied loosely at the base of my head. I hadn't had the time to make myself look good.

"Have the two of you eaten?"

"I have," I said, and Taro nodded.

"Good. I've been dispatched by my lady to show you the house. It's possible to get lost here, and we want you to be comfortable. It's your home now, and it's been quite a while since Taro lived here. He might not remember everything."

"I would be delighted to see the house," I said. "But Taro might have a report to write to the Triple S." Taro didn't have any such report. As a rule, Sources didn't write reports. But I thought he might not wish to face all the memories that might be lurking in his childhood home.

Taro frowned at me. "Was there anything about my writing a report in that letter you got?"

"No."

"Then I'm good to go."

All right, if that was what he wanted.

"Good," said Dane. "I figure we should start at the court room and we'll work our way up. We ask that you never go up to the fourth floor. All of the servants' quarters are up there and we want their privacy to be undisturbed."

We followed him down a different set of stairs from the one we'd taken up the night before. We took two flights and ended up in a long room with a bit of a throne-like chair at one end and rows of seats along the walls.

"This is the court room," Dane announced. "This is where the people of Westsea come to ask for assistance, make complaints, and hear news from away. There is no judge in these parts, so Fiona hears disputes as well. She sits once a week."

That would be a tough job, making those kinds of decisions. I wouldn't want to have to do it. It would have been interesting, though, to watch Taro doing it. He could be very lordly when he wished. "So everyone waits in those chairs?" It was considerate, I thought, to make sure the petitioners were comfortable.

"Those are for the spectators."

"People who have no stake in the disagreements watch them?" As though it were some kind of entertainment?

"Aye. It's considered important for people of the area to see justice being done and all that."

"So who are the usual spectators?"

"The High Landed, mostly."

Ouch. So some average person would have to beg for assistance with all those aristocratic strangers watching and probably commenting. That was a harsh test of fortitude. I supposed, though, it would discourage inappropriate or vexatious suits.

We followed Dane from the court room to the sitting room we'd been in the night before, through that room and into the second largest dining room I'd ever seen. A wide table of blackwood stretched from one end of the room to the other, long enough, I figured, to comfortably seat about sixty people. It was bare, gleaming in the morning light shining through the row of windows in the northern wall. Candelabra peppered the southern wall, and the eastern and western walls were painted with more landscape murals.

"We don't eat in here much," Dane told us. "The servants expected us to, when we first arrived, but it would be ridiculous, the four of us eating at this enormous table."

"Were all the staff here when you arrived?" I had no idea how that sort of thing worked.

"We brought some people with us, and we had to let a few go because they weren't able to tolerate the change in titleholder"—I wondered what that meant, exactly—"but it's mostly the same people who were here under the Duke." He headed toward another door, which opened into a tiny alcove and then another door. "This is the kitchen. Attention, everyone!"

For this room, unlike the others, was full of people working. They all halted their slicing of vegetables and scrubbing of pans to look at Dane. Then they looked at us, some with interest, some with indifference, and a couple with scowls. I wondered how we'd managed to annoy them so quickly.

"I just wanted to introduce you all to Source Karish and Shield Mallorough. I expect you to show them the same quality of care you've shown my family."

His words made me a little uncomfortable. They seemed to imply the staff didn't know how to do their jobs without being told. It was kind of insulting.

"Now, Shintaro, Dunleavy, are you able to cook for yourselves?"

That was an unexpected question.

"I can," Taro answered. "I wouldn't expect much from Lee."

Prat. "I can cook," I added. Just not very well. And I hoped he wasn't suggesting we demonstrate right then. The long row of scrubbed stoves looked different from anything I'd seen before, and they were intimidating.

"We ask that should you wish for something during the night, you prepare it yourself. We prefer that the staff isn't disturbed, once they've bedded down."

"Of course," I said, but I wouldn't be doing any cooking while half-asleep. I'd probably burn the whole place down. "What's that?" I asked, pointing at an odd figurine on the wall in one corner of the room. It had a star shape for the head, its body was made by a circle around a cross, and its limbs were all different lengths. It was quite ugly.

"It's a kitchen guardian," he answered. "It's to protect the food from rotting and poison."

Interesting. I wondered if it actually worked.

The next room was the ballroom. I looked around, noticing details I'd missed before, distracted as I was by the fight between Fiona and Dane. The floor was wood instead of the marble that seemed to have been laid through most of the rest of the first story. There was a large musicians' alcove at one end. The walls were vaguely reflective. On the ceiling was a chandelier so large I couldn't help thinking it was destined to fall. On the east side of the room were a line of smaller rooms where guests would rest and refresh themselves in privacy.

The next room had a huge piano in it, a bass fiddle, and some music stands. "Do either of you play any instruments?" Dane asked.

We both shook our heads.

"I always thought it strange you didn't play anything," Taro said to me. "Music affects you so powerfully."

That was a polite way of saying music could make me

act like an idiot. Shields tended to be sensitive to music, to the point that a martial air could make us violent, or a love song make us willing to sleep with someone we normally wouldn't go near. I was more sensitive than most. That was the reason I didn't play anything. It would be particularly embarrassing if I caused myself to be stupid with my own music.

"Fiona and I can't play anything, either. Maybe we can get Stacin started on something. It seems a shame to leave such a beautiful room unused." Then it was through a hallway and into what could only be a library. The room smelled of leather, the furniture brown and comfortable looking, with stacks upon stacks of books.

"Oh, no, we'll never get her out of here," Taro muttered.

Dane chuckled. "Fiona said you're fond of books."

Then Taro must have told her that, for I never did. I wondered why they'd be discussing me. "I am."

"You'll be interested in this." He opened a drawer and handed me a small book, the cover made of a hard substance I wasn't familiar with. It opened with a crack and the paper felt unlike any paper I'd seen before, very slippery. And the words . . . "I can't recognize this writing."

Dane grinned. "We found it in one of the caves in the cliffs. The cliffs have shifted some because of the earthquakes. We've written to Academic Alex Reid. Have you heard of him?"

I nodded. He was a noted linguist and historian.

"He's written back. He says he thinks this book is from the Landing."

I stared at him. Seriously? The Landing? When our ancestors traveled from somewhere in the stars to our world with incredible machines that had all been rendered useless and destroyed by natural disasters? That Landing?

My awe must have shown on my face, because he laughed and gently plucked the book out of my hand.

"You're free to look at it at any time. I just ask that you don't take it out of the library and you always return it to this drawer." And he put it back in the drawer.

Damn the tour. I wanted to look at the book and see if I could figure out some of the words.

"Reid has agreed to come and look at the book, tell us what it says."

I would have the chance to meet Alex Reid?

"I don't think I've ever seen her so excited about anything," Taro commented with amusement.

I closed my mouth in an attempt to look less foolish.

Dane laughed and led us out of the library and back up the stairs.

The second story held the titleholder's huge study, with almost as many books as the library, a receiving room for the titleholder's spouse, private rooms for the butler and housekeeper, and rows of guest bedchambers. Aside from the books in the study, there was nothing of interest on that floor.

The third floor was purely for the family's bedrooms. These were all larger than the bedrooms on the second floors, all of them with private sitting rooms, dressing rooms and water closets. They were similar to our suites in the Triple S residence in High Scape, only much grander, and with bellpulls.

Again, nothing of real interest there, until we came to a particular room at the northeastern end of the house. A large room, but without the additions of the other suites. The walls were cream colored, there was only a small fireplace, and the bed was that of a child's. There was a trunk in one corner, and empty shelves lined one wall.

"We're not sure what to do with this room," said Dane. "It's so much starker than the others. We thought about making it into a nursery, but the servants don't like coming in here. Some outright refuse."

Taro froze, shaking. I suspected I knew why. I guessed this was the room Taro had spent most of the first eleven years of his life locked in. Banished from family and possible friends because his parents interpreted his common Source trait of occasionally spouting nonsense as a sign of madness. Left in the single room for eleven years where, as far as I could tell, his parents never visited him and his significantly older brother spent his idle hours tormenting the younger boy by tossing him about and screaming at him.

Taro dashed out of the room.

"What's wrong?" Dane asked, perplexed.

"Bad memories," I muttered, furious at myself for not anticipating this and warning Dane. I followed Taro out, but he was down the stairs and around a corner, and the house had suddenly become a maze. He was gone.

Chapter Four

I looked for Taro but was unable to find him. If he wanted so badly to hide from me, he wouldn't listen to anything I had to say even if I could find him. So I went back to our rooms, where he could find me when he wanted to. I decided I might as well write those reports for the Triple S.

So, how to write a report that would satisfy the Triple S council without actually telling them anything. Because I wasn't going to tell them why the Empress sent us to Flatwell. I didn't yet know how Taro would handle events. And I didn't know what to tell them about the Emperor. Maybe I would use a ridiculous amount of multisyllabic words and make each sentence at least half a page long. Whoever was forced to read it would get sick of it and put it aside for later, and eventually they'd forget all about us.

Sure, that would work.

I decided I'd write a letter to Aryne first. She was the descendant of the collateral line the Empress had been looking for. The Empress hadn't liked her, after Taro and

I had spent months looking for her, but as Aryne was also a Source, we'd left her at the Source Academy. I wrote to her occasionally, so she wouldn't think we'd forgotten her.

And while I was writing to her, I might get some decent ideas about what to write to the council. It wasn't at all about procrastinating.

Before I finished the letter, Taro came into the room. I looked up at him, but he didn't look at me. He just paced.

"Maybe we shouldn't live here," I found myself saying.

"Don't start that again. We've been posted here."

"No, I mean maybe we shouldn't live in this house."

"Where else would we live?"

"I'm sure we could find an inn or something." That was what Pairs often did.

"And we would tell my cousin what as we throw her hospitality back in her face?"

"Blame it on artistic temperament."

"Mine, I suppose."

"We can claim it's mine, if you want. I don't care." Actually, it would irk me a little, but that was better than having Taro tied in knots all the time.

He snorted. "You must be really worried about me if you're willing to admit to any kind of emotional turmoil."

Hey, was he trying to claim I actually had emotional turmoil? He was the moody one. "Your mother lives right next door, Taro. I'm more than willing to put some space between us and her."

"Oh, my gods." He put a hand over his eyes. "Her."

Actually, I found it strange that she hadn't come over yet, but I didn't say so. Speaking it out loud, I feared most irrationally, might actually make it happen.

"I don't think we should move," said Taro. "It makes sense for us to be here. It is the place that has the most empty space, and we're family. I'm just being ridiculous.

You're supposed to smack me up the back of the head and tell me to be sensible."

"You're too far away." And as far as I was concerned, he had every right to feel weird about this place. Maybe I should keep an eye out for a better place for us to live. I'd rather insult Fiona than have Taro assailed by bad memories every moment of every day. "I'm writing a letter to Aryne. Do you want to add something?" I could tell he was about to shake his head. "You should. You didn't write anything in the last one."

"I can never think of what to write," he muttered as he came to where I was sitting.

"I don't think it matters." She had no one in the world, and Taro and I were poor substitutes for family. The least we could do was write her regularly. "It's important that she knows we think about her."

Taro shrugged and I let him have my seat at the secretary. In my mind I tried to compose a convincing letter to send to the Triple S.

Suddenly Taro straightened in his chair. "Are you ready?" he asked.

That meant he was feeling the approach of a natural disaster, and he was going to channel. "Aye."

The inner protections he had, guarding a mind that would directly touch the forces of the world, faded away, allowing the forces attached to the natural disaster to flow through him. I erected my Shields around him, letting him do his work while guarding him from the forces he wasn't manipulating. I calmed a mind straining with exertion, and slowed blood that threatened to burst from veins and heart as Taro's whole body reacted to forces the human vessel wasn't really designed to interact with.

It was something I usually enjoyed doing. It was a wonderful stretch of mind and concentration, to feel what Taro was doing and make sure he was protected while he did it. I had trained most of my life to do this, and I knew

I was fortunate to be able to do it for someone as worthy as Taro. As there were more Shields than Sources born, I was aware that there were many Shields who never got bonded and therefore were never able to Shield. And there were some Shields bonded to unworthy Sources who dragged them down into infamy with them.

I liked the challenge of Shielding, but of late most of the events we channeled were unusual in nature. It looked like this one would be the same, for all of a sudden the forces started rushing through Taro at a faster pace, and faster again. His blood started pumping harder, his mind working more intensely. This wasn't good. "Slow down, Taro!"

"I can't!" he snapped.

Images started slamming into the back of my mind, images I had seen before. Waves crashing into high, dark cliffs. The images brought other impressions. Salt water filling my mouth and stinging my nose. The screeching of seabirds piercing my ears.

No, not again.

It was going too fast, too fast. My Shields felt like they were stretching. "Slow down!"

There was no reaction from Taro. Maybe he hadn't heard me. Usually we could speak while channeling, but I wouldn't be surprised if all of Taro's attention was on the forces. Mine should be, too. I felt like I was holding his moist beating heart in my hands and trying to stop it from beating so hard. I felt like I couldn't breathe without dragging in pounds of salt.

I thought my Shields might start to burst apart at any moment.

And then I felt trembling. Actual physical trembling. It wasn't me. It was happening around us. Were we letting the earthquake through? "Do you feel that?" I demanded.

"Aye," said Taro.

"We have to do something."

"I'm open to suggestion."

The trembling continued. It didn't get to be very strong, just causing rattling of the wall hangings.

And then, suddenly, it was over. Thank Zaire. I was exhausted and drenched with sweat. I was about to rub at my face, but I stopped and looked for blood on my hands. That was foolish. It wasn't as though I had been literally holding Taro's heart in my hands.

"Hell," Taro said weakly. "What was that?"

"That was the same kind of channeling you were doing at the end of our stay in High Scape."

He shook his head. "It never felt anything like that."

It felt the same to me.

Lila walked in. Again, without knocking. Really, was that normal?

I expected her to make some comment about the tremors, but the first words out of her mouth were, "Her Grace, the Dowager Duchess of Westsea, is here."

Ah, damn it. I knew I shouldn't have spoken of her out loud.

"Are sir and ma'am receiving?"

"No," Taro said shortly.

"Of course they are," the Dowager Duchess said, sailing in. Which meant she hadn't bothered to wait wherever she had been told to wait.

There was no mistaking that the Dowager Duchess was Taro's mother. She was small and fine-boned, with black hair untouched by gray, and black, slightly narrowed eyes. However, aside from appearance, the two were nothing alike. Thank Zaire. The Dowager was just too poisonous to bear. I would have been miserable dealing with that kind of personality on a regular basis.

I hated that woman. More than I'd ever hated anyone. Including the crazy Source who'd had Taro abducted and had threatened to kill us. We were strangers to him, while the Dowager Duchess enjoyed tearing strips off her own son.

I was pretty sure Taro hated her, too. He didn't rise

from his chair as he normally would when someone entered the room. "You're not welcome here," he told her.

"Don't be ridiculous. This was my home longer than it was yours." Cold black eyes racked over my form. "Shield Mallorough, you're looking terrible, as usual."

"And your manner sets an example for us all," I shot back. If Taro had loved her or sought her respect, I would have been polite to the woman no matter what she did. But he didn't, and previous attempts to keep to the high road had been disastrous. So I said whatever I felt like, knowing though I did that the Dowager could be far more insulting than I.

"Shall I fetch some refreshments, sir?" the maid asked Taro.

"No, she's not staying."

"Tea would be appropriate," the Dowager countered.

"Lila," Taro said firmly. "None of us require anything. Please stay close so you can see the Dowager out in a few moments."

Lila curtsied and withdrew to the sitting room. I would have preferred she leave altogether. She was going to witness some nasty behavior.

"I thought you were supposed to stop the earthquakes," the Dowager commented.

"I drained away most of its power."

"I understand we're not supposed to feel anything."

"We just got here. It takes time to adjust."

"Let us hope we all survive your period of adjustment." Seriously, shut up.

"It's appalling that I had to learn of your transfer from the servants," the Dowager said. "And of your arrival last night."

Who in this household was running off to tattle to the Dowager?

"You eat what you cook," Taro muttered.

"None of your nonsense mumblings at me, Shintaro," the Dowager snapped. "It is hopelessly ill-mannered."

It was said that Sources couldn't help sometimes expressing their thoughts oddly. It was just the way their minds worked. Apparently the Dowager had never accepted that. I couldn't understand why. Even though she clearly didn't like the fact that her son was a Source, what was the point in denying that he was one, and all the things that went with that? What did she hope to accomplish?

I wondered if she ever regretted locking Taro away all those years. Did she have it within her to admit, if only to herself, that she had made a mistake? Perhaps that was why she treated him so badly. He reminded her of her errors.

"What do you want?" Taro demanded.

"Are you not going to offer me a seat?"

"No."

She sat down anyway. "Do grow up, Shintaro."

Telling another adult to grow up was one of the most obnoxious things a person could say. In my opinion, the people who said such things were those suffering from the greatest lack of maturity.

"I have work to do, Your Grace, which is something you would know nothing about. A transfer means a lot of paperwork. Say what you came to say."

"You think I know nothing of responsibilities? Who do you think managed this estate before your brother?"

"My father."

"Sometimes, my dear boy, you are so delightfully naive." She nodded at me. "Send your little friend away."

"This is Dunleavy's room. If anyone is going to leave, it's going to be you."

"Actually, I don't mind—" I really had no problem with leaving, I had no interest in what the Dowager had to say, but before I could get the words out, Taro shot me a filthy glare. So I sat down.

"You're always so melodramatic, Shintaro." His mother

sighed. "I merely wished to inform you of all that has been going on in Flown Raven."

"Fiona has been keeping me informed."

"I have no doubt she has been. And that's part of the problem. She hasn't exactly been fitting in here. Has she told you that?"

"She has said everything is going well and that the only flaw in her ice is you."

"I don't doubt that is the way she feels. She thought she could fly into the ancient seat, having never been here, and order everyone about with no understanding of their character and no willingness to learn from those of us with years of experience."

"Your Grace, with the way you treat people, a drowning man wouldn't take a rope from you."

"Such a man would be an idiot, wouldn't he?"

Aye, he would be. I had to give her that. Good advice should be considered no matter what the source.

Was Fiona the sort to blunder around blindly in a new place? I had no idea. She had struck me as sensible, but I barely knew her.

I knew the Dowager only slightly more, but she had never struck me as particularly intelligent. She was just mean. And I would wager she never bothered to learn about people before ordering them about. She'd certainly never bothered to learn anything about me.

She probably resented Fiona because the current Duchess wouldn't let the Dowager walk all over her.

"Fiona is not as well liked as she might have led you to believe," the Dowager went on with a certain banked glee. "The people here don't take to strangers. They're used to having our family hold the title, and Fiona is disturbing all of them, but she ignores their concerns. It is more than two years that she has been here, but she's not finding her feet and the people are suffering for it."

"Even if that were true," said Taro, "it has nothing to

do with me. I'm just the Source posted here. Politics and money are none of my business."

"It's so embarrassing that my one remaining child is so ignorant," the Dowager said, her exasperation clear. "You haven't been just a Source since your brother died. That you seduced the Empress into allowing you to abjure your title won't change the fact that you should be holding this duchy and protecting the interests of these people. It's what you were born to do."

"It was not," Taro retorted. "Nor was it what I was raised to do. You made sure of that."

"Stop being so childish."

Could she just stop with the insults? I wasn't comfortable with how badly I wanted to slap her.

"No," was all Taro said.

She sniffed. "As I was saying, Fiona has not won the trust or respect of the people, and she has offended His Imperial Majesty greatly."

"He was demanding taxes he had no right to ask for."

"Others were more politically astute and met his demands, and they are now the better for it. Sometimes insisting on one's rights is not wise. She still had to pay the taxes after the coronation, plus a few extra fines for annoying His Majesty. What did she accomplish?"

"Pride in knowing she won't be bullied?" Taro suggested.

"There is no pride to be felt in stupidity," she informed him.

I was kind of curious as to whether the Dowager had given way to the demands of another. Her husband, perhaps. Maybe she was so bitter because she had suffered some poor treatment in the past.

I felt no compassion for her if she had. Did that make me a bad person?

Lila walked back into the room and dropped into a curtsy. "Forgive me, Your Grace, sir, madam. There are four of His Majesty's Imperial Guard here. They wish everyone in the manor to gather in the ballroom."

Well, that was unexpected. Imperial Guards. The Imperial Guards were the protectors of the Emperor and sometimes the enforcers of his laws. I could think of no reason why they would be here in Flown Raven, but it probably wasn't anything good.

Then again, maybe it was good. I had no way of knowing. Sometimes I was just too pessimistic.

"What do they want?" Taro asked.

"I don't believe they've said, yet. They've only just arrived."

"And they want to see us all right now?"

"Yes, sir."

Well, at least it cut short our painful visit with the Dowager.

"You may escort me down, Shintaro," said the Dowager.

"I'm sure you can find your own way down," said Taro. "After all, you've lived here much longer than I have." He held out his hand to me, I took it, and we headed down to the ballroom.

Fiona and her family were already there, and more servants were coming in all the time. Taro and I stayed in the back of the crowd, hopefully out of sight of the four Imperial Guards at the front, resplendent in their bronze armor and red capes.

A few moments later, Fiona said something to one of the Guards, and he nodded. "Everyone," he called out in a strong voice. "I am First Lieutenant Corvis. This is First Sergeant Evanov, Second Sergeant Haasen and Corporal Oteroy. We are here by order of His Imperial Majesty, Emperor Gifford."

Hells, what did he want now?

"As you may be aware, there is, springing within normally sensible people, a belief that spells and casting are real, that by mixing the right ingredients and speaking the right words unnatural things can be made to happen. As you might not be aware, there have been disastrous consequences to these attempts to cast spells. A fire was started in Silver River, destroying dozens of houses and killing eight people. Wells all over Slight Peaks were poisoned, resulting in twelve more deaths. People in High Scape were murdered by those wishing to have their ashes for use in their spells. And every day, more examples of death and ruin come to His Majesty's ears. He has decided he can no longer delay stamping out these erroneous beliefs."

I wondered if First Lieutenant Corvis knew that the Emperor actually believed in the power of spells, and used them himself.

"The Emperor has heard many disturbing rumors about Flown Raven and Westsea. Rumors that the pretense of casting spells is prevalent, that it arises in nearly every family and is condoned by your titleholder." The Guard sent a look of rebuke Fiona's way. "I take this opportunity to remind you all that pretending to cast spells is illegal, and carries with it harsh sanctions. We have been given the authority to carry out those sanctions against anyone found in possession of the tools of casting."

"Enforcing His Majesty's laws in Westsea is my responsibility," Fiona objected.

"There will be no interference with your duties in any other area, but we will be dealing with all offenders of the casting laws."

This had the potential to be a nightmare. If the people resented Fiona as an outsider, how would they feel about these Guards from the other side of the continent poking their noses in and asking questions?

Maybe that would make the people like Fiona more.

Of course, we had only the Dowager's word that the people disliked Fiona. That wasn't worth anything.

"It is the duty of all of you to cooperate with us," the

Guard continued, pitching his voice over the rustle of whispering that was rising up. "I expect you to turn yourself in if you have attempted to cast spells."

Well, he was an idiot.

"I expect you to come to me with information about others who you know are attempting to cast spells."

What a dirty little plan, expecting people to spy on each other.

"If I learn that you have been aware of attempts to cast spells and have failed to report it to one of us, you will face the same sanctions as the perpetrator. These sanctions are public floggings and constitute the following: a single lash for any item purported to be used for the casting of spells, a single lash for each book of spells, five lashes for performing any alleged spell or ritual for the purpose of casting, an additional lash if it's a love spell, an additional ten if the attempt to cast harms another person, another fifteen if it damages someone's property, twenty lashes for each instance of collecting, possessing, selling or consuming human ashes."

The whispering got louder. I thought of the carriage driver and his alleged spell to stop the hail. Was he still about? I hoped not. He was harmless and didn't deserve to be flogged.

According to the First Lieutenant, I had a duty to tell him about the carriage driver. I wouldn't tell him, though. I wasn't going to tell him about anyone. It was disgusting of him to ask.

And when the First Lieutenant found out about what I wasn't telling him, would he really have me flogged? As a rule, Shields and Sources were spared sanctions for criminal behavior. We were considered too valuable to be locked up or executed or otherwise rendered unable to channel. But Taro and I were out in the middle of nowhere, the only Pair about. There was nothing stopping them from having us flogged and asking for forgiveness after.

People died when they were flogged. If I died, Taro would die with me. That wasn't fair.

I still wasn't going to tell them anything.

The First Lieutenant pulled a folded parchment from his purse and held it out to Fiona. "These are orders from the Emperor stating that you and your people are to assist us, and that you personally are to provide us with bed and board."

Fiona's expression was blank as she accepted the parchment. I would bet everything I owned that she was actually fuming. My guess was supported by the fact that she didn't just take the Guard at his word but insisted on reading the missive. "Understood," she eventually said. Nothing about cooperating, just that she understood. Interesting. "Cekina, please find the Guards suitable accommodation. Please stay with them until their every need is seen to."

Fiona's housekeeper strode out of the crowd and approached the Guards. She said a few words to the First Lieutenant, who nodded. The four Guards bowed briefly to Fiona and then followed Cekina out of the ballroom.

The whispering of the crowd rose into loud objections, and Fiona had to clap a few times to get their attention. "I know you all have concerns," she said. "I will be in my office shortly. I ask you all to bring"—heavy emphasis on the word "bring"—"your concerns to me as quickly as possible. You are all relieved of your duties for a short while so you can do this. Off with you. Source Karish, Shield Mallorough, I ask you to remain behind."

It was weird seeing so many people curtsy and bow all at once, practically simultaneously. Then they quietly drained out of the room. Taro and I joined Fiona and her family at the head of the room.

"Daris and Tarce, you can go if you want," Fiona said to her siblings.

"Ooh, you have secrets we're not important enough to hear, is that it?" Daris drawled.

"Not at all," said Fiona. "You can stay if you like."

"I'd rather see what those louts are up to," said Tarce, heading for the nearest door. "Obnoxious nest of twits, aren't they?"

Daris crossed her arms. "So talk," she ordered in a tone of challenge.

"Shintaro, Dunleavy," said Fiona. "I felt tremors. Were they signs of an earthquake?"

"Aye," Taro answered.

"Why did we feel them? Are we supposed to?"

"No, we're just adjusting to a new post."

"Does what you do to prevent earthquakes or whatever involve the casting of spells?"

"Certainly not," said Taro.

"Are there any books about it?"

"There are books that try to explain it," I told her. "But they don't tell anyone how to do it. There's no learning how to do it. You have to be born able to do it, and at the academies we only learn how to control what we can do." And ethics, and laws, and how to read and write and figure.

"Are there any tools you use, or any little rituals?"

"No, nothing like that."

"Shintaro, please tell me exactly what you do when you do . . . whatever it is you do."

Looking a little baffled, Taro described what he did when he channeled, going back over details when Fiona asked him to, answering questions that first got very precise, then went a little strange and irrelevant. After Taro had been questioned for quite some time, Fiona turned to me.

Daris huffed and left.

As soon as the door was closed again, having driven her sister away with trivial questions, Fiona stepped closer to us and whispered, "I have an important and dangerous favor to ask of you."

"All right," said Taro.

"There are spell books in the library," said Fiona. "Some of them have been in the family for generations. I don't want them lost." She didn't mention the fact that she could be flogged for having them. Or could she? It was a difficult thing to punish an aristocrat. "And I know some of the staff have little trinkets that might be considered tools for casting. I am sure the Guards plan to search the manor and I don't want to see any of my people flogged."

"Of course not," said Taro. "This is all nonsense."

"While Cekina is keeping the Guards busy, I would like to have everything transferred to your suite while the Guards are here."

That was a lot to ask. A whole lot to ask.

"You can't be punished for being in possession of these things."

"We can't be sure of that," I objected.

"But I can be sure that anyone else caught with these things will be punished. If they do find it in your room, I will insist the Triple S council be contacted before any punishment can be meted out. There are only four of them. They can't do anything if we stand against them."

"That won't win you any favor with the Emperor," Taro warned her.

"He doesn't have any favor for me now anyway. Will you do it?"

Taro and I looked at each other. I hated the idea. I really did. "But when they search our rooms . . ."

"Your rooms were used by a former duchess," said Fiona. "She had a lot of secrets. There are places to hide everything. It's highly unlikely the Guards will be able to find anything."

"But not certain."

"No, not certain. Look, I may not be able to protect my people if any of them are caught. I know I can protect you two because of your position. Please."

It was a horrible idea, but I couldn't bear the thought

of people getting flogged just because I wanted to be a coward. "It's fine with me."

Taro nodded.

Fiona grinned. "Thank you." Then she shocked the hell out of us both by giving each of us a hug. "Go up to your suite. We'll bring everything to you."

Feeling unnerved, I followed Taro back up to our suite. We waited a short while, and then there was a knock. Only it wasn't a knock on our door. We looked around for a few moments, and then I heard something in the bedchamber. I stepped into it to see a wall made of bookshelves swing open. Fiona and Dane stepped in, Fiona carrying two cloth sacks and Dane burdened with arms full of books.

A secret passage. It was like something out of a book. I hadn't thought anyone actually had them.

"We got this just in time," Fiona said. "They've already started searching the servants' quarters."

This was such a bad idea. "Where can we hide them?"

"Watch me." She headed straight to the fireplace. "Come see what I'm doing." Taro and I stood next to her. I watched her grab hold of a small iron cube set into the back of the overmantel. She pulled it out, revealing it to be an iron bar about a hand in length. She put it on the floor, and then she pulled off the front of the overmantel, revealing that it was hollow.

That was kind of interesting.

Dane started packing the books within the overmantel. Fiona began pulling items out of the bags. Black candles, slim knives with white or black handles, sticks of incense, lengths of bone, the kitchen guardian, one really disgusting bundle of black hair. Once everything was packed in, the front of the overmantel was locked back into place.

Looking at the overmantel from the front or the sides, it didn't look like it could come apart. At least, not to me, but I wasn't an expert. Maybe criminals hid things in such a way all the time.

"Thank you again," Fiona whispered, and she and Dane disappeared back behind the wall.

"Did you know about the secret passages?" I asked Taro.

He shook his head.

I sat in a settee close to the door to the corridor. Taro paced. We waited for the Guards to show up.

The heavy knock on the door sounded just under an hour later. I jumped to my feet and stood beside Taro when he opened the door.

"You're not coming in here," he told the Guards.

"Stand aside," the First Lieutenant ordered.

"No."

"We are under the orders of the Emperor."

They were Imperial Guards. They were always under the orders of the Emperor.

"Once we moved in here," said Taro, "these rooms came under the control of the Triple S. The Emperor has no jurisdiction here."

"You can't just take a room and treat it as a separate property."

"Watch me."

"Stand aside. Now."

Taro crossed his arms. "You're going to have to move us."

I didn't think daring them to lay hands on us was the greatest idea, but the Guards were clearly reluctant to do so. That was interesting.

"Are you in possession of paraphernalia related to the attempt to cast spells?"

"Of course not!" Taro sounded thoroughly scandalized. He really was a good actor.

"Then why don't you want us to look?"

"Because you have no right to, and this whole incident is offensive."

"Stand aside."

"I will not."

There was a heavy silence as Taro and the First Lieutenant settled into a staring contest. I had no doubt who would win. Taro had faced much scarier people than an Imperial Guard. I looked at the other three Guards, a woman and two men. The woman and one of the men were watching expressionlessly. The other man seemed to find his own feet more interesting.

"The Emperor will hear of this," the First Lieutenant threatened.

"Send him my regards," Taro answered lightly before closing the door in the Lieutenant's face.

I took a deep breath. That had been tense. And it wasn't over yet. The Guards hadn't said how long they would stay. What if someone told them everything had been hidden in our rooms?

We'd have to deal with that if and when it happened. In the meantime, I wouldn't be able to relax until they were gone. Not the best state to be in at a new post.

Chapter Five

The next morning, Taro and I enjoyed our breakfast in the main-floor sitting room. It consisted of fruit, bread, fish and an amazing egg mixture that included cheese and herbs. Fiona clearly had an excellent cook. I was embarrassed by how much I ate, but not so embarrassed that I didn't eat as much as I could.

The whole house seemed very tense. Lila had been silent as she built the fires in our suite. I wondered if she had a clue what was hiding in the overmantel she stood before. The maids laying the food in the sitting room barely looked at each other. Did either of them use spells? Did the staff know who had the tools of casting? Would anyone tell the Guards? So far, it appeared that no one had admitted to anything yet.

Fiona, Dane and Tarce were in the room with us. Tarce was sipping coffee and staring out the window. Fiona and Dane were pushing their food around their plates without eating anything.

"Dunleavy, Shintaro," Dane said suddenly. "After

you've finished eating, I'll show you the shoreline. It's important you know how dangerous it is, and you won't know until you see it."

"We've been to waterfront areas before," I said.

"No waterfront like this, I'd wager."

"Unfortunately, I won't be able to go with you," said Fiona. "The Guards, having found nothing of interest in the manor, have decided to violate the privacy of all our tenants. I think it best that I go with them."

"But there are hundreds of tenants," said Taro.

"I know. All of my footmen had to visit every single one of them to, ah, let them know the Guards would be coming."

"I'll accompany you on your little jaunt, Dane," Tarce announced.

"That bored, are you?" Dane asked wryly.

"The air in the manor has grown foul."

"Can't argue with that."

We left after breakfast by a rear entrance of the house. We crossed a large expanse of dark green grass, and I was entertained by the wide berth Dane gave the dowager house. I hadn't heard him speak of Taro's mother, but obviously she had made an impression on him.

The ground grew rocky, and it sharply rose up into the range of hills. We weren't to climb over it, thank the gods. I had neither the will nor the boots for that. Dane led us to a small path that pierced through the range at the base, a strangely twisted little path through the rock, doubling back on itself a half dozen times, the walls of it worn smooth and showing hundreds of layers of multicolored rock.

On the other side of the range was a different world from what we'd left. A world without grass or trees, the rocky ground stretched out before us, and then a sudden drop to the shore lining the sea. Stone cottages were built against the ridge, but they all appeared to be empty.

The sea was beautiful, gray blue in color, waves jagged

and frothy. I could hear the waves moving, fresh and harsh as they crashed against rocks. Through an unfamiliar, unpleasant odor, I could smell the sea and taste it, an edge of salt in the air. Above our heads, white birds whirled in the sky and screeched.

These were the sensations I had experienced while channeling the events of Flown Raven, though not as extreme. It wasn't normal for me to see visions or perceive tastes. Did Taro have some kind of connection to the land that caused me to experience those sensations when we channeled? Was that sort of thing possible?

"I'm taking you first to meet someone very important," Dane said. "You have to know what she does and recognize what she does, for your own safety." With that mysterious announcement, he headed off toward a stone structure that I was surprised had survived the earthquakes.

It was a tower, about three stories high, and beside it was an odd structure. A kind of arch with something that looked like a slab of stone somehow suspended within it. A path had been worn in the rocks to the door at the base of the tower. Dane rang a bell hanging by the door.

After a few moments, we heard footsteps, and the heavy door was opened by a beautiful young woman with thick black hair, warm brown skin and lovely brown eyes. She was small, too, no taller than I.

I looked up at Taro, waiting for his reaction to this beautiful woman. He was smiling politely.

"Source Shintaro Karish, Shield Dunleavy Mallorough," said Dane, "this is Wind Watcher Roshni Radia."

Radia smiled, a brilliant smile of beautiful white teeth.

I looked up at Taro again. He was still smiling politely.

"Wind Watcher?" I asked, as I had never before heard the term.

"Please come in." Radia stood back to let us pass, then closed the door behind us.

"That's very gracious of you," Tarce said, which was, I thought, kind of a strange thing to say. His tone was just shy of snide. Radia ignored him.

The room we entered was the shape of the round tower, which felt wrong and odd. Along one side was a cooking area with a plain solid table for eating. The rest of the room was taken up with leisure seating. It was a dark room, with few windows, dark walls and dark furniture, and rugs and wall hangings consisting largely of dark red.

"Please have a seat," Radia invited. "Would anyone like some coffee?"

Dane, Tarce and I said yes, and Taro refrained, having never learned the benefits of the bitter drink. Radia fiddled with her stove and I admired one of her tapestries, which was full of detail one didn't notice until one got really close. It was a scene of a ball, dozens upon dozens of figures in circles and rows. I could almost see them moving.

"Beautiful, isn't it?" Dane stood beside me. "Roshni wove it."

"She made this?" What was it with all these people and their multiple talents?

"I have a great deal of time for such frivolous pursuits," Radia said dismissively, bringing over a tray of cups and coffee fixings.

"That's not what you told me," Tarce commented. "You said you had no time for frivolous pursuits."

Radia glanced at him. "That's not precisely what I said."

"Aye, that's true. You said I was trivial and you didn't want to waste time on me."

"Are you trying to start an argument?"

"Of course not. I would never win. You're far too clever for me."

"Yes, I am. You might as well just accept it."

"Really, I should never talk to you at all, but I, unlike you, have scads of time on my hands. All sorts of time for trivial pursuits."

For the first time, Radia looked annoyed. "I am not a trivial pursuit."

Tarce's face flushed. I wasn't sure whether he was embarrassed or angry.

"What is a wind watcher?" I asked, partially for the goal of derailing whatever argument appeared to be brewing.

"It's very simple, really," Radia said in her original friendly tone. "When the wind is strong enough to make the wind rock move, I warn everyone, to make sure everyone stays indoors."

"The wind rock is that slab of stone suspended from the arch?" I asked. Radia nodded. "The wind gets strong enough to move that? It's huge."

"It also gets strong enough to blow people and animals off their feet," said Dane. "It blows carriages over, and capsizes boats. It's just too dangerous for anyone to be out."

"Can't people figure it out for themselves when it's too windy?"

"People anxious to get work done will ignore it. The warning is like an order from the titleholder to stay inside."

"My family have been wind watchers here for generations," said Radia. "It's an honor to be able to serve Flown Raven in this way."

"And you must stay here all the time in case the wind gets too strong and you have to give the warning?" That sounded horrible.

She laughed, a pleasant, throaty sound. "Nothing so grim, Shield Mallorough. I do spend a lot of time here, but I have the freedom to be out and about when the weather is fine, and usually I can predict when the wind might get too strong, and it gives me the time to return to the tower."

"How can you predict something like that?"

She shrugged. "I just can. My father could, too."

Huh. Interesting.

"I felt some tremors earlier," Radia said. "Are we supposed to be able to feel that with you here?"

I was going to get sick of that question. Taro gave her the standard lie about having to get used to the post.

After our coffee had been consumed, Radia took us to the second floor, which was, she said, where she slept.

"That's a huge bedroom you have," I exclaimed.

She laughed again. "No, no, it's divided into four rooms. If I ever have a partner and children, they will live here with me."

"Of course, you'll never have either if you insist on hiding in your tower," Tarce said. Radia said nothing.

The top floor was all stone and huge windows. Within the bare room was a loom and a huge, long brass instrument, some kind of long horn, on a stand. The horn had no keys, and was just a mouthpiece attached to an ever-widening tube. "This is how you warn everyone?" I asked.

"I'll show you," she said, standing on the small stool that sat beneath the mouthpiece. "I'll blow a light note, so you'll recognize it when you hear it again, but it won't be as loud as I usually blow it. I don't want anyone else to hear it and get confused." She put her mouth to the mouthpiece, pulled a breath from deep in her stomach and blew.

The sound that came out was like the lowest, most rumbling trumpet note I'd ever heard. It made the pit of my stomach vibrate.

Radia took her mouth away. "I usually play three notes in succession, again and again, until I see black spots in front of my eyes. That gives everyone time to hear and understand. And I only play when I see the slab move. I don't play for entertainment or other trivial reasons."

"And when you hear it, you get inside," Dane told us. "Drop whatever you're doing and run to the nearest shelter, whatever it might be. No one will deny you shelter. And you don't delay. I don't care how important whatever you're handling is. You run. People have been killed by the wind."

"How often does this happen?" I asked.

"It varies. Not every day. Not even every week, usually. But it's very unpredictable."

"So it's not according to season," I said.

"No."

It seemed to me a lonely life. I wouldn't like it. Yet while Radia offered an open invitation to visit when we left, she didn't seem desperate for company.

As soon as we left Radia's tower, the odor hit me again. I couldn't help wrinkling my nose. "What is that smell?"

"I'll show you," Dane said.

"I think I've had enough fresh air," said Tarce. "Have a glorious day." Without waiting for a response, he headed off toward the ridge.

Dane took us down a rocky path to the waterfront, and then along it, around a sharp bend that suddenly revealed to us the sight of a huge carcass on the rocks. It was a whale, an animal I'd only ever read about and never thought to see. What I saw was a disgusting violation of the animal. And it stank.

It was a gigantic creature, even stripped of its fins and tail. Swaths of skin had been peeled away, and people were engaged in the process of cutting out strips of fat and dumping them into large copper cauldrons.

"They're rendering the blubber into oil," Dane explained. "Much of the duchy's wealth comes from whale oil."

That surprised me. I didn't think I'd ever encountered whale oil in my life. And when I thought of Flown Raven, I'd always thought of farming.

"Please don't get too close," Dane said. "The oil can spit, and your clothes aren't fit for protecting your skin."

I had no intention of getting any closer to that smell. And

the people working around the whale and the cauldrons were not only covered in leather but seemed really competent as they moved about. I would just get in their way.

As we walked about, I noticed people spotting Taro, nudging their neighbors, and then all of them watching him. I assumed they were merely taking note of his beauty. That was what such attention usually meant. But then a man came charging over, glaring at Taro, and it became clear that admiration was not what motivated him.

"You're the duke's kin," the man accused Taro. "You were supposed to take the title after him."

That was what they were angry about? What the hell? He didn't even know Taro. Why would he want Taro as the titleholder?

"Now, Leland," Dane said in what was clearly the beginning of a placating comment.

"You whisht," Leland snapped, shocking the hell out of me. Was that any way to talk to his duke? "Not talking to you. I'm talking to you." He nodded at Taro. "You're of the family. This is your home. These things mean nothing to you?"

Actually, they probably didn't, but Taro wasn't stupid. He wasn't going to admit to feelings either way in this situation. "I wasn't born to be a duke, Leland. And I was never trained for it. I was born to be a Source."

"Family is more important than any of that tripe."

I couldn't believe he could feel that way after the community had lost two children to earthquakes. Did they really not understand what Sources did?

"Didn't they teach you anything about loyalty in that fancy school of yours?"

They certainly did. Loyalty to the Triple S.

"What I didn't learn, at the Academy or anywhere else, was the first thing about taking care of a duchy of this or any size."

"It's not about what you know," Leland said. "It's what you are. It's your blood."

"It's your duty," a woman added. "Our families have given your family everything we've got for generations. You can't just step out of your obligations because something more interesting comes along."

"I'm a Source," Taro protested. "I can't be a title-holder."

"You could if you gave a damn," the woman accused him. "It's been done."

"That's enough," I warned her. Yes, it had been done. I knew of Sources who'd taken hereditary titles. But there weren't many, and the Sources involved hadn't actually lived in the lands of the estates. And none of this gave these people the right to attack Taro. It didn't even make sense to want Taro as a titleholder. Fiona had experience running an estate in Centerfield. Didn't they know their own best interests?

"Is it you, then?" the woman demanded, looking at me. "Are you keeping him from taking his rightful place?"

"I couldn't do that even if I wanted to."

"I have no training," Taro insisted.

"It's not training. It's blood."

"Fi— Her Ladyship shares my father's blood."

"She's not a direct heir. You are. It was your duty to come here. And since you've neglected your duty, the sea has gotten angry. Deaths are up and numbers are down."

Please tell me these people didn't actually believe the sea was capable of having moods.

"That's not true," Dane objected. "I've shown you the books. There have been no more casualties than earlier years, and the catches have remained similar."

"Books." The man spat in an expression of contempt. "You can write whatever you want in books. I know what I've seen. We all have eyes."

"And we never had earthquakes before," the woman added. "You can't write that away in your books."

"And now we have a Pair to deal with the earthquakes,"

Dane reminded them. "Source Karish can't have both responsibilities."

"If he'd come when he was supposed to, we would have never had any earthquakes, and Parcin Woodward and Jeeno Drake wouldn't have died."

I wasn't brave enough to tell these hostile people that I was actually the person responsible for the deaths of those children. I was the one who had convinced Taro not to channel the events from Flown Raven. All right, so I hadn't known the events Taro had been feeling in High Scape had been from Flown Raven, but I'd made no effort to find out. I should have.

"I'm sorry you feel ill-used," said Taro. "But there is nothing to be done about it now. The title is held by Her Ladyship. That's the end of it."

"There is always something to be done," the man said in a tone I found threatening.

But Dane didn't seem to feel it. He just rolled his eyes. "We apologize for disrupting your work." It was a clear dismissal of the discussion. "Come along, Shintaro, Dunleavy."

So the Dowager had been telling the truth when she said Fiona didn't have the affection of all the tenants. I hated it when the Dowager was right. She was such a nasty creature that it seemed fitting that she be wrong about everything.

But were the tenants correct in their perceptions? That was the question. I didn't want to think Fiona was actually failing in her duties. I liked her.

Not that it was any of my business. My sole job was to help Taro channel events. It was not my place to even think about politics.

Well, unless things got violent. Then it would become my business whether I liked it or not. I could just see the two of us running from a crowd of furious whalers. They'd all been big and strong and handy with their instruments.

"Sorry about that," Dane said. "There were many in the community who made it clear they would be unhappy with any titleholder who wasn't a Karish. There are those who believe there is magic in the bloodlines that protect them."

"I thought we'd be getting away from the use of casting here," I said.

He frowned. "Why would you think that?"

"Why wouldn't I?"

"Spells have always worked here."

That was an odd way to put it. "It only became well-known in High Scape over the past couple of years." Though there was evidence casting had been practiced by some for years. Maybe generations.

"How odd," said Dane. "But then, I heard High Scape is an odd place. Everyone so crowded together, it's sure to make everyone strange."

What an unusual opinion. "Do you believe spells actually work?"

He looked as though he thought that was a ridiculous question. "Of course."

Of course. Sometimes I felt like the only person who hadn't.

Chapter Six

I woke to the sensation of something stroking over my right eyebrow. I opened my eyes, a little befuddled, to see Taro leaning over me.

He smiled sheepishly. "I'm sorry. I didn't mean to wake you up."

I didn't mind. I felt loose and warm and utterly comfortable. The simple, light touch felt nice. And now that I was awake, his finger moved around more, down the slope of my nose, over my lips, along my jaw.

I smiled at him.

And Lila walked in, cutting short any possible further activity.

That was going to get annoying.

The maid curtsied. "Her Ladyship and His Lordship invite you to join them for breakfast in the sitting room."

I guessed that meant we were supposed to get up.

"We'll be there shortly," Taro told her, and she curtsied again before leaving.

I wondered if that was hard on the knees.

"Are they really supposed to just walk in like that?" I asked as I scrambled out of bed.

"Aye. You're supposed to ignore them unless you absolutely have to talk to them."

"But that's so rude." All of it. The servants just walking in. Our ignoring them.

"It's what everyone expects and feels comfortable with, I suppose."

"I'm not comfortable with it," I mumbled. And the other side of that coin, it looked like privacy was something else we were losing to this post. Really, was this woman going to be popping in on us all hours of the day?

We found Fiona in the sitting room, drinking coffee, while Dane sat on the floor tormenting his young son by tickling him. The boy was gasping as he laughed and I wondered if that was good for him. They both did seem to be enjoying themselves.

"I'm in the mood to celebrate," Fiona announced.

"I always enjoy celebrations," said Taro. "They do make life much less dreary."

I glanced at him. There was something vapid about his tone. I wondered what, in particular, was bothering him now.

"May I know what you're celebrating?" I asked.

Fiona grinned. "It appears that none of my tenants are in the habit of casting spells. Or, forgive me, are in the habit of pretending to cast spells."

So the Guards hadn't found anything. I was relieved. Flogging was reprehensible, and I would have hated knowing that any of the tenants had suffered it. I agreed that there were people who were trying to cast spells without knowing what they were doing, and that the results could be dangerous, but the way to deal with that, I thought, was to teach people how to do it and build sensible laws regulating the casting of spells. Trying to convince everyone that casting had no power at all seemed futile and foolish.

Fiona rubbed her hands together. "The weather is perfect for visiting the caves. They were opened up by the earthquakes. They're fascinating."

"They're dangerous," Dane countered.

She waved him off. "Only for idiots. We'll take precautions."

I couldn't help frowning. "You go into caves for . . . entertainment."

She laughed. "The look on your face! But there's something astounding in this particular cave. So have some breakfast and change into something sturdy. You won't regret going, I promise you."

Crawling through caves would have never been anything I chose to do, but I could think of no polite way to get out of it. So Taro and I ate and changed our clothes and headed out with Fiona. Dane chose to stay behind and play with his son.

We hiked through the hill range and then scrambled up the other side. Fiona was carrying a rope and a lit lantern. I didn't like the possibilities that leapt to mind concerning the rope. I was not going to be suspended into any hole by a rope. I was putting my foot down at that.

The entrance to the cave wasn't the circular shape I'd envisioned. It was a strange, irregular shape, as though it had been torn open by the top and bottom of the cliff grinding in opposite directions. The floor wasn't smooth, either, but full of jagged protrusions. We'd have to be careful about how we walked.

There was an iron peg pounded at the floor of the entrance. Fiona leaned down to tie an end of the rope securely around the peg. "So we can find our way back easily," she explained.

She went in and I followed her. After a few steps, I realized Taro wasn't following me, and I looked back. He was standing at the entrance of the cave, his hand against one wall, and his shoulders were slumped. "I can't go in," he said.

"Why not?" Fiona asked.

I studied him, or I tried to. I couldn't really see his face with the sunlight coming in behind him. "Do you feel there is something dangerous about it?"

"There's not enough air in there."

"It's perfectly safe, cousin," Fiona assured him. "I've been here many times."

"It probably is," said Taro. "But I can't go in there." And he turned and headed back down the hill.

I strode to the mouth of the cave. "Taro," I called, and he waved at me over his shoulder. It was a dismissive gesture. He didn't want me following.

"Are you going to go after him?" Fiona asked.

"He wants to be alone." Or, at least, not with me. I had no idea why he was so alarmed by the cave. Was it the darkness? Was it the weight of all the rock resting on top of us?

I was almost talking myself out of this. But Fiona was looking disappointed. There was something she wanted to show us. I'd feel churlish if I refused now. "He'll be all right."

"Maybe when you tell him all about it, he'll change his mind. Come this way."

I followed Fiona. Carefully. I tripped twice and had visions of falling face-first into the rocky floor. I might end up with an eye gouged out. It got worse once we took a couple of bends and the sunlight faded.

We definitely needed the rope Fiona was awkwardly unwinding as we walked. The cave, to my surprise, branched off and branched again and turned in on itself. We lost all sunlight and our voices echoed off the walls. Soon our entire world was nothing more than what lay within the glow of the lantern.

"I love it in here," Fiona said with enthusiasm. "It's like being in a different world."

It was indeed. A dark, damp world, where the world I

was used to was separated from us by miles of black rock.
A world with no color, where our voices scattered into
pieces and came back to us in distorted waves.

But really there was nothing to see. We took a few
more twists and turns with nothing new happening and I
was wondering why we were there.

"Here it is," Fiona announced. She tucked the rope into
a crevice in the floor and held the lantern up.

I gasped. I was looking at a huge cavern with walls
covered in chunks of transparent white and blue stones.
The chunks varied in size from the size of the tip of my
finger to my clenched fist. The floor was covered with
them, and so was the ceiling. The light of the lantern
bounced off thousands of tiny surfaces. It was beautiful.
It was breathtaking. "What kinds of stones are these?" I
reached out and carefully touched a few clusters.

"I'm not sure. I'm tempted to think diamonds and sap-
phires, but I don't think they develop together like that,
and they need polishing to get that shine. But wouldn't it
be amazing if they were?"

"You'd be wealthier than the Emperor." Or so I guessed.
I had no idea how much money the Emperor had.

"Only if I chose to have them mined."

"You might choose not to?"

"This cave is a wonder. It would be a shame to strip it
bare just for the sake of money. I have enough money.
That's one reason I haven't told any of the tenants or the
servants about this place. They might be tempted to come
in and take some of this, and end up getting lost in the process. These caves are dangerous if you don't take care."

I had to admire her willingness to consider leaving the
cavern untouched. While on Flatwell, I had been forced to
earn money, as the residents had refused to provide Taro
and me with the services and goods that were our due. I
had some experience with having no money when money
was needed, or having some money and worrying about it

running out before I could make some more. I imagined most people, upon finding such a cave, would order it stripped without a second thought.

Of course, Fiona had been wealthy her entire life. Perhaps that gave her a sense of security most other people lacked.

The cavern was not a perfect sphere, of course. There were jagged little alcoves here and there, and I noticed in some of the alcoves strips of solid green. It looked like jade. Really, how had all these different elements been brought together like this?

"I wonder if the Dowager Duchess knows about this. She'd be furious that it wasn't discovered while under Karish control. She'd spit nails."

Fiona chuckled. "She's hilarious when she's angry."

Not what I would call it, but Fiona wasn't as vulnerable to the Dowager as was Taro. "Maybe you should tell her just to torture her." That would be something I would like to watch.

"Come over here," said Fiona. She was standing in another of the alcoves, a deeper one, I thought, from the way the light of her lantern was reflected. I carefully made my way over to her and looked at where she was pointing.

The sound I made was not a shriek. Of course, I shouldn't have made a sound at all, but I'd never seen a skeleton before. The fact that it was still dressed in odd-looking clothing made it all the more grotesque.

Fiona laughed at my nonshriek.

"Who is that?" I demanded.

"I imagine it was someone who was stuck here in an earthquake that shifted all the caves, but of course I can't be sure."

"Why hasn't it been taken out and cremated?"

"It has some historic significance, don't you think? I'm not sure I should move it."

"It doesn't seem right to just leave it there."

"I'm going to ask Reid to take a look at it when he gets here. I'll do whatever he suggests."

There was something in the skeleton's hand. It was thick and rectangular and made out of a slightly shiny black material that I had never seen before. "What is that, do you know?"

"No idea."

A thought struck me. "How old do you think this skeleton is?"

"Have no idea about that, either."

In my excitement, I couldn't help touching her arm. "Do you think it could be one of the First Landed?"

Her eyebrows rose. "That doesn't seem likely, does it? Surely the skeleton would have completely disintegrated by now."

I knew nothing about that sort of thing. "The clothes are strange." All black with pockets in weird places, like down the leg of the trousers. "That's some kind of little machine." That was one of the First Landed. I was sure of it. A professor at the Academy had had little machines that belonged to the First Landed that had been similar in size and shape.

I stared down at the skeleton. I wondered whether it was male or female. I wondered what his name was, and what he thought of our world. What had his occupation been? Did his language sound anything like what we spoke? Had he had family? Was he happy to be here?

I reached out to touch the machine. The skeleton's finger fell off.

I shrieked then, I wouldn't deny it, and I jumped. I fell against Fiona, who dropped the lantern as she grabbed onto the wall to keep her balance. The lantern smashed and we were drowned in darkness.

"Hell!" said Fiona, her voice sounding distant in the thick, pressing darkness.

I couldn't see anything, no matter how hard I stared.

I couldn't remember how we'd gotten there or where the entrance back to the cave mouth was in relation to our position. How the hell were we going to find our way out?

"Stay right here," said Fiona. "I'm going to find the rope."

"It's pitch-black in here," I said unnecessarily.

"That's why I want you to stay where you are. So I can find you again."

Really, I couldn't even see any shadows or traces of light anywhere. This was a nightmare. I'd known this was a bad idea.

Where was the skeleton's finger?

I listened to Fiona. I heard her carefully leave the alcove. I heard her swear under her breath. I heard her slowly shifting along the floor of the cave. What if she left me? She might end up scuffing away, down one of the paths I'd seen running off in different directions. And then she would get lost and no one would find either of us.

I was so stupid. This was all my fault. It had been ridiculous of me to jump that way just because that skeleton's finger fell off. I wasn't a child. I was a Shield, damn it. I was supposed to stay calm at all times, especially in the face of the unexpected.

"Hell," I heard from Fiona.

"What else is wrong?" I asked, and I cringed at the waver in my voice. Damn it, couldn't I at least appear calm?

"I can't find the rope."

"The rope that's supposed to lead us out?"

"That's the one."

No no no no. We were stuck in here. We'd never get out of there. "How is that possible?"

"Hold on. I'll keep looking," she said, but she sounded like she had no real hope of success.

"What if you can't find it?"

"Calm down, Dunleavy. It will be all right."

"You have no way of knowing that."

She didn't answer, which I took to be a very bad sign. There was some more scuffling, and then I heard her back at my side. "I can't find the rope," she said. "We'll have to wait until the others come to look for us."

"That could be hours," I complained. I was ashamed of myself, but I couldn't help it. We were stuck there in the middle of a mountain with no way out. The whole thing could collapse in on us and smother us.

"Aye, it could," said Fiona. "But we're safe in here. Nothing can happen to us in here."

Oh, I could imagine all sorts of things. And the very fact that she had said nothing would happen made it a certainty that something would.

And wasn't that a foolish thing to think? Not to mention superstitious. So I would stop thinking that way immediately.

"Here, we'll sit down right here," said Fiona. "Dane knows where we are. When we don't show up, he'll come looking."

I sat down. The rocky floor bit into my behind. It was impossible to get comfortable. "Is there no way we can find our own way out?" Because I hated the thought of just sitting and waiting.

"No," was her immediate answer. "With neither a lantern nor a rope, we'll get turned around and we'll go the wrong way and no one will be able to find us. Dane knows about this cavern. He knew this was where I was bringing you. He'll know to come here."

"All right." I sighed.

"Just sit tight. It'll be fine."

Aye. It'll be fine. Wonderful.

Chapter Seven

"So," Fiona said after a few moments, "Shintaro's manner is unexpected."

I stiffened. "Taro's a fine man."

She chuckled. "I have no complaints, Dunleavy. He's just much more serious than I expected."

"Really?" I couldn't imagine anyone calling Taro serious, but then, he had been pretty grim since coming to Flown Raven. "There are things he is serious about, but overall he's fairly vivacious."

"Vivacious." Fiona sounded out the word as though testing it for suitability. "I didn't really know what to expect. There's what we heard before Shintaro went to the Source Academy, and what we've heard since."

"What did you hear of before he went to the Academy?" I knew what they would have heard after he was released for field training. The same that the rest of us had heard. That he drank and gambled and slept with anything on two legs. I'd also heard that he was shallow and arrogant. I'd heard all of this before being bonded with him, and I'd believed it all, which had led to some real difficulties between the two of us, to my shame.

But what rumors were passed among his extended family? I had no idea. I was almost afraid of finding out. It was sure to infuriate me.

"That he was a half-wit, mostly," Fiona said with an ease I disliked. "That for his own good he was kept in a room in the cellar, for significant exposure to others exacerbated his imbalanced sensibilities. That he didn't have mind enough to speak properly, never mind reading and writing or moving about in the open world."

"That's appalling." I felt sick. Who had spread such foul ideas?

Well, I knew who had started those rumors. His own parents. The Dowager had once said in my hearing she didn't want people knowing about Taro's peculiarities, because they embarrassed her, but who else could have told everyone about Taro?

Then again, the servants could have spoken out. I always forgot about the servants.

Did that mean I was a bitch?

"Aye, I know," said Fiona. "When we learned he'd been taken to the Source Academy, I remember wondering why they even wanted him, no matter what his talent. He surely couldn't be useful as a Source. But I'd assumed it was something legal, that the Triple S had to take him no matter what was wrong with him."

Actually, they probably did. I'd never thought about it, but it made sense. And I remembered seeing at the Shield Academy some people, children and adults, who never mixed with the students and never went to the classes. Were they damaged people who just happened to be Shields?

"We don't hear anything for five or so years, and then we start hearing that he's growing up to be some kind of hellion and everyone loves him."

I had a feeling not many people actually loved Taro.

They'd merely enjoyed his fine form and maybe his talent. However, I had no reason to believe he hadn't enjoyed the attention. He'd been a young man, after all.

"I'd never seen him, had no contact with him before he sent me the code. Surprised the hell out of me. I'd assumed he would take the title and run the estate into the ground. It had never occurred to me he would ever, in a million years, abjure the title. His letter came out of the blue. I couldn't have been more shocked."

"Were you happy to get the title?" I asked.

"Not happy, so much. Dane and I were doing well in Centerfield. Our tenants were successful. But I felt I could do a good job running Flown Raven, and I was the first choice of the heir apparent. I felt a sort of duty to take it."

I wondered if she still thought she could do a good job. I wondered if the claims of less successful fishing and whaling were true.

"I did feel really grateful to Shintaro for choosing me. I thanked him for his sacrifice several times, but he kept saying it was no sacrifice to him, that he felt nothing for Flown Raven and it would prosper in my hands. I get the feeling he would be happier if he'd never had to come to Flown Raven, and I feel bad about it. I never expected to get your Pair when I told the Triple S we needed one. And I never expected the Triple S to turn the request over to the Emperor. He's not usually involved in the posting of Pairs, is he?"

"You directed your request to the Triple S?" I asked.

"I understood that was what one did."

So how did the Emperor learn of the request? I could see no reason for the council to tell him. How did he know that the Triple S council hadn't already assigned someone to Flown Raven when he'd ordered us here? Knowing him, he hadn't, and hadn't cared.

"Then I finally meet Shintaro and it turns out that my

cousin is personable and of sound mind, and maybe he should have taken the title after all, if he is going to end up living here for the rest of his life."

"It's unlikely to be the rest of his life." It had better not be. "And even if it were, he's here as a Source, not a duke. There's no reason to expect him to take both roles."

"The people here believe very much in tradition. The Karish family has held the title for generations. And I think they felt it as a personal insult when Taro abjured the title, like he was rejecting them. Some of them have been very vocal about their displeasure at my being here. And the numbers are down."

I didn't point out that Dane had claimed to some tenants that the numbers weren't down. I didn't blame him if he was lying. "I don't know anything about it, but couldn't the numbers fall for reasons that have nothing to do with you?"

"Certainly, but you can understand why they think the way they do, can't you? And you can see the logic of Taro taking the title, can't you? If he's going to be here anyway, why not have him be duke?"

Because he didn't want it. Because I didn't want it. Because I hoped we would be transferred to another post in a few years. "Are you thinking of offering to give the position back to him?"

"Oh, no. It would be illegal for him to take it."

Thank gods.

"It's just hard not to see that he would be a better fit."

"He has no training in estate management."

"All he would need are the right advisors."

But how could he find the right advisors if he didn't know what he was doing in the first place? "Well, believe me, he doesn't think he made a mistake in abjuring, so neither should you."

She was silent after that, and I wondered if I'd spoken too firmly. Some people found that offensive. I shifted, trying to find comfort on the uncomfortable ground. I couldn't believe my eyes still hadn't gotten used to the darkness. I needed to talk to distract myself.

"What's it like having to make legal decisions?" I asked her. Not many titleholders had to do that.

"It's horrible," she said. "I don't know what the hell I'm doing."

That had been emphatic. "How can that be?" I asked. "All you do is listen to two stories and choose the better one."

"That's what makes it so horrible. Usually both sides have merit, you know, and it isn't obvious who is right. And there are some wonderful liars in the world. What if I'm totally taken in by one of them?"

"Surely everyone in your position feels the same."

"I don't know. Everyone else seems pretty confident in what they're doing."

"Maybe everyone is just fooling everyone else."

"That's a depressing, pessimistic thought."

I shrugged, forgetting that she couldn't see me.

We sat in silence for a while. And it was silence. I couldn't hear anything. It was like we were cut off from the rest of the world. And then my mind went off in ludicrous directions. Maybe we were cut off from the rest of the world. Maybe the rest of the world had been destroyed by a disaster while we were stuck in the cave. Maybe we were the only two people left alive and there was nothing left but this cave.

That was stupid.

I itched to look for the rope myself, and that was stupid, too. If Fiona couldn't find it, I certainly couldn't. I just hated waiting there for someone else to find us. There had to be something we could do for ourselves.

If I were Taro, I could alert him that I was in trouble by starting an event, and if he were me, he would be able to feel that was what I was doing, know I was doing it because I was in trouble, and start looking for me. I hadn't been thrilled when he had done that in the past, but I could certainly understand the temptation. I would do it right then, if I could.

"Do you have any appointments today?" I asked Fiona hopefully. If she didn't show up for a meeting, Dane would start looking for her.

"I have a meeting with Roshni but that isn't until late afternoon."

Damn.

"Don't worry. Dane thinks this whole place is a death trap. He won't wait long to look for us."

Something about her words made me remember some things Dane had said. "Is he not happy to be here?" I asked, worried that I might be overstepping my bounds.

"He was content at home. I discussed with him taking the title, of course, and he agreed to the move, but now that we're here he isn't thrilled with the differences. Or the people."

"Do you think he'll get used to it?"

"He'll have to, won't he?"

That seemed a little callous. And shortsighted. It was bad enough that Taro and I resented being here. It would make for a miserable household if Fiona and Dane hated it, too.

Time passed. Or I assumed it did. It was hard to tell, stuck in the cave.

I was thirsty. And hungry. And I felt dirty.

I wished I'd gotten a better look at that machine, because I would never be seeing it again. Once I got out of the cave, I was never going back. Ever.

The ground seemed to be getting harder. My knees felt like they were locking up. I shifted in preparation for standing up.

"Where are you going?" Fiona demanded.

"I just want to walk around a bit."

"Don't. It's too easy to get turned around and you won't be able to find your way back. If you're not in this chamber, there's a good chance we won't be able to find you at all."

I sighed and settled back down.

We waited some more. I needed to relieve myself. That was too embarrassing.

I couldn't believe how long they were taking to find us. We must have been gone long enough to be missed. Why weren't they here?

Maybe they couldn't find us. Maybe they'd somehow moved or pulled up the rope and they were going down one of the branches of the cave. Maybe they were lost somewhere in the cave. Maybe we were all going to die in this black, silent little world.

All right, now, that was ridiculous. I was scaring myself. I could feel my pulse in my throat. That wasn't accomplishing anything.

Breathe. In two three four, hold two three four, out two three four.

"What are you doing?" Fiona asked.

"Breathing," I answered.

"You're awfully loud," she complained.

I had a feeling shrieking like a child would be even louder, so I continued with my serenity breathing.

"They will find us, Dunleavy," Fiona said. "Don't worry."

"I'm not worried," I lied.

"We just have to sit and wait."

"I'm good at sitting and waiting." No, I wasn't.

Fiona chuckled.

I hadn't been trying to be funny.

I swore the seat of my trousers had to be torn to shreds. I wouldn't be decent enough to leave the cave. I would have to walk around in front of all those strangers, hanging out of my trousers. They'd lose any respect they ever had for me. They'd smirk every time they looked at me.

"Do you hear that?" Fiona asked.

Finally. "You hear them looking for us?"

"I don't—" She broke off. "There, that. Do you hear that?"

I listened. I strained to hear something. "I don't hear anything, but that doesn't mean anything. My hearing may not be as acute as yours." Shields tended to have duller senses.

"Shh!" A few more moments of dark silence dragged by, then Fiona shouted, "We're in here! We're in the crystal cave!"

Her voice seemed to echo in the dark. Once it finally faded, I listened for any new sounds. I still heard nothing.

Could she be hearing things, hearing what she desperately wanted to hear? Maybe she was more frightened than she was letting on. Fear could do strange things to a person's mind.

"There it is again," she said.

I still heard nothing. Was I going deaf? Maybe it was my own mind upon which fear was working.

"Over here!" Fiona shouted.

"Who's making that racket?" a voice thundered out.

"Dane!" Fiona sighed, and I felt her rise to her feet.

"You're getting loud in your old age, woman."

"You've never complained before."

"What did you do with the rope?"

I could see a glow then, and it was only then that I felt a little spurt of joy and relief. We were finally found. The glow grew stronger and came around a corner. It was Dane, Taro following behind.

Thank Zaire. I gratefully climbed to my feet, which was harder than it should have been. My legs felt numb.

Fiona threw herself into Dane's arms, which seemed to surprise him. "What took you so long?" she demanded.

"We didn't think you were still in here."

"Why the hell not?"

"The rope was gone. What did you do with it?"

"We didn't do anything with it. Can we just get out of here?"

I was all for that.

Taro crooked an arm for me to take. I was grateful for it. I was stumbling a little on my numb legs. "Are you all right?" he asked.

I was then. Also extremely relieved. I had been really starting to worry. "Aye. Wouldn't want to have waited any longer, though." We followed Fiona and Dane, the latter of whom was coiling a rope as they followed it back to the mouth of the cave.

"What was that about the rope?" I asked him.

"The rope you tied to the peg was gone. That's why we took so long. After an hour we came back, and found the rope gone, so we figured the two of you were out and about somewhere and we didn't need to worry. But a few more hours passed, and we asked around a bit if anyone had seen you, and no one had. Dane decided to go as far as the crystal cave, because he knew Fiona had wanted us to see it."

"Did you get a chance to see it?" I hadn't noticed him react to the cavern at all. "It is truly beautiful."

"I really don't give a damn. I hate it in here."

I would tell him about the cavern and the machine at a better time. "I don't know what happened with the rope. We had it with us all the way to the machine, but when we looked for it again, it was gone."

No one commented, but I supposed it was a mystery best left for another time. I was desperate to get out, too. In fact, once we were finally out in the afternoon air, I drew in a deep breath as though my breathing had been restricted before.

And despite my sincere worry about the matter, my trousers were unscathed.

Chapter Eight

We returned to the manor to find that a guest had arrived. Alex Reid, the Alex Reid, had appeared while the men were out looking for us. I was surprised by the little spurt of excitement I felt at the news. I didn't get excited about people. It was embarrassing.

"Thank you, Bailey," Fiona said. "If you could let Academic Reid know that I need to freshen up and that I'll be with him as quickly as I can."

"Of course, my lady."

Although I hadn't seen a mirror, I was sure I looked a complete mess. "If you all would excuse me," I said, and I headed for the closest access to stairs.

"What's going on?" Taro asked, striding along behind me.

"Academic Alex Reid," I said, taking the stairs in the court room.

"What about him?"

"He's Academic Alex Reid!"

"So what?" he growled.

"He's a brilliant historian, and an excellent writer. I can't believe he's here." I'd had so many questions to ask him while I was still a student. I couldn't remember any of them right then, damn it.

"Sounds pretty boring to me," Taro muttered.

"Only because you don't enjoy history. Among those who do, he's highly admired."

We entered our suite.

Which had been ransacked. Cupboards were left open, knickknacks were out of place, clothes had been pulled out of the wardrobe and drawers, and the mattress had been flipped and left half off its frame. All I could do was stare, stunned.

Taro swore at length, his diatribe finally ending with ". . . damned Guards."

"That's who you think did this?"

"Who else could it be? Servants would only be looking for trinkets, and they wouldn't have to search the whole room to find them. They would have left everything as they found it to avoid immediate detection. Only the Guards wouldn't care if we knew it was them who had done this."

Bastards.

I went to the overmantel and unlocked the front portion. All the casting tools appeared undisturbed. "It might be a good thing they searched our rooms. Now they won't suspect us."

"They had no right to do this," Taro snapped.

"Of course not. But the fact that they did might make everyone safe."

"I still think you should write a letter of complaint to the Triple S council."

"Certainly." Not that I thought it would accomplish anything. The Triple S seemed to be powerless in the face of the Emperor's encroachment.

We spent some time straightening up the suite. I felt

odd knowing people had been rifling through our things. Had they gone through my correspondence? I still had a half-written report to the Triple S in the secretary. They had no right to be reading that. I would have to start locking the secretary.

I washed up, and when I changed into fresh clothing I felt uneasy knowing unfamiliar hands had touched them. If I hadn't thought it was ridiculously extravagant, I would have requisitioned an entire new wardrobe. The clothing felt dirty against my skin.

Taro freshened up, too, changing into trim black trousers and a gorgeous red shirt, leaving his luscious black hair loose. He looked delicious. I wondered why he was making so much of an effort for a man he claimed to have never heard of. Then again, Taro always did his best to look good. We went down to the sitting room.

Academic Alex Reid was a man in his late forties. I knew that from reading his autobiographical works. What I saw was a tall, lean man with shoulder-length brown hair, graying in places, with brown eyes and rather pale skin. He was almost plain, except when he first saw us. Because then he smiled, and it was a warm, spontaneous smile that completely transformed him into something lovely.

"You must be Source Karish and Shield Mallorough," he said, holding out a forearm.

"I fear I must," Taro said in an almost flirtatious tone that I hadn't heard from him in a while. "For such is what I was born. It's such an honor to meet you." And he gave the man a bone-melting smile.

What the hell was he playing at?

I stepped forward. "Please call me Dunleavy," I said, offering my forearm. "I am a great admirer of your work."

"I have to admit I always love hearing that," he said.

"You made an investigation into the evolution of the tax laws seem interesting. That must have been quite a challenge."

He laughed, and it was a delightful sound.

"It looks like you have been grossly neglected," Taro commented, cutting into Reid's laughter. He was looking at a tray with an empty plate and an empty cup. "Shall I ring for more?"

"Truly, I've been very comfortable. I'm happy to be here under any circumstances. Just to be given a chance to look at Flown Raven is an unanticipated opportunity."

We were all still standing, which looked silly, so I sat down, and the men followed suit. "Why is Flown Raven so interesting?"

"It is believed to be one of the areas most settled by the First Landed. Who knows what kinds of discoveries might be waiting here? Historians have been trying to explore this area for decades, but the previous titleholders wouldn't allow it. To be the one given this chance is an enormous honor."

"Are you going to write a book about Flown Raven?" I asked. That would be exciting.

"It depends on what I find." He looked at Taro. "Source Karish, it would be invaluable to get your input."

Taro gave him a languid smile. "How so?"

"You lived here as a child, did you not?"

"Ah, my dear man, that was so very long ago, but it will be my pleasure to do all that I can for you."

I really didn't like the way Taro was talking to Reid.

Fiona and Dane came in then, and it was a good thing, too, because I was getting confused. Introductions were made, and Dane served liquor from one of the side bars.

"I would like to thank you again," said Reid once we were settled again. "To have found that book, that is exceptionally good luck. I am honored to be invited."

"You should be honored," Daris said as she stepped off the last step at the back of the room. "I live here and I'm never invited to anything. I might as well be Shintaro when he was a child, locked in a room and forgotten."

I was stunned that she would say that in front of a stranger and an outsider. What a bitch.

Reid was obviously confused. He frowned and glanced at Taro, quickly glancing away.

"I'm starting to understand why you drink so much, cousin," Taro drawled. "Even you find you unpleasant."

She sent him a hand gesture that none of us needed translating. "So why are you really here?" she asked Reid.

"I don't understand," the professor said.

"You're living off my sister just to read a book? I don't think so."

"Some find the study of history very valuable."

Daris snorted into her glass of whiskey. I wondered if that hurt. Whiskey was a nasty drink that burned like hell. "Fiona doesn't."

"Please feel free to ignore my sister, Academic Reid. Everyone else does."

"You're such a fraud," said Daris. "You love history so much? You admire this historian so much? Name something he's written."

I didn't blame Fiona for not being able to come up with a title right then. I had read many of Reid's treatises and couldn't remember the exact title of any of them, and I wasn't the one being put on the spot.

"I never claimed to be a historian myself," said Fiona. "We have found ancient things on this land and it would be idiotic not to have those things examined by experts. Now, are you here for any reason other than to cause a scene?"

"No," said Daris, and she crossed the room to sit too closely beside Reid. "You're not good-looking," she announced. "But you are a fresh face, and you are unescorted. Has Shintaro offered you his bed yet?"

Reid blushed. I found that odd in a man his age.

"That's enough, Daris," Taro snapped.

"Don't even think you have any influence over me, Shintaro," Daris retorted. "You gave up any chance of that when you handed the title to my younger sister."

"What do you do anyway?" Taro demanded. "Do you just lie about all day getting drunk?"

Daris ignored him. "Really, sister, tell the delicate historian why he's really here."

"He is here because we found machinery and a book we believe to be extremely old, and his name was recommended to us," Fiona answered with forced patience. "I really have no idea what you're insinuating."

"Of course not," Daris sneered.

Really, what was she hinting at? What was so unusual about a wealthy titleholder hiring an expert to evaluate unexpected finds on her land? Or was Daris just making accusations for the sake of causing trouble? She seemed the sort to do that.

"How thoughtless of me, Academic." Fiona suddenly stood and reach for the bellpull. "You haven't been shown to your room."

"No, not at all," said Reid, which didn't quite make sense, but I had a feeling he was still flustered by Daris's behavior. A maid, Vora, came to show him to his room, and I had the feeling he was happy to escape.

I was trying to think of a way that I could escape, too.

"What are you up to this time?" Fiona demanded of Daris.

"I have no idea what you're talking about, sister."

"Are you going to drive him away just because you can?"

"What an excellent idea. I never would have thought of it myself."

"Did you take our rope today?" Fiona demanded. Taro and Dane looked as shocked by the question as I felt.

"Rope?" said Daris.

"You knew we were going to the caves. You would

have seen Shintaro come back without us. It would be your idea of fun to take the rope while we were inside."

"True," said Daris. "But, to my shame, I didn't. I didn't actually know where you were. I don't spend all my time watching you. You're not that interesting."

Really? Then why was she wasting her time with us right then?

But I couldn't believe anyone would deliberately remove the rope. That was a horrible and dangerous joke to play on someone. It was possible that we could have been permanently lost in there and died. How could anyone think that was funny?

Unless someone had done it with the intention of harming either Fiona or me. But that was ridiculous. No one would dare injure a duchess, and I hadn't been in Flown Raven long enough to seriously annoy anyone.

"If I find out you did it, I'll—"

"You'll what?" Daris challenged with a complete lack of concern.

"I'll ban you from Westsea and from Centerfield. Who'll pay for your alcohol then?"

Why were they having this dispute in front of the rest of us? Had they forgotten we were there?

"You would never banish me," Daris said with ridiculous confidence. I'd certainly banish her. "You're too obsessed with things like family and honor."

"You may prove to be the exception to the rule."

Daris laughed. "Go ahead, Fiona. Try it. Dare to have the neighbors whisper about your shocking behavior, casting out your penniless sister when you have so much to share. I would worm my way back within a day." She poured herself another whiskey. "I'm off to talk to the shy academic. He may prove to be entertaining." She headed back to the stairs.

"You leave him alone," Fiona ordered.

A laugh was the response.

"She wouldn't have taken the rope, Fiona," Dane said.

"You don't know her."

"I've lived with her for years." And he sounded less than thrilled about it.

"You've only seen what you've been allowed to see."

All right, if she was that bad, why was she living there? So what if she was family? So what if she had nowhere to go? If she was ungrateful and dangerous, kick her out.

Obviously, it was not my place to say anything like that.

"It was probably an animal," Dane suggested.

"What kind of animal do we have around here that could do that?"

They were gearing up for an argument. I had no interest in witnessing that. Taro and I left the room without saying anything. Fiona and Dane didn't seem to notice.

Supper was held in the formal dining room, and it was an uncomfortable affair. We were all seated around one end of the table, and it was clear Fiona and Dane were still feeling the effects of their argument. Daris said nothing that wasn't an insult. Tarce looked bored and uninterested with his food. I was dead tired and would have preferred to be in bed. Taro was just acting weird.

So, this was what family life was like. I was happy to have been spared it so far.

I was desperate for conversation that didn't cause tension. "Have you come across other books written by the First Landed, Academic Reid?" I asked.

"Yes," he answered eagerly. "Two. One in the library in Erstwhile and one under the ruins of Velia. It took years to translate the first one. It seems our language has drifted a great deal from the one the First Landed wrote and spoke. But having translated the first one, the second went much more quickly."

"What were the books about?"

"The one found in Velia was a book of theories about what form of government would be most suitable for the people living here. It is fascinating, the different models that were described, and there were examples taken from their other worlds. That one was a real find. The one found in Erstwhile was a book of spells."

The mention of spells made most of us glance toward the door. Damned Guards. I wondered where they were. Maybe Fiona had told them they weren't allowed to eat with the rest of us.

"Unfortunately," Reid continued, "once we determined that that was the nature of the spell book, we lost access to it. I understand the Emperor doesn't approve of such things."

"But you're sure the book was made by the First Landed?" I asked.

"As sure as I can be."

"You're saying you think the First Landed used spells?" He couldn't be saying that. We knew the First Landed had all sorts of wondrous machines. What need did they have for casting?

Reid opened his mouth, paused and shut it with a wink. "You've gotten me talking when I should be listening. And a good historian doesn't reveal his theory without having a few facts to support it. I'm not there yet."

Damn. That was enticing. And annoying.

"Tell me, Academic Reid, is my sister paying for your expertise?" Daris asked.

"I don't believe it is appropriate to discuss that," said Reid, a little coolly.

"Which means that she is."

"Leave it alone, Daris," Fiona ordered.

Daris, of course, didn't listen to her. "Knowing my sister, you're not getting much."

Reid looked down at his plate. "There are things more important than money."

Daris laughed. "There is nothing more important than money."

"Not everyone thinks as you do, Daris," said Fiona.

"Maybe you don't, but that's because you've always had scads of it. You've never had to worry about it."

"You've never been without."

"Scraps from your table."

Why were they arguing in front of us? I would have expected better manners from Fiona, at least. Or maybe that was how all families behaved, guests or no. Certainly, the Duchess never let an audience keep her from being obnoxious.

I turned back to Reid. "Will you need some assistance while you're here? I have a lot of free time and would be happy to contribute." I didn't think my research skills would be of any use, but I might be able to make copies of the documents for him, if he needed.

"Now, Lee, don't seek to dominate the poor man's time," Taro chided. "You'll have him working all the time, and that's no fun."

Reid frowned in confusion before saying, "I'll need to start before I can know what the workload will be."

"And you'll want to savor the delights of Flown Raven while you're here," Taro added suggestively.

Reid flushed again. He would have to get over that. I watched him as he appeared to be searching for something to say, and failing.

Fiona took pity on him. "You know, I don't understand why we can't read their books. I thought we spoke the same language."

"Actually, the First Landed spoke several different languages, though as far as we can tell they also all spoke a common language. We think what we speak is mostly the common language, with some influences from the other languages, but with some drift due to the passage of time and the experiences we've had while living here. The way we shape letters has changed, too, partially because of the tools we've used to write. With all of the changes, the average person looking at a First Landed book probably wouldn't be able to read it. I would, because I know what to look for."

Reid spoke at length about language and its historical importance. I didn't understand a lot of what he said—I was starting to suspect he wrote better than he spoke—but his words seemed to suppress all the tensions at the table, and for that I was grateful.

Unfortunately, he couldn't follow Taro and me up to our suite, where Taro demanded as soon as the door was closed, "What the hell is the matter with you?"

As far as I was concerned, that came out of nowhere, so all I could say was, "Huh?"

"You were drooling all over him!"

I stared at him, shocked. "Are you insane?"

"You think I'm going to watch you grovel for some man without saying anything?"

"There was no groveling." Except by Taro. "There was no drooling. He's a respected historian. I enjoy history. You know this."

"Offering to be his assistant? Are you serious?"

"We don't have regular watches here. What are we supposed to do with our time?"

"I didn't know seducing people was a viable option. I'll have to keep that in mind."

"I am interested in the books he has written, and what he might find here. I have every right to speak to him and show my appreciation for him."

"That wasn't appreciation. That was—"

"You do not tell me how to behave. And talk about drooling, you were the one who was flirting with him." And what had that been about? Reid didn't seem Taro's type, a little too serious with rather tame pursuits.

"According to you, I flirt with everyone all the time. I thought he might like to see how it was properly done."

I rolled my eyes because all I could think of was to

call him an ass. Name-calling was an indication of a weak argument, even if the other person really deserved it. "I'm not being inappropriate and I'm not changing my behavior."

He crossed his arms. "Then neither am I."

Sometimes I just wanted to smack him.

Chapter Nine

We went to bed angry, but I slept surprisingly well. It had been a long, trying day, and I didn't appreciate being shaken awake.

"I'm going to kill you, Taro," I muttered.

"Shh," a voice said. "Get up."

That was a woman's voice, and when I cracked my eyes open I saw it was Fiona. And that it was barely dawn. I couldn't hit Fiona, unfortunately. "Something wrong?" I asked in a sleep-roughened voice.

"Shh! Get dressed," she whispered. "Wear something warm. Bring a coat or something."

"Taro—"

"Not him." She left the room then.

If Taro didn't need to be awakened, it couldn't be an emergency requiring immediate attention. I was tempted to go back to sleep. It would have been so easy. But I supposed that would be rude. I sighed and pulled myself from the comfortable warm blankets—it was a little chilly—and dressed in trousers, a shirt and a cloak.

Fiona was waiting in our sitting room. "What's going on?" I asked.

She put a finger to her lips. Really, what was with all the melodrama?

I followed her down to the kitchen. Radia was there by the back door. I wondered if we were going to indulge in secret feasting. I wouldn't mind getting up early for something like that.

But Radia disappointed me by opening the door, and we all walked out into the cool, moist morning air. Whisps of fog were clinging to the ground, and the silence was heavy in the air.

"What's going on?" I asked in a hushed voice.

"We're going for our morning constitutional," Fiona answered.

"Your what?"

Radia snickered. "A walk."

I knew what the word meant. "That's very nice," I muttered. "Why do I have to go with you?"

"Because it's good for you," said Fiona.

"Sleep is good for me," I retorted.

Fiona laughed. "You need to get familiar with the area and the people. You're going to be here for a while."

Not if the Triple S transferred us. I still had hopes for that.

But the fresh, cool air was nice, I had to admit, and I felt a little more energy and a clarity of mind as we walked around the house and headed in the direction of the village.

"I have begun the wall hanging for Lord Serilin," said Radia.

"Excellent."

"How did you learn to weave that way?" I asked.

"My mother taught me. She was a merchant's daughter, and her family dealt in wool. She had little to do once she moved here."

"Where are your parents now?"

"My father died. My mother moved back to Soothing Way. Flown Raven was too remote for her. She is happier with her family in a larger city."

"I'm sorry." It must have been difficult to be left behind.

She shrugged. "My father loved it here. So do I."

"What about siblings?"

"I have an older brother. He left with our mother."

"How was it decided that you would be the next Wind Watcher?"

"I have the talent," she told me.

"And your brother didn't?"

"No."

"How exactly does it work?"

"I really don't know. I just feel something that tells me I need to stay close to my tower in case the wind gets too strong."

Huh. That was interesting. What was such a thing the result of? Was it something like casting? Was it somehow like being a Source and a Shield? I'd never heard of such a thing.

"I have heard grumbles," Radia said to Fiona.

"People are always grumbling," Fiona said dismissively.

"I believe the grumbling is getting stronger rather than dissipating. More and more people are saying you're failing as a titleholder. I think some kind of display is in order."

Fiona frowned. "What kind of display?"

"I don't know. Something that shows off your power. Something splashy."

Fiona raised her chin. "I am the rightful titleholder. They owe me their loyalty. I don't need to entertain them like some kind of jongleur."

"That is, of course, up to you," Radia said mildly.

"Besides, I'm getting to think the only way to impress these people is to kill a whale and drag it in and render it all by myself. I mean, what do they want?"

"A Karish," said Radia.

"Who doesn't?" I murmured.

The two women looked at me. "What do you mean?" Radia asked.

"Nothing of any sense," I said. "I really don't understand why they care so much. Taro has no training. He wouldn't know what he was doing. Wouldn't that cause them some concern?"

"To the people here, tradition and custom are very important," said Radia. "Change alarms them."

"We've been through all this before," Fiona complained. "They just need time to see I can do the job."

"It's been more than two years," Radia reminded her.

"Merely a blink of an eye in the long term."

I had a feeling Fiona was aping a certainty she didn't feel. Was she hoping that if she appeared confident, she would inspire confidence in others, or was she merely in denial?

Then again, what option did she have but to appear confident? She couldn't afford to appear weak. People would walk all over her.

Did she have the option of handing the title to someone else? She was in a different situation from Taro. He'd never had the title. Could Fiona, having accepted the title, now give it away? Would that be the best thing for her?

"So, Roshni, my love," Fiona said in a completely different tone of voice. "When are you going to take pity on my poor brother and give him a smile?"

Aha. I was right.

"I fear what encouragement he might derive from a smile."

"And why should you fear what encouragement might bring? Is he not handsome? Is he not young? Is he not attached to the highest of families? And it would be so convenient for you. You wouldn't even have to move."

"All this is true."

"So what objections could you possibly have with my perfect younger brother?"

Radia grimaced. "Please don't make me say it."

"What? You mean that he's arrogant, idle, and ill-mannered? But what obstacles can such things be in the path to true love?"

"Your brother does not love me. He sees me as a challenge, and once the challenge is conquered, he will lose all interest. I'm not a horse to be broken."

"I don't know," Fiona said. "I think he's serious this time."

"Then he shows it ill."

I had to agree with Radia on that. What little I saw in Tarce's interaction with Radia certainly hadn't impressed me. I wondered if he had started with the more traditional route—sweet words and trinkets—and, when that didn't work, either got bitter or was trying a unique and risky tactic.

We were approaching the village as the sun rose high. "What's that building?" I asked, pointing at a taller, slim building with some kind of wheel apparatus partially submerged into the river next to it. I'd seen buildings like it before but had never thought to ask about their purpose.

"It's a gristmill."

"What's a gristmill?"

Both Fiona and Radia snickered. "You're such a city girl," Fiona teased.

"Yes," was all I could think to say.

"It grinds grain into flour."

"Ah."

"The miller also makes the richest, most fragrant bread, and she probably has some coming out of the oven right now."

I was starving. I would say yes to anything.

The miller was a tall, slim, angular-looking woman with her iron gray hair bound into a braid that fell to her waist. Her face had deep wrinkles and it was very red. She was indeed in the process of pulling loaves of bread out of a large oven. Their aroma flooded my mouth with saliva.

"Good morning, my lady, Madam Wind Watcher," she said. She looked at me with her eyebrows raised.

"Shield Mallorough, this is Miller Ena Geller."

We clasped forearms.

"How are you finding Flown Raven, Shield Mallorough?"

"It's very beautiful." In a chilly sort of way. "I'm used to having my time rather rigidly controlled by the Triple S. The level of freedom here will take some getting used to."

"Shouldn't you be with your Source in case something happens?"

"The bond allows for some distance. The village is close enough to the manor for me to Shield Source Karish should he channel."

"Really?" said the miller. "I had been told that you couldn't be more than a few feet away from each other without suffering crippling pain."

That was a rumor I hadn't heard before. I wondered if it was the result of Taro telling the Empress he couldn't bear to be parted from me for long. The Empress, enjoying Taro's company, had been keeping Taro in Erstwhile and leaving me useless in High Scape. So Taro had lied to her to convince her to let him go.

Would that story have spread so far as to reach Flown Raven? "There are a lot of rumors about Pairs that aren't true. That would be one of them."

The miller leaned closer. "Is it true that Sources and Shields always fall madly in love with each other?"

"No."

She looked disappointed. "So you and your Source aren't in love with each other?"

I hesitated. I didn't want to talk about my personal life with this stranger, but I wasn't comfortable lying. It would feel like I was denying something, as though I was ashamed of it.

Fiona rescued me. "Ena, we were hoping to break into some of your delectable bread while it is still warm."

"Of course, my lady."

The warm bread, fresh butter melting into its nooks and crannies, was sumptuous. I could have probably eaten a whole loaf by myself, but I couldn't act the glutton in front of strangers. It did make the early start worthwhile.

After the miller, we stopped in at the blacksmith's, the cheese maker's, and the milliner's. They were all up and working at an ungodly hour. Had people in High Scape had to wake so early?

It was a thriving village of a fair size. I wondered how often they put on plays. Or if they received new books on a regular basis. Or if there were any talented alto or bass singers in the area.

"The next person we're going to introduce you to is very important," Fiona told me. "She's the healer, and she's excellent. If you know of anyone having any difficulty, send for her. We're lucky to have her."

We were taking the path from the main road to a small cottage that was set farther back than most of its fellows. It was made of stone, was small but well kept, but it had an odd smell. Not unpleasant, but not pleasant, either. It almost made me sneeze.

Fiona knocked on the door. I could hear a lot of footsteps shuffling around. Was someone hiding?

The door was opened by a woman only slightly taller than I, blond, and younger than I would expect a healer to be. She was frowning. "My lady."

"What's wrong, Healer Browne?" Fiona asked.

"Those Imperial Guards are here."

I was surprised by the anger that swelled up in me at the mention of the Guards. I hadn't seen any of them since they rifled through my suite. I'd hoped they'd slithered off somewhere, never to be seen again.

"I thought they already searched your home?"

"They decided to search it again."

"May we come in?"

"Of course."

I could hear things being shifted, cupboards being opened and closed, and I could see the four Guards moving about in the kitchen that seemed to make up the front half of the cottage. "What do you think you're doing?" Fiona demanded.

"You know precisely what we're doing," the First Lieutenant said as he fingered the contents of a bag the size of his hand. He pulled out his fingers, covered with fine white powder, and sniffed at them. "What is this?"

"It's aminak," Browne answered impatiently.

"What does it do?"

"It soothes stomach cramps. Look, you've been through here before."

"I wasn't present the last time your residence was searched. From the reports I received, you required a closer look."

"Your handling is spoiling my supplies," Browne complained.

"At least you're here while they search," I said, the words coming out without permission from my brain. I hadn't planned to speak at all in the presence of the Guards, but their arrogance infuriated me. Every time I dressed I had to wonder what they had done to my clothes. "They waited until Source Karish and I were away to turn our rooms upside down."

"I'm sorry, Shield," the young female Guard quickly said, "but we—"

"You do not apologize for doing your duty!" the First Lieutenant snapped at her.

"You should be ashamed for acting like thieves," I said, before wondering if they could do anything else to me if I irritated them.

"You would not grant us permission to enter your suite."

"And so you did anyway. And did you find anything? No."

"We have His Imperial Majesty's orders to search everywhere."

"For tools of a trade that His Majesty won't even admit exists."

The First Lieutenant looked at me with an interest that made me uneasy. "Are you saying you believe casting is a genuine skill?"

See, that was why I should never speak. "I am not qualified to make that judgment, but I am certain there are more serious crimes to be investigated. Murder, rape, treason. You are wasting everyone's time with these trivial pursuits."

"His Majesty is of a different opinion, and his is the opinion that matters."

"His Majesty is of the opinion that my people should be continually harassed?" Fiona asked coolly. "One search was more than enough, and more than my people should have endured."

"Do you think we're not aware that you sent servants out to warn everyone to destroy or hide anything incriminating?"

"Of course I didn't," said Fiona. "My people aren't involved in criminal activities. None of them are pretending to cast spells."

"If that's the case, then none of them have anything to worry about."

"They shouldn't have to worry about people like you stomping through their lives with all the finesse of a great whale. Believe me, I will be reporting your behavior to His Majesty. If he feels this is the way to treat the people of another titleholder, he needs an education."

And she was the one to give it to him? I didn't know anything about politics, but that seemed a risky thing to suggest.

The First Lieutenant didn't appear overwhelmed with either concern or remorse. "You do what you feel you must."

He was a cocky little bastard.

They continued to go through Healer Browne's possessions, and they were suspicious of many of her powders and serums, but they finally decided to leave without taking anything or arresting her.

"And this will be the last time you put her through this, I take it?" Fiona said to them.

"We will decide when we are finished," the First Lieutenant said coolly before leading his colleagues out the door.

"I'm very sorry, Healer Browne," Fiona said to the annoyed woman.

"Would the Emperor grasp so far if a Karish were the titleholder, I wonder?" Browne mused.

That was a little harsh.

Fiona flushed in anger.

"It depends on why he's doing it," I said.

"What do you mean?" Browne asked.

"I haven't heard of him doing this anywhere else. Certainly, the laws were made more stringent in High Scape, but there weren't any searches going on, and as far as I can tell they weren't searching in any of the places we passed through on the way here. Why is he being so obnoxious about Flown Raven?"

"It is a very large and wealthy estate," said Browne.

"With significant political power," Radia added. "Or the potential for it."

I didn't see how that could be possible when Fiona apparently didn't spend much time at the Imperial court. "Wouldn't he then want to court Fiona rather than do his best to alienate her?"

"He could be trying to punish me for refusing to pay those taxes until I absolutely had to."

"That seems a petty reason to be disrupting your people this way. He can't just do whatever he wants to do."

"Unfortunately, there's no practical way to stop him. Not without garnering a great deal of support from other powerful titleholders."

"Which you can't really do without spending more time at court," I said.

"Probably not."

"Why don't you go to court?"

"I'm needed here."

That was probably true, especially as the tenants weren't as supportive of Fiona as they should be.

"Well, we might as well get on with why we came," said Fiona. "Shield Dunleavy, this is Healer Nab Browne."

We clasped forearms.

"So what about you, Shield?" Browne asked, challenge drenching her tone. "Do you believe casting is real?"

"I'm not in a position to judge," I said, because I was a coward.

Browne rolled her eyes. "I'm asking for your opinion. Don't be ridiculous."

I sighed. Fine. "Yes, I think it's real." I hoped I didn't get into a whole hell of trouble for admitting it.

"And why is that?"

"I'm not telling you that."

"Fair enough. Do you believe it should be considered criminal behavior?"

"I believe it should be regulated, but no, I don't consider it criminal." Why was I telling this to a stranger?

On the other hand, what harm could it do for people to know I thought casting was real? They might think I was foolish. So what?

"If you find yourself with nothing to do in the evenings," said Browne, "you should come by. We have the fiddle and the squeeze box here most nights."

"Thank you. I might do that." I actually might. I had no doubt I would find myself at loose ends most evenings.

We left shortly after that.

"She likes you," Fiona told me. "Believe me, that's rare."

"It's always good to have the healer like you," Radia added.

"Then those Guards have something to worry about."

"Believe me," Fiona chuckled. "They have no idea."

Chapter Ten

It was Decision Day, when Fiona sat in the court room all day and heard complaints. She invited Taro and me to witness her work. I agreed to it with pleasure, but Taro declined. He was going to find someone to gamble with.

There was, Fiona told me, a precedence involving the seating of the spectators. The highest rank of spectators sat in the chairs closest to Fiona's throne-like chair. This was the best place for viewing the parties in dispute. The seats farthest away were often empty, for they didn't allow people to hear everything that was said. I planned to stand to Fiona's left, rather than picking a seat and ruffling people's sense of importance. I didn't plan to stay all day, and I didn't want to cause any disruption when I left.

We stood at the top of the stairs, watching as various members of the community seated themselves. Fiona pointed out several people and gave me their names and backgrounds. Then she emitted a noise that sounded half gasp, half laughter, and she grabbed my arm. "That man down there," she whispered. "The white-haired, rotund man just entering."

"I see him."

"His name is Petro Rosen, Baron of White Locks. He was given his title by the Emperor, and no one knows why, because he certainly didn't have the money to buy himself a title. He was just a barrister before, and to listen to him you'd think he'd been born to the highest title in the world. Whatever you do, don't look him in the eye, or he'll lumber over to you and talk to you. And talk to you. And talk to you. For hours. All of it about how wonderful he is. It's unbearable."

I thought she might be joking in some way, but when I looked at her, she was dead serious. "That doesn't seem so bad."

"You haven't had to sit through it. If you're not careful, you will."

The four Guards strode in, standing behind the throne. "What the hell do they want?" Fiona growled. I had no answer for her.

I noticed Radia sitting about halfway up the room. She was chatting easily to one of the women beside her. I hadn't thought Wind Watcher was the equivalent to an aristocratic title. Or perhaps she operated outside the ranking system, as did Shields and Sources.

Once the court room was as full as it was going to get, Bailey and two footmen, Daniel and Sam, stood beside the throne. That, apparently, was the signal for Fiona to proceed down the steps. I followed her. Once she was seated, Bailey announced in a booming voice, "Her Grace, the Duchess of Westsea, will hear your submissions. All seeking her counsel may step forward."

I had been informed that all petitioners and respondents were gathered and supervised in the foyer. Through the door from the foyer, two men were escorted by two burly footmen, Rikin and Hiroki. One of the applicants looked familiar, a lushly handsome man with bright blue eyes and curly brown hair.

The other one was unfamiliar, and was not so grand to look at, being scrawny and pale with uncombed red hair. To my shame, I was already inclined to believe the handsome one. I knew it was wrong, but I couldn't help feeling I'd seen him before, and that we'd met under somewhat pleasant circumstances.

"Merchant Jem Carther is the petitioner," Hiroki announced. The handsome one bowed deeply. "The respondent is Merchant Chris Demont."

"I didn't do nothing," the other man alleged.

"I shall hear Merchant Carther's submission first," said Fiona. "No interruptions, Merchant Demont, if you please."

"My petition involves a theft that took place four days ago," Carther announced. "The day started like any other day. Up too early and limiting myself to only one cup of coffee because beans are scandalously expensive in this place."

"Too true," uttered an older man sitting near us.

"I was in the market square at my usual place. Scrubbing all the bird feces off my stall, because bird droppings just don't inspire people to plunk down their money. Once that was done, I cleaned myself up and wandered down to the bakery where I purchased this delicious cheese pastry from the equally delicious Baker Tracy."

There were some appreciative whistles at that. I grinned. I'd met Baker Tracy. She was a handsome woman.

"I unlocked my stall. I set out my wares. I sell jewelry, a range from light and sweet to dense and expensive. All are welcome at my shop.

"There was nothing unusual about the day, and I didn't notice anyone watching me while I was working. The morning passed as it usually did, and I was bringing in fairly good trade. And then this . . . well . . . creature came up. A frightful-looking block of a man, with unnaturally black hair all greased up into a cone on the top of his head, this weird green and blue paint smeared about his eyes, and the most hideous triple-striped shirt with indecently tight trousers. And really, a man so poorly endowed should not be so eager to show everyone his poverty. Either way, the man looked like a clown and I asked him where his players were. Now"—Carther lowered his eyes in an expression of remorse that I didn't believe for a moment—"I know that was rude of me, but he also smelled like a privy, and I was worried he would drive away all the customers from the stall.

"He seemed offended by my question, though I smiled so sweetly when I asked it. And he started shrieking, his voice quite grating, and he accused me of having sold him an inferior product. Well, I knew immediately that something was off, because I never sell inferior products, and I didn't care how this creature had tarted himself up, I have a gift for remembering voices and I would have remembered that one. I'd never served him before. So I ignored him and continued the discussion with the customer I had been assisting before he'd arrived.

"That incensed him, so he grabbed the front of my shirt, and he was stronger than he looked, for he pulled me almost off my feet and pushed me out onto the street, all the while screaming that he would have me whipped like a dog. For some reason, he didn't seem like someone I should be taking seriously. So I twisted his hands off my shirt and headed back to the stall.

"That was when I saw this mousey fellow in my stall, surrounded by all these people who apparently were too engrossed in the clown to notice what was going on right beside them. He had one of my strongboxes, and his furtive movements made it clear he had no intention of paying for anything in it. Or the box itself. Those things cost a pretty coin, I tell you. Anyway, my plan was to dive at the fellow and flatten him, but the clown tackled me mid-flight and down I went.

"They both ran off, and I reported the theft here. Demont, the mousey one, was caught by some of your people, but the blocky one escaped."

"Bailey?" Fiona asked.

"That's correct, my lady. We have been unable to find anyone matching the description of the accomplice."

I imagined the accomplice had changed his appearance by the time anyone was looking for him.

I sneaked a look at Fiona. She had been aggravated to learn Taro and I had been robbed. What did she think of this second example of crime? Or was it only the second?

"What about the jewelry? Was that found in Merchant Demont's possession?"

"No, Your Ladyship."

"I see. Merchant Demont, what is your description of events?"

"I wasn't in the market that day," that man said.

"Where were you?"

"At home."

"Where is your home?"

"I don't live around here."

"That doesn't answer my question. Where is your home?"

"I live in Little Rock."

"That's within a day's ride from here."

"That's not close," Demont insisted.

"So you don't use our market."

"No. No, I mean yes. But not that day."

"Why not? That's the principal market day for the week."

"I was in Red Bird."

"You just said you were at home."

"No, I forgot. I was in Red Bird."

"There's no market of note in Red Bird."

"There is a fine market in Red Bird."

I didn't know if disagreeing with the adjudicator was the smartest thing a party could do.

"I open the question to the court," Fiona said. "Did anyone witness these events?"

A woman halfway down the left side of the room raised her hand.

"What did you see, Baroness Graydon?"

"I was in the market the day of the theft. I saw a man such as Merchant Carther described assaulting him."

"Did you see Merchant Demont steal anything from Merchant Carther's stall?"

"No, my lady."

"Did anyone see anyone stealing anything from Merchant Carther's stall?"

There was no response.

"Did anyone see Merchant Demont anywhere on the day in question?"

There was no response.

"Then I have nothing more to rely on than the words of the parties. I find Merchant Carther more credible and that Merchant Demont did commit the theft."

"No!" Demont shouted, and Rikin and Hiroki moved closer to him. "That's not right!"

"Everything Demont owns shall be given to Merchant Carther immediately. This matter is settled."

Carther bowed again and left. I didn't know what to think about the verdict. Had Fiona believed him merely because he was more articulate? Maybe Demont had merely been rattled answering a bunch of questions in front of all those people. I knew I would be. Could she really make such a drastic decision based on so little evidence?

But I had to admit that some instinct was telling me the petitioner was telling the truth. Maybe Fiona had had the same instinct.

The next petitioner was a woman seeking money for a

child from one of Fiona's servants, one I couldn't remember meeting. I thought he was an under gardener. The petition gave a detailed account as to when she met him, where they engaged in their affair, and her failed attempts to get support once she realized she was expecting.

"It's not mine, Your Ladyship." He scowled.

"And how do you know that?" Fiona asked coolly.

"She's no better than she should be," he declared boldly. "She's had every man in the community."

"Including you?"

He didn't confirm that, but he didn't deny it, either. He just looked down at his feet, then scuffed the floor. I decided right then that I didn't believe a word he said.

"I declare Manin Ford is the father of—"

"Your Grace!" he shouted in protest.

She pointed a finger at him. "If you wish to avoid responsibility of a child, you will refrain from the activities that create them. I declare that Manin Ford is the father of Ilya Wright, daughter of Julia Wright. Ford will pay to Wright four coppers a month. My stewart will see that the money goes to the petitioner."

"You have no right to do that!" Ford objected.

"Rikin, please help Ford out."

Footman Rikin put a hand on Ford's shoulder. Ford shook it off but headed toward the door without further protest. I supposed he was smart enough to want to keep his job. Wright, who looked grimly satisfied, left unattended.

What followed was a dispute over a land boundary, a complaint from one woman that another had lured her cook away, which Fiona dismissed as too trivial for her attention, and a charge of the sale of an inferior pig. I saw none of the uncertainty Fiona had claimed when we were stuck in the cave.

I wondered how well Taro would do this job. He was clever, and he seemed to understand people better than I. He could possibly charm both sides into believing they had won.

On the other hand, people thought of him as either a half-wit or a philanderer. Would they have respected him?

Why did these people want someone of his reputation as a titleholder?

Maybe they thought he would be weak and easy to manipulate.

In time, Fiona called the midday break. She withdrew, but I stayed behind to watch what happened. The doors to the foyer opened and maids pushed in trays covered with platters of sandwiches and jugs of coffee and tea. Those seated in the spectator chairs headed down to partake in the refreshments. I decided to join them. I was feeling peckish.

I didn't look at him, I swear I didn't, yet Rosen ended up beside me anyway. "Good day," he said. "I am the Baron of White Locks. I take it you are Shield Dunleavy Mallorough."

Immediately, his accent annoyed me. There was something pompous and artificial about it. "I am." Unfortunately.

"I was almost a Source, you know. I was taken to the Academy because I had all the qualities of a Source. Only once I had been there a few months did they determine I was not in fact a Source."

What was it about him that made me think he was lying? It wasn't as though such things never happened. I knew that they did. It was just that Fiona's description of him was shaping my thoughts. I shouldn't be letting that happen. I couldn't seem to help it.

"It was just as well, of course. I think being raised among one's family is more normal and much more healthy. It leads to a sharper mind, you know."

Did he know he was insulting me by saying that? Did he care? And there was nothing I had ever seen to suggest children raised among their families were any healthier than those who weren't. Crazy people showed up everywhere.

But Rosen needed no answer from me. "My family were tenants on a beautiful estate just outside Westsea. My father was the blacksmith and my mother worked the land. They both knew I was too intelligent for any such trade, so they concentrated on and paid more for my education than that of my brothers and sisters. My siblings were happy to make the sacrifice, knowing I would go farther than any of them."

My gods, he was telling me his life story. Literally. Right from the first moment of our meeting. I'd never met anyone who did this. It was strange.

"I did very well as a student, you know. The best in all my classes, and the tutors appreciated my intelligence. They ran out of materials years before I was old enough to be finished with my schooling. One of my tutors was an intimate acquaintance of a world-renowned barrister, who took me on as an apprentice. I was with him only a few weeks before he told me I had an exceptional legal mind."

Really, I could only stare at him. So many boastful statements crammed together. Who spoke like this? Was this a joke? Was someone setting me up for something?

"From the beginning, I was involved with complex and important files, and my files were always successful. I have appeared before adjudicators all over the world, including in the Southern Islands and before Her Imperial Majesty Empress Constia."

I would have dearly loved to see this pompous individual interacting with the brutally honest residents of Flatwell. The people of Flatwell would have no problem telling a person he was an idiot right to his face. I was wishing for that kind of bravery right then.

"I was a regular confidant of the Empress and performed many services for her. Upon his ascension to the throne, the Emperor granted me the barony as a sort of payment for my work for the Crown."

How could he think anyone wanted to hear this? It

might be interesting to friends and family, but not to a stranger. How could he not know this?

"The Emperor is a brilliant man, don't you think?"

What, he actually wanted me to contribute to this conversation?

Suddenly, Radia was at my side, curling a hand around my arm. "There you are, Shield Mallorough," she exclaimed. "I've been looking everywhere for you." I could have pointed out that there weren't so many in the large room that one would be hard to spot or reach, but I was sensing an opportunity to escape and I wasn't going to curdle it. "Please excuse us, my lord," she said. "We have important Shield and Wind Watcher business to discuss." And she pulled me away from him before he could answer.

She steered me toward the refreshments. "Didn't anyone tell you not to look him in the eye?"

I laughed.

After the break, the first petitioner was almost visibly bubbling with rage, Rikin following him closely. Fiona spoke before the petitioner could say anything.

"No, Callum," she said as soon as he reached her platform. "My decision was final."

"Thought you might have come to your senses," he grumbled.

"And I thought you might come to yours. It looks like we were both wrong."

"You have no right to deprive me of my livelihood!"

"You violated a whole raft of sea laws. The *Sea Wind* was unseaworthy. You patched ice damage with barely secured tin. You didn't use a compass or lead lines. You overcrowded your passengers to an appalling degree, packing them like cargo. It's a wonder you didn't kill anyone."

"The old Duke never minded," he said mulishly, and I wondered if he meant Taro's brother or his father.

"I can't speak for anyone else on that matter," said

Fiona. "As long as I'm the titleholder, the laws will be obeyed."

"I've debts coming due. If I don't pay them, I go to jail. Then there is no money coming in. What's my family supposed to do? The youngest is only four."

"These difficulties are due to your behavior, not mine," Fiona said resolutely.

I admired her for that. I would have had trouble sticking to my decision once the four-year-old was brought into it. I would have been trying to reach some kind of compromise to make sure no one would be left coinless.

"So my family can all starve, is that it?" Callum's face, already red, seemed to glow.

"Or you can find some other employment and perform it properly."

"You know nothing!" Callum accused her, a vein pulsing in his forehead. "You weren't born for that seat. That seat is meant for one born and bred here, one who understands and cares what this place is about. That is not you. Get out of that seat!"

"Calm yourself, Callum."

"I will not calm myself! You holding that title is a . . . a . . . a miscarriage of justice. It's unnatural. You have no right to that title. Get out of that seat!"

"You have my permission to withdraw, Callum."

"I don't need your permission for anything! Get out of that chair!"

The next thing we knew, he had punched Rikin in the face, a brutal blow right to the nose and mouth, and then he was rushing the throne. He pushed Bailey, who had instinctively stepped forward, right out of the way with so much force that Bailey fell and slid a short distance away. He grabbed Fiona by the shoulders, pulled her from the chair and sent her sprawling to the floor. "This isn't your place!" he shouted, kicking her solidly in the stomach with his heavily booted foot. "You don't belong here!" Another kick, higher and in the chest. "Get away! Go away!"

He pulled back for another kick, but Hiroki tackled him and sent him to the floor. Callum managed to dislodge him with a punch to the face. Bailey and Rikin, blood pouring from his nose, jumped on him and flattened him firmly to the floor.

"She'll ruin all of us!" Callum shouted. "The Imperial Guards wouldn't be here if we had a proper Karish in the title. She can't stay here!"

Hiroki and Rikin dragged him, yelling all the way, out the door to the foyer. Everyone in the spectator seats was twittering and rumbling. They all looked excited, the prats.

And the Imperial Guards had done nothing but stand there, the useless bastards.

I knelt beside Fiona on the floor, where she was curled into a ball. I stroked back her hair for some reason. As though that would accomplish anything. "Can you move?" I asked her. "Does anything feel broken?"

"Get everyone out," she gasped.

I stood and faced the greedy eyes of the spectators. "Her Grace will hear no more submissions today," I announced. Now, what was a good way to tell them to get out? "She thanks you for coming and bids you good day."

Not a one of them so much as shifted in their seats.

"Her Grace orders you to leave," said Bailey.

That got people moving. As a Shield I was taught to be circumspect. I kept coming up against situations where a more direct approach was needed.

I sat back down beside Fiona, trusting Bailey to arrange for Healer Browne to come.

I couldn't believe the proceedings had just exploded into violence like that. I was surprised that Fiona hadn't handled it better, after practicing with Dane. Perhaps she had never been attacked before.

Well, I hoped she hadn't.

I stroked Fiona's hair until Dane came, at which point

I withdrew. They deserved privacy. I went to my bed-chamber so I could calm down after the violence I had seen. I didn't deal well with brutality. It made me jumpy.

I learned later that Fiona had suffered no real injury, only pain and bruising. To me, that was bad enough. I'd never thought being a titleholder could be dangerous.

Chapter Eleven

I woke up extremely early the next morning. I couldn't understand why I was waking up so early; it was very unlike me. I spent some time trying to determine what had woken me. I looked at Taro, who was sleeping deep and still on his side of the bed. I listened for any sound, but if there had been one, it wasn't repeated.

There was a strange quality about the darkness and the silence, a quality that made me uneasy. I was unable to go back to sleep, though I tried for quite a while. At length, I slipped from the bed and dressed silently. I wasn't sure what I was going to do. The house was still asleep.

The library, I thought. I could stay out of everyone's way for a while in there. I lit a candle in our sitting room and descended the stairs that took me to the court room. It was then that I came across a window that had been left unshuttered. Immediately beyond the glass was the thickest, darkest fog I'd ever seen in my life. I could see nothing else out the window, not even the grass growing immediately outside.

I couldn't resist it. I ignored the library in favor of slipping through the kitchen to the back door and stepping out into that glorious, deep fog. The light of my candle rebounded off it. It seemed as though I could feel it against my skin. It was entrancing and eerie. I took a few paces out into it. I could see nothing, not the path that lay before the steps, not even the house that I had just left. How extraordinary.

I breathed it in. It felt different to breathe. I closed my eyes, just listening. I imagined I could hear the sea lapping against the rocky shore, the sound carried to me by the fog. I craved to walk out in it, but I wasn't that stupid. I would too easily be turned around and would lose my way.

Dane wasn't really being paranoid when he spoke of the dangers of this place. I could easily see someone ending up injured or dead by walking lost in the fog. I'd have to ask him at breakfast if there were any other life-threatening conditions inherent to Flown Raven. We could end up killing ourselves in ignorance.

There was an enticing beauty about it. It was inviting me to walk into it and be transported to a strange new world. High Scape had had nothing so entrancing as this.

I heard a scuffle, and the next thing I knew I was shoved from behind, hard, forcing me off the path and causing me to drop my candle. Then my arm was caught, pulling me this way and that, jerking me around, keeping me off balance so I couldn't even strike a blow. I was pushed again, hard enough to send me tumbling to the ground. Then I was left alone. I heard some sort of scraping, and then nothing.

I heard nothing. I could see nothing. I didn't know where I was in relation to the house. I was completely vulnerable to whoever had attacked me. I waited for another blow, and waited, and waited until I had to decide that my attacker had left.

Who had attacked me? Why? Who had I managed to infuriate this time?

How the hell was I going to get back?

All right, I didn't have to panic. I wasn't in any danger, as apparently my attacker had left. So no danger. Unless he chose to come back. I wasn't going to think of that right then. I was going to stay calm. I was going to sit still and wait until the fog cleared. Daylight would burn it away.

I felt so foolish. How did I get into these predicaments? Was there something about me that called out for abuse?

If I wasn't careful, I was going to start believing in things like bad luck.

It had to be my proximity to Taro. He called to trouble like a child to its mother. I just got caught in the cross fire. It wasn't fair.

I was hungry and craving coffee. And I was chilly. I wasn't dressed to be outside.

No, of course, it wasn't bad luck, and it wasn't Taro's fault. I'd been stupid to go outside when I could see the fog was this thick.

On the other hand, I should have been able to stand right outside the door without any difficulty.

"Dunleavy Mallorough, where the hell are you?" I heard Taro roar. From behind me. I'd thought I was facing the house. Of course, that was assuming he was in the house.

Oh thank gods. "Keep talking!" I called as I rose to my feet.

There was a pause. Then he said, "What the hell are you doing out here, you madwoman? Did you leave all your good sense back in High Scape?"

"I'm always sensible."

"The current evidence suggests otherwise. How did you come to be out here?"

"I'll explain once I'm inside. Just keep talking."

"Oh, I'll keep talking, all right. It's handy to have you

forced to listen to me. Since when are you such an early riser anyway? And why do you never wake me up? Do you not understand how much fun we're missing out on?"

Finally, I could see a glow in the fog, and a few steps later I was at the door. As soon as Taro saw me, he grabbed me by the hand and yanked me into the house, where he wrapped me in a tight embrace.

"Why do you keep doing this?" he demanded, speaking into my temple. "What's going on?"

"I'm not doing it on purpose," I objected. "No harm done."

"This time. You've got to be more careful."

"I'm always careful."

Taro scowled. "We have to call off the search." He slung an arm around my shoulders and escorted me to the sitting room, where Fiona was stretched out on a settee with Stacin tucked in beside her and our own maid, Lila, attending to her.

"Dunleavy!" she called out as soon as she saw me. "What the hell are you playing at?" She gestured at Lila to pull the bellpull.

"I wasn't being stupid on purpose," I protested. Why did everyone assume the worst? "Why was there a search?"

"Because we couldn't find you anywhere in the house," Taro snapped.

"I take an early-morning walk over my land every single morning," said Fiona. "It's my way to reinforce my connection to the land." That sounded very ritualistic to me. "The only things that prevent me from taking that walk are excessive wind and fog. Shame on you. Lila, go find His Lordship."

I was embarrassed to have caused so much upheaval. "I was being careful," I said. "I planned on going only a step beyond the door, and I did, but then I was pushed."

Taro groaned and covered his eyes.

"You were pushed?" Fiona asked. "You're sure you didn't slip?"

"Positive. We had a sort of fight afterward."

"What the hell does 'sort of' mean?" Taro demanded.

"It means there were no blows landed." Or thrown, as far as I could tell. "The person just pushed and pulled me around until I was totally disoriented and then left."

"What did he look like?"

"I have no idea. I couldn't see him in the fog. I had an impression of dark cloth, that was all."

"What about their voice? Did they say anything?"

"Nothing."

"Damn it," Taro muttered.

"This must have been some kind of prank," I said. "I was in no danger. I just had to wait until someone found me." And yet, though I felt compelled to dismiss the act as a joke gone wrong, I had difficulty believing that was all it was. This was the third odd, potentially dangerous event to take place just since my arrival. The paranoid side of my nature felt something must be going on.

"You were not necessarily safe," said Fiona, stroking her son's blond hair. "Sometimes people panic. You could have run off to somewhere dangerous, some of the rocky areas in the back, or onto the road. And these fogs can last for days. Who knows what kind of trouble you could have gotten yourself into?"

I resented the implications that I was getting myself into trouble deliberately. Really, I didn't lack for attention, and that was the only reason I could think of for a person choosing to get into scrapes.

"Everyone knows to treat the dangers of the fog seriously," continued Fiona. "I can't think of anyone who would pull such a dangerous prank."

I had nothing to say in response. Either I insisted on suggesting that the action had been a joke, contradicting my hostess, or I accused someone in Flown Raven of wanting to do me harm. Both options would make me look ill-mannered.

Dane came storming into the room. "What happened?"

"Dunleavy stood outside to admire the fog," Fiona told him. "Then someone pushed her into it."

"Are you sure you were pushed?" he asked.

"Yes," I said with forced patience.

"Did you see who it was?"

"No."

"Are you all right?"

"I'm fine."

"Hm," he said. And then he smiled with a sparkle of mischief in his eyes. "Maybe it was the harlin."

Fiona rolled her eyes. "Lords, Dane, don't start."

"What? There's said to be one around these parts."

"You're being ridiculous. This is a serious matter."

"A harlin," Dane said to me, "is said to have been the essence of a whale whose young were killed by human whalers. She takes the form of a human woman in order to wander about the land where whalers live, to kill the women who would bear the children who would take the whale's children. She is said to be nothing more than a dark cloak riding the fog, with a form of the coldest mist you've ever felt. If she touches you, you'll freeze solid and stay solid until spring, where you will melt into nothingness."

"Stop trying to scare her, Dane," said Fiona.

"That's really not a problem, Fiona," I said. "This person touched me, he didn't feel cold, and I'm definitely still alive. And any children I have are not likely to be whalers." If I had anything to say about it.

"Don't be too sure of that, Dunleavy," said Dane. "It all depends on what the parents do. Shintaro, have you ever been on a whaling boat?"

"No," Taro answered, sounding appalled.

"We'll go as soon as the fog clears up."

"No, thank you."

"We have to toughen you up. Look at your hands."

Taro held out his hands. He looked at them. I looked at them. They seemed fine to me. "I'm a Source."

"Is that all that you are?"

"Pretty much," said Taro.

My mouth nearly dropped open in shock. What a horrible thing for him to say. And it wasn't true. He was so much more than a Source. He was a truly good and decent man. He was an excellent friend. He could ease people's pain with the touch of his hands. Why would he think of himself as nothing more than a Source?

"Then it's time to change that."

"Why aren't you asking Dunleavy if she wants to go?"

I suddenly lost all sympathy for him.

"Dunleavy, do you want to go whaling?"

"Not at all."

"There you go."

I didn't understand why all I had to do was say no to get me off the hook when that apparently didn't work for Taro. I wasn't going to fight it, though.

"You don't have the kind of distractions here that High Scape offered you," said Dane. "You have to find something to occupy your mind."

"Perhaps, but that something is not going to be whaling."

"You won't know until you try. And really, whaling is exhilarating."

Taro growled in that way that meant he was conceding and hated it. Everyone seemed to recognize it for the capitulation that it was.

Stacin wiggled down from his mother's side on the settee, making her grimace as he obviously hit some tender spots. "Don't leave the room, pudding," she said.

I looked at her with surprise at the name with which she had cursed her son. She blushed, so I didn't tease her. But really, poor Stacin. "We have to decide what to do about this person who attacked Lee," she said.

"We can ask everyone where they were this morning," said Dane.

"The person who did it will lie," said Fiona.

"We might be able to tell who's lying. We can be subtle. I'll ask the questions."

"Why you?"

"I'm harmless. All the servants like me. Some still think of you as a usurper."

Fiona scowled but didn't dispute his assertion.

"Then I should do it," said Taro. "There's no one more harmless than me."

"Don't talk that way," I snapped.

He just raised one eyebrow, as though I were the one who was being unreasonable.

"Thank you for the offer, Shintaro," said Dane. "But I don't think you know the servants well enough to determine whether they're being truthful."

"I suppose," Taro admitted.

Stacin, who had been exploring the room largely by falling against furniture, fell against Taro's leg. Taro jumped slightly, and looked down. "Good day, there."

Stacin stared up at him for a moment. It was cute, the blond toddler looking up at the grown dark-haired man.

"Treat," Stacin said clearly before launching himself off Taro's leg.

"Treat?" Taro asked.

Fiona grinned. "Usually he says that when he wants something to eat. He doesn't usually talk to strangers. You must be special."

"I'll start talking to the servants now." Dane headed for the stairs. "I promise you, Dunleavy, whoever did this will be dealt with appropriately." He left.

"What does 'appropriately dealt with' mean?" I asked Fiona. I didn't want anyone exiled to a life of starvation or anything like that.

She shrugged. "We won't know until we find out who it is or what the circumstances are."

All right. That sounded fair.

"I'm so sorry, Dunleavy," said Fiona, cuddling Stacin, who had returned to her side. "All these things have been happening to you and in front of you. Believe me, this isn't normal."

"Maybe I've brought bad luck."

"I know you say that in jest, but I do think something odd is going on. And it doesn't coincide with your arrival. Odd things started happening shortly before that. The chandelier fell during a party. Fortunately, it creaked loudly before it came down, warning everyone. No one was hurt."

I knew that chandelier was dangerous. What had possessed Fiona to put it back up?

Taro had taken a seat beside Fiona's settee. He was threatening to touch Stacin's nose with his finger, and the child was giggling and ducking down behind the armrest of the settee to avoid him. It was adorable.

"I'm thinking of getting a reading done," Fiona said. "On the house."

"I don't know what you mean."

"There's a man among the tenant families who can use a spell on a house to see if there's anything malignant about it."

I wasn't sure how to react to the assertion that a house, an inanimate object, could be malignant. I'd never heard of anything like that. "You think there's something wrong with the house?"

"I believe it's a possibility."

"You have felt this way for a while?"

"Not really. Just since this run of bad luck. But there may have been negative things going on before, that I haven't been aware of."

"I see." I had been wrong about so much in the past that I didn't want to dispute with Fiona. Not to mention that it would be rude. But I couldn't believe in a house causing bad luck. "What about the Guards?"

She snickered. "The Guards don't know what the hell they're looking for. I'll figure out some way to get them out of the house."

Taro managed to touch Stacin's nose, and the child laughed.

Chapter Twelve

The fog didn't burn off with the morning. It didn't look as entrancing once the sun was up, but it was just as thick, and I found myself stuck in the house with nothing to do. Taro was edgy and not the best company. Fiona wasn't up for much beyond lying down. Dane was questioning the servants. I didn't want to spend time with either Tarce or Daris, even if either one of them wanted to spend time with me, which I was pretty sure they didn't.

So I went to the library, looking for something to read, and found Reid there, deep in the book and writing furiously on paper. I passed him without talking to him, thinking it was the perfect kind of day to read something frivolous. A scan of the stacks showed me a wealth of novels, plays and poetry. No philosophical, historic or geographical tomes. That amused me, for some reason. Clearly the titleholders of Westsea didn't feel the need to impress others with their collection of books. I pulled out a few books at random, and kept the one that was able to appeal to me on the first page.

I paused by Reid on my way back to the door. I knew I shouldn't disturb him, but I was curious. I stepped loudly to give him warning that I was approaching the table, then said, "Academic Reid?"

"Hm?" was his response.

"Can I bother you for a moment?"

He looked up, his expression vague. Then he blinked, his gaze clearing and sharpening. "How can I help you, Shield Mallorough?"

"I'm wondering if you have found anything interesting about the book." It was probably too early for him to say anything, but there was no harm in asking.

"Well, I shouldn't tell anyone but Her Grace, as she is the one who retained me, but you're a Shield. You know how to be discreet. Please, have a seat."

I eagerly did as I was bid. "Is it a book from the First Landed?"

"I'm pretty sure it is."

And I had to suppress the urge to take the book from him and get another look at it. That book was hundreds of years old. It had actually been made by the First Landed. That was incredible. "How could it have survived so long?"

"The materials they used for constructing the books appear to be particularly durable. For example, this"—he tapped a page—"doesn't seem to be paper."

"What's it made from, then?"

"I really don't know. I've only seen this in the other two books. We haven't been able to figure it out. But look." He bent the corner of a page, and before I could gasp out a stunned objection, he unbent it. There was no crease in the paper.

Huh.

"Did you know there might be a First Landed machine in the caves?" I asked.

"Her Grace told me. I look forward to seeing it. However, I have no expertise in such matters."

"Who does?"

"Academic Joanna Barker."

"I've read some of her work." I frowned.

Reid grinned. "You're not impressed with her?"

"She claims there were already people living on this world when the First Landed got here, and it was when the two bred together that Sources and Shields came into being." And that struck me as plain ridiculous.

"And you disagree?"

"Of course. We all know there was no one here when the First Landed came. To claim otherwise strikes me as being contrary for the sake of being controversial. And she seems to be reaching ridiculously far for evidence to support her theories."

"You don't believe the ruins of Masai and Balance support her conclusions? They don't seem to resemble any structures we've found to be built since the Landing. They seem to predate the Landing."

"How can the age of such things be determined?"

He winked. "I'm afraid I can't give away our trade secrets."

Would it be rude to ask what kind of trade secrets historians could possibly have? "So you agree with her?"

"I don't entirely. I don't entirely disagree, either. After all, this world is one on which people can live. It would seem wasteful if there were no people living on it until the First Landed arrived."

"But our own records state that Sources and Shields were born centuries after the First Landed were cut off from their home. What is the explanation for taking so long to breed?" Of course, maybe they had hated each other at first. It would make sense that if there were people on the world before the First Landed arrived, they would hate their conquerors.

"Our records could be wrong."

"Really?" I stared at him. "How could they be wrong?

That wrong? That seems like something very significant to omit."

Reid laughed. "The people who wrote them were nothing more than people, with flaws and motives. The only way to be certain of any period of history is to live through it, and even then there would be substantial gaps in your knowledge."

I put a hand to my forehead. It felt like my brain must be spinning. Much like it had when I'd first read Barker's works.

"Why does it distress you?" Reid asked.

"Because it doesn't make sense. The world was full of natural disasters. These first people couldn't have survived."

"Our people managed to survive between the Landing and the development of Sources and Shields. But it is possible the natural events only became constant after the First Landed arrived."

"But why would the history books not mention the presence of people here when the First Landed came?"

"Maybe the information got lost. Things were very chaotic for a while. Or perhaps something shameful had occurred. After all, if there were people here, this was their world, and apparently the Landed just took it from them."

That was disturbing. Could this be true? Did my ancestors come to this world and take it from its people?

Then again, our history was full of people taking land from other people. That had never bothered me. It was what happened. It still happened, titleholders taking each other's land by applying to the monarch. Why was I letting something that had happened hundreds of years ago upset me?

"Now," said Reid. "In that book I told you about, the First Landed book about what kind of government would work best here, there was no mention of any kind of government already in place. I would think there would be, if there were people already living here."

That made me feel better, for some reason. "Do you think this book will have any information about that?"

"I can't be sure, yet, but it looks to me like it's about the weather."

"The weather?" I was disappointed. We knew all we needed to know about the weather.

He smiled. "We can't expect all the books we find to alter everything we believe in."

Perhaps not, but it would be better for us if the book addressed something we didn't already know. Like what kind of music the First Landed listened to. What they ate. A book of manners.

"So here you are," Taro said from the doorway.

I opened my mouth to explain why I was there, but Taro wasn't looking at me. He was looking at Reid. I didn't know how to respond to that.

Neither did Academic Reid, from the looks of it. "My lord?"

"Tsk, tsk. Taro, please." Taro sat on the edge of the table, facing Reid. "I have barely seen you since you arrived. And here you are buried in work without so much as a cup of tea to quench your thirst."

"That is no matter. I tend to forget myself in work. Tea would grow cold before I thought to take a sip."

"I do admire people who take their work so seriously. It's refreshing."

Hey, I took my work seriously.

"Are you being treated properly by everyone?" Taro asked.

Reid hesitated before saying, "Of course."

Taro picked up on that pause. "I hope you trust me enough to come to me with any problems. I can assure you that I can work things out to your satisfaction."

I couldn't properly see Taro's expression, but something about it seemed to make Reid blush. "Thank you, my lord. Ah, Source Karish."

"Now, I told you to call me Taro," my Source chided him.

"Aye, that's right. Uh, sorry."

What the hell was Taro playing at? Was he actually flirting with the man? I wouldn't have thought Reid was his type.

Then again, I wouldn't have thought I was his type, either. But maybe I was. That had never occurred to me. Perhaps Taro had a special liking for quiet, studious people.

But surely Taro wouldn't seriously flirt with someone else right in front of me? He wasn't that tactless.

But then, he had been acting somewhat strange since we'd come to Flown Raven. Maybe he didn't really know what he was doing.

I just wished I knew if Taro was serious in his flirting. I had been expecting him to lose interest in me since I first started sleeping with him. Was it actually happening?

Just thinking about it caused a burning sensation in my stomach.

"Can I convince you to break from your labors for a little while?" Taro asked in his smoothest voice. "You'll be the fresher for it."

"Ah, I am, uh, honored," Reid stammered. "But I'm here by the Duchess's grace. I wouldn't feel comfortable taking more time than is absolutely necessary to translate this book."

"Well." Taro leaned forward and touched his shoulder. "Let me know if you change your mind." He slid off the table and gave me a hard look.

I tried to tell him he was being an ass with the power of my gaze. It didn't seem to make any impact on him. I was happy to see him leave the library.

"I'd like to stay here to read," I said to Reid. "There is

something soothing about reading in a library. Will that disturb you?"

"Not at all. I enjoy the company."

So he went back to his book, and I cracked open mine. Only a few pages in, I realized the story was about political intrigue. That was not my first choice for light reading— all the alliance-making and betrayal made me tense—but the author had a light, wry touch that I enjoyed.

It was not much later when the First Lieutenant swept into the room with a confidence that made me clench my teeth. This was someone else's home he was swanning about in. A home to which he had not been invited. How dared he stride about so easily?

"What are you reading?" he demanded of me.

"A novel."

"Does it address casting?"

Oh, how ridiculous. Even fictional accounts of casting were under suspicion. "It doesn't seem to."

"You will tell me immediately and hand the book over to me the moment you suspect casting will be addressed."

Really, who the hell was he to be giving me orders? No one, that's who. But I had to respond to him to get him to leave me alone. "Understood." Not that I was actually going to do as he demanded. The prat.

"Don't take that book from the library," he told me. "Don't take any books from the library. We don't want any of them going astray."

"Understood." Was it my fault he wasn't asking if I had already removed any books from the library?

The First Lieutenant turned to Reid. "What is the nature of the book you're studying?"

Reid looked him straight in the eye and said, "I haven't determined that yet."

"How is that possible? You've been working on it for days."

"The wording the First Landed used is not natural to me, and I have to be very careful not to mistranslate any part of it. This will take me weeks."

"I'll see your notes, then."

Reid gathered them up and held them to his chest. "These notes belong to the Duchess."

The First Lieutenant scowled. "I am here on behalf of the Emperor. When I speak, it is as though he were speaking."

"So you say. To me you're just a soldier. The Duchess has retained me, and if you want to see these notes, you'll have to address that with Her Grace."

"I'm ordering you to give me those notes."

Reid abruptly stood and left the table, striding to the fireplace in which flames danced with crackles and pops. Reid held the pages over the flames. "I'll burn them right now and write nothing more."

"You do that and I'll have you arrested."

"For what?" Reid challenged.

"For obstructing an Imperial investigation."

"I'm not obstructing anything. If you want to see these notes, you need merely apply to the Duchess. She will then direct me."

"There is no need to ask her. Everything that belongs to the Duchess belongs to His Majesty."

"Not according to the Icene Treaty."

It was clear that the First Lieutenant didn't know what the Icene Treaty was or how it restricted the powers of the monarch. He looked furious. "You're choosing a very dangerous path, Academic."

"Standing up for one's rights should never be dangerous."

That, I thought, was ridiculously naive, but it seemed to make an impression on the First Lieutenant. He glared at Reid before making a neat turn on his heels and striding out of the room. I released my held breath and let the tension flow out of me.

"That was risky," I said to Reid.

He shrugged. "I despise bullies. I've encountered too many of them in my life."

Still, that had been brave. It was another reason to admire him.

Chapter Thirteen

The day Taro was dragged out whaling, before dawn, no less, I received a second letter from the Triple S council, complaining that I hadn't responded to the first one yet. I thought they hadn't waited a reasonable length of time to get any response. And I hadn't known what to say about our last channeling. On the one hand, it had been successful, in that no damage had been done. On the other, it hadn't been successful, as people had been able to feel it.

I didn't know what to tell them, so I was tempted to say nothing. Really, what could they do if I didn't respond to their letters?

I dressed and went down to the family sitting room to eat with whoever else was there. For some reason, in Flown Raven I found I preferred eating with others if that was an option.

Fiona was there with Stacin. She was alternating between eating morsels of bread and cheese and watching her son eat slices of apple. "Good morning," I said as I crossed to the breakfast side bar.

"Good morning," Fiona said. "Stacin, say good morning to Dunleavy."

"Good," he mumbled around his current slice of apple.

"Good morning, Stacin." I stifled the urge to ruffle his hair, baffled as to why I felt it in the first place.

He continued to munch on his apple. He had his priorities straight.

"I know I should make him eat in the nursery," Fiona said apologetically. "I enjoy having him with me."

"He is your child and this is your house. I would say the only person's opinion that counts on the matter is yours." I scooped up some omelet, some toasted bread, some apple and some cheese. I was always so hungry in the morning, and I really liked this idea of having food ready-made when I woke up.

It was because of the servants that this food was ready-made, I berated myself. Don't get used to it.

"Some people feel the presence of children shouldn't be inflicted on them."

That prompted an unworthy thought. "Did one such person happen to be the Dowager Duchess?"

She grimaced. "She's poisonous, isn't she?"

"I can't believe Taro is her child." Though he was probably spared much of her influence. That was one good thing about him being locked away during his formative years.

There were more important topics than the Dowager to discuss. "How are you feeling?"

"Tender," she admitted.

"What happened to the man who attacked you?"

"I stripped him of his land and banished him."

"Really? He's lost his home?"

"Of course. He's lucky I didn't fine him on top of that."

"What about his family?"

"It is unfortunate that they suffer with him. I have spoken with his partner and offered her a place without him, but she has chosen to tie her life with his."

Of course she would. She had children with him. Everyone would think less of her if she chose security over him. "Will they be able to get land from another title-holder?"

"Perhaps, but if any such titleholder contacts me for information about why Callum left, I will tell them the truth."

That was harsh. I didn't blame her for her choice of punishment, and I certainly had no sympathy for anyone who would attack another person so brutally. Still, he had gone from operating his vessel under the rules he assumed the titleholder approved of, to having lost everything, all in a matter of weeks.

Tarce wandered into the room, looking tired and lazy. Despite appearing as though he was a couple hours' short of much-needed sleep, his hair was perfectly coifed and he was sharply dressed. He helped himself to the coffee but didn't touch the food.

Fiona grinned. "My, my, dear brother. You're up early. What's the occasion?"

Tarce glowered at her. "The wind was screaming last night."

"Really? I didn't hear anything. Did you, Dunleavy?"

"No, not at all." That didn't mean it wasn't. I could sleep through such things.

"Well, it was. Kept me up all night and then I couldn't get back to sleep."

"Poor boy."

"Shut up." He took a seat a little away from us.

It was true that Tarce hadn't yet joined us for breakfast since I'd come to Flown Raven, but I had no reason not to believe Tarce about the reason why he was there, until Radia was escorted in. Then I had to hide my smile with my coffee cup. Now, how had he known Radia was going to visit?

"My Lady Westsea, Lord Tarce, Shield Mallorough," she greeted us.

"Good morning, Roshni," said Fiona.

"Good morning, Wind Watcher," I added.

Tarce said nothing.

"Please help yourself to some breakfast." Fiona waved her hand at the breakfast bar and Radia smeared some jam on toast before taking a seat. "Do you have any news for us?"

"Nothing of any real note, my lady. The weather has been fair."

"No strong winds last night?" Fiona asked with an impish glance at Tarce.

"Not that I noticed. Nothing sufficient to make the wind rock swing."

"How would you know the wind rock is moving while you slept?" I asked.

"There are clappers attached to the sides. They cut through the wind and I've gotten used to waking when they sound."

"So you never sleep soundly?" I asked, appalled.

She smiled. "Don't worry, Shield Mallorough. I sleep well enough."

"If you had a partner," Tarce said suddenly, "you would have someone to share the load."

"No doubt," said Radia. "But that's no reason to acquire a partner."

I imagined it would be hard for a wind watcher to find a suitable partner. She was rather isolated in Flown Raven. The tenants would need a partner who could move in with them, not the other way around. A partner for Radia would have to give up their home and work to live in the tower. That probably wouldn't appeal to many.

It was becoming increasingly clear that Tarce would be willing to make that sacrifice, but he was the clumsiest suitor I'd ever encountered. I didn't understand his difficulty. He was handsome, he appeared reasonably intelligent, and he was wellborn. Why was he so bad at this?

There was a pause as we waited to see if Tarce would come up with something clever in response. He didn't.

"I received a letter from the Earl of Gray Rocks," Fiona said. "He wanted to know if you would weave a tapestry for his daughter. She is getting married. He has indicated his preferences as to form and color."

Radia nodded. "What is he prepared to offer?"

"The first foal dropped by Swiftfoot."

Radia looked surprised. "You're thinking of participating in racing?"

"Not at all, but the foal's descendants will be very valuable."

"When does he want it?"

"That's the hitch. He wants it in time for the wedding."

Radia pursed her lips. "That will depend on what he wants."

Fiona took a folded piece of paper and handed it to Radia.

"You're using her, Fi," Tarce chastised her.

"I am happy to contribute to the wealth and prestige of Flown Raven," Radia muttered as she read the letter.

"You spend all your time weaving. It gives you no opportunity to do anything else."

"I enjoy weaving."

"What else would you have her do?" Fiona asked him with a grin.

"Anything that's more pleasant."

"I enjoy weaving," Radia repeated.

Seriously, Tarce was so very bad at this. It was painful to watch. No wonder Radia was completely disinterested.

And right then, I felt Taro's protections fall. I raised my Shields just as a slew of forces came blasting through Taro. "Oh, gods," I said.

"Dunleavy, is something—"

I put up a hand to stop Fiona. "Channeling," I explained curtly. Then I wrapped my hands around the arms of my chair, and hung on.

I needed to hang on. The pressure of the forces gave me the impression that I was going to be swept away. The water filled my mouth and nose, making it difficult to breathe. The crashing against the rocks was so hard I thought my bones might shatter. The screaming of the birds was so loud and so constant it flooded my mind and made it hard to remember what I was doing.

Pounding pounding pounding.

Hold on hold on hold on.

I could barely feel Taro through all the chaos. I remembered he was on a boat. Whale hunting, of all the imbecilic ideas. Someone had better be looking after him. If he drowned, I'd find a way to mete out some punishment before I died.

Then the water swirled harder in my brain, and I couldn't think of anything more than keeping my Shields up. The forces rushed on and on, Taro's mind and body working harder and harder to channel them.

Was that something bursting? Were my Shields failing? I scrambled as best I could, but I couldn't hold on.

The tremors returned. Damn it, we couldn't make it work. We were failing.

And then, suddenly, I felt nothing from Taro at all. I gasped and opened my eyes to see Fiona, Radia, and even Tarce looking at me with concern. I was curled up in my chair, my hands white-knuckled on the arms of the chair.

"Dunleavy?" said Fiona. "Are you all right?"

I uncoiled and relaxed my hands. "Taro's channeling ended too abruptly." As soon as I said it, I regretted opening my mouth. That was not the sort of thing to be telling regulars.

"Do you think something happened to him?"

"Oh, no," I lied. "That sometimes happens. It doesn't mean anything."

But maybe something had happened just as his channeling was finished, something to do with whatever those
idiots did when they were out killing whales. He could be
badly injured and on his way to death, and I'd have no
idea until he actually died.

Why the hell hadn't I objected to his going whaling?
When did I get so stupid?

I had to get out there. I jumped to my feet and ran out
of the sitting room, hearing, "Dunleavy, where are you
going?" from Fiona behind me. I didn't stop to explain. I
ran to the kitchen and out the back door, blind to everything that wasn't immediately in front of me.

I crossed the gardens at a run, trotted through the
strange twisted path through the ridge, and had to skid to
a stop, as the loose rock on the other side made for some
unstable footing. I picked my way down a tiny path worn
into the cliff and down to the rocky shore.

There were no docked boats yet, but one was rowing
up to the shore, and Taro was in it. Sitting up and unsup-
ported, thank gods. I breathed a deep sigh of relief.

Sometimes I thought I shouldn't let him go anywhere.
Bad stuff always happened to him when I wasn't around.

Tarce caught up with me, gasping. "You run damned
fast."

I didn't answer, too busy watching the small boat that
was bearing my Source back to land. Two men were rowing the boat with long, sure strokes, two others were just
sitting there, and Dane was leaning close to Taro and saying something to him. Everyone looked all right.

After an age, the boat pulled up to the wide strip of
rock that served as a beach. The two rowers jumped out
and pulled the boat more firmly onto the shore. Taro and
Dane jumped out with, again, no sign of an injury. The
two rowers immediately pushed the boat back off the
beach and began rowing back out to sea.

"What happened?" I demanded.

"He just went blank," Dane said, though I hadn't been

asking him. "I never even thought about the possibility of him . . . uh . . . having to do his thing in the middle of whaling."

"Don't feel bad. Neither did either of us. Taro?" I prompted.

"We'll talk about it later," Taro snapped. "Do you know what that is?" He pointed out at the water.

"Water?"

"No! What we were traveling in!"

Zaire, calm down. "The boat."

"What kind of boat is that?" he demanded.

How the hell did I know? I thought about the boat I'd seen. Sturdy, kind of wide for its length, which had been about four men long. "Some kind of shore boat for the whaling boat."

"That *is* the whaling boat!" he nearly shouted. "A whole group of idiots go out in a bunch of boats like that, and they attack a whale! They find a whale and get as close as they can to it— Do you hear me? They get close to it! And the strongest idiot throws a harpoon at the whale, with some kind of floating weight attached to it."

"A drogue," Dane supplied helpfully.

"And the animal thrashes about, and nearly kills us all, but instead of doing the intelligent thing, all the boats get closer, and all the other idiots throw their spears at it, and it was dangerous and careless and just completely insane." Then he glared at Dane. "What is wrong with you people?"

Dane laughed and slung an arm around Taro's shoulders. "It's the right kind of insanity, my friend. But not for you. Those little spells of yours are too dangerous. Now, it's time to go back to the house. You need a whiskey."

Taro didn't object. So we all went back to the house and then to the sitting room, where Dane insisted that Taro drink a whole tumbler full of whiskey. It was a good thing Taro had a head for alcohol.

After he had obediently downed the last drop, I announced he and I had Triple S business to discuss and we went back to our rooms. I looked in every corner to make sure Lila or someone else wasn't lurking about. When I felt we were clear, we sat in the settee closest to the center of our sitting room. "What happened?" I demanded.

"Nothing happened. The event was successfully channeled."

"We felt tremors here. Didn't you?"

"I couldn't feel anything but the boat," he muttered.

"That is the second time we . . . leaked. That's a problem."

He scowled. "Fine. All right. I channeled, but I couldn't control the forces the way I should be able to."

And that was very, very dangerous. Sources were supposed to be in complete control of the forces they were channeling. Too much could go wrong if a Source lost control. It would kill the Pair and leave the people vulnerable to whatever event was happening. "In what way?"

"They went faster than I liked. And there was a raw quality to them, as though there was nothing between me and the forces. I never thought there was anything between me and the forces before, but now I can feel the difference."

"It didn't feel like that when you were channeling Flown Raven events while we were still in High Scape?"

"No. Channeling events from Flown Raven has always been strange, but I never felt so out of control. Maybe the distance helped me in some way."

"If I tell the Triple S we're having trouble, they're likely to transfer us." Which would be the best for everyone, I thought, though I had already gotten to like Fiona and her little family. "They're already displeased about you being here."

"No!" was his emphatic response. "Don't tell them anything."

"I know you don't like any contact with them, but they already suspect you're going to have trouble here."

"Suspecting isn't knowing."

"And if we can't do this—"

"I can do this. We just have to work on it."

"Work on it how?"

"You'll think of something. You always do."

Wonderful. Put all the responsibility on me. "This place has a bad effect on you. You were almost lordly in your delegation."

He grimaced and shoved his hands in his hair. "I hate this place," he muttered.

Ah. For that, I couldn't blame him. "Then let's do something that will get us out of it."

"By telling the council we're failures? How can you be willing to do that?"

"We're not failures. We just shouldn't be here."

"We will not leave by claiming I can't channel. Don't you tell them I can't channel."

"I won't write anything without your consent." I took his hand. I wanted to get him to relax. It seemed to me he'd been tied into knots since we got here. We sat on a settee, and I sat close beside him and laid my head on his shoulder. I breathed in, slow and deep, and let it out. In and out. And as I listened for Taro, I was aware when his breathing imitated mine.

Next step: with my free hand I trailed patterns on the back of his, keeping my touch light and teasing. He pulled his hand from under mine and reached across to trail a fingertip over the shell of my ear. It tickled and I lifted my head. Taro chuckled and leaned forward to kiss me.

But just before our lips met, Lila walked in. "A message for you, my lord."

"I'm not a lord," he grumbled. "I'm a Source."

The maid extended the silver tray. Taro snatched up the missive and waited for Lila to leave. He frowned at the seal at the back. "It's from Her Grace."

"You mean your mother?" I asked, just to make sure. "Her Grace" could almost mean Fiona, though I'd never heard him refer to her by anything other than her personal name. And Fiona would never be so pompous as to send him correspondence while he lived in her house.

He stared at the envelope for a while, and I could tell he was deciding whether he should even open it.

He opened it. He read what appeared to be only a few lines. Then he tore the paper into pieces and left the settee so he could throw the pieces into the fireplace. "I'm to attend her at her residence immediately," he told me. "I've been ordered to leave you behind."

"Are you going to go?"

"No."

"She's just going to come here."

"So let her. I don't follow her orders."

"But if you hear her out, she might then leave you alone."

He snorted in derision. "You have met her, haven't you?"

"She lives on the property. If we're going to stay here, you have to figure out a way to deal with her." Maybe that would convince him we should try to get transferred.

"Ignoring her has worked for years now. I learned it from the best."

Aye, but unlike Taro as a child, the Dowager Duchess wouldn't let herself be ignored. Still, it was Taro's problem to solve and I wasn't going to nag him about it.

"I have to go . . . be somewhere," Taro said, and he practically ran from the room, making it clear that my presence was not welcome.

I sighed and picked at a loose thread in the cushion of the settee. So much for my ability to make Taro feel better.

Chapter Fourteen

A loud bang woke me and had me jerking upright, looking about without, at first, seeing anything. Then I blinked and Lila was there, at the window. "I'm sorry, ma'am," she said as she messed about with the window. "I have to tie the shutters down." She did so after a few moments, and then she closed the window.

"What's going on?" It sounded like the world was being torn apart out there, the very ground being ripped up into the air.

"The wind is kicking up."

Oh. That seemed an insufficient cause for Lila's behavior. But then, I hadn't grown up in a place where the wind regularly knocked over carriages. "Did the Wind Watcher sound the alarm?"

"Oh, no. It's not that bad. A good thing, too. Her Ladyship has to visit the families of the tenants lost in the whale hunt yesterday."

"People were lost? I'm so sorry. I didn't know." Whaling was that dangerous? And Dane had had Taro doing it? What was the man thinking?

"Jacob Ikubi and Eller Le Royer. It's my lady's duty to give her condolences to the families as soon as possible."

"But she doesn't go out in the wind." She had said so.

"Only when the Wind Watcher blows the horn. She hasn't. It's my lady's duty to go out today. It has to be as soon after the deaths as possible."

"Were one of those men someone close to you?" I asked gently.

Lila appeared offended. "They don't need to be kin for me to feel for them."

"No, no, of course not." But it would better explain, I thought, why Lila was so emphatic in her assertion that Fiona had to go out that day, despite the fact that the wind, while less than deadly, was still pretty nasty. "We would hear the horn all the way out here?"

"The horn can be heard everywhere," Lila said firmly. "Has ma'am decided where she will take her morning meal?"

I guessed that was the end of that conversation. "I'll go down to the sitting room."

"The others have already eaten, ma'am."

Zaire, did that make me feel lazy. Still, I wasn't about to order breakfast be brought to my room. That was a little too aristocratic for my taste. "That's all right. I have no difficulty with eating alone." In fact, sometimes I preferred it. I wasn't always at my best in the morning.

The sitting room was empty, aside from the maid who was in the process of clearing away the remains of breakfast. I rescued some cold toast and lukewarm coffee and sat listening to the wind. It was so loud, crashing about beyond the shutters and wailing over the roof. It seemed pretty dangerous to me, even if it wasn't strong enough to warrant the horn. I wouldn't go out in it. Fiona was crazy.

So I went to the library. Reid was there, the table covered with papers and scrolls. He wasn't working, though. He was watching three of the Imperial Guards, who were pulling books out of the shelves, flipping through them and dropping them on the floor.

I didn't think their superficial search method was going to be fruitful, even if they actually stumbled across a book of spells. All the spell books I had seen didn't have titles easily identifying them, and their nature couldn't be determined by flipping through the pages. You had to actually read them.

I took a seat at Reid's table. "Having trouble working?"

"They do make a racket."

"You could give us a hand," the Second Sergeant complained.

"That is not why Her Grace hired me."

"I don't understand you people," the Second Sergeant spat. "People are causing a lot of pain and damage trying to fix their lives with spells. This is dangerous. It's for their own good to have this trash collected and disposed of."

I doubted the books were to be destroyed. They were no doubt to be sent to the Emperor. Did they know His Majesty was using spells himself? Did they believe it was something only the royal could or should use? Or did they truly believe casting was nothing more than pretense and fraud? I wouldn't blame them if they did. That was what I had thought not too long ago.

The Second Sergeant had been waiting for an answer, and when neither of us gave him one, he made a sound of disgust and resumed ransacking the library.

It was an appalling way to treat books. I couldn't bear to watch it for long. I smiled at Reid and left the library.

The books in the library weren't the only books in the house. And the Guards had already searched our suite, the bastards. The door to our suite had a lock. It should be safe enough.

As I was climbing the stairs, I became aware of a noise pulling at my mind. I ignored it at first, but it nagged at my mind and teased my ears. Then I listened to it, and I finally realized what it was.

The warning note from the Wind Watcher.

Where was Taro?

I ran up to our suite. Taro wasn't there. I checked with Cekina and with Bailey, and neither of them knew where Taro was. I tried all the rooms on the main floor, and Taro wasn't in any of them, with no evidence that he ever had been.

Now I was really starting to panic, because where else would he be? The only other place remaining was the kitchen, and he wasn't there, either. If he was out in that wind doing something stupid and reckless, I was going to kill him.

The staff in the kitchen seemed disturbed by my presence. "Is there something I can fetch for you, ma'am?" one young girl asked. "If you tell me where you'll be, I'll bring it to you."

No, damn it, I didn't want anything. Did they think I ate all the time? "I'm looking for Source Karish," I said. "Has he been here?"

The young woman exchanged a look with one of her colleagues.

What the hell did that mean? Was he sleeping with someone? That was damn fast, and he could have told me.

"He's gambling with a few of the lads in their quarters, ma'am," the servant said.

"Hush, Demis!" one of the older servants snapped.

"I don't think a man should be playing loose with his money without his woman knowing," the young girl retorted stoutly.

"Ah," I said, nearly sighing with relief. "So he's inside." Really, that was all I cared about. Other than him sleeping with someone. I'd rather he'd been sleeping with someone than gallivanting about in the wind, but not by much. I did wonder how he'd gotten his first ante for the game. All of his coins had been stolen.

"Yes, ma'am."

"What about Her Ladyship? I understand she was to be visiting some of the families today."

"She's not returned, but she would have gotten shelter in one of the cottages as soon as she heard the horn. I wouldn't be concerned."

I couldn't help but be concerned, but there was nothing I could do about it. Having lost all interest in reading, I went back to my suite, lit a candle, sat on the floor and tried to stay calm.

The wreckage I could hear being done outside was unnerving. What if Fiona and Dane hadn't been able to get to safety before the wind got really bad? What if they were both dead?

That would be horrible. I liked them both. And who would raise Stacin? It would be tragic if he ended up an orphan. Did Fiona have any relatives more reliable than Tarce and Daris? Did Dane?

What would happen to Flown Raven if both Fiona and Dane died? Fiona had said she had already chosen an heir, and I assumed she meant Stacin, but Stacin couldn't take the title as a child. He was too young to learn the code. That would leave Flown Raven vulnerable to challenges to the title. It would be a nightmare.

As far as I knew, the only people who knew the code needed to inherit were Taro and his mother. He didn't want the title. Maybe she would take it. I didn't know if a title could go back up a generation once it had progressed to the next one. It seemed to me that if that were possible, the Dowager Duchess would have taken the title once her elder son had died.

It was so frustrating to worry about things about which I could do nothing.

I didn't see Taro until I went to the sitting room for supper. Tarce and Reid were there. Fiona and Dane were not.

"I understand you and Academic Reid were hard at work all day in the library," Taro commented, the faintest edge to his voice.

"I wasn't in the library long at all."

"You should not be disturbing Reid in his work."

Condescending prat.

"Not at all," Reid said. "I find Shield Mallorough's presence very restful."

Restful. Hm. Interesting description. I wasn't sure I liked it.

I saw Taro's eyes narrow briefly. Then he smiled brightly. "Not too restful, I hope. You wouldn't want to fall asleep in the middle of translating a sentence."

Tarce snorted. I had no idea why. The comment hadn't been funny. Taro usually had a much more delicate touch.

"Lee, my dear," said Taro. "You shouldn't be disturbing the academic this way. He'll never get his work finished and then he'll never go home."

And Taro really wanted Reid to go home. He was being ridiculous.

"While I would do nothing to extend my time here," said Reid, "I'm in no particular rush. And perhaps Shield Mallorough can provide some useful input."

Taro grinned. "She's convinced you she is an expert in history, has she?"

Hey, I knew more about history than a lot of people did.

"She doesn't need to. Good ideas can come from anywhere." He wiped his mouth with a serviette. "Speaking of which, I should get back to it. If you all will excuse me."

Tarce watched him leave, then he sat back in his chair, crossed his arms and watched Taro and me.

Just what did he find so interesting?

"What are you going to do this evening, my love?" Taro asked me.

Oh, no, don't you dare use that careless, flyaway tone with me, not after what you just said. "I'll be in the library." That had been my original intention, after all. I wasn't going to change it just because he was being ridiculous.

"Then I'll find someone to play some cards," Taro said in a challenging tone, as though he expected me to object.

"You do that. Have fun."

And then I was left with Tarce. He smirked at me. I glared at him.

"I thought Shields were supposed to know exactly what to say in all occasions to make everyone feel better."

We were, actually. I'd never been good at it. My first, strongest impulse was to tell him to shut up, and that would only prove my point. "Have a good evening," I said instead, and I left the room.

This behavior on Taro's part was cause for concern. His dislike of Doran, a man with whom I had kept company in High Scape, had been out of proportion, but it had had a logical basis. Doran and I had had a relationship before Taro and I started sleeping together, and Doran, though I hadn't been entirely aware of it at the time, had been trying to rekindle that connection.

With Reid, however, there was nothing. He wasn't interested in me, and I wasn't interested in him. There hadn't been any kind of spark when we met. I hadn't been engaging in behavior that was the slightest bit inappropriate. There was a complete absence of reason for Taro's behavior. So what did that mean? Was I not supposed to talk to anyone ever again, just to spare Taro's feelings?

It was so strange. I'd have never thought of Taro as a possessive lover. He'd never appeared so about anyone else, at least not in my hearing.

I did go back to the library. Neither Reid nor the Guards were there. I spent some time trying to find the novel I'd been reading before, a substantial task with the mess the Guards had made. I was unable to find it. The place was a mess. So I decided instead to put the books back on the shelves and start to organize them. It was engrossing work and I felt I was doing something productive. I spent a few hours at it, though, without getting a whole lot done. It was a big job.

Twice more I heard Radia blow the horn. Clearly, the wind was still vicious. I wished Fiona and Dane were back in the house. It was too easy to imagine the worst.

In time, I went up to the suite I shared with Taro. I was sort of dreading it. What if Taro was still in his odd mood? I hated arguing right before bed. It made it hard to sleep.

I entered the sitting room of our suite. I noticed immediately that one of the heavier chairs had been shifted around to face the fireplace, and there was a basin of some sort on the floor before it. There was a pot on the hearth, and as far as I could tell there was nothing more interesting than water in it. Towels were warming above it, and towels were laid out on the floor around the chair.

"Take off your boots." It was Taro, coming into the room from the hall with a bottle of wine and two glasses in his hands.

"What's going on?" I asked.

"Just take off your boots." He put the wine and glasses on a small table next to the chair. "And your stockings, then sit down."

I did as ordered, relaxing into the comfortable chair. Taro went into the bedchamber for a few moments and returned with some odd little earthenware bottles I didn't remember seeing before. He put the bottles on the table next to the wine. Then he filled the basin with the contents of the pot, testing the temperature. He picked up one of the earthenware bottles and poured something amber into the water. Immediately, a fresh, woody scent drifted into the air.

With a light touch he prodded my feet into the water. It was just shy of too hot, and all the muscles in my legs were forced to relax. "What's all this for?" What did I do to deserve it? I thought he was angry with me.

"Because I feel like doing it." He poured a glass of white wine and placed it in my hands. Then, after rolling up his sleeves, he poured a clear liquid from another earthenware bottle into the palm of his hand. He rubbed his hands together, then put my wet right foot against his left thigh.

He rubbed the oil over my skin, calf and foot, gently working the muscles. It felt marvelous. "When did you learn to do this?" For while Taro had rubbed my foot before, he hadn't done it with quite that level of skill.

"Remember when we went to Williams's bordello?" Taro asked.

"Very much." It had been, after all, the only time I'd ever gone to such a place. It hadn't met expectations.

"I went back there to learn how to properly rub feet."

I frowned at him. "You went to a bordello?"

"Just to learn about foot rubbing."

What in the world for? "And nothing else went on there?"

"Of course not."

It was a reasonable question, I thought. And if he could get strange over my merely talking to a man, surely I had good reason to be suspicious of his going to a place where sex was sold.

Not that I actually did suspect him of anything. If he said nothing went on, then nothing went on. However, I felt like pretending to disbelieve him, after his behavior earlier that evening.

He sighed. "I'm trying to do something nice for you here. Can't you just enjoy it?"

I didn't know if I could, but I could see Taro had gone to a lot of effort. I didn't want to spoil it any more than it had already been spoiled. I relaxed in my chair and sipped at my wine. Taro always remembered I preferred white.

He firmly pressed his thumb to the bottom of my foot, and arousal thrummed through me. I emitted a gasp and Taro gave me a cocky grin. "Told you I went there to learn," he almost taunted as he did it again, with identical results.

"I approve of acquiring knowledge." I sighed, and he began to work on the other foot.

He really was so good with his hands. It seemed that every time I turned around, he could do something new. Did he understand how talented he was? Maybe he didn't, and maybe that was part of the problem. Maybe I should be telling him that sort of thing, even though he never seemed to believe me when I complimented him. Maybe I just didn't do it often enough.

Who would have thought the Stallion of the Triple S would need to be reassured about his abilities?

Taro moved the basin away, and he started massaging the muscles in my thighs, expert strokes by long, golden hands. I suspected I knew where this was going and I heartily approved. The chair would make for an interesting location.

And then we heard a noise. Taro looked around the chair and scowled. "Yes?" he demanded.

That meant someone was there. I could have died of embarrassment. I rearranged my skirt.

"Academic Reid would like Shield Mallorough to visit with him as early as possible tomorrow," I heard Lila say.

I could see Taro stiffening. "I'll see she gets the message," Taro answered, barely hanging on to his pleasant expression. "You can go now." He straightened away from the chair, cleaned his hands on the towel and went to the bedchamber. I waited a little while, but he did not come back out.

Lila had the worst timing in the world.

Chapter Fifteen

I was pleased to see Fiona and Dane in the family sitting room early the next morning, enjoying their breakfast with Stacin. It would have been horrible to have something happen to them. "I'm relieved you suffered no injuries yesterday," I said to them as I sipped on some excellent coffee. It seemed they always had excellent coffee.

"It was a near thing," Fiona answered. "There was all sorts of debris whipping around. In fact, a wagon went flying by. We were lucky we just happened to be out of its path. I doubt we would have been able to get out of the way fast enough."

That was insane. Surely the horn should have been blown before wagons started flipping around.

It would have been interesting to see.

"Where did you end up staying?" I asked.

"With the Isha family. They were very good to us. They fed us well. We sang songs and told stories. They told us that there were fewer fish running this year—everyone seems compelled to tell us that—but they were perfectly nice about it."

"Dane has said that the books say the fishing is the same."

"Well, they're bringing in the same numbers in their hauls, but we had a particularly harsh winter last year. That usually means less fish are born. The problem is that while they're catching as much fish as usual, there are fewer fish than usual in the water. That worries them. It shouldn't, because it's happened in prior years, but they're uncertain about me as a titleholder and they're looking for bad signs."

"I see," I said, though I really didn't. There were fewer fish than usual, but the fishers were catching the same amount. How did that work?

It was starting to disturb me, all the examples of the lack of confidence the tenants felt in Fiona. I wanted her to do well. The people deserved that. I wanted her to justify Taro's choice of her.

And I didn't want the Dowager Duchess to be right.

Bailey came into the room. "The Wind Watcher was wondering if Her Grace is receiving."

"Oh," said Fiona. "Certainly, if she doesn't mind an audience."

"I shall inquire." Bailey sailed back out of the room.

I wondered if Taro and I should leave. I didn't want to, having dished up a plate full of eggs and cheese and bread. I looked at Fiona and Dane, and neither of them was looking back at me. So I sat still and kept eating.

Radia was frowning as she was led into the sitting room. She was also carrying what looked to be a very heavy bag. "I'm sorry to be disturbing you and yours so early in the day," she said. "But it's vital that you know this as soon as possible. Yesterday, before I sounded the alarm, I saw that the wind rock had been braced with this." She pulled out, with some effort, a stone at least a hand thick and twice as long. "It stopped the rock from swinging."

Fiona took the stone with a small grunt at its weight. "I can't believe the wind would kick up something like this."

"I don't think it did," said Radia. "It was wedged in there by someone."

"No!" Fiona stared at her. "No one would do that."

"I'm sorry, Your Grace, but that's the only way this could have been forced between the rock and the arch."

"But this would endanger everyone. It's the stupidest prank I can imagine."

"There are plenty of stupid people about."

"Would this be the same kind of stupidity that would cause a person to pass the mouth of a cave, see a rope and take it?" I asked.

Now everyone was staring at me. "What makes you think that?" Fiona asked.

I didn't know why my mind linked the two. Except the two were actions with dangerous consequences and no benefits. "It just seems to me that the two events would require the same kind of thinking."

"No one here would play such tricks. Even with people they hated. Especially something like stalling the wind rock. That would endanger just about everyone."

I shrugged. It was just an idea.

"We need to stop this from happening again," said Radia.

"We will tell everyone this was done," Fiona responded. "Everyone will be on the lookout for anyone doing it again."

"That may not be sufficient," Radia warned. "People can sneak around at night."

"Then what do you suggest?"

"A gate with a locked entrance."

"I can't do that," Fiona objected. "You know as well as

I that the wind rock is an emblem of good luck. People touch it for luck all the time. I can't deprive them of it."

Huh. I hadn't known that. Did the Imperial Guards? Would they consider that a form of casting? I would like to see them try to take that huge rock.

"At least you're finally demonstrating some understanding of the value of tradition, my dear," said the Dowager Duchess as she glided into the sitting room with all the ease of someone who felt she belonged there. No doubt she thought she did. "Shintaro, are you never alone? One would almost think you disliked your own company."

Shintaro's only response was to pop a piece of bread in his mouth.

"Attend me, Shintaro," the Dowager Duchess ordered, striding back out of the room.

We all watched her leave and kept eating.

It was too much to hope for that she wouldn't return, and I was right, for return she did. "Must you always cause a spectacle, Shintaro?"

Taro took a slow sip of tea.

"That Academy of yours taught you terrible manners. You don't even know enough to answer?"

"Do my answers matter?" Taro challenged her.

She ignored that, as she seemed to ignore all things that displeased her. Except Taro. She seemed unwilling to ignore him since his brother had died, though she had easily ignored him before then. "It would have been decent to answer one of my messages."

"I thought a lack of answer was the best answer of all." Taro turned to me. "Her Grace wants to introduce me to some woman."

"Not some woman, Shintaro," the Dowager chided. "Lady Simone Frezen. A lovely girl."

"Apparently since I can't marry you, Her Grace wants me to meet a woman I can marry."

"I see." He couldn't marry me? Why the hell not? True,

there was no point to him marrying me—our bond was unbreakable and neither one of us could leave the other—but that didn't mean he couldn't.

"She's dragged this woman all the way from Erstwhile."

"Ah." I had a suspicion this woman was beautiful and elegant and knowledgeable in the ways of the aristocracy.

"Come along, Shintaro."

"Don't be ridiculous," he said loftily.

"As your mother, I have the right to a certain amount of respect."

"One would think so, wouldn't one?"

Her eyes narrowed. "Lady Simone has traveled a great distance to meet you."

"That is not my responsibility."

"You are really so childish that you won't even meet this poor girl who is so far from home and everything she knows?"

Oh, I despised such people, those who manipulated circumstances so one suffered while another appeared selfish for not behaving in the desired manner. It was the manipulator who was cruel, but the manipulated was the one who appeared heartless for not falling in with the plan. Even I, right then, half felt that Taro should just go meet the girl, if only to tell her he wasn't interested and that he thought it unfortunate she had come all this way for nothing. It wasn't her fault the Dowager was a wench.

"I'm not available to marry, and if that is the lady's expectation, there is no point in my meeting her."

"I am disappointed in you, Shintaro."

"When are you not?"

"I insist you come with me."

"Insist away."

"This behavior is inexcusable."

"Blame it on my upbringing."

The Dowager Duchess was fuming. I supposed she was genuinely surprised. Before we came to Flown Raven, Taro had almost always gone to her when ordered. She clearly didn't know how to deal with him now. She gave me a poisonous glare—why was she annoyed with me? I'd said nothing—and swept out of the room.

It always seemed to me that people needed time to recover after being exposed to the Dowager Duchess. Certainly, we all took a moment to collect ourselves.

"Shintaro, would you mind terribly if I killed your mother?" Fiona asked.

"Feel free."

I knew it made me a terrible person that I kind of wished they weren't kidding. I couldn't help it.

"My lady, we must make a decision about the wind rock," Radia reminded Fiona.

"I won't deprive everyone here of access to it," Fiona said firmly. "There's enough bad feeling as it is."

"Two people died in the wind yesterday," Radia announced.

That made us all hesitate. Personally, I was all for gating the rock. Superstition was no cause for endangering everyone.

"Who died?" Fiona asked.

"Little Issa Cornwell, when she was sent out to gather eggs. The wind pushed her off her feet and she hit her head on a stone. Darol Tensen's boat capsized and he drowned."

I watched Fiona think about that. I was trying to silently convince her to do the sensible thing by thinking "locked gate" at her over and over. There was a vicious prankster about. In my opinion, extraordinary measures were needed until the person was caught.

My mind clearly had no particular power, for Fiona said, "We'll let everyone know about the deaths, and offer a reward for good information about who tampered with the rock."

"Yes, my lady." Radia clearly didn't agree with Fiona, but wasn't going to push it further. And that was too bad, for a lock was an obvious solution. Then again, I wasn't going to push it, either, because it wasn't any of my business.

I just wouldn't go outside when it was at all windy.

What followed was a sort of exodus from the room. Taro stormed out, teeth clenched, and I knew better than to follow him. I would be only an aggravation to him right then. Radia nodded to Fiona and Dane before taking her leave, and Tarce, feeling his reason to stay was gone, drifted out moments later. Dane kissed his wife and muttered something about bookkeeping and slipped out. I lingered over my coffee.

"Forgive me for asking," I said, "but is the wind rock's accessibility as a good-luck symbol really so important?"

"It's vital, one of the things I learned almost immediately after moving here. They cast even more spells here than they did in Centerfield, and the rock is a feature in a lot of spells."

Ah. So it would be something in which the Imperial Guards would be interested. If they knew about it. They were still crawling around looking for evidence of casting, and from the looks of it, they were getting nowhere. Could an entire community be so silent? Was there not a single person who could be swayed by threats and bribes?

"You seem uncomfortable talking about casting," Fiona observed.

I shrugged. "I didn't know casting was real until a few months ago. Before then, I thought it was nothing more than a plot device for plays and novels."

"How strange, that nowhere in a Shield's education is there discussed the practice of casting. Is not what you do a form of casting?"

Why did so many people leap to that conclusion? "Not at all. There are no spells, no special ingredients. And a person has to be born able to be a Source or a Shield. It seems to me anyone can cast spells."

"No, not anyone can. I can't. I've tried."

I was surprised. Fiona seemed an intelligent, strong person. That seemed to be the sort who would be able to cast. "That seems a dangerous pursuit. The Emperor has increased the sanctions against the use of spells."

"No," said Fiona, "he's increased the sanctions against the act of pretending to cast spells."

"That's a pretty fine distinction."

"But a significant one, according to the adjudicator."

Fiona was in charge of enforcing the law. She could ignore whatever she chose. But she was accountable to the Emperor, though to my knowledge, the monarch hadn't interfered with how a titleholder enforced the laws in generations. "Many people here seem comfortable with the use of spells."

"Of course. They grew up with their grandmothers showing them how it was done."

"But life seems rather harsh for many of them. If they can use spells, why isn't life better for them?"

"There are limits to what spells can accomplish. And as I said, not everyone can cast them."

"It's just—it seems to me that this belief in spells sprouted out of nowhere. I know there have been some who always believed, but why is it that I never heard of it before?"

"Well, there seems to be less use of it in the East."

"I don't understand."

She shrugged. "Life in this part of the world is harsh and dangerous. I've never seen anywhere else quite like it."

I hadn't, either. "I see."

"But surely you have heard of the Reanists."

Everyone had heard of the Reanists, and my exposure to them had been far too thorough. "What have they to do with anything?"

"Some say they are well versed in the act of casting."

My stomach tightened in revulsion. "They don't cast." And yet, when they had attempted to kill all the aristocrats in High Scape, they had sat us in a carefully prepared room and served unusual food. Could that qualify as a spell?

Fiona raised her eyebrows at me. "What makes you say that?"

The fact that Reanists were homicidal as well as crazy. I was sure a whole lot more people would be dead if Reanists could cast. "I suppose I feel that they, too, would have better circumstances if they had access to that sort of power."

"I don't think many people know the Reanists' true circumstances. But we heard that Reanists were killing the High Landed in High Scape a few years ago, with the goal of stopping natural disasters from occurring."

"Yes." They'd tried to kill Taro. And that was after they'd asked him to sacrifice himself willingly. Was that not proof of insanity? Who would agree to that?

"And now the Triple S is transferring Pairs from High Scape without replacing them, presumably because it's gone cold."

"Sites go cold," I said. "There's no predicting which ones will."

"But the timing is suspect, is it not?"

"Not necessarily." I was being pointlessly stubborn. I knew that. I just hated the idea that sacrificing aristocrats the right way could actually work. And if it was true, it was a dangerous idea to have bandied about. I might think most aristocrats were a waste of air, but I didn't think they should be slaughtered. And my own Source was an aristocrat. No one had the right to hurt him for the sake of a spell, even if it meant halting all natural events. Pairs halted natural events, and no one had to die over it.

"What do you know of casting, Dunleavy?"

"Virtually nothing," I admitted. "I mean, I read some books in High Scape, and I've seen some spells performed."

"Perhaps you should take this opportunity to educate yourself."

"This seems a particularly bad time to indulge in such an education, with the Imperial Guards running about."

"Ah, but although the Guards watch us while they are in the manor, they are often about the countryside, spying on my tenants. And regardless of what my tenants may think of me, they are developing no love for the distant and arrogant Emperor. The Empress used a rapier; her son swings an axe."

"If casting is as widespread as you would have me believe, the Guards will surely discover something of what they are looking for."

"They are all Easterners. They know nothing of this area, what tools are needed to whale and fish and plow and which might be used in casting. Their ignorance will keep my people safe."

"But what if someone is caught?"

"No one shall be flogged on account of these ridiculous laws. The Emperor can take it up with me if he chooses."

"You seem determined to make an enemy of the Emperor." When it would be far more practical and healthy to do her best to avoid his notice.

"I am merely determined to do my best for the people of Flown Raven. I have seen nothing about the Emperor but his wish to inflict the force of his authority on us all. That is not enough to gain my loyalty."

"You swore an oath of fealty to him," I reminded her.

"By sending his Guards to me, expecting his Guards to be able to punish my people, he has violated codes of procedure and honor that have been in place for centuries. He has broken his vows, and that allows me to break mine."

"I hope he will interpret his actions in the same manner as you." Of course he wouldn't. And I couldn't help but feel Fiona was taking foolish risks. I really hoped that she didn't suffer for it. I liked her. She took her responsibilities seriously.

And on a purely selfish level, I would have to be in close contact with whoever replaced her. If the Emperor somehow managed to have her replaced, his chosen title-holder would no doubt be someone I couldn't tolerate and couldn't trust. I wanted Fiona to just concentrate on the well-being of her tenants and stay out of the Emperor's way, for her sake and ours.

Chapter Sixteen

Reid walked in, and I remembered Lila's ill-timed message from the night before. I would have forgotten all about it if he hadn't wandered into my view. That embarrassed me. "I was going to see you as soon as I'd finished breakfast," I lied.

He looked puzzled. "I fear I don't understand."

"Did you not ask Lila to tell me you wanted to see me this morning?"

"Who's Lila?"

Why would she have told me that if it weren't true? But perhaps there was some miscommunication involved.

"But now that you mention it, you might be interested in what I've seen so far. Will you join me in the library after breakfast?"

"I'd be delighted." Maybe he'd forgotten he'd told Lila to give me that message. Academics were supposed to be forgetful about real life, weren't they?

I had another cup of coffee while Reid ate, and after Reid had eaten we headed toward the library.

He didn't speak once we had entered that room. First he looked in every nook, then closed the door and gestured me to the farthest corner behind the stacks. "It's a book of spells, I think," he whispered. "And I believe the spells are meant to control the natural disasters and weather."

"I thought the First Landed had machines for that."

"The machines didn't work."

"And the spells did?"

"I don't believe they did."

"Why would they write a book about it, then?"

"From what I read in the other spell book I mentioned, their spells did work in the beginning. When they first came, they used their machines. When that didn't work, they tried casting. From what I've read so far, some spells did have an effect, but in time even they didn't work."

"Why not?"

"The book says they think the magic faded from the world."

I frowned. "The magic faded?"

"The theory in this book suggests that all the machinery they used was so powerful it caused damage to the world itself. The weather and the natural events became more destructive. Some of the water and soil was destroyed. Even the air was fouled. And the magic of the world was suppressed in some way. They mention being able to feel the power of the world when they first stepped on it, but that they quickly lost that feeling. And something of particular note is that Flown Raven, though it was called something different in their time, was a place where spells were more easily cast. It appealed to them, and one of their first and largest settlements was in this location."

That was something I wished I could have seen, their steel roads and their tall buildings with their flying machines dotting the sky. "That may be why the machine is in the cave."

"Perhaps."

"Why are people able to cast spells now?"

"Perhaps the world is finally healing, and the magic is coming back."

"Healing. The world is not a person."

"It doesn't need to be a person to suffer injury and to heal."

I wasn't sure I agreed with that, but he seemed so confident about it.

"Flown Raven was also one of the places hardest hit by earthquakes shortly after the First Landed were established here. You know that part of history, do you not? That their machines all failed and their cities were buried by natural disasters?"

"We learned about that in the Academy," I told him. "I was never taught the slightest thing about magic, though."

"No. That sort of thing was never mentioned in approved scrolls."

"Why is that?"

He shrugged. "It was hundreds of years ago, and for most of that time, magic didn't seem to function. People wouldn't believe it. A serious discussion of magic in any historical text would have made the work lack credibility."

"Do you really think that's the reason?"

"I can think of no other reason to neglect to address the issue."

Neither could I, but that explanation seemed to me to be too weak. Too forgiving. Too naive.

On the other hand, I was getting to be too suspicious of everything. It was tiring.

"The thing is, the magic is coming back, as you know. And it would be interesting to see if Flown Raven resumes its prior position as a place where magic is most powerful. That should be of interest to you."

"Why?"

"You're a Shield who's been posted here. You've grown up performing one form of magic"—I grit my teeth; Shielding was not magic—"and you're in a place where magic may become most potent. You know, since meeting you, I've become more interested in the role of Sources and Shields through history. It's interesting, don't you think? The machinery of the First Landed is destroyed. Magic, it appears, is eliminated. A few centuries later, all of a sudden, a Source is born, and then more, and then Shields. Do you know the numbers of Shields and Sources have increased from one generation to the next, practically from the time they were discovered? And for the past few generations, the magic has been growing stronger. It's an interesting coincidence, don't you think?"

"I don't think channeling and magic have anything to do with each other."

He shrugged. "Maybe not directly. Maybe they're both connected to something else."

"Like what?"

"That might be something I can discover in time."

I rubbed my forehead. He was saying so much that didn't make sense. I was feeling a little confused.

There was a solid, loud knock at the library door, making us both jump. We both looked around the stacks. It was Taro, and his expression was blank. "Lila said you were looking for me," he announced.

I frowned. "No, I wasn't."

He assumed a bright smile. "You two. Always together, always working so hard. The moon is eclipsed." He sauntered into the room. "What conversation do you have that is so very fascinating?"

"We're discussing a historian we've both read," Reid answered.

I looked at him, surprised by the lie. Why was Reid willing to tell me about the book, but not Taro? How could he imagine I would be comfortable with that?

"Lee, my love, you know it isn't good for you to spend so much time reading. You'll wrinkle your lovely brow."

He trailed a fingertip over my forehead. "You don't want to ruin your looks."

That had to be one of the most ridiculous things I'd ever heard. I didn't say that, though. I was the master of restraint.

I had an idea why he was acting like this. Or, at least, I had a couple of theories. He didn't like me spending time with Reid, for no good reason. Living in the manor where he had so many bad memories was probably making him crazy. And his mother was right next door.

Taro smiled at me, the slow, sensual smile that still made my stomach clench. "Surely you can think of better things to do than spend every day and every evening in the library."

We couldn't have sex all the time, though I had to admit the challenge of trying might be fun. "You spend all day and all night playing cards."

He tsked. "Now, that's not true. And it's a terrible thing to accuse me of when you really don't know what I do all day."

"So what do you do all day?"

He winked. "Follow me and find out."

I didn't want to. Not when he was in that kind of mood. He was only trying to get me away from Reid. I resented it. But I didn't know how to refuse without looking like a wench. "Of course. I'll see you later, Academic Reid."

"Of course."

I followed Taro out of the library. After a quick glance around to make sure no one would overhear us, I said, "You can't keep acting this way."

"I don't know what you mean."

"I'm not spending an inordinate amount of time with Reid."

"Every time I see you, you're deep in some kind of intimate conversation." A bit of bite slid into his tone.

"That's just been a weird coincidence. Really, I spend more time with Tarce. You're not bothered by him."

"Tarce is a fool," he said sharply.

I followed Taro out of the house. Where were we going? "Aye, he is."

"And handsome."

"I suppose."

"And does nothing useful with his time."

"Not that I know of."

And that seemed to be all he had to say about Tarce. Which was fine. Tarce wasn't that interesting, and it wasn't as though I actually wanted Taro to get upset about Fiona's brother. "I am getting very tired of you acting like I'm going to commit some indiscretion."

"Now you know what it feels like."

"I never thought you would start sleeping with someone else without telling me first."

"You honestly think that makes any difference? Whether I'm told first or not?"

"I do. It makes a huge difference."

"It still amazes me how little you understand about things that really matter."

"Well, why don't you enlighten me?"

He stopped and stared down at me. "Fine. I will. Being told in advance makes no difference at all."

I crossed my arms. "I disagree."

He rolled his eyes. "Of course you do. Zaire forbid I should know anything about anything."

He was clearly not ready to be reasonable about this, so I let him walk on. I stopped following him and headed for a nearby bench. Maybe I would try again when he was calm.

I really couldn't believe that he thought I would possibly throw him over for Reid. Reid was completely uninteresting to me in that way. And Taro and I had already agreed we would have no such relationships with other people. Did he think I hadn't meant that, or had forgotten, or something?

This place was making him irrational. Was there any

way we could make Flown Raven less unbearable to Taro?

Get his mother to move.

Hm.

What were the arrangements for her to live at the dowager house? I had no idea. Did she have any money of her own, or was she given an allowance by the Westsea estate? Could she be persuaded to leave if offered more money? That would be up to Fiona, but Fiona despised her, too. Maybe she would be willing to pay extra for the privilege of the absence of the Dowager.

It was a plan, but a weak one. Knowing the Dowager, the mere fact that we wanted her gone would make her resistant to inducements. But it was a start. I had to think about it.

I went to our suite. I locked the door. I took apart the overmantel and picked a book at random.

It turned out to be a book of glamors, or something along those lines. A spell to whiten teeth. A spell to perfect skin, or change its shade. Spells to appear as other people. Spells to change the color of one's hair.

And that was when I was gripped by a truly stupid idea.

What if I could do this? Apparently, lots of people could, and they didn't need any special training to do it. Wouldn't it be amazing if I could do it?

No, it was ridiculous. Nothing I had ever done suggested I could cast spells and have them work.

Although Reid, who appeared a smart fellow, seemed to think there might be some connection between being a Shield, or a Source, and the casting of spells. He believed Flown Raven itself might be a place of some kind of power. The combination would suggest that I had a good chance of succeeding in casting a spell, wouldn't it? And to reject the knowledge of something while everyone else was embracing it could be disadvantageous.

What could it hurt to try?

All right, slow down. It would hurt a lot if I was caught.

So I just wouldn't get caught. The door was locked. And I would have to hope no one other than Fiona and Dane knew about the secret passage.

And if I paid the proper amount of attention, I wouldn't light the place on fire. I would start with something harmless.

The instructions to change the color of one's hair were short and looked simple. True, the spell was meant to hide gray hair, but there was no reason to believe the spell wouldn't work on red hair. And I'd always wondered what I would look like with hair of a more normal color. Black would be striking.

I needed a candle—these things always called for a candle—ash from a fireplace—supposedly the ash of a pig but I'd have no way of knowing what kind of ash would be in the kitchen, my best source—the sap of an oak, water, soap made from the lard of a lark, and a quail's egg. Regular soap and a chicken's egg would have to do. The juice of grapes—wine—and, of course, drops of my blood. I was supposed to fast for twenty-four hours before I performed the spell, but I didn't want to wait that long. Fasting couldn't really make a difference to something like this. How would the spell know?

I gathered the ingredients. The sap was a challenge, as it didn't run freely that time of year. And I got strange looks as I scooped up some of the ashes in the kitchen. I washed my hair as instructed. I dressed in only a dressing gown and sat cross-legged on the floor beside where I'd set up all the ingredients along with the required copper bowl and a wooden spoon.

I lit the candle. Then, referring to the book, I spread the ashes on the floor in a thick layer. Using the middle finger of my right hand, I drew a circle in the ashes, and within the circle the figure of an eye, the symbol of blood, a collection of wavy lines that was supposed to signify hair, and a horizontal line that was flat on one end and wavy on the other. Then I put the bowl on top of the ashes.

Into the bowl I cracked the egg and poured the sap, the wine, and the water. I sliced my palm and let some blood drop in. I mixed the ingredients.

I felt foolish at several points in this process, and I almost stopped, but I kept convincing myself to go on. I wanted to see if it would work, and it would cause me no harm if it didn't. None of the ingredients was dangerous.

Once the mess I was going to be putting in my hair was the right consistency, I referred to the book again and spoke the incantation written there. "Oh, forces of the world, hear my plea, change the adornment to one of youth, to one more pleasing to the eye. I offer to you the emblems of youth, the fruits of spring. Adorn me with the feathers of youth."

I repeated the nonsensical paragraph several times until I had it memorized. I continued to repeat it as I bent over the bowl and, with some effort, sank all of my hair into the mess. I recited the incantation eight more times, my neck and back aching due to the unnatural position. The combination of the ingredients was more potent than I'd thought, for I was feeling a little dizzy and jittery.

Once I'd repeated the phrase twenty-eight times, I pulled my hair out and wrapped it in a towel that I'd lined with dried mint. The worst part of this process was that I'd have to keep my hair wrapped up until the following dawn. It didn't make sense to me that something that was supposed to be an illusion took so long to set in. It probably wouldn't even work.

And I'd ruined a towel that didn't belong to me. I would have to give Fiona a gift.

I heard pounding on the door to our suite. I ran to it. "Who's there?"

"Why the hell is the door locked?" Taro demanded.

"Is anyone with you?"

"No. What's going on?"

I opened the door. He walked in. He appeared agitated and his hair was in disarray. "What's happened?" I asked.

His eyes narrowed. "Are you sick?"

A valid question, as it was early in the day for me to be in my dressing gown. Clearly I should have waited until the evening to try the spell. "I'm trying to dye my hair."

"You're what?" he demanded, his voice cracking high.

He heard me. "I'm trying to dye my hair."

"What the hell are you doing that for?"

That was a rather explosive reaction to the news. "I've often wondered what it would be like to have black hair."

"Black? Are you insane? That will look terrible with your coloring. And your eyebrows will still be red."

Oops. I hadn't thought of that. But surely the spell would address my eyebrows, too? "I'm trying a spell."

"You're trying a spell?"

"Aye, I wanted to see if I could do one."

"So you chose to start by changing the color of your hair?"

That seemed more disturbing to him than the fact that I was trying to perform a spell. He had the queerest priorities at times. "Why not?"

"You didn't even ask me!"

One of the maligned undyed eyebrows rose. "Excuse me?"

"You heard me!"

"When did you develop the delusion that I need to have my physical appearance approved by you?" Arrogant ass.

"Don't be ridiculous," he said, sounding just like his mother. "What if I thought to shave off all my hair? If I just went out and did it without telling you first? That wouldn't disturb you at all?"

Well, to be honest, aye, it would. A lot. But I didn't

have to admit that, and if it had happened, I would have kept my displeasure to myself, because I wasn't an arrogant ass. "You hacked off most of your hair when we were in Flatwell. You didn't talk to me first."

The look on his face implied that he had forgotten about that completely. "I was roasting," he said in what I considered a lame attempt to justify his behavior. "It was hotter than hell."

"My hair was longer than yours, and I didn't cut it." I did enjoy being right.

"You didn't feel the heat like I did"—which was true—"and you did plenty else."

Which was also true. "None of that matters. You set a precedent that I'm following now."

"Fine. Whatever." He threw up his hands. "It doesn't matter."

"So what's happened?" I asked again, because he looked ready to start pacing.

"What?" he responded with an air of distraction.

"You were upset before you saw me."

"Her Grace," he muttered.

"What did she do?"

He pulled in a deep breath and then slowly let it out. "She accosted me in the garden. She got a grip on my arm and I wasn't prepared to shake hard enough to be free of her."

"Was she trying to drag you to the dowager house to meet that friend of hers?" I should have expected something like that.

He laughed a little hysterically. "If only it were something so simple. She told me the Emperor would support me if I chose to pursue the title again."

I stared. What? I mean, what? I thought this had all been put to bed. And, what? "Is she insane?"

"I know," he said wearily.

"Fiona has the title."

"I know."

"She's already picked an heir, so that even if something did happen to her, you wouldn't be first in line for the title."

"I know."

"What is she thinking?"

"She said . . . She hinted—" He broke off, biting his lower lip.

"What?" What was the crazy old bat thinking now?

"She seemed to imply that there were ways to remove someone from a title."

"My gods." Would she never give that up? "What's the Emperor's interest in this? He doesn't even like you." Then again, I didn't think he'd liked Taro the first time he'd tried to bend the laws to get Taro the title after he'd abjured it. "What the hell is he up to?"

"I thought this was over the last time." Taro's shoulders slumped in fatigue. "I really don't understand all this interest in my life. I can't imagine she was so active in my brother's life."

"Maybe if you had the title, she'd leave you alone."

"That possibility is almost enough to make having the title an attractive prospect, but that's not going to happen. I have her attention now and it seems I can't lose it. I don't understand why she can't just forget it all. It doesn't affect her life at all."

Truly, I didn't understand her interest. I was sure she didn't either like or love Taro. So why did she care? Why did she waste the effort and attention? It couldn't purely be because the current titleholder wasn't a Karish. That just made no sense. "What did you tell her?"

"That I wouldn't take the title. That no matter what happened, if the title was presented to me on a platter, I'd find another relative to give it to."

"And she said?"

"Something along the lines that I didn't know what I

wanted, and I let you influence me too much. And to remember I had the support of the Emperor."

"I influence you too much?"

"She said that it was in your best interest to keep me as your Source, because if I became a duke, you wouldn't be any use to anyone."

Those were concerns I had had the first time it seemed he might end up with the title. But Flown Raven had been a cold site back then. Now that it had become active and needed a Pair, the situation was different. "If you actually wanted the title—"

"I don't, all right?" he said impatiently. "I never have. But she talks at me like she thinks I did. That you were the only reason I abjured the title. That I have no mind of my own."

That bitch. We had to find a way to keep her away from Taro. She was just too poisonous and relentless, and someday he was going to snap and throttle her. Then he would be weighted down by guilt for the rest of his life.

Taro paced for a while more, but it seemed to wind him up rather than relax him. He announced he needed to move and he left. I had to hide in my room, so, as uncomfortable as it made me, I asked to have my meals delivered to me, and wrote letters. Taro hadn't returned by the time I went to bed.

Sleeping was a challenge, awkward because of the wrap I wore around my head. That was why I didn't appreciate Taro's startled shout early the next morning. "Who died?" I asked in a thick voice.

"Your hair!" he practically shrieked.

My hair had died? "What?"

"Your hair!"

Oh. I guessed it had worked. That gave me a little glow of accomplishment. It didn't make up for being roused at a ridiculously early hour of the day. "It can't look that bad." I snuggled back down in bed.

"Oh no? Take a look in the mirror."

"I will. When I get up."

He tapped my forehead, and kept tapping until I opened my eyes. So I could see the strand of hair he'd pulled before them.

It was green.

Green. Not greenish. Not with a green tinge. Green as grass. My hair was green.

With a cry of dismay, I flew from the bed and flung open a window before seeking a mirror. In the bright light of the morning, I looked at my reflection. My hair, every single strand, was the same unrelenting shade of green.

My gods, what had I done?

Taro started laughing. And he didn't stop. I could have thrown the mirror at him, only it wasn't mine. "Will you stop?"

"That's what you get for meddling with what you were born with."

"It wasn't supposed to do this." How could I be seen by anyone like this? My eyebrows were practically gleaming in orange contrast. And the color was thorough, every hair, right to the skull. Green. What was I going to do?

Taro was still collapsed on the bed laughing.

"Keep laughing, my lord," I said sourly. "You'll have to go to the market for some hair dye."

"How do you plan to make me?" he snickered.

"You'll make me go out like this?" I asked, surprised.

"I think you should have to suffer for doing this without talking to me first."

"Fine. If that's the way you want to be about it." It would be humiliating, of course, but there were worse things in life than green—green!—hair. I would go to the market myself, if I couldn't wash this out or change it back.

"What's that supposed to mean?"

"Maybe I'll start a new fashion."

His laughter stopped abruptly. "You're going to go walking around with green hair?" He looked appalled.

"I have no choice, do I?"

His eyes narrowed. "You wouldn't dare."

"We'll see, won't we?"

Oh my gods. My hair was *green*.

Chapter Seventeen

I didn't have a scarf that would cover my hair. After a frustrating expanse of time I managed to pin a pillowcase to my head in a manner that covered all my hair. It looked ridiculous, but less ridiculous, I thought, than my green hair.

Every single servant I passed on the way down to the sitting room turned and stared at me. I thought servants weren't supposed to do that sort of thing, express shock at the strangeness of the guests. Surely I didn't look weird beyond all comprehension and experience.

Fiona was with Stacin in the sitting room, and, like her servants, she stared at the pillowcase on my head. "Good morning," I said, hoping I sounded like I thought everything was normal.

"What the hell is that?" she demanded.

So much for normal. "I just washed it."

"And that requires a pillowcase because . . . ?"

"Pillowcases provide the optimum combination of exposure to air and protection from dust." Hey, that actually sounded plausible.

"Really?"

"You've never heard of that?"

"Can't say I have."

"Imagine that." I headed for the coffeepot. I really needed coffee. "Does your market have a dye maker?"

"There is no market today."

Oh, hell. "When is it?"

"Two days from now. It is held once every other week."

"Damn it."

Fiona's gaze drifted up to the pillowcase again. "You need dye so desperately?"

"It's not desperation," I lied. "I was just hoping to get some things done today."

"I'll tell you how to find the dye maker if you tell me what color you've dyed your hair."

So much for lying. "That's not necessary." Damn it, I wanted to know.

"So you're going to wear that pillowcase for two days, and then wear it to the market with everyone there to see it?"

If I had to. I was not going to tell her my hair was green. I was not telling anyone. It was bad enough that Taro had seen it. And if he told anyone, I would kill him.

If Fiona could tell me where the dye maker was, so could others. Others who wouldn't feel they had the right to ask me why I needed the dye, no matter how strange I looked.

I grabbed a couple of pieces of bread and hunted down Bailey. He stared at the pillowcase for only a moment, and cleared his voice before giving me the directions to the dye maker's home. I headed out immediately.

It was drizzling outside, but not enough to divert me from my goal. Apparently it rained a lot in Flown Raven. I couldn't let it stop me from doing whatever I wanted to do, or I'd never leave the manor.

Apparently I was due only so much humiliation that

day. I didn't pass anyone on the way. Would I be so lucky on my way back?

The dye maker's name was Tish Rounder, and she lived in a small cottage set a little apart from the rest of the village. I could smell it long before I could see it. It was a horrible, gagging layer of stench, bringing tears to my eyes, and I almost turned back.

But I had green hair. I pressed on.

I knocked on her door, breathing through my mouth. That didn't really help much. The air tasted foul.

The woman who answered the door was a stocky brunette a good many years older than I. Sweat shone on her face, explained by the blast of heat from the interior of the cottage. Her leather apron was stained various colors and her hair was tightly tied back from her face.

She looked at my pillowcase and laughed.

I had the feeling that reaction would be getting really annoying really fast.

"Good day," I said, struggling for decorum. "I understand you make and sell dyes."

"I do," she said with a smirk. "Dye for what?"

What did she think? She was going to make me say it? "For my hair." And I didn't have the slightest snap in my tone. I was pleased.

"Please come in." She stood aside.

Did I have to? It was sure to smell even worse. I stepped through the door, and yes, it definitely did. How did she bear it?

"My apologies for the disorder, my dear," the woman said. "I'm making indigo. That's always aromatic."

"Aromatic" was a cruel understatement. The stench was as brutal as a weapon, sending edges of steel scraping out the back of my nose and clogging my throat. It was vicious. "Ah," I said.

"Let's see it, then."

"I beg your pardon?"

"Your hair."

Blunt people made me insane. "Is that really necessary?"

"I have to know what you've done before I can know if I can fix it."

I supposed that could be true, though I suspected it was more a matter of her wanting to entertain herself. Reluctantly, I unpinned and unfolded the pillowcase from my hair. She started laughing before my hair was fully free.

"If you're quite done," I said.

And she laughed a few moments more before calming down and saying, "You didn't dye your hair that color."

"I certainly wasn't born with it."

"I mean you didn't dye it to get it that color."

"No, I wanted it to be black."

She looked frustrated and I didn't blame her, for yes, I was deliberately misunderstanding her. Her enjoyment of my embarrassment annoyed me. "How did your hair come to turn green?" she demanded.

I wasn't going to tell her that. Casting was illegal. Or pretending to cast was. Certainly, possessing the tools of casting was illegal. I didn't want this woman running to the Imperial Guards.

She took the choice out of my hands. "You tried some kind of spell, didn't you?"

"I most certainly did not."

"There's no dye that can get a color that solid, that thorough. That's a spell."

"No, it wasn't." I should just shut my mouth. The more I spoke, the less convincing I sounded, even to my own ears.

"I can't help you," Rounder told me. "Nothing I make can do anything about that."

She couldn't help me. Really? My hair was going to stay green? For how long? Until it grew out? That would take years. And in the meantime, I would have to shave myself bald. Because regardless of what I'd told Taro, I wasn't prepared to walk around with green hair.

"You need to see Healer Browne," she told me.

"I'm neither sick nor injured."

"You need to see Healer Browne," she repeated with greater emphasis on the words.

"Do I?" Was she saying Browne knew something about casting? Did Browne cast herself?

"She can help you if anyone can."

"Thank you." My hope renewed, I gladly left the malodorous cottage and hoped I didn't carry the stench with me.

If the grimace on Browne's face when she opened the door was any indication, I did indeed stink. "I was just at the dye maker's," I said quickly.

"Why does that mean you have to come here?" she demanded.

"Dyer Rounder suggested I come here."

"Why?"

I pulled the pillowcase off my head.

Predictably, Browne laughed. For a long time. "I guess I don't have to hide from you the fact that I cast spells. Did you follow the spell exactly?"

"No."

"You didn't?"

"Not precisely."

"That was fairly stupid, don't you think?"

"It's a spell. It's not supposed to work."

"So why were you doing it?"

My idiocy laid bare, I shrugged.

"I'm not sure," she said, "but I imagine it's meant to be only temporary. Your hair will probably change back in time."

That was a relief, sort of. "How much time?"

"Didn't the instructions say?"

"No." I was pretty sure they hadn't.

"And yet you tried it anyway?"

"I really hadn't expected it to work at all."

Browne snickered.

"Can you do anything for me?" Or not, I wanted to ask as well, but that seemed too obnoxious.

"I can brew you a cup of tea and listen while you tell me exactly what you did. Maybe there is a way to fix this."

I didn't want to linger. I wanted to be told how to end the spell and to run back to the manor to hide. But she was filling a kettle and I felt obligated to stay, so I did, sitting at a table that was piled high with chopped greenery and vegetables. I wondered whether they were ingredients for healing, casting, or breakfast.

Having given up on trying to be discreet about my behavior, I was brutally honest with Browne about the steps that I had skipped or adjusted, and in each case Browne tsked in disapproval. "These things are written as they are for a reason," she chided.

"To make them appear more impressive." It wouldn't create much awe if there weren't a series of tests to meet first, would it?

"Why do you dabble in things for which you have no respect? That is the worst sort of person."

Really? The worst sort of person? Worse than murderers and tax collectors?

Though I could understand, a little, what she was getting at. I shouldn't be interfering in things I wasn't prepared to take seriously. I knew the power of casting was real. I had seen spells, performed poorly, do a great deal of damage. I had been stupid.

But here was the thing. I had cast a spell. That reality was taking a while to seep into my brain, but that was the truth. People all over the world had believed in casting for years. More and more people were coming to think that casting was real. A spell had been cast on my person. And now I had cast a spell, though I had made a hash of it. It was remarkable. "So you are an expert in the use of spells?"

"I wouldn't say I'm an expert. I know certain things. And I can cast spells and have them work."

"But it appears not everyone can. Why is that?"

"There are a number of reasons. For some, reading isn't easy. Casting a spell needs a strong will and sharp focus. Those can be improved upon with training and practice, but not everyone has those qualities, while some have them in abundance. Like everything else, there are those who will take to it easily and those who will never be able to do it at all. And then, of course, spells won't work at all unless they're performed in a place of power."

"Place of power? The book didn't mention that."

"Are you sure? There was no mention in the chapter at the beginning that told you how to prepare yourself?"

That would have been the chapter I'd skipped as unnecessary. Because I'd learned about preparation in other books I'd read while still in High Scape, and now that I thought of it, I obviously hadn't remembered enough about it. Because I remembered now reading about places of power, namely, where the three rivers met. People had been anxious to have control over that area. "Not that I recall."

"Hmph," said Browne, and I had a feeling she didn't believe me. "It is said that only certain places foster the ability in people to cast spells. There are few such places now, but they are growing in number."

"Really."

"My grandmother would tell stories of when she was a girl, that that was when the power started coming to Flown Raven. It was weak at first, and grew stronger over her lifetime."

"Do you think it's as strong as it's going to get?"

"Not at all."

That was a horrible thing to hear. Because if this thing was growing, and more people were going to be using it, there would be chaos. I just didn't trust people to use this properly.

Shortly after Taro and I had been bonded, a bitter rogue Source named Stevan Creol had abducted Taro. Creol had discovered how to create disasters and had been using that ability to attack High Scape. Taro, the most able Source in High Scape, had been able to stop Creol's attacks. And so Creol had had him kidnapped.

Witnessing Creol's behavior had enabled Taro to imitate it. He could create disasters and, like Creol, could cause small areas of soil to shift. Off his own bat, he had the limited ability to heal.

None of these was a traditional Source ability.

Just as my ability to tamper with the weather was not a traditional skill of a Shield.

Was it all connected? Reid sort of suggested it could be. "What do you think I should do?" I asked.

"Wait a few days to see if your natural color returns. If it doesn't, try for black again using the proper steps. A properly cast spell should allow your hair to change back to its natural color in time."

"I don't know how to get lark's lard," I protested.

"Send word to me. I'll get you all the proper ingredients."

"Really?" That was generous of her.

"And sometime, when I need help, you can do me a favor."

Ah. See, that was the problem. She was required to give me what I asked for.

Except I wasn't asking for healing. I was asking for supplies for spells which, as far as I knew, weren't part of her trade. A Shield couldn't just go around demanding the personal possessions of people. Especially when said possessions were sort of illegal.

But a Shield wasn't supposed to be beholden to anyone.

"Is there a problem?" Browne asked in the face of my indecision.

This wasn't just about my hair. People were using spells, and I had the ability to understand what they did. It was important that I know what casting meant. "No, none at all." I would deal with the repercussions when I had to.

"Do we have an agreement?"

"We do." I would just hope my hair changed back naturally. And if it didn't, well, I'd figure something out.

I left Browne's cottage soon after that. Unfortunately, I passed three people on the way back to the manor. All three of them stared at the pillowcase I'd had difficulty repinning to my head, and then grimaced and cut me a wide berth. This made it brutally clear that I carried the stench of the dyer's cottage with me. What would they think of me?

Then I entered the manor, and found Bailey blocking my path. "Something wrong, Bailey?"

"My apologies, Shield Mallorough," he said, and from the way his hand lifted from his side I fancied he was an instant away from holding his nose. "Though it may cost me my position, I can't let you in. The smell will get into everything."

"I don't want you fired, Bailey," I grumbled. "But how am I to rectify the situation if I can't bathe?"

"Please go around to the back near the kitchen," he said. "Maybe I can arrange something."

All right, this was getting ridiculous. If he wanted to smell something bad, he should go to the dyer's cottage. And the healer seemed to have endured my scent without real difficulty. But I traipsed to the back of the manor, where a bathtub had already been carried out and a stand placed beside it. Three roasting irons had been plunged into the ground, forming a triangle around the tub. Two maids were engaged in suspending sheets from the irons in order to, I assumed, provide me with some privacy while I sat in the tub.

Bathing outside. Just lovely.

One maid grimaced, presumably at the smell I carried. The other slapped the first maid's arm in rebuke. "We're boiling water for you now, ma'am," the second maid said. "And we've got women guarding all the windows, so none of the men get a peek."

I hadn't even considered the possibility of men watching through the upper windows, and I would have preferred to remain ignorant. It was embarrassing enough that the whole household was involved in giving me a bath because I stank so badly they couldn't let me in the manor.

Oh, but the embarrassment didn't end there, for once the tub had been filled with steaming water, the maids collected from me everything I wore, for the purposes of burning it. That included the pillowcase on my head. There was nothing for it. I took out the pins and revealed my grassy green hair.

The maids stared at it, openmouthed. "How did you get it that color, ma'am?" the first one asked.

"I'm not prepared to say."

"But why is it—" The second maid slapped her again, to shut her up.

What a perfect day.

I got in the tub and scrubbed until my skin was pink. Once the water cooled, the tub was emptied and filled again, for the smell was still strong. The upper maids, the housekeeper, the kitchen staff, all the women of the household stopped by to recoil at my scent and offer me bizarre methods of getting rid of it.

Oh, but the best moment had to be when my sophisticated, beautiful, never-a-hair-out-of-place Source arrived and looked over the barricade of sheets. "They taught me about Shields at the Academy," he said. "I was told Shields were sober people, cautious in thought and deed, temperate of mind and mood."

Oh, shut up.

"Where were all those Shields at my Matching?"

If I had had something to throw at him, I would have.

"Surely I deserved such a worthy creature."

I had all sorts of ideas about what he deserved.

"That figure of grace and discipline who never—"

"Do you want me to cut off all your hair while you sleep?" I asked him. "Because you're riding to it."

He grinned and then winked, the prat.

I spent several hours bathing, scrubbing until the skin around my nails began to bleed and it was deemed unsafe for me to continue scrubbing. My curiosity as to whether the smell I thought was still clinging to me might be only in my mind was determined for me when Taro forced me to sleep on the settee in our sitting room. He was laughing as he did it.

On a more positive note, when I woke the next day my hair had resumed its natural hue.

Chapter Eighteen

The day was to be spent in mourning, both for those who had been lost while whaling and those who had died in the wind. The bodies had already been disposed of by their families; it was time to honor their characters. From what I understood of the rites, the morning was to be solemn, remembering what was lost. The afternoon was to be a little lighter, remembering the joy the deceased had brought to the community. In the evening, everyone would disperse into their own homes and sing to lull the world into acceptance of the loss of its members.

Everyone gathered in the early morning just beyond the gardens behind the manor. The sky was heavily overcast, turning gray, and there was a faint drizzle dampening hair and clothing. I would say that the weather matched the mood of the people, except it seemed truly sunny days were rare in Flown Raven.

A fire had been built on a large square of hammered copper set on the grass. Most of the others in attendance stood in a wide circle around the fire, so Taro and I followed suit. A man holding a wooden flute was standing near Fiona, and they were talking in low voices.

Dane was there, holding Stacin. Tarce and Radia stood near them. Daris was absent. That was no surprise to me. I rarely saw her, and her drunken bitterness would be a disastrous addition to the proceedings.

The Guards were there, too, and I couldn't figure out why. Did they think spells were going to be cast during the funeral? Couldn't they just let it rest for a day? Their presence stirred up a lot of resentment, and no one needed that.

Everyone spoke in low voices, even the children, and they didn't speak much. I didn't want to say a word if I didn't have to. I was often clumsy with words, especially with strangers, and I was sure anything I said would do more harm than good.

Taro's mother showed up. Of course she did. I was aware of Taro growing tense beside me, and I wished she would just die already. She was going to cause an argument in front of all these people—I just knew it.

Except she didn't seem to spare a glance for Taro. She appeared much more interested in Fiona. She didn't join the circle, and she had with her three women who carried unfamiliar rods, red in color and about the length of a man's arm each. I wondered what that was about.

I directed my gaze away from them. This day was for the dead and those who mourned them. I would give them the attention they deserved.

Fiona had told me what would happen. These people who believed so much in ritual and magic had a rather simple ceremony for saying good-bye to their dead. Ritual, she said, created a distance between the dead and the living that was unhealthy. Grief could be more easily exercised through simplicity. I thought I might agree with her.

Four preadolescent children stood far outside the circle, one each at north, south, east and west. They represented those who had died, and were usually but not necessarily members of the families of the deceased. Each wore something belonging to the deceased, an article of clothing, a pendant or a handkerchief, and each carried an item of significance to the deceased, chosen by their families.

Fiona held a rattle that she shook every few moments. The flutist began to play a mournful, light tune. More people gathered. Fiona began to speed up the shaking of her rattle. A short time passed, and I believed just about everyone in the community was there. Fiona quickened her rattle until its ring was constant.

The four children ran up to the circle. That was the signal for everyone to clasp hands. I had Taro at my right and a stranger at my left who held my hand too tightly. Fiona stopped the rattle.

"Four lives have chosen to leave our home," she announced. "We don't wish them to leave."

And that was our cue to prevent the youngsters from passing through into the circle. The children let themselves be held back, not ducking under the linked hands.

"But all lives must come to an end," Fiona continued. "If they did not, we would not value them as we do. Holding on to these lives poisons us as we attempt to move forward, and insults the memories of our loved ones, by wasting the efforts they made on our behalf while they lived. And so we must release these lives." She shook the rattle again, just once.

That was the signal to unclasp our hands and let the children through. Once they were all inside the circle, they each took a place around the fire at north, south, east and west.

"We bid farewell to Issa Cornwell," said Fiona, and one of the children threw a doll into the fire. "We bid farewell to Darol Tensen." Another child threw a smoking pipe. "We bid farewell to Jacob Ibuki." The third child threw some kind of small tool I didn't recognize into the

fire. "We bid farewell to Eller Le Royer." The final child
threw in a small framed portrait.

Fiona then spent some time talking about the four deceased and their places in their families and communities.
Jacob Ibuki had been an experienced whaler, always the
best teacher for the young ones starting out. Eller Le Royer
had hated whaling, but had done his best at it because of
its importance to the community. Darol Tensen had had
an acute sense of humor that everyone enjoyed. Fiona
couldn't say much about the child, though she mentioned
that one of the girl's first words was "bicci" for biscuit,
and that she'd had an uncanny ability to escape almost
every kind of confinement placed on her. Fiona was a
good speaker and was able, even, to make people chuckle
once in a while. I hadn't been to many ceremonies honoring the dead, but this was one of the least oppressive I'd
attended.

Fiona wrapped up her presentation by saying, "I invite
others to celebrate the lives of the lost."

And one after the other, individuals within the circle
described the people they had lost. Some, in anticipation
of this moment, had substantial speeches prepared. A few
said nothing more than something like, "He was a good
man, and I miss him," which I found just as effective.

After a good many people spoke, there was a silence,
and no new people volunteered to speak. That suggested
to me that the solemn part of the occasion was over. It was
time to move on to the celebratory part of the day.

Then the Dowager Duchess cleared her throat.

That couldn't be good.

Everyone went still.

"Our community has lost four dearly beloved members
within a few days," she said, and I would have been surprised if she could have named any of those people before
today. "This is a serious injury to all of us, an injury from
which we can never fully recover."

If she gave a serious damn about a single person who'd

died, I'd eat my boots. If she didn't care about her son, she couldn't care about virtual strangers. Well, maybe she did; I was sure her priorities were pretty screwy. But I doubted she felt the slightest shred of emotion for these particular strangers.

"To lose so many at once is unprecedented in our community."

Really? It seemed a dangerous place to live. The wind alone could kill people.

"These unprecedented deaths are part of a disturbing trend of bad luck that has been cursing Flown Raven."

Oh no. Muttering began among many in the crowd. I was furious with the Dowager. This was supposed to be a time to soothe grief. She was using the occasion to stir up ill will against Fiona.

I wished I was an articulate, persuasive speaker. Then I might be able to shut the woman up in a way that would discredit her before the others. I looked at Fiona, but she didn't appear prepared to speak to defend herself, her expression blank.

"I know many of you have been feeling you have been left to fend for yourselves, and you would be right."

How would she know? She didn't see how Fiona spent her days.

"The titleholder has not been whaling, as is the tradition of every titleholder in Flown Raven."

Taro's brother went whaling? I found that difficult to believe. I didn't know much about him, and I had never met him, but I found it hard to accept that the man who had apparently spent his days drinking and whoring cared much about tradition when it might inconvenience him. Nor did I believe that if it were such a tradition, Fiona wouldn't do it. She took her responsibilities seriously.

"The fishing has been depleted. Crops are not looking as healthy as they have in past years. Whales have not come as close to shores. And the titleholder has done nothing."

And what, realistically, could Fiona do about such things?

"There has been an increase in criminal activity in the area. Our very own Pair"—hey, we were not hers—"were robbed not far from here. Thieves are breaking into homes. There has been no reaction from the titleholder. And when the titleholder learned of the tampering of the wind rock that caused the deaths of two people, she did nothing."

The Dowager had agreed with the decision to leave the rock without a gate, but one would never know it by the look of baffled indignation on her face. And the very people for whom Fiona had made that decision, so that they would have access to the rock considered so important to them, began to look angry.

"The disintegration of your lives has been going on for more than two years," the Dowager continued. "With no signs of abatement. How long are you to be expected to bear this?"

"Aye!" shouted a tall, stocky man. "This was a prosperous area, once."

"And it can be again," the Dowager added. "If the land and the sea are properly managed."

I really couldn't believe she was doing this in front of all these people.

"The elders among you may be aware that Flown Raven has a unique custom, called retesting. It has not been performed for decades, but it is still a valid and legitimate custom."

Oh, lords. I had read about this sort of thing in history texts. This was bad.

"A titleholder may be called to face retesting every two years by any resident of Flown Raven," said the Dowager. "Should the titleholder refuse or fail the retesting, the title becomes free to be assumed by a more worthy person."

Son of a bitch.

"The Duchess has been the titleholder for more than

two years, and has never undergone any retesting. Does anyone wish to call a retesting?"

"I do," a man called out, a big, strapping man I remembered seeing before. He was a whaler, I thought.

"James," Fiona said in protest. I guessed she'd thought he liked her.

He looked her in the eye, not a trace of shame about him. I expected him to say something to justify his behavior, explain why he was doing this. Apparently he didn't feel the need. Probably the Dowager had told him to keep his words few in number.

I wondered what the Dowager had promised him to have him do this.

"You'll lose your residency if you lose the retest, you know that," Fiona warned him.

"I won't lose."

Damn it, this wasn't right. Being a titleholder had nothing to do with fighting. If there were going to be things like retesting, it should focus on things that mattered, knowledge of the law or the ability to fish or something like that. Why was fighting always supposed to be the solution to everything?

Fiona was going to lose to this man. There was no doubt about it. Could she really lose the title because of it? Did that mean pressure would be placed on Taro to seek the title? Was that what the Dowager had meant when she'd spoken of ways to free up the title?

I didn't want to go through that again.

"Wind Watcher," the Dowager called. "It is your task to judge the retest. You will be objective."

"I know my responsibilities," Radia responded calmly.

The Dowager gestured. Her servants moved away from the crowd and, with the rods they carried, created a circle on the ground. It didn't look big enough to hold a proper fight.

"I will return," Fiona said loudly. "I must change my

attire." She was dressed in a dark purple gown with a wide skirt and wide sleeves. She would drown in that in a fight.

"You are not to leave the field of the retest once it has been called," the Dowager objected. "Wind Watcher?"

"That is the tradition," Radia admitted with obvious reluctance.

"Fine," said Fiona with an angry edge to her voice. She spoke quietly to her lady's maid, who was standing behind her. Frances looked shocked, then moved forward and began to unlace the back of Fiona's dress.

And before us all, the Duchess of Westsea stripped down to her undergarments and her bare feet. On top of that, she ripped up the sides of her shift so her legs were perfectly free.

I noticed that most of the men didn't know where to look. They were sneaking glances at their titleholder, of course, but seemed unable to look at her for more than a moment. Even James seemed discomforted. In less serious circumstances, I would find that hilarious.

Fiona pushed her blond braid over her shoulder and strode over to the circle, where she stood and waited.

This was stupid and barbaric. I didn't want to watch it, but I feared walking away might imply I didn't respect Fiona.

Did this sort of thing happen in High Scape? I'd never heard of such a thing. But then, Flown Raven was kind of remote. Maybe old traditions had lingered.

James lumbered over, but without the confidence Fiona exuded. I wondered if things were already deviating from what he'd expected. Maybe he'd expected her to try to get out of it. Did that mean he didn't know she'd been practicing with Dane? Was that possible? I assumed that servants gossiped about their employers, and there was no way the servants didn't know about Fiona and Dane's fighting lessons.

All the mourners shifted over to surround the circle. Was their grief forgotten because of this spectacle? Why had none of them spoken up on Fiona's behalf?

Why had none of her family? Dane looked furious, his lips pressed hard together. Tarce looked shocked, a surprisingly honest expression. Neither defended Fiona.

Perhaps they felt that doing so would undermine Fiona's authority in some way.

When everyone seemed ready, Radia called, "Begin."

James charged at Fiona, his hands held in fists up near his head. He swung at her face. She blocked James's right arm with her left and shoved the heel of her hand into his nose in an upward motion. He wheeled away, and a few instants later there was blood pouring from his nose.

I would have thought that would be the end of it, but James seemed to shake it off and came back swinging. Right and left and right again, Fiona dodging each blow. I noticed that they fought very differently. James relied solely on his fists, it seemed, while Fiona seemed to move her body more fluidly, moving her feet more.

Fiona was caught off guard when James aimed for her stomach. That blow landed hard and solid, and Fiona curled over. James brought up his knee to smash Fiona's face with it, but she seemed to collapse before his knee could reach its target.

Fiona fell to the ground and rolled right to the other edge of the circle, James stepping after and attempting to kick her. He looked very awkward as he moved, and he seemed to be experiencing some difficulty with his balance.

Fiona stopped rolling just short of the rods. Passing over the rods would have lost her the fight. She grabbed onto one of James's legs and drove her thumb into the back of his knee. He fell with a shout and Fiona scrambled to her feet. Once up, she kicked James in the face.

She knelt, pushing at James to try to roll him over the rods. Before she could accomplish this, James grabbed one of her hands and I could hear the snap as one of her fingers went back.

I glanced at Dane. He was frowning in concentration. He didn't appear at all frightened. I looked at the Dowager. She looked angry. I supposed she'd expected it to go faster.

James wrapped his arms around Fiona's neck and was trying to roll her over him and over the rods. She dug her knees into his back and made herself impossible to shift. She struck out ineffectually a few times, her arms obstructed by James's hold around her neck. She slid her head down a little and bit, hard. James's arm jerked and Fiona reached around to grab at his face, sinking her nails into his cheek. That made him jerk again, and Fiona wiggled up and away.

She sank a knee into his stomach. She clenched her two hands together and pounded them into James's face. He pushed her off. She dug her heels into his side and pushed.

James rolled out of the circle.

He scrambled to his feet and charged at Fiona again. Fiona backed up.

"Hold!" Radia shouted. James kept going. "I said hold!"

James stumbled to a stop.

"The retest is complete. The titleholder retains the title."

Fiona spent a moment to straighten her dirt-streaked shift. "Now that this nonsense is finished," she said coolly, "I invite you all to partake of the refreshments laid out in the garden and use the remainder of this day for its intended purpose: honoring the lives of those who have been lost."

I looked at the Dowager. Her expression revealed no knowledge that she was the target of Fiona's chastisement. She just looked angry. Her plan hadn't worked. And so she had no use for anyone present. She turned and left, her servants following.

The residents noticed the hasty departure, and there were a few grumbles of disapproval. Ha. Maybe they realized they'd been used. Maybe they would wonder if they really wanted a Karish as a titleholder after all, if she was any example of how they behaved.

Healer Browne ignored James and headed to Fiona, intent on seeing to what I guessed was a broken finger. "We don't have time for that now, Healer," I heard Fiona say. "There is the rest of the mourning."

"I can see to that," Dane objected.

"It is my task and I will perform it," Fiona insisted, accepting help from Frances to step back into her gown.

"Fiona—"

"Leave it."

I was embarrassed. I hated hearing people argue. I looked away.

And saw two people walking from around the manor. They were heading toward the group of us. At first, I thought they were more tenants, but I couldn't imagine any of the residents being late for the funeral.

People began drifting toward the gardens and the refreshments. I drifted with them, keeping an eye on the approaching couple. In a few moments, I saw piercing white against the left shoulder of one. A Shield.

A replacement Pair? I felt a spurt of excitement. I wouldn't mind that at all. It would be the solution to all our problems.

"Taro," I said, gesturing at the two.

He squinted at them. "Are they coming to assume the post?"

It was good to see we were in the same place on that topic.

"I hope not," said Fiona, who had apparently chosen to hover near. "You just got here."

We waited, and the forms took on more detail. The Shield was an older man, bald and slim. His Source

seemed a bit younger, dark haired with a full beard, and
stockier. They were no one that I knew.

"Source Karish and Shield Mallorough?" the Shield
asked once they were in comfortable speaking range.

"Aye," I said.

"This is Source Evro Pedulla. I am Shield Neil Kaagen. We're on the Triple S council."

I practically felt Taro freeze beside me. I resisted the
urge to touch him. "I see." I should have said it was a
pleasure to meet them, but I was too sure it wouldn't be.

"We have some questions to ask you," said Kaagen.

"And you came all the way out here to ask them?" I
said.

"We could hardly have you come to us. You're the only
Pair here."

That wasn't what I'd meant. The situation had to be
pretty serious if they felt the questions couldn't be addressed through correspondence.

Of course, I hadn't yet responded to their last piece of
correspondence, but surely that didn't warrant their coming out.

"We didn't pass anything that looked like a tavern
nearby," Kaagen said. "Could you recommend a place
for us?"

"You can stay with us," Fiona interjected. Her manor
was getting fuller by the moment. Surely she was going to
run out of rooms soon. And, of course, there were taverns
in the village. Either they didn't look hard enough or they
wanted to be on top of us.

Why did she invite them in? I didn't want them close
and comfortable. I wanted them distant and uncomfortable.

"Thank you, ma'am," said the Shield. "That's most
generous."

"I am Lady Westsea. This is my husband, Lord Westsea. Our entire household is engaged in a solemn duty. If

you will join us, we will see to your needs as soon as our obligations are met."

The abundance of purple worn by everyone would have alerted the Pair to the nature of our gathering. "It will be an honor to participate," said the Shield.

In Fiona's garden, food and drink were consumed. Stories were told and songs were sung. People roared with laughter and screamed with anger and grief. And through it all, I was distracted.

Members of the Triple S had come to talk to us. That just couldn't be good.

Chapter Nineteen

That night in the dining room, the council Pair joined us for supper and some painfully polite conversation. They didn't speak of why they were there, despite some subtle probing. Or Fiona asking them straight out. They said only that it was Triple S business.

That didn't stop Reid from peppering them with questions about all sorts of aspects of Triple S life and the council in particular. The Pair evaded the questions more often than they answered. I had behaved in a similar manner in the past, and had been much less dexterous about it, yet I found it embarrassing that they weren't more forthcoming. Perhaps because Reid was so eager for information, and so clearly knew he was being given the brush-off.

After supper, Fiona and her family and all the servants collected in the ballroom to sing. Taro and I joined them, though neither of us knew the songs being sung. The songs were not mournful. Neither were they joyous. If anything, they sounded like lullabies. Reassuring, promis-

ing that all was well, it was all right to close one's eyes.
Everything was fine.

While not mournful, the music still made me want to
cry. I managed to avoid it, barely, by blinking a lot. No
one noticed, not even Taro, and for that I was grateful.

And the music distracted me from thoughts about the
Triple S council. I lay in bed that night, and instead of
twisting myself into a knot worrying about why Kaagen
and Pedulla were there, I heard the songs run again and
again in my head. I was lulled into sleep, which meant I
was refreshed in the morning, all the better to deal with
what was sure to be a very stressful day.

At breakfast the next morning, Shield Kaagen said to
me, "Lady Westsea has given us permission to use her
library while we discuss matters."

"While you and I," said Source Pedulla to Taro, "will
be using the music room."

"How appropriate, my dear," said Taro. "Did I tell you,
I can't tell one note from another? Did you want me to
play something for you?"

Pedulla looked confused. I could sympathize with him.

They were going to speak with us—no, let's call it what
it was: interrogate us—in separate rooms. That couldn't be
good. What did they suspect us of?

I noticed Kaagen had notes.

We sat at the largest table in the library so Kaagen could
sit far away from me and I couldn't see what was written
on his paperwork. He took out from his bag a quill and an
inkpot, and he started writing immediately. "Tell me, when
was the first time you heard about Source Karish?"

"The first time?" I hadn't been expecting that. I'd been
expecting questions about how well Taro was handling
the events taking place in his birthplace.

"I assume your Matching wasn't the first time you
heard his name."

"No, I heard about him while I was still attending
classes."

"When?"

"I don't remember." Not exactly. He was seven years older than I, and he had begun his training outside the Academy when he was sixteen and I was nine. I didn't imagine I would have heard anything of him before then. I didn't know how much more I could narrow that down.

"Try."

I shook my head. "I can only say that I was aware of him in at least my last two years at the Academy. I think."

He wrote something down. "And what sort of things did you hear of him?"

"That he was an excellent Source."

"What else?"

That he would sleep with anything on two legs, but I wasn't going to admit that. "That he was a lord."

"What else?"

"I really don't remember."

"You must remember more."

Why must I? "It was years ago. I had no idea he was going to be my Source. I had no reason to think about him or pay any particular attention to the stories about him." Sometimes I wished I could go back to that state, where I didn't think about him all the time. I loved him, but I really wished he wasn't the center of all my thoughts so incessantly. It seemed unbalanced.

"So there were stories about him."

"Yes, some."

"You just don't remember them."

"Correct."

"You said you heard he was an excellent Source."

"Yes."

"What made him an excellent Source?"

"He could channel very powerful events. He felt them early and channeled them quickly." He was handsome and entertaining and enjoyed a good time.

"What else?"

"What else is there?" No, no. I shouldn't have said that. It sounded challenging and defensive. Like I had something to hide.

"You tell me."

"That's all I remember."

More scribbling. "And when you met him, what did you think of him?"

"That he was very sophisticated." And condescending and a little smarmy. Sometime I would have to ask him if he had been nervous that night.

"And?"

And? "He was polite and friendly."

"Anything else?"

"Not that I can recall."

"Your Matching is not a day that stands out in your memory?"

Sarcastic prat. "It does."

"Yet all you can remember thinking about Source Shintaro Karish was that he was"—Kaagen referred to his notes—"sophisticated, polite and friendly."

"And handsome." There, that was four things.

"Anything else?"

"No, that's all."

"Are you sure? After all, it took a few moments for you to remember you thought he was handsome."

I would not glare at him, no matter how much he deserved it. I would be the epitome of the serene Shield. "I'm afraid that's all." What good would it do anyone to tell him I'd been disappointed to be chosen by Taro? That I'd had my eye on another Source with a reputation for being serious and calm? What did any of this have to do with anything?

"How did you get along with him in the first few days you were bonded?"

I didn't want to talk about that. I'd been a perfect bitch to him for the first few weeks of our relationship. It was hard enough to admit that to myself. I didn't want to discuss it with anyone else. "It was an adjustment."

"Can you elaborate?"

No. "We had to get to know each other. There was a lot of talking"—that wasn't true—"and some arguing"—that was true—"but it didn't take long to settle into a smooth working relationship." That was kind of true.

"Tell me about the first time the two of you channeled, or don't you remember that?"

Whether he believed it or not, I had to think about it. "We were in a tiny settlement. A cold one. It was a cyclone."

"And Source Karish channeled it."

"Yes."

"Was there anything unusual about the way he channeled?"

"Not at all." The only matter of note was that I'd been able to Shield him so well after such a short acquaintance.

"The event was channeled successfully?"

"Of course." I would have reported it if it wasn't.

"Had there ever, in your relationship, been an event that Source Karish couldn't channel?"

"No," I answered, a reflexive response. That was true, too. Taro was in danger of losing control of the events he was channeling in Flown Raven, and the regulars had felt tremors, but to date he had not failed to actually channel any event since coming to Flown Raven.

And the event he had stopped channeling in High Scape, we didn't know if he couldn't. He'd just stopped because I told him to.

Something told me I should be telling Kaagen about our difficulties. The only reason I didn't was because I knew Taro would explode if I did. And that was so stupid. We could be sent somewhere else. He had to want that. All it would take was telling Kaagen.

Why would Taro care whether people knew he had difficulty channeling the events of his place of birth? It was no reflection on his abilities. It was expected.

Kaagen noticed my distraction. "Have you remembered something?"

"No, I was just checking. No incomplete channelings."

I watched him write in silence.

"Now, tell me about the first time you channeled in High Scape."

The rest of the morning was spent going over in painful detail Taro and my channeling history during our first few months. I didn't have to lie or smooth out details much. I'd written reports for most of it, reports Kaagen had brought with him, and I'd been honest in them. There had been no reason to be anything but honest at that point.

When the light streaming through the windows announced it was past midday, Kaagen used the bellpull and asked the answering maid for refreshments for the both of us. It didn't surprise me that we had more to discuss, but I was getting tired. I would have appreciated a chance to stretch my legs and to get away from a room that I'd once thought lovely but was now finding suffocating.

Then Kaagen got to Stevan Creol, and I began to feel even more uncomfortable. "Source Karish wrote in his report that Source Creol was able to use his abilities to create events."

"Yes."

"Why did Source Karish write that report? It is your task to write reports."

"He wanted to do it."

"Why?"

"I think he felt that as he had been abducted by Creol and had spent the most time with him, he would be better able to write an appropriate report."

"I see." He jotted something down. "How did Creol create events?"

"I don't know." That was the truth. I still had no real idea how Taro did it, really.

"But you believed him when he said he could do it."

"He demonstrated he could do it."

"How did he do that?"

"He caused a flood."

"Did he? That's not mentioned in Source Karish's report."

"Karish wasn't there when the flood happened. I guess I forgot to mention it to him."

"You forgot to tell him that Creol could cause events," Kaagen said in a flat tone.

"He already knew Creol could create events by the time I found him. I guess that detail got lost in all the other things that were going on."

"But how did you know Creol caused the event?"

"It was a conclusion I came to afterward, due to the timing of it. Also, I could feel it when I Shielded him."

"You Shielded him?"

"Aye."

"Why did you do that?"

"He wasn't bonded. He said an event was coming. He asked me to Shield him, so I did."

"And you were able to do so."

"Yes."

"Without difficulty."

"With little difficulty." It was always a little difficult to Shield a Source I wasn't bonded to.

"That's fairly unusual, wouldn't you say?"

"It's not unheard of."

"Have you, since bonding, Shielded any other Source who was not Source Karish?"

"Yes, Source Tenneson. I happened to be there, so I Shielded him."

"With no difficulty?"

"With little difficulty."

He appeared annoyed by the qualification. I was merely

being accurate, and someone of his experience should have better control over his expression.

"You never reported that unusual skill to the council."

"I wasn't on duty. It wasn't my place to write a report."

"That's a specious excuse."

"I assumed Shield Ogawa wrote a report. She and Tenneson were recalled shortly thereafter."

"To my knowledge, no one has reported this little ability of yours to the council. You should have."

"I see." I wasn't going to apologize. It wasn't unheard of for Shields to be able to protect Sources not their own.

"Why did the timing of the flood alert you to the possibility that Source Creol was causing the event?"

I honestly couldn't really remember. It had been a confusing time. "I think it was because Middle Reach is a fairly cold site, and he was talking about events, and all of a sudden one happened. It seemed a little too coincidental."

"I see." There was a long period of scribbling then. "Have you ever Shielded another Source who could cause events?"

"No." There, that was a lie. And I hoped Taro was telling Pedulla the exact same thing.

But what if he didn't? What did it matter? What would they do to us if we lied? I really had no idea. Could they send us to a cold site for that?

"Are you sure?" Kaagen asked.

Did he have to make me confirm every single answer? "Quite sure."

The maid who had taken Kaagen's request returned with a tray of water, bread, cheese and dried fruit. I wasn't hungry, but I took a small portion anyway. It would help to keep my head clear.

"Now, did you see the report Source Karish wrote con-

cerning his and your time in Middle Reach?" Kaagen
asked after the painful silence of our meal.

"I did."

"Did it not appear to be lacking in detail to you?"

"No. And we received no request for a follow-up from
the council."

"Do you have any idea how many reports we receive?"
he demanded.

I'd never thought about it. "Meaning you don't read
them all."

"Of course we do," he blustered. "But it may take longer than we'd like to get to them."

Ah.

"Source Karish's report says that the two of you, as
well as a handful of other Sources, were kept in a hole that
Source Creol had created in the ground with this talent
of his."

"Yes, that's right."

"And it was sealed over you?"

"Yes."

"Then how did the two of you escape?"

Ah, hell. Think think think. "Creol left it open the last
time," I lied.

"Why would he do that?" Kaagen asked skeptically.

"I'm not sure," I said, thinking frantically, drawing out
my words to give myself time. "But I have a theory."

"Please be so good as to share it."

Pompous git. "There were a couple of things at play, I
think. All of the Sources aside from Karish had been in
the pit for several weeks. All of them, including Karish,
were very weak. I think Creol felt we wouldn't be able to
escape the pit even if the top were open, and there was no
one outside the pit willing to help us. So there would be
no harm in leaving it open. As well, I believe that shifting
the soil was very taxing, and the attack on High Scape
would be even more so. He wanted to save his strength."

"I see."

I didn't think he believed me. That wasn't fair. That was a reasonable explanation, even if I was just making it up as I went along.

"So the Sources were able to garner the strength to get out?" Kaagen asked.

"One of Creol's followers had earned his disfavor and was put in the pit when I was. With his help, Karish and I were able to get out. Eventually, after Creol died, we were able to arrange to get the others out."

"And how exactly did Creol die?"

I'd killed him. Taro had felt him causing the event. Taro had fought him while I Shielded Taro. I'd been able to tamper with Creol's Shield, so that the forces he was manipulating weren't properly released. The pressure had, according to reports, caused him to literally explode. "I'm not sure." My voice was strained to my ears. "Something went wrong."

"Were you there when he died?"

"No."

"You didn't see it?"

"No."

"You seem affected by it."

"It's one thing to hear stories of channeling going wrong. To know it actually happened is disturbing."

"I see." Kaagen put aside his paperwork. "This wasn't in any report, per se, but we heard stories that Source Karish performed his own events while in Middle Reach."

"No," I said firmly. "He threatened to, to ensure our safety and the safety of the other Sources. They didn't know the pit had been left open. He claimed to have opened it himself, and convinced them that he could do what Creol could. He can be very convincing when he wants."

"No doubt," Kaagen said sourly. "But the stories said he convinced them by demonstration."

"He didn't. I don't know what else to tell you."

"You are telling me that Shintaro Karish, touted as the most talented Source of his generation, cannot perform a skill a Source who couldn't even bond could perform?"

"To my knowledge, there was no doubt about Creol's skill, only his character."

Kaagen shuffled through his papers for several moments. "Let's move on a little."

Gladly.

"High Scape suffered a period of highly unseasonal weather not too long ago."

"Yes, the residents call it the Harsh Summer."

"It was during that summer that rumors started about Source Karish having the ability to heal."

"Aye, I know about those."

"Can Source Karish heal?"

"Of course not."

"Then how can you account for the rumors?"

"The regulars were angry with us for not normalizing the weather. In an attempt to garner goodwill, Karish visited ill and injured people in the hospital, where he would talk with them, flirt with them, fetch things for them. He made them feel better by giving them attention. That's all." I was proud of that answer. It seemed a particularly good one to me.

"And that was enough to have people lining up in front of your door last fall looking to be healed from that plague."

Ah, that. I knew that would come back and bite us. "People lined up, but Karish couldn't do anything for them." And that was the truth.

"They don't seem to feel that way. People who saw him said he made them better."

How did he know? Who had he been talking to?

"He might have made them feel better. He has an excellent manner with people. But he couldn't heal them."

Kaagen sighed loudly, putting down his quill. "Shield

Mallorough, all morning I have been dismayed to feel you have either been lying to me or omitting the truth in an attempt to mislead me."

I suddenly felt ashamed, because that was true. But I didn't speak as he was clearly waiting for me to do. I couldn't give anything away.

"What has anyone in the Triple S done to make you feel you needed to be dishonest with us?"

Nothing, really. Except Taro was so afraid of them, and he didn't scare easily. And I'd killed a man and I didn't want to be punished for it. And I'd never heard from my cousin Caspian since he had been recalled to Shidonee's Gap. And a dozen little things that made me think the council didn't have the best interests of the individual members in mind.

"Have you nothing to say?" Kaagen prodded.

"No."

Kaagen glared at me.

There was a knock on the door.

"Not now!" Kaagen snapped.

"It's me," his Source said through the door.

Kaagen went to the door and opened it just a little. "I'm in the middle of things."

"I can't deal with him anymore," Pedulla hissed. "He's making me crazy."

"Keep your voice down!" Kaagen stepped out into the hall and closed the door behind him.

I grinned. I guessed Taro was engaging in his useless lordling routine, pretending to misunderstand questions and giving vapid answers. People did find it infuriating. I wished I could watch.

I sighed and laid my head against the table. I was getting a headache.

Chapter Twenty

Kaagen came back into the library and I sat up, embarrassed that he had seen me so weak. He picked up his notes. "Source Pedulla will be speaking with you for the rest of the day," he told me.

"Oh," I said. So now Kaagen was going to be driven crazy by Taro's act. He totally deserved it.

Maybe I should take a leaf from Taro's book. I could be convincing in behaving vapidly. I was sure of it.

Kaagen left, and in a few moments more, Pedulla came into the library. I noticed he had far fewer notes than Kaagen had had. He sat down in Kaagen's seat.

"I would like to talk to you about your first visit to Erstwhile," he said. "How did that come about?"

That seemed an abrupt change from what I'd been talking to Kaagen about. Did that mean anything? "We received a summons from the Empress."

"What was the reason for the summons?"

"I believe she thought Karish had something to do with stopping Creol and his attacks on High Scape."

"What made her think that?"

How was I supposed to know the mind of the Empress? "Nothing we said."

"So other people were saying Shintaro stopped Creol?"

"I don't know. They never said so to us."

"What did Shintaro do to kill Creol?"

He really had very dark eyes. They made me want to stare into them. It was distracting, and if I was distracted, I would say something stupid. "Karish didn't kill Creol."

"Are you sure?"

"Yes."

"How can you be sure?"

Because I killed him. "He was with me when Creol died, and we weren't anywhere near Creol."

Pedulla leaned back in his chair and stared at me. I stared back, but it was hard. His stare had a weight to it that I wasn't used to.

"How did it come to be believed that Shintaro caused Creol's defeat?"

"I really have no idea." Because the residents of Middle Reach had said so. Because the Shield protecting Creol had felt my meddling and, once she had gotten over her hysterics at his death, had told everyone that we had killed him. At least, she spread that story until her bonded Source was killed by the residents of Middle Reach, and she had died with him.

Pedulla pursed his lips and tapped his paper. I waited in silence. After a long while, he asked, "What did you do while you were in Erstwhile?"

"Read a lot. Went to the theater and to music halls. There was a lot to do in Erstwhile." Not as much as in High Scape, but certainly more than Flown Raven.

"How much time did you spend with the Empress?"

"Karish and I?"

"No. Just you."

"Not much." The Empress had had no interest in me.

"Yet you were in Erstwhile for months."

"I wasn't." And damn, I hadn't meant to say that. Though, really, it was something they could learn on their own.

And he confirmed that. "No, you weren't. After a few weeks, you were sent to High Scape while Shintaro remained in Erstwhile for months after. Isn't that true?"

"Aye." Unlike all the questions Kaagen had been asking, this was a topic the Triple S had never investigated. I wasn't sure what to say.

"Why do you think she did that? Have Shintaro stay there on his own?"

"I think he amused her."

"Really? You think the Empress would have a Source removed from the roster merely for her entertainment?"

"That seemed the sort of thing a monarch might do." I wasn't being facetious. Royalty did as their whim moved them, regardless of the consequences, or so it seemed to me.

"You don't speak of the royalty with respect," said Pedulla. "That's unusual."

"Is it?"

"Very. What did the royal family do to make you speak of them so?"

"Nothing." Besides pulling us this way and that, the bastards. "I was being inappropriate. I'm like that sometimes."

"Not an admirable trait in a Shield," he chided me.

Oh, go to hell. What did he know? Had he ever had to deal directly with royalty?

"What did Shintaro do for Her Majesty?"

"Sit with her. Talk with her. Did some errands, I believe."

"That's all?"

"That's all I know of." And I didn't think Taro would lie to me about it.

"For months?"

"That's what he said."

"Are you sure that's all? He didn't do anything else?"

"What do you suspect him of doing?" Surely they didn't think he'd slept with her? That was vile.

"I will ask the questions, Shield Mallorough."

Well, yes, sir. "And I'm answering. That's all he did. That's what he told me, and I believe him."

"Why in the world would she disrupt his duties for such trivial activities?"

"She enjoyed his beauty."

"Surely you're not so naive as to believe that."

I was, actually. Pedulla just didn't understand. He clearly hadn't seen the way people reacted to Taro.

"Was that why the Empress called the two of you to Erstwhile over a year later? To enjoy Shintaro's beauty?"

The question was asked sarcastically. I answered it with sincerity. "It's very possible." There was no better reason for sending us on that ridiculous hunt of hers.

"Shield Mallorough, we know you didn't spend the entirety of your absence from the roster in Erstwhile. Where did you go?"

Hell, these questions were annoying. I was getting a headache. "I'm not allowed to tell you that."

"Who told you that?"

"The Empress. She made it clear that we would be hanged if we told anyone."

Pedulla pulled in a breath of shock. "Are you sure that was what she meant?"

"She was very clear about it."

Pedulla stood and walked around his chair, tapping the back of it with his fingers.

Maybe I shouldn't have said that, but how else was I going to get out of telling them where we'd been?

"Surely you knew the Empress wouldn't have carried out that threat."

"Of course she would have. She was the Empress."

"And you're a Shield. A member of the Triple S. Under our jurisdiction, not hers."

And he called me naive. "Who was to stop her if she decided to carry out her threat?"

"We would."

"How? She had the army."

He chuckled. "So you believed . . . what? If you told us, she would send the army after you?"

It was possible to make anything sound ridiculous. Prat. "I mean she had the means to enforce her wishes."

"Military might is not the only way to accomplish things."

"What other way do you have in mind?"

He cleared his throat and avoided answering. "The Empress is dead," he said.

"Her son is not."

"You think the Emperor might carry out her wishes?"

"He might." Actually, I didn't think it would be the Emperor carrying out her orders. He probably still didn't know what we'd been doing, or who Aryne really was. But if the Empress had picked people as unlikely as us to look for Aryne, she probably had other unlikely people doing other unlikely things.

Would someone given the job to kill us if we talked still find themselves obligated to carry out her orders after she was dead? I had no idea, and I wasn't going to find out.

"So you are refusing to discuss your time off the roster."

"I am."

"You were gone for over a year and you won't explain yourself."

"I can't explain. I've told you why."

"And you don't feel worried about what form of punishment we might choose to deal out for this gross dereliction of duty?"

"You won't kill us." I hoped. Maybe I was being the naive one after all.

Pedulla drummed his fingers against the back of his chair. "I suspect you are relying on your Source's value to shield you from any punishment at all."

I honestly hadn't thought of that.

Pedulla sat down. "Emperor Gifford has expressed notable interest in Source Karish."

"I don't know enough about the Emperor to know whether his interest in Karish is notable."

"But you will acknowledge that the Emperor has shown interest in Shintaro."

I guessed I had to. "Aye."

"Offering to violate the law to enable Shintaro to get his title after abjuring it."

How the hell did he know that? "Aye."

"That's extraordinary, don't you think?"

"I do."

"What in all the land did Shintaro do for the Emperor to gain such a favor?"

It was more a matter of what Taro's mother had done, and I didn't want to think about that. I couldn't imagine how she had convinced Gifford to give Taro another shot at the title. "Nothing."

"The Emperor violated the law out of the goodness of his heart? He, too, thought Shintaro was beautiful?"

Why couldn't the Emperor think Taro was beautiful? Taro was beautiful. "I can't speak to the Emperor's motives, but I know Karish did nothing for him to earn that favor. Surely it is obvious that Karish turned down the opportunity to regain the title."

"And perhaps he changed his mind. Perhaps living at his birthplace, even without the title, was something he wished for after all? So the Emperor obligingly transferred him?"

I wasn't going to tell this stranger why Flown Raven was the last place Taro wanted to be. "Again, I can't speak to the Emperor's motives. I can only tell you that Karish did no favor, and the Emperor's decision to transfer us surprised Karish as much as it did me."

"And you never thought to question the Emperor's right to transfer you?"

Should I say I knew the Emperor hadn't had the right? I'd already accused the Triple S of not being able to protect us from the Empress. "I assumed he had your approval. You were transferring other Pairs from High Scape."

"He did not get our approval. He did not even seek our counsel."

I wasn't at all surprised.

"Are you aware that the Emperor had transferred other Pairs, also without consulting us?"

I frowned. I didn't know what to feel about that. It was annoying enough that the Emperor had transferred us. I had the feeling the Emperor was suspicious of us, or something. But to learn that he was manipulating other Pairs as well really bothered me. That was not within his authority. "I had no idea."

"Tell me, why is it that our members feel the monarch can give the Triple S Pairs orders?"

"He's the Emperor. He's our ruler."

"He's not an authority over you."

"Someone needs to tell him that. And it's not us."

"And by 'us' you mean—"

"Anyone who is not on the Triple S council." To expect any regular member of the Triple S to say no to the Emperor was just stupid.

"Despite his interference with other Pairs, the Emperor has shown more direct interest in Source Karish than any other member. Tell me, was your transfer to Flown Raven the last contact you've had from the Emperor?"

"There are Imperial Guards here, looking for evidence that people are pretending to cast spells."

That seemed to surprise him. "Really." He tapped his quill against his paper. "What have they found?"

"To my knowledge, they've found nothing."

That surprised him even more. "How is that possible?"

"I don't understand."

"The people of Flown Raven have a long tradition of casting spells."

"You mean a long tradition of believing spells can work. Or trying to cast spells. Or pretending to cast spells."

Pedulla hesitated a moment before saying, "Yes, of course."

Gods. I knew what his original choice of words meant. The council of the Triple S knew spells actually existed. How could that be? How could they not educate us about the use of spells? Really, what was going on?

They knew people in Flown Raven cast spells. Would they tell the Guards?

"Shintaro swore fealty to the Emperor," Pedulla said finally. "Why did he do that?"

"The Emperor told him to do so."

"A member of the Triple S has no right to be swearing loyalty to the Emperor. The only institution to which any of you are loyal is the Triple S."

I didn't like being told to whom I may be loyal. "You would have expected him to refuse?"

"That is what he should have done."

"He couldn't refuse an order from the Emperor."

"What would the Emperor have possibly done to him if he had?"

"Taro wasn't about to find out and I thank Zaire for it."

Pedulla looked at me narrowly. "That reminds me of another area of inquiry."

Oh, wonderful. Really, I wondered what would happen if I just got up and left, just refused to answer any more questions.

I wished I were braver, sometimes.

"It has come to our attention that you and Source Karish have entered into an intimate relationship."

Gods, didn't people have anything better to talk about?
"Is this true?"

"That is none of your business." I was not going to talk about that.

"The functioning of every Pair is of concern to us."

"We function perfectly."

"That's an arrogant statement to make. It's clear that Source Karish has been an unfortunate influence on you."

What a catty thing to say. "Can you point to an example when we have performed inadequately?"

"When you left for over a year. In fact, when you left to look for Source Karish when he was taken by Source Creol without seeking permission. This is not behavior we admire."

I shrugged. "There was nothing else to be done."

"That was not for you to decide."

"Shield Kaagen admitted it can take a while for the council to read its correspondence. It was very likely that had I asked for permission, I wouldn't have received any kind of answer before Karish was killed. And then I would have been dead, too."

"That is no reason to ignore responsibility and procedure."

"Are you serious?"

Pedulla glared at me. "You don't show proper respect for the council or for your role as a Shield."

"I'm not going to let procedure or expectations stop me from doing what needs to be done."

"So you're saying if you had to do it all again, you'd do the same?"

"In a heartbeat."

"Then there is nothing more to be said." He rubbed his forehead. "Just go."

Really? That was abrupt. But I wasn't going to wait until he changed his mind. I stood, and I was a little wobbly, as I hadn't moved in hours. I went straight to my suite, made use of the facilities, then summoned Lila for a meal. I still felt awkward having food brought to me, but it was well past the supper hour and I was both starving and thirsty.

And yet it was a good couple of hours before Taro made his way up, carrying with him a mug of water and a plate of cold meats and dried fruit. "Gods, that was hell," he said in a gravelly voice.

"What did they ask you?"

"Everything," he said, collapsing into the nearest chair. "My favorite color. How often I piss each day."

"Seriously."

"I am serious. That's what it felt like."

"Kaagen asked a lot about whether you had any unusual abilities."

"Me, too."

"I tried not to answer, but Kaagen thinks I'm a liar."

Taro grinned. "He thinks I'm an idiot." He popped a slice of apple into his mouth.

"Maybe that will make him think you're incapable of special abilities."

"That's the plan."

I let Taro eat and worried about Kaagen and Pedulla in silence.

I waited until we were both ready for bed and slipping between the sheets before I asked, "How worried should we be about all this?"

"I have no idea," was his less than reassuring response. "Nothing came of it the last time they questioned us."

"They had more material this time. And they seemed more hostile."

"Probably because of that stupid oath I made to Gifford. They don't like his poaching on their territory."

"It's up to them to educate the Emperor on their territory, not us," I grumbled.

"Do we have to talk about it? I've been answering questions about it all day."

"You have a point." I was still worried and resentful

about it, but there wasn't much I could do except stick to my story and see what happened. Worrying about it would accomplish nothing.

Besides, there was something more interesting to do, something we hadn't done in a long while. I stroked his nearest cheek with a finger. He smiled. I kissed him.

There was the sound of a throat clearing from the door. Taro and I broke apart and I bit back some inappropriate language. It was Lila. Again.

"My apologies, sir, ma'am. Shield Kaagen and Source Pedulla wished you to know that they want to speak with you as soon as possible tomorrow."

They were still up? That couldn't be good.

"Thank you, Lila." Taro sighed.

After that, I was too embarrassed to participate in anything other than sleep.

It took a while for me to fall asleep, however, tired as I was. And when I did sleep, my head was filled with disturbing dreams that I forgot as soon as I woke up. And when I woke up, I remembered that first thing in the morning I would be enduring more questions from the council Pair.

I made sure to have breakfast first.

Kaagen and Pedulla met with both of us in the library. They sat in the only two chairs at the table, and it was clear Taro and I were expected to stand. Taro dragged two chairs over to the table so he and I were sitting as well.

"I'd like to begin by saying we're disappointed in you both," said Kaagen. "You both went to great lengths to avoid answering questions. We expect better from our members."

Neither Taro nor I gave a response to that. I was disgusted with myself for feeling ashamed. We had good reasons for being careful with what we said.

"However, your evasions were as informative as your answers would have been."

I was pretty sure that was just a ploy to make us feel uncertain.

"For example, without either of you answering the question about the nature of your relationship, we have confirmation of it. You would have merely denied intimacy if there were none. As well, we have confirmation from one of the servants here."

Lila, probably. That girl was annoying.

"I would think the council would have more important things to worry about," said Taro.

"You feel violating one of our most stringent taboos is unimportant?"

"It's not a taboo," I interjected. "It's merely discouraged." But at least he wasn't calling it a perversion. I'd been accused of that, too.

"And discouragement isn't enough?"

"People discourage all sorts of things for all sorts of reasons."

"What is that supposed to mean?"

I really wasn't sure. It had just sort of come out of my mouth without my mind's direction. "Other Pairs have engaged in intimacy. You never did anything about it." As far as I knew. "Frankly, I believe it's none of your business. Especially as none of the reasons for discouraging such relationships have occurred. We function perfectly well."

"And what happens when the relationship ends? Can you guarantee that you will continue to function well?"

"Of course." I would see to it.

From my peripheral vision, I was aware of Taro looking at me. What, was he about to disagree with me? Did he not think we could be professional even when things went wrong?

"This is just another example of a habit of defiance you are exhibiting."

"We're not being defiant." We were doing what we had to do. And no, they didn't understand that, and I couldn't tell them that, but they were creating another complication that we really didn't need.

"We disagree. And we will be keeping a close eye on you. Expect more visits from us. Shield Mallorough, it is your task to write the reports, not Source Karish's. We will be expecting them more often and in greater detail. Do you understand?"

"Of course."

"And I would encourage you to dissolve the unnatural aspect of your relationship."

Oh, go to hell.

I was pleased to see the back of them. They wanted more detail? I'd give them detail. I'd tell them the exact shade of green of the grass. I'd tell them how many birds were in the sky. I'd give them so much detail they'd come to hate the sight of any correspondence from me.

Chapter Twenty-one

Taro was gone when I woke the next morning, as was his custom. I was used to that. I didn't know what he did all day. Gambled, I supposed. I realized I had seen far less of him since we reached Flown Raven than I had at any other time since we'd been bonded. I missed him.

Maybe this would end our allegedly inappropriate relationship. Not the opportunity of another lover, but the dearth of common interests, which was made obvious in all the free time we had. That seemed worse, somehow, than losing him to someone else.

I went to the sitting room for breakfast. Reid was there, but no one else. "Good morning, Shield Mallorough," he greeted me heartily.

"Good morning, Academic Reid," I answered. "You seem in high spirits."

"I am. In fact, I'd like you to come to the library after we eat, if you can spare the time."

Time was all I had. "I would be delighted."

"Your hair is lovely, by the way," he added with an artificially innocent air.

Of course, everyone knew what had happened to my hair. I had put out the rumor that I had merely dyed it back to orange. The only people who I was sure believed me were the Guards, because none of them came to interrogate me about it.

The Guards didn't seem terribly bright.

Reid had a satchel with him. It seemed to me that he was always carrying it. When we got to the library, he closed the door behind us, then took paper and the book from the satchel, laying them on the table. Then he pulled open the hardened bottom of the satchel—a secret hiding place?—and pulled out more paper. "I really shouldn't show you these, yet," he said in a low voice. "But I know this is of great interest to you, and relevant to what you do. Just don't tell anyone, all right?"

"Of course."

"Please take them to the corner." He pointed. "You'll be out of sight from the door. If anyone comes in, I'll sneeze and you'll have to hide the paper."

"Certainly, but what will you be doing while I'm reading your work?"

"Working on the papers I plan to give the Guards." He grinned.

Sneaky fellow.

I went to the corner of the room, the one hidden by one of the stacks. I unfolded the papers. I started reading. Most of what I saw was a long-winded version of what Reid had already told me. Then I came to a description of a spell, a spell meant to call rain.

Could it possibly work? Maybe it hadn't worked for the First Landed, but apparently the magic of the world had been fading under their regime. Would someone be able to work that spell now? Would I? After all, I was already able to affect the weather to some degree. Would this spell allow me greater accuracy?

I heard a creak, and Reid sneezed. I silently folded the paper and hid it behind four books. Then I took a book from a different shelf and opened it at random.

"Good day, darling."

I blushed. I hadn't been expecting anything like that. It definitely wasn't one of the Guards.

"Good morning, Lady Daris," I heard Reid say.

"Find anything for me?"

That was a curious question for Daris to be asking Reid.

"I don't know what you mean," Reid answered firmly.

"Of course you do." There was a bit of a pause, the sound of wood creaking, and then, "Anything in that ancient book that can help me?"

"I've already told you, Lady Daris, this book has nothing to do with politics, and little to do with history. I can't imagine how it can help you."

"Alex, Alex, Alex." Daris sighed. "You have a remarkably narrow scope for an academic. There's no telling how information can be used. All it takes is a little imagination. And I have a great deal of imagination."

I didn't. What was she after?

"I was hired by Her Grace to study the book and report my findings to her." Reid sounded indignant. Like he would never dream of letting anyone see his notes before Fiona. So, really, why was he letting me?

"And how much," Daris said, her voice lowering into a throaty murmur, "is my sister offering you for your services? Room and board and a few coins? I can give you so much more."

I heard Reid clear his throat with a nervous air. "I study for the joy of knowledge, not for what can be done with that knowledge."

"Can you not see how limiting that is?"

"Perhaps, but that is my role, and I don't care to deviate from it."

"Then don't. All I'm asking is for you to hand that knowledge over to me before you give it to my sister, and I will determine whether it is useful to me or not."

"That is not why I am here. I have an obligation to honor my contract with Her Grace."

I heard the clink of metal hitting wood. "Think about it," Daris whispered. There was another creak of wood, and then I heard the library door open and close.

Well, that had been distasteful.

"Shield Mallorough?"

I replaced the book and retrieved the papers, then left my little corner. The first thing I noticed was Reid's radiant flush, followed by the scatter of coins on top of the table at which he was working.

Reid rubbed his face. I took a seat at the table and tapped a coin with a tip of my finger. "I'm going to guess that she's hoping you can help her get the title from her sister."

He gaped at me. "You think she wants the title?"

I couldn't think of any other reason Daris would care about the book. She didn't seem the sort to waste the effort to put a spoke in Fiona's wheel just for the hell of it. "I think she's bitter that she didn't get it. I didn't think she was so bitter she actually wanted to do something about it. What else does she want your help for?"

"She hasn't said, and I haven't wanted to ask. She just asked me to report my findings to her before I did to Her Grace." He rubbed at his eyes. "She has suggested that doing so would help her address some great injustice. I never thought it had anything to do with the title."

I could be wrong. I didn't know Daris well enough to guess at her wishes. I just knew she'd made a spectacle of herself the first night Taro and I had gotten here, and her anger was directed at Taro for giving the title to Fiona instead of her. So it seemed reasonable to me that if she was scheming about something, it would be about the title.

I wondered, if she had known about the retesting, would she have fought for the title herself? Maybe hearing about what had happened had started her own little evil mind working.

I tapped the coin again. "This is a bribe?"

He nodded. "More money than I've see in a handful of years."

"What are you going to do with it?"

"Leave it for the servants to pick up."

That impressed me. "You're not going to help Daris?"

He leaned sharply back into his chair, gaining some distance from something distasteful. "Certainly not."

"What does it matter to you who has the title?"

"Nothing, but there is something . . . dark . . . about Lady Daris. I think she would be a terrible titleholder. When she speaks of justice, I see only greed. She has said nothing to me that makes me think she has been done wrong by anyone. I can't imagine she would do anything useful or right with any power she might have, no matter what the nature of that power is. I don't believe being in association with her would be in my best interests. I have heard some whispers of her treatment of the servants. At some point she would become displeased with me, and there is no telling what she would do to me."

"But really, how could this book help her?"

He shrugged. "What she says is true. There is no telling how information can be used. It takes only a fertile mind and the will to use it."

I hoped I was being ridiculous, and Daris was only playing a game. For it seemed to me that Fiona was facing opposition on all sides, and it would be particularly disgusting if her parasite of a sister, who had received everything from Fiona including the coins on the table, was aiming for her as well. "What exactly does she want you to do?"

"For now, tell her any interesting findings before I tell Her Grace, and not tell Her Grace anything until Lady Daris gives me leave." He sighed. "The academic world is not without its politics, but if this is some kind of maneuvering over a title the likes of Westsea, with the kind of twisted bitterness I've seen in Daris, I've never been put in the middle of such things. I have no interest in starting now."

The solution seemed simple to me. "If you told Her Grace about it, it might disentangle you."

"On the contrary, Lady Daris will see me as an active enemy, and then what might she do to me?"

"What can she do to you?" Daris didn't have any power of her own, did she?

"I don't want to find out."

We were talking in circles, and it seemed to me that Reid was trying to avoid making a decision. I didn't blame him, but dithering in the middle of the road would likely get him run over.

We both turned our heads at the sound from the doorway. It was Taro. I repressed a sigh. Here it came.

I was expecting some kind of accusation. Instead, Taro smiled at me, slow and sweet. "You work too hard, my love," he said in a throaty voice.

It was the middle of the day in front of another, not alone in our bed at midnight.

Reid went red. I didn't blame him. Taro was being ridiculously blatant.

"I'm not working," I said.

His eyes widened in feigned shock. "You're not distracting poor Alex, are you?" His gaze shifted to Reid. "She can be so deliciously distracting, can't she?"

Now it was my turn to blush. Damn him. "We're merely discussing history."

"That's work," he declared, "and you're doing far too much of it. Come." He held out a hand. "Let me be the one to distract you."

I hated being propositioned in front of other people, especially when I thought the person doing the propositioning was insincere. But I didn't know how to react. I couldn't bring myself to just say no—that seemed too blunt—but I sure as hell wasn't going to say yes.

I put the pages on the table in a manner I hoped was subtle. "Actually, I'm feeling quite unwell." I hated using a complaint of ill health as an escape. I just couldn't think of anything else on the fly. I put a hand to my stomach. "I'm just going to lie down by myself for a while."

"I'm sure I can make you feel better," Taro smirked.

"All I need is some sleep." I escaped from the library.

Taro didn't follow me. I was relieved but also puzzled. If he had believed my excuse, he would have wanted to escort me to the bedroom and made sure I had everything. If he didn't, he would have wanted to torment me.

He was acting so strangely. It had to be this house. And his mother. They were dismantling his character before my very eyes. I hated it, and I didn't know what to do about it.

I went to our suite and stared out the window for a while. Then I picked up my current novel, but it didn't hold my interest. I had to do something, or I would brood about Taro, and that would make me crazy.

I knew what I wanted to do. I wanted to try casting again. I wanted to get it right. I was sure I could do this. I had will and focus. I was apparently in a place of power. I just had to make sure I followed the instructions exactly.

Could it really be that easy?

I opened the overmantel again. I avoided the book I'd looked at before. No more glamors for me. I wanted something really simple, something that wouldn't cause trouble if it didn't work. And what I found, both surprising and disturbing, was a child's book of spells.

It was horrible to be teaching children how to cast spells.

That was my first reflexive thought. But, really, why? Unless I thought there was something wrong with casting spells.

Well, there was something wrong with casting. It was unnatural.

If it was unnatural, how was anyone able to do it?

Oh, just read the damn book.

The book began with a chapter explaining why it was important for children to learn about spells as early as possible. Spells, if held out as something only adults were allowed to do, would be irresistible to children, tempting them to experimentation with unfortunate results. It was better to allow them to learn spells within the scope of their abilities. As well, it was best to teach ethics and responsibility to young minds when they were at their most open and impressionable. Which, I thought, made a certain amount of sense.

Still, the thought of it made me uneasy.

The next chapter was filled with games for children to play, games meant to encourage concentration and focus. Memorizing items on a tray, counting backward from a hundred by twos, threes, or fives, drawing through drafted mazes, and finding patterns in a series of simple pictures. I started with counting back from one hundred by threes and found it easier than expected. The other games proved to be equally simple, though my recall wasn't perfect.

I had the spell I wanted to try in mind. It required being outside, so I headed out through the back door. I decided to go out to the grass beyond the garden. I would look odd out there, but I would see anyone long before they were able to hear me, and the curves of the yard would shield what I was doing.

I should be able to perform a child's spell, shouldn't I?

It was a beautiful day. The sun was shining for once, there was a gentle breeze, and the temperature was pleasantly cool. And no one was working in the garden; another rarity.

I sat in the grass for a while, enjoying the silence and the solitude. It had never been so quiet in High Scape. I wondered that the constant racket hadn't made me a little crazy.

I breathed with concentration, as I had been taught to breathe in the Academy when I needed to be serene. Breathe in all the annoyance created by Taro being an idiot; push it all out in one slow exhalation. Breathe in all the aggravation of knowing Taro's mother lived only a few steps away; push it all slowly out. And so on until the knot was gone from my stomach, my shoulders were down and my mind was comfortably blank.

I crouched down low on the grass and focused on a single blade. I imagined that it was blue. I could see it in my head, a blade of grass as blue as Fiona's dark blue eyes.

"Calling on east,
"Calling on west,
"Change the hue of this blade,
"At my behest."

I blew on the blade of grass.

I felt a strange buzzing sensation.

And the grass turned blue.

Oh my gods.

It worked.

It couldn't be that simple.

And as soon as I thought that, the blade faded back to green. But I could make it blue again, as long as I concentrated. I could make other blades blue, too. And though the explanation of the spell didn't call for it, I changed the blades to red, then purple, then pink. The pink looked the most disturbingly unnatural.

Still, I couldn't believe I'd actually done it. This was a spell, it was real, and I'd done it.

I didn't want to believe in it. I didn't want to have to face the fact that any idiot could pick up this book and cast a spell. The possibilities were terrifying.

That was what bothered me the most about casting.

Not that the existence of spells didn't make sense. Not even that it was a tool used by people unwilling to work for things the natural way. The worst thing about it was that there was no control over who learned what and how they used what they learned.

The Emperor was trying to control it, of course, by outlawing the possessions of the tools of casting. I didn't think that was the right way to go about it, and not just because I never thought he did anything the right way. I couldn't imagine outlawing any kind of knowledge ever made it go away completely, and that meant someone was in possession of it, using it in the shadows. Wouldn't it be better to have those people and what they were doing out in the open, with rules they had to follow for safety? How could anyone protect themselves against the use of something they didn't know anything about?

I searched for another spell. My goal was to successfully perform every spell in the book. Even if I had to go back to Nab Browne for supplies.

I looked up just in time to see one of the Imperial Guards approaching me. It was Corporal Oteroy, the female Guard. My heart beating faster, I slipped the book under my skirt and spared a thought to be relieved that this book of children's spells didn't require any tools.

She stood before me, and I, sitting on the ground, had to look up at her. I felt vulnerable.

"Shield Mallorough," she said.

"Corporal Oteroy," I answered.

"What are you doing out here?"

If she had not been so blunt, I would have given a more civil answer. "That's no concern of yours."

She sighed. "I wouldn't have thought you had been here long enough to catch the belligerence of the local residents."

That meant the residents weren't cooperating. Good for them. "They resent the Emperor prying into their concerns."

"He has every right to pry! He's the Emperor!"

She seemed rather emotional about this. She was younger than I. Perhaps I was witnessing the fervor of youth. "He might try using a palm instead of a fist."

"It isn't our place to question the methods of the Emperor," she declared pompously.

"It's our duty to question the Emperor in everything he does. We're not mindless animals."

"We've sworn an oath of loyalty to him," she said hotly.

"I never swore any such oath."

She gasped. "You feel no obligation to obey the Emperor?"

"I have obeyed the Emperor. He sent my Source and me from High Scape to Flown Raven. Only the Triple S is to decide where Pairs are to be posted, yet we obeyed the Emperor."

"Of course you did. The Emperor's is the final word in all things."

I pushed out a long breath. I was wasting my time. "Is there something I can do for you, Corporal?" I could feel the book against my leg. What was I going to do if she tried to make me stand up?

"I understand that of the Pair, the Shield is the more responsible and dutiful."

"That's the common rumor. Like anything else, it depends on the people involved."

"So I can rely on you to inform us of any incidents of the pretense of casting spells, or any incidents of possession of casting tools."

"I'm not going to spy on people for you," I said sharply.

"You have to."

"I most certainly do not."

She glared at me. "Facts concerning your cooperation or the lack of it will be reported to the Emperor."

"Tattle to him all you like. Clearly you have found

nothing and you're getting desperate. I'm not going to help you invade the privacy of these people any more than you already have."

"You'll regret this."

"I have no doubt, but that's all you're getting from me."

She stomped away. I waited until I was sure I was alone, then I took my book out of hiding. There were more spells to try.

Chapter Twenty-two

There were a great many High Landed living around Westsea's borders. Not as many as lived around Erstwhile, but more than lived around High Scape. None held a title equal or superior in power to Fiona's. This meant, apparently, that to show their true worth, said titleholders had to wear the most colorful clothes and piles of glittering jewelry when attending a ball given in honor of a Source and Shield.

Taro and I looked like paupers among all that finery. Taro looked a little out of place in solid black. He was pretty enough, however, to pull that off. I wore a blue gown that had been in style when I'd had it made in High Scape, a low neckline with a tight waist and wide sleeves. Lila had tied my hair up rather elaborately. I, like Taro, had no jewelry to wear. I looked nice enough, but nothing like the ladies with their wider skirts, higher hair and mountains of gems.

That was all right. I'd wager I was far more comfortable.

The ballroom, like the court room on the other side of the manor, had a wide staircase from the first to the second floor. Taro and I had to wait out of sight on the second floor while all of the several dozen titleholders and their spouses and grown children were announced. Then, when it was decided everyone who was going to come had arrived, Fiona stood at the base of the stairs. That was our cue. I took Taro's offered arm and we stepped out from the shadows.

"It is my great honor and pleasure to present to you," Fiona announced, "Source Shintaro Karish and Shield Dunleavy Mallorough."

And they applauded as we descended the stairs, which I hadn't expected.

And then, as we reached the floor, Fiona said, "His Lordship and I are privileged to grant the honor of the first dance to our Source and Shield."

I sure as hell wasn't expecting that. Why had no one warned me? I shot Fiona a hard look. Her grin in return was unrepentant.

So everyone stood in a circle to watch Taro and me dance. The music started up, and I realized, to my annoyance, that the piece was a long and slow one, not one that would make me act irrationally, but was sure to keep us in everyone's view for a good long while. Once again, I thanked the forethought of my academy instructors for insisting we all learn to dance. It had seemed a frivolous pursuit at the time.

"So, my love," Taro said in a low voice. "You've been spending a lot of time in the library lately."

He stroked his thumb along the underside of my wrist, and it made me shiver. "Not really."

"And yet I catch you in there with him all the time."

"Every time I've been in there, you've walked in." Which was unbelievably bad luck.

"Just what are you and Academic Reid talking about so intensely?"

I rolled my eyes. "He's translating the book." Should I tell him?

He was being a prat.

That was no reason not to tell him, damn it. I whispered, "It's a book of spells for controlling the weather."

"A book of spells about the weather," he said with his voice a little louder than I liked.

"Shh!"

"And you're truly interested in this."

"Of course."

"You burned all the spell books you were reading in High Scape."

"Because people were getting crazy about casting and I didn't want to get caught up in it. People treat it more naturally here. Besides, it's Fiona's book. And it was created by the First Landed. I wouldn't dream of burning it."

"You're being evasive."

"I am not."

"Pedantic, then."

"How am I being pedantic? Are you just throwing words out there until one sticks?"

He scowled. "After what you did to your hair, a sensible person would have nothing more to do with spells."

"I can't give up after one failure. That would be pathetic. Besides, I have nothing else to do."

"You can't give up?" he demanded. "Have you been making other attempts?"

"I don't know that 'attempts' is the right word."

He ducked his head a little closer. "You've been casting spells?" he hissed.

"Aye. Four spells successful, so far." I grinned.

"What kind of spells?"

"Really simple, harmless ones." That thrilled me all the same. I couldn't believe I'd managed to do it. I hadn't expected to be able to do it.

"You look almost gleeful about it," he accused me.

"Why shouldn't I? It's a new skill."

"A skill that will get you in trouble."

"That doesn't stop you," I reminded him.

"That's different."

"How?"

"What I do is a natural outgrowth of what I'm supposed to do."

"There are many who would disagree. Which is why you're so desperate to keep it hidden."

"Is that why you're doing this? To be even with me?"

"Of course not. I'm not in competition with you." What a horrible thing to suggest.

"Then what is this all about?"

"I'm bored. And it's interesting."

"It's illegal."

Well, yes. There was always that little hiccup. "Nobody here thinks it's illegal."

"Nobody here makes the laws."

"But it's up to the people here to enforce them, and they're not going to. Besides, I'm not going to make it obvious that I'm doing it." Though talking about it in the middle of the ballroom wasn't the smartest thing I've ever done. But really, no one around the area was going to care. No one about seemed to think much of the new Emperor or his laws, and it appeared no one was giving the slightest assistance to the Imperial Guards.

Who were not present. Interesting.

"I can't believe you're risking our lives to play with this garbage."

"We won't be killed even if we get caught."

"We'll get sent to a cold site."

"And would that be so bad? You hate it here."

"That hasn't got anything to do with it. You're flinging this thing around with no concern for the repercussions."

"How is this any different from you creating disasters whenever you feel like it?"

He opened his mouth to give an inadequate response to

my valid point, but he didn't speak as we realized people were applauding. Apparently, we had finished the dance and bowed to each other without noticing. That was embarrassing.

Taro escorted me to the side of the room, and as soon as we were free of the dancers swinging into circles, Fiona was grabbing his other arm. "I'm getting a crack at you before everyone else stakes their claim," she announced, and he was gone.

Leaving me, I noticed, beside Tarce. Who wouldn't ask me to dance. And I wasn't about to ask him.

"Look at them all," he drawled as he watched the dancers. "Wearing their finest. Straining their minds for witty conversation. Why do you think they do it?"

Why did anyone do anything? "There must be something about it they enjoy."

He chuckled. "You are naive for one so worldly."

I wouldn't have thought of myself as worldly.

"No," he continued. "They all want something."

Most people did. "Such as what?"

"Allies in their little games. Lovers. Making their power and appeal known."

"I see."

"And then there are all the unmarried guests," he added. "They're all here for me."

I didn't bother to fight a smile then. "Really."

"You think I'm being arrogant."

"I do indeed."

"The Westsea family is the premier family in the area. The title itself is among the highest in the world."

"You don't have the title."

"No, but being as close to it as I am is appealing enough to most people hoping to marry. Look at them," he said with disgust. "Eyeing me like I'm a horse at market."

So I looked. It was true that some young people were sending covetous glances toward young Lord Tarce. Many were doing the same with Taro, although he was pretending to ignore them as he laughed with his cousin. The majority of people, however, seemed to be looking only at the people they were with, which made sense.

"And what do they see?" Tarce said. "What I look like. What I have. Nothing else."

"What else do you have to offer?" Ouch. I really hadn't meant to say that out loud. He glared at me. I kind of deserved that, but it was a valid question. "Look at how you treat people. Like they're beneath your notice. Like their concerns are too trivial for you to bother with. You're not going to find someone interested in your personality. Except people with defective personalities of their own who like to be abused."

"What the hell gives you the right to talk to me like that?" he demanded.

"You being ridiculous."

"Remember your place, Shield," he growled.

"I do," I said. "And it is not beneath you."

He walked off. As far as I was concerned, that meant I won.

"That was cruel," a low voice said from behind me. I turned. It was Radia.

"It was true," I said.

"And you think the truth can't be cruel?"

No, but the fact that it was true and that the person receiving it was being an ass made it forgivable. "Do you think he'll contemplate what I said?"

"No. He's a young man. It's against their nature to listen to anyone, especially young women."

"Is that why you're hiding from him?"

She smiled. "I am a responsible Wind Watcher. I hide from no one."

"Uh-huh." I wondered how she, surrounded by the noise of the ball, would be able to perceive the warning signs of a coming wind, but to ask would be to imply she didn't know her own business. "I think you would be good for him."

"Of course I would be, but he'd be terrible for me."

I couldn't deny that.

The music stopped midpiece. That got everyone's attention. His boots thudding against the marble floor, Bailey walked from the musicians' alcove to the principal entrance to the ballroom. Over the whispers he announced, "Her Grace, the Dowager Duchess of Westsea. The Honorable Lady Simone of Eastbrook."

Oh, of course. How did I manage to forget? I watched the two women glide down the steps, the focus of everyone's attention.

Simone was breathtaking. Slim, tall, with golden blond hair, light eyes and perfectly chiseled features. Her gown was rather simple in cut but dramatic in its deep red color. She wore little jewelry, the only real extravagance the lightly jeweled string of gold threaded through her hair. Her expression didn't give her emotional state away, but she certainly seemed calm.

It was my intention not to stand next to her. Ever.

"Where is my son?" the Dowager Duchess asked in a commanding voice.

She just never skipped an opportunity to embarrass him.

"In the middle of a dance," he called back.

"Resume the music," Fiona ordered, and whatever the Dowager Duchess had been planning to say was drowned out by the instruments.

I really liked Fiona.

Taro couldn't stay out on the floor on a constant basis, but he was able to work around that. I watched him lead Fiona to the side of the room and his mother lead Simone over to him. Before they could reach him, however, he picked another willing partner and was back out on the floor. I watched the Dowager watch her son, trying to figure out where he would end up by the end of the piece, and she was fairly accurate, just not accurate enough to reach him by the time he had scooped up another dancer.

And that was what he did at the end of every piece. I
watched the Dowager drag Lady Simone from one end of
the ballroom to the other without quite catching Taro. It
was hilarious.

But he could do that for only so long. In time, the
Dowager was able to corner Taro with Simone in tow.

I wondered what Simone thought of all this. Did she
know of the Dowager's plans? Did she approve? She had
to know something was odd about having to follow the
Dowager all over the ballroom.

I saw Taro glancing about, and when he caught my eye
he gestured me over with an imperial jerk of his head.
"Excuse me a moment," I said to Radia.

"Are you kidding? I want to see this."

So Radia and I fought the wave of the crowd surrounding the dancers. I thought it would be better to have the
confrontation in private, though I could understand why
Taro would be unwilling to discard any sense of restraint
witnesses might impose on the Dowager. When we
reached them, Taro put his arm around my shoulders and
pulled me close to him.

"That is no way to behave before others," the Dowager
chided him.

"And you're the authority on appropriate behavior,
are you?"

"You're not needed here, dear," the Dowager said
to me.

"But she is welcome here," Taro responded for me.
"By me, and that is all that matters."

"There is no reason for you to make a drama of this,
Shintaro. All I wished to do was introduce the two of you.
Lord Shintaro Karish, this is the Honorable Lady Simone
Frezen, daughter of the Baroness of Eastbrook."

Taro did know how to be a gentleman. He released me
and bowed low, and Simone curtsied in return. "I regret
that you came to Her Grace's attention, Lady Simone," he
said. "Whatever plan she has will not come to fruition."

"Certainly, it will not," said Simone, "should I not choose to accept the Dowager's proposal." Ooh, aye, she had a nice dollop of arrogance going there.

Proposal. That was an odd choice of words. Proposals usually had benefits for both parties. What would the Dowager get out of a relationship between Simone and Taro?

"Perhaps I can save everyone's time by saying no right now," Taro said with a trace of desperation.

"You have not investigated my circumstances."

"Your circumstances are irrelevant."

"That is an unwise position to take in any situation," Simone said coolly.

At least she wasn't trying to seduce him with sweetness.

"Well, I'm foolish like that. I'm sure Her Grace has told you that."

"She told me that the bond between Source and Shield is completely unlike marriage."

That was a sharp conversational curve to take. And blunt, considering the audience.

"That's nothing you need to concern yourself with," Taro said coolly.

"I have also been informed that your Shield is involved in an irregular relationship with Academic Reid."

I had planned—hoped—to stay out of the conversation, but I couldn't let that slide. "That's not true," I said. Bitch. Though I supposed I should have saved the irritation for the person who told her the lie. That would be the bitch standing next to her.

"None of that matters," said Taro. Not a rejection of the woman's allegation, which I found disappointing. "Listen, you're just a victim of Her Grace's manipulations. I don't hold you responsible for that. But I have no intention of having anything to do with you. So you might as well go home."

"I'm not a romantic, Lord Shintaro. I am quite capable of accommodating your other relationships as long as you're not ridiculous about them."

Hell, that was cold. "I'm not," I said.

She looked at me for the first time. "After all this time, he hasn't married you. What does that tell you?"

"That he has no political alliance to build or land to trade."

"If he truly loved you, he wouldn't need such reasons. You are merely an entertainment for him until he meets someone more appropriate."

Did she really think the words of a complete stranger would make me doubt the words of someone I knew? Was she really that stupid?

"I need to dance with Lee," Taro announced. "Ladies." He steered me toward the dancers.

They had already begun their sets, but Taro and I were able to join them without causing any disruption. It was a pleasant dance, not too demanding, and I was able to think of other things. Unfortunately.

I couldn't believe the Dowager was telling people I was sleeping with Reid. Was that something of which she was trying to convince Taro? I was pretty sure he wouldn't believe it—he'd better not—but he didn't need to be hearing that trash.

What was she trying to accomplish? Simone was mentioning marriage, which was just ridiculous for a first meeting. She had to be responding to some kind of invitation or suggestion from the Dowager. Why did she want Taro to marry Simone? How could Taro marrying Simone result in him getting the Westsea title, which was the Dowager's ultimate aim? Was she merely torturing us both for her own pleasure?

Clearly, the woman needed something harmless with which to fill her time. Like knitting. Or steeplechasing.

At the end of the dance, a young woman claimed Taro

for the next set, and I was free to move back to the side, where I engaged in idle chatter with anyone who cared to talk to me.

That dance ended, too, and there was a bit of a pause. Then all the musicians seemed to dive into the next piece with unusual vigor. It was an odd piece, strident and fast. What kind of dance could be performed to music like that? Apparently a lot of the dancers felt the same, for they stood in the center of the floor and looked confused.

I took a deep breath. My heart had picked up its pace a little, and I felt uneasy.

And oddly invigorated.

One of the fiddles screamed into high notes. It pierced my ears and seared through my mind.

What was going on? Something was happening. No one played that kind of music for entertainment.

It was a sign of something, I realized. I was in danger. So was Taro. I had to get to him. But there was something wrong with my eyes. I couldn't see. I couldn't see Taro.

Someone was trying to hurt us. I had to find them. I had to stop them.

My mind was racing. I couldn't think.

Someone touched me, and I struck out. I felt soft flesh under my fingers. Someone was trying to hold me in place. I couldn't let them. Taro was in danger.

I ran. I hit something and pushed it out of the way. Why were all these things obstructing me?

Because they were all my enemies. They wouldn't let me find Taro. Well, I wouldn't let them stop me. I balled my hands into fists and swung them in every direction.

Someone from behind grabbed me by the waist and lifted me clear off my feet. I kicked and punched but I couldn't hit anything. Panic flared up in me. I was helpless, but I had to get to Taro.

"Calm down!" a familiar voice snapped, piercing through the music in my ears. "It's over. It's stopped. It's all fine."

The words were said again and again. In time, I recognized the voice as Taro's. A few moments later, I couldn't hear the music anymore.

Taro lowered me to my feet. I was gasping for breath. I felt all tied in knots.

And then I noticed the complete silence. And the fact that absolutely everyone was staring at me. How humiliating. I wanted to crawl under the floor. Or leave. I could do neither. Taro had a tight grip on me.

"It's because of the music," Taro said, his voice sounding very loud. "I can't say I admire your repertoire, cousin."

Music could make Shields react in overtly emotional ways. A song of unrequited love could drive us to tears. A pounding song of lust could cause us to sleep with whoever was handy. And a martial tune could make us violent.

I was more sensitive than most. I had been humiliated several times in the past.

"I didn't pick that piece," Fiona said, striding over to the musicians' alcove. "What are you playing at, Dicer? You can't even dance to that."

"We were told Your Ladyship requested it," the fiddle player protested.

"Who told you that?" Fiona demanded.

"One of your maids."

One of her maids. Why would they meddle with the music selections? They just wanted to watch a Shield go berserk? Some people were just sick.

"Which maid?" Fiona asked. "What did she look like?"

The fiddler shrugged and looked at his colleagues. None of the other musicians seemed able to add any information, either.

"Play something more appropriate," Fiona ordered. The music started up again.

It hurt my ears, which had grown sensitive under the earlier assault.

Taro led me toward one of the walls. "I'm afraid you have a few people to apologize to, Lee."

"Damn it, did I hurt anyone?" I was so embarrassed. I hated this, hated that mere music could turn me into a madwoman.

It turned out that I had struck three people in my attempt to get to Taro. Lady Edith, Lord Camer, and Sir Sugra. They were clustered together.

I curtsied as low as I could without falling over. "I am deeply apologetic," I said. "I hope I have done no lasting harm."

"So do I," Sir Sugra snapped. "I don't know what is acceptable in the wilds of High Scape, but here we all know what kind of behavior is considered civilized."

"Oh, climb down, Grady," said Lady Edith. "Shields are like that with music. She couldn't help it."

That didn't make me feel any better.

"Then she shouldn't be going to balls," said Sir Sugra.

I was starting to feel the same way.

I felt Taro's tension through his hands. "I checked the planned dances and music myself," he told them. "There was nothing dangerous in the approved selection. Clearly, there was some kind of miscommunication."

"I still say she shouldn't come to balls, if she is so easily turned into a violent brute."

I heard Taro draw breath to respond. I spoke before he could. "You're quite right, Sir Sugra. And in that spirit, I shall leave right now. You don't have to come with me, Taro."

"I find myself disenchanted with the company," he announced loftily, and Sugra choked on his offense.

I thought we should leave before we offended anyone else. I pulled Taro away.

Dane met us at the door. "I'm so sorry about this," he whispered. "We were very careful about the selection of music. I can't imagine how this happened."

"It's not your fault," I said. I just wanted to go. I didn't want to talk about it.

"Well, it's someone's fault, and we mean to find out whose. We'll be holding a little meeting after all the guests have left. Someone saw something, and they'll either tell us or risk all of them getting fired."

"Don't do anything extreme for my sake."

"It's not just for your sake. You assaulted some of our guests. I know it's not your fault, but we don't want it happening again."

I really didn't want to talk about it anymore. I had acted like a mindless child in front of all the aristocrats in the area. They would be talking about it. They would be telling those who hadn't been in attendance. It was awful. I wanted to move away and never come back. "I understand," I said, just to end the conversation. "Thank you."

"It's my duty and my pleasure. Have a good evening."

Well, that would be impossible, but getting away from all those eyes was a wonderful start.

Chapter Twenty-three

I woke up feeling unusually warm. And confined. I wasn't used to that, so it took me a few moments, sleep muzzled as I was, to realize Taro was spooned up behind me and holding me tightly. It was nice, and I smiled.

Then I remembered he was desperately unhappy.

I wasn't sure what was going on in his mind. I didn't blame him for having dark feelings, but it would only be better for him if he could put them aside. Was there any way I could help him do that? A way that didn't include never talking to Academic Reid again, because that was just ridiculous.

It didn't help that he had so little to do with his time. No racing, no tavern treks with his crowd of friends. I didn't think even he could play cards all day every day.

He needed some friends. That was it. He'd had flocks of friends in High Scape, but he was now sticking close to the manor. That couldn't be good for him. I had to figure out how to get him out and about with like-minded people.

Had he managed to make any friends at the ball? I hadn't seen him stay with anyone any longer than a single dance. But at least other aristocrats knew he was there, because of the ball. Maybe some of them would now invite him to their house parties and their hunting clubs. Not that I thought Taro had ever gone hunting before, but he would have to learn to adapt to keep from getting bored. He didn't deal well with being bored.

Taro seemed to become aware that I was awake, for he snuggled even closer and pressed in to kiss my ear. I giggled and squirmed so I could turn over.

A throat was cleared at our door. Why was that damn door always open? "Her Grace has asked all the members of the household to meet in the ballroom," Lila informed us. "Immediately."

I wondered if someone had come forward with the name of the person who'd requested that strange piece of music. I wondered if Fiona would actually fire everyone if no one had. That seemed harsh, and would also leave the household at a standstill until new staff could be brought in.

Taro and I dressed quickly and went down to the ballroom, where everyone in the household had gathered. Fiona didn't actually look that angry, though she was very pale. Dane, however, looked furious. So, a mass dismissal it was.

Standing with Fiona and Dane was a young man, short and slight with dull brown hair, pale skin and plain features. He wore the garb of a tenant farmer, though he didn't have the build for it. A large purple sack was slung over his shoulder.

"If I could have everyone's attention," Fiona said loudly. "It's time to begin. No one has admitted to requesting the Tower March last night. No one has reported seeing anyone else make the request. I will be questioning every single one of you on this matter. Perhaps whoever had done it had meant no harm. We are not used to having

Shields around here, and perhaps not all of you understand how Shields need to be handled."

Handled. Like an animal or a child.

"However, there have been a lot of little accidents happening around here, some of them potentially dangerous.
Of course, I want everyone to be more careful, but I don't
think being careful is enough. These little accidents have
been going on since my family took residence, and I am
aware that this establishment was not a calm or happy
place before my family's arrival." She put a hand on the
shoulder of the young man standing beside her. "You all
know Cavin. You know his special sensibilities." I didn't.
"We are going to go over this house, room by room, until
we find the source of the discontent. You will all remain
here unless you are called for, to identify anything unusual found among your possessions."

Fiona had mentioned to me her suspicion that the house
was bad luck. Sometimes people said that sort of thing
without meaning it. Did she actually believe it was the
house that was causing all her difficulties? The accidents,
the disapproval of her tenants? Wasn't that kind of ridiculous? Especially when there were so many other probable
causes, like human fallibility, dangerous surroundings
and a Dowager Duchess who was stirring up disgruntled
tenants?

Fiona reminded me of Atara, the leader of the troupe
Taro and I had traveled with when we were searching for
Aryne on Flatwell. She had believed a curse was responsible for the deaths among her troupe, when it was really
a combination of bad luck, a dangerous lifestyle and her
vengeful brother following them around and causing them
as much trouble as he could.

Except now, I knew magic existed. If I had known then
what I knew now, would I have believed in the curse, too?
But we knew her brother had been causing accidents.
We'd seen him at work.

Ergh.

"You can't go through our private things," a maid whose name I hadn't learned objected.

And Fiona didn't bother to answer her. "You may begin," she said to Cavin.

"Did you draw the water yourself, my lady?" he asked her.

"Yes, it's on the table."

Cavin drew from his purple sack a small copper bowl and filled it from a jug on an end table. He held it delicately between the tips of his fingers. "I will need silence from you all," he said. He began to hum, tunelessly and at a very low pitch. The sound hovered over the barrier between pleasant and weird.

Were they crazy? This was a spell. There were Imperial Guards crawling all over the estate looking for evidence of this. How could they risk this?

I sidled up to Fiona and asked in a whisper, "Are you sure this is a good idea? The Guards."

"Have been told by someone very discreet that a burned-out cottage at the edge of the property is a site for casting spells. They'll be gone for hours."

Several more moments later, Cavin announced, "This room is not the source of the distress." Then he headed to the antechambers, where people could rest in privacy during a ball. He hummed at his bowl in each one, and when he finished his face was bright red. Taro chuckled.

"What?" I asked him in a whisper.

"Perhaps his little bowl showed him what people get up to in those little rooms."

"They're meant to be a respite during a ball."

"People find respite in a variety of activities."

I stared at him. People had sex in there? "During a ball?"

"The chance of discovery can add an extra spice of enjoyment."

"Can it, now?" I was giving him plenty of opportunity to add something along the lines of "So I've been told." He didn't take advantage of it.

"Those rooms are clear," Cavin told Fiona.

"All right, Bailey, you will come with us," Fiona said. "Avkas, it's your responsibility to see no one leaves. Tarce, Source Karish, Shield Mallorough, please come with us as well."

I was glad to be included. This looked like it would be interesting.

We went to the kitchen, which I'd never seen so empty of human life. Cavin hummed at his bowl. It was an odd thing to do, I thought. How did he learn of it? Did he read of it in a book? Did he make it up himself? Was it passed down to him by a family member?

Cavin spent more time in the kitchen than he had with the ballroom, opening drawers and cabinets, holding the bowl over shelves and all other surfaces of the room. Then he pronounced it clean, and we moved on to the dining room.

I revised my earlier opinion. I could see this getting boring pretty quickly. And I was hungry and in desperate need of some coffee.

Tarce, apparently, was of a similar opinion. "Can we just declare my suite the source of all evil and be done with this?"

"You wish your suite were that interesting, Tarce," Fiona retorted.

"This is a little ridiculous, don't you think?"

"Do you have a better idea?"

"No, but Dane did. Fire the lot of them. We'd have better luck with better servants."

"That's an incredibly callous thing to say."

Tarce shrugged. "Blame your husband, not me."

Nothing interesting happened in the dining room, or in any of the other rooms on the first floor, though a ring Fiona had been missing was found in the music room.

We went to the second floor and started with guest bedrooms. They were dustier than Fiona liked. The third one
made Cavin blush again. And Fiona noticed.

"What's been going on in here?" she demanded.

"Some . . . intimate activity. A fair bit of it."

"No one has stayed in this room for years."

"The activity is frequent, long-standing and recent."

"I believe that's something I can address," said Bailey.

Ah, so servants had been having sex in that room. A lot
of them, I guessed. Maybe it was a bit more of that spice
Taro was talking about, the chance of discovery and the
opportunity to use more luxurious surroundings than they
would normally enjoy.

The rest of the guest rooms revealed nothing, and
neither did Bailey's private room. The housekeeper's private room, however, was discovered to possess a strange
sort of book full of nothing but drawings of naked young
men. I wouldn't be able to look at the woman in the eye
again.

I found it ironic that the Guards' rooms were searched,
too. Their doors were locked, but Bailey had keys to
everything. Nothing was found there. I was kind of surprised. They were causing a lot of bad feeling. If rooms
could develop atmospheres based on bad emotions, surely
Cavin should have been able to feel something there.

We went to the third floor, and the first room we went
to was the master suite. There was no reaction from either
the bowl or Cavin. There was no reaction in Tarce's suite
or even Daris's, which I had thought would be another
likely location. There was nothing in Stacin's nursery. Except for Stacin himself, of course, and he was adorable as
usual.

It was in Taro and my suite that we finally got a look at
what the bowl and the water were supposed to be doing.
When Cavin started humming, the water rippled. Cavin
frowned as he continued to hum.

"What does this mean?" Fiona asked him. "Is this it?"

Cavin stopped humming. "I don't think so, my lady. There is some darkness here, but it isn't strong enough to be causing your difficulties."

Darkness? I didn't like the sound of that. Was he sensing Taro's emotional discord? That was no one's business.

And I didn't appreciate the contemplative glances we were getting. What did they think darkness meant? The possibilities—violence, verbal abuse—were distasteful to contemplate.

Fiona touched my arm and gave me a look of sympathy. I responded with the blankest expression I could muster.

Cavin resumed humming for a while, but he eventually shook his head. "This isn't it."

We moved on to the bedrooms that were empty. Again, there was nothing.

We finally reached the room that had been Taro's when he was growing up. I felt Taro grow tense as soon as he stepped over the threshold. It seemed to me that Tarce wasn't too happy to be in there, either. Did he object to it in the same manner as did the servants?

Cavin held up his bowl. He hummed. The water exploded out of the bowl and splashed to the floor, to be joined by the bowl itself. Cavin had jerked his hands away as though his fingers had been burned. I looked at his face and saw that he had gone very pale.

Then he jolted out of the room. He didn't go far, just over the threshold, but it was abrupt enough to let us know he'd found what he considered the origin of the problem.

So there was a source of bad luck in the house. The room where Taro had grown up. And everyone, including Bailey, looked at him. Except me. I wasn't going to help humiliate him.

Fiona cleared her throat. "What needs to be done?"

Cavin was taking deep breaths, his color slowly returning. "Cleansing," he said. "Fire and water."

"What it needs is an axe," Taro muttered, not quite under his breath.

"You must perform the cleansing yourself, my lady," Cavin said with an apologetic air. "As the titleholder seeking relief, the cleansing will take best if performed by Your Ladyship's hand."

"Wonderful," said Tarce. "So the rest of us can go, aye?"

"Witnesses make all acts stronger, more binding," said Cavin.

"This will ultimately benefit us all, Tarce," Fiona told him.

Tarce rolled his eyes. "How much can any of us accomplish if this fellow can't even stay in the room?"

Cavin coughed in embarrassment and walked back through the door. "My apologies, my lady. The reaction was very strong."

"Think nothing of it. What is to be done?"

"The water Your Ladyship drew needs to be brought from the ballroom."

"Bailey?"

"Right away, my lady." Bailey left the room.

Cavin went to the nearest window with the clear intention of opening it. He was unable to. "Are these painted shut?" He looked closer. "I believe these are nailed shut, my lady. From the outside."

Dane checked the other windows. "They all are."

The windows were sealed? For how long? Surely not from the time that Taro had lived there. Surely he hadn't been stuck in this room for years without even the possibility of fresh air?

I really wanted to go find Taro's mother and beat her.

Two footmen were given the unenviable task of crawling around outside the house to pry out the nails. Fiona asked us all to remain in the room while the two men worked. I wanted to get Taro out of there. I thought it was heartless of Fiona to insist Taro remain, but Taro was being stoic and I knew he wouldn't appreciate being singled out by me to leave.

Once all the nails had been pulled out, Cavin opened all the windows. Then he reached into his bag and pulled out a smaller leather bag.

"What is that?" Fiona asked.

"Fire powder."

"That is a dangerous substance to be using indoors."

"I won't be using much of it, my lady." He deposited little piles of the black, powdery substance in each corner of the room. Bailey returned with the jug of water, which Cavin took from him and gave to Fiona. "I will light the powder. You must douse the flame when I tell you, my lady." Fiona nodded her understanding.

Cavin lit the nearest pile of powder, which flashed bright enough to hurt the eyes. "Douse the flame," he told Fiona. She did so. They repeated the process with each pile.

It raised a horrible stench in the room.

"The windows should be left open all day and through the night," Cavin said. "I will test the room again tomorrow morning."

"So that's it?" Tarce asked. "Not the most impressive display of casting I've ever seen, I must say."

"Forgive me, my lord, but it isn't a matter of casting spells."

"Then what is it?"

"Merely my greater connection to the air around us."

Oh, lords, not another form of discipline that made no sense and accomplished unpredictable results.

Taro was the first out of the room, his strides long and purposeful. I didn't follow him. He would come to me when he wanted to be soothed. If I followed him, I'd only end up aggravating him, and not in a healthy, productive way.

I ended up not seeing him for the rest of the day. I worried, of course. I asked around. No one seemed to know where he'd gone. I had no idea where to look. All I could do was wait and hope he wasn't getting himself in any trouble.

He did return in time, crawling into bed beside me. I pretended to be asleep, fairly sure he wouldn't want me asking him a bunch of questions.

We all met in the same room the next morning. Cavin held up his bowl and hummed. The water exploded out of the bowl. I hadn't been expecting that.

"What does that mean?" Fiona demanded.

"The cleansing didn't work." Cavin picked up his bowl in shaking hands.

"What is the next step?"

It seemed to me that the next step should be having Taro perform the cleansing, because that was what this was about, wasn't it? Taro had been kept in the room for years, scared and lonely and miserable. That was the source of whatever was allegedly going wrong with the room and its influence on the house. I could understand the significance of the titleholder performing the ritual— there was a belief in a special bond between a piece of land and its titleholder—but if Taro's history in the room was part of the problem, wouldn't the ritual be more powerful if he were the one performing it?

"This is beyond my ability, my lady," said Cavin.

"You're saying we just have to leave things the way they are? That's unacceptable."

"The only other solution I can think of is the complete destruction of the room."

"What do you mean? It's part of the house. I can't just carve it out."

Cavin shrugged. "I can think of no other solution."

Fiona looked up at the ceiling and thought and apparently came up with no solution of her own. "Thank you, Cavin. Bailey will see to your compensation."

"Thank you, my lady." Cavin bowed. "I am truly sorry." Cavin and Bailey left.

"At least we know there is a cause for all that discontent and it's not all in our heads," said Dane. "We can investigate ways to deal with it."

"If a spell won't fix it, what will?"

"He said it wasn't a spell that he was doing," I pointed out. "So maybe a spell can fix it, if we find the right kind."

I felt odd making the suggestion. Yes, I believed spells had power. Yes, I'd been casting them myself. But I still wasn't comfortable talking about it all so casually. I could just imagine what my classmates and professors would think to hear me now. Or the other Pairs in High Scape. They'd all think I was crazy.

"Do you have any ideas?" Fiona asked.

"Oh, no, none at all. I'm just suggesting a place to start looking. Though not a convenient place, with these Guards hanging around."

Fiona sighed rather explosively.

We all left the room and went off in different directions. I went back to the suite I shared with Taro, opened the overmantel and started looking through the books, hoping to find a spell that dealt with draining negative emotions out of a room. Because clearly there was something meaningful going on in that room. And if Fiona was right, the accidents were going to keep happening until whatever was wrong with that room was fixed.

Chapter Twenty-four

I couldn't have been more surprised when I received a summons from the Dowager Duchess, informing me I was to attend her at her home, immediately and without Taro. Of course I was tempted to respond with a rude refusal, or to give no response at all, but I was curious. The Dowager usually worked pretty hard to pretend I didn't exist. To invite me alone into her private den struck me as uncharacteristic, and I wanted to know what goal she thought I could or would assist her with.

I didn't bother changing my clothes or dressing my hair for her. I just left the Dowager's note on the table beside our bed and left the suite, heading straight out. A fanciful part of me thought I should make sure someone knew where I was going, in case I was never heard from again.

I crossed the large gardens and the small brush of trees to the dowager house. I was let in upon knocking and was shown into a small sitting room to wait. I supposed the Dowager hadn't expected me to show up immediately after all. I had time to examine the decor, which was very, very spare. The furniture was made of a very dark wood, the wood itself lacking in any extra ornamentation, and the cushioning was minimal and of a single solid color. In the room there were two chairs and a settee and four end tables, and that was it. There were no knick-knacks anywhere, and nothing hung from the walls. While I appreciated the lack of clutter, it came off feeling cold. I couldn't imagine anyone being comfortable there.

Maybe that was the point.

In time, I was shown to another room, a salon that was no more comfortably furnished. I sat through another short wait, and then the Dowager entered. I stood but I didn't curtsy. Strictly speaking, I didn't have to curtsy to anyone but royalty, but I still tended to do it if I cared about a person and didn't want to annoy them for no good reason. The Dowager didn't fall into that category of person.

"Shield Mallorough, I hope you are well," she said as she sat in one of the chairs. I noticed her back remained straight, and she didn't rest against the back of the chair. Taro used to sit like that a lot.

Her greeting carried a warmth I had never before heard from her. I found it unnerving. "I am in excellent health, thank you for inquiring."

"And how are you enjoying living in Flown Raven?"

"It is a beautiful area, and Fiona and her family have been very hospitable."

"Still, you are an intelligent woman, used to city life. There cannot be a great deal about to engage you."

That was a strange thing to say. "I must disagree."

"Really?"

"Yes. There are many diversions about."

A maid came in with a tea tray, and once she left, the Dowager fixed me a cup of tea without asking me if I wanted any. "Is that why you're spending so much time with Academic Reid?"

Not this again. "I actually spend little time with Reid."

"That is not what I've heard."

"Rumors are often inaccurate."

"My dear girl"—I nearly swallowed my tongue in shock—"I would be the last to berate you for seeking the academic's company. My Shintaro has many admirable qualities, but a fine mind is not among them."

I glared at her. "I disagree."

She chuckled, and that was another shock for me. "You may be sure, my dear, I have never doubted your loyalty to my son. It is only what he deserves, of course, but one rarely gets what one deserves in life."

"That is true." Because she deserved to be rolled down a hill in a barrel full of spikes or something equally painful.

"That is why I wished to talk to you, to discuss what Shintaro deserves. And you as well, my dear. You are a good person who clearly takes her responsibilities seriously."

Really, who was this woman? "I see."

"Have you ever heard of Matt LeBarr or Winel Taroque?"

"I'm afraid I haven't."

"They are a Source and Shield, respectively. A Pair. And their personalities were so disparate, leading to such violence, that eventually the Triple S council agreed they did more harm than good and let them separate."

I searched my memory for those names, of even a rumor of such circumstances, and I came up with nothing. "That's impossible. The Triple S never allows Pairs to be wasted that way." Well, beyond sending Pairs to cold sites, though the theory was that they would be returned to proper duty once they were properly punished for their crimes.

"The Pair was useless as it was. There was a concern they would actually kill each other in the violence they perpetrated against each other. It was feared such an incident would poison the respect people felt toward the

Triple S. LeBarr and Taroque were sent back to their respective academies, to teach or some similar task."

"I haven't heard anything of this."

"Secrecy was a condition of separation."

"Then how have you learned of it?"

The Dowager laughed, and I couldn't help it. I just stared at her. Had Taro ever in his whole life witnessed her like this? She seemed almost human. "I have been alive a great many more years than you, Dunleavy, and have been so fortunate as to be in such circumstances that I know people in all sorts of positions. And if I don't know them, a friend does. All kinds of information comes my way."

I would have never suspected the Dowager of having friends. Allies, maybe, but not friends.

"And, of course, as my son is a Source, I've had particular interest in the workings of the Triple S. My friends and other acquaintances know this, so they relay to me everything they hear. I believe I know more about all that the Triple S does than any Triple S member. Most of you pay little attention to each other."

That was a chilling idea, that someone outside the Triple S would have a more accurate view of us than we did ourselves. Someone like the Dowager. And I couldn't even disagree with what she was saying. I, for one, had lost touch with most of the people with whom I went to school.

"I have to confess a secret, my dear." And she leaned slightly forward, as though she were really afraid of being overheard. "When I learned my son had been bonded to a member of the merchant class, I truly feared that I would be hearing too much from your family seeking connections and favors." I opened my mouth to object—my family were not social scroungers—but she spoke before I could. "I heard nothing at all. But you must forgive me, for all my life I have been surrounded by people who were interested only in alliances and negotiations and benefits.

It was strange to come across a whole family of those who cared nothing for such things."

I wouldn't have said my family cared nothing for such things. They were, after all, a normal merchant family. My parents considered alliances and benefits when it came to my brothers and my sister. However, I was not part of the family business. It had probably never occurred to them to seek benefits through me.

"Everything I have heard of you is that you are a decent, honorable person, and a worthy Shield for any Source. I admit I have had difficulty believing such salutations, but I assure you that believing such is what I have come to do."

Thank you, and I don't believe you, not for a moment.

And I was realizing Taro had inherited more than his looks from his mother. They could leap from one topic of conversation to another with equal dizzying ease.

"However, I have heard other things as well. How disappointed you were when Shintaro first Chose you."

How the hell did she know that? I hadn't told anyone, and it hadn't been long before it wasn't even true anymore.

"And that his lifestyle, his gambling and his intimate exploits embarrassed you."

"Taro has never embarrassed me," I objected.

"You don't need to defend him to me, Dunleavy. I know my son."

"On the contrary, I don't believe you know him at all."

Her expression became serious, and I thought I would be blasted with a more characteristic insult. Instead, she said, "I don't blame you for feeling that way. I have not always known best how to talk to my son. But you have never seen us interact alone. Can you concede that Shintaro behaves differently when you're in the room?"

"I don't know why he would."

"My dear, your opinion means a great deal to him."

"As his does to me."

"Does it? I know he is very upset about you spending so much time with the academic, and yet you continue to do so."

He wasn't very upset. Kind of irritated maybe. That was no reason not to talk to Reid whenever I felt like it. And that didn't mean I didn't value his opinion. It just meant I wasn't letting him control me. And I was sure he didn't want to, even when I annoyed him.

"Don't misunderstand me. There is nothing wrong with what you are doing, but you can understand why he's upset. He does not have the finest mind, and you choose to spend all your time with a man who lives by his intelligence."

Taro couldn't possibly feel that way.

Could he?

There was nothing wrong with Taro's mind, damn it. Just because he didn't spend all his time reading didn't mean he wasn't smart.

"You're not happy in Flown Raven," said the Dowager. "I can see it. So can many others. And you must be aware that the reason you're here is because the Emperor feels this is the best place for Shintaro."

Actually, I doubted very much that the Emperor cared at all for what was best for Taro.

And all right, so I wasn't overjoyed to be in Flown Raven, but that didn't mean I was miserable. What was she seeing? Did other people see it, too?

"There is reason to believe that Taro will spend the rest of his life here," the Dowager said.

What a horrifying thought. "It is the custom to be transferred every few years."

"I have reason to believe Shintaro will be treated differently from other Sources. After all, it is not Triple S custom to post their members in their places of birth, is it?"

Why did she have reason to believe any of this? Where was she getting this information?

And was she really intimating that the Emperor would be messing Taro about indefinitely? What the hell had Taro done to deserve that?

"Now, be honest. It is not your desire to spend the rest of your life in Flown Raven, is it?"

"No." I saw nothing wrong with admitting that. "But it isn't Taro's, either."

She sighed. "I fear Taro won't often be given the freedom of doing what he wishes. It is the nature of the position he was born to."

"He was born to be a second child." And you treated him like trash.

"It is more complicated than that. He has captured the interest of the Emperor."

And whose fault was that? If she hadn't gone running to the Emperor to try to get Taro's title back, the Emperor would have never known Taro existed. "He belongs to the Triple S."

"The Triple S has ceded authority over Shintaro to the Emperor."

That was not what their letters suggested. "I think they might be surprised to learn that."

"They allowed the Emperor to transfer you here, did they not?"

I didn't think "allowed" was quite the right term. It was more likely that they had been so appalled by the Emperor's audacity that they hadn't known how to react. I got that way when people were spectacularly rude to me.

"I fear that Shintaro will be in a position of service to the Emperor for the rest of his life. But you needn't be. You can seek separation, just as LeBarr and Taroque were granted."

"We don't have anything like their reasons." If that had ever actually happened. Was there a way to find out? If secrecy was a requirement, no one would tell.

Except Aryne. She was at the Source Academy. She'd know if LeBarr was there. I'd have to write to her.

"That doesn't matter. Once a thing is done a first time, it is far easier to arrange matters to have it done subsequent times."

I didn't want to be a part of that. If people knew they could leave their partners, they'd never put any real effort into working with them. We didn't always get to like the people we worked with. "I have no interest in being separated from Taro."

"Because you're in love with him."

"Because he's my Source." That mattered more than everything else.

"You don't wish to be free of his burdens to the Emperor? Of his irrational possessiveness? Of his philandering ways?"

"Taro doesn't philander anymore."

She frowned in sympathy, and she lightly touched the back of my hand. "You don't really believe that, do you? You are not so naive?"

"Taro has told me so, and I believe him."

"My dear, there are rumors."

"Like the rumors that had me sleeping with Academic Reid?" The rumors she'd been spreading?

She drew back. "I do apologize. I was so worried for him. I know now that I had no reason to be."

"You have no reason to be worried for me, either." And she wasn't, of course. She was merely trying to separate us. And why was that?

"I just want you to think about the possibilities. How much easier your life would be, if you didn't have Shintaro's burdens to deal with."

Really, I didn't know what to say. She was acting so warm and friendly and I didn't know how to respond to it. The one thing that was certain was that I wasn't going to let her think she'd won me over. If there was any hint I might for a moment consider leaving Taro, she would run to him and tell him, and wouldn't that be a fine mess? "I'm quite happy with Taro, and I wouldn't dream of asking to be separated from him, even if such a thing were possible. So while I thank you for your concern, it is entirely misplaced." Just shut up, already.

"You just think about it," she said.

That was my cue to leave. I was happy to do so. The Dowager's pleasant demeanor made my spine twitch.

The first thing I did was hunt for Taro. I wanted to talk to him before his mother had a chance to fill his head with lies. He proved to be harder to find than I expected. He was not gambling with off-duty members of the staff, and no one could recall seeing him recently. After an hour or so of searching, I gave up and went back to our suite.

I was really surprised to find the woman in our bed. I stopped in the doorway between our sitting room and the bedchamber, blinking. Was I in the right place?

She turned over, and I saw it was Simone. I should have known from the hair.

She sat up, the blankets falling from her naked torso. "Oh," she said, her eyes carefully widened. "Taro said you'd be in the library all day."

So she was supposed to convince me she and Taro had been indulging in secret assignations. "Lords," I muttered. "Are you a rotten actress."

"I'm terribly sorry. I didn't want you to find out this way."

"So you're going to follow your script no matter what I say?" I looked for Simone's clothes. She could cover up those breasts anytime.

She raised her knees, resting her arms on them. She smiled, a pretty little smile, and she seemed to gleam in the soft afternoon light. I could see why someone would find her alluring, graceful in her nudity.

Still, a really bad liar.

"I can understand why you don't want to accept what you see."

"I see nothing to worry about. It seems to me people can wander around this house at will."

"My dear, it was bound to happen sooner or later. Taro is a charming fellow with a voracious appetite."

I crossed my arms as I thought about her little display. "How did the Dowager convince you to do this? Surely it's beneath your dignity. It's like something the saucy maid would do in a comedy."

She flushed. She didn't like that.

"What are you supposed to get out of this? Even if it worked, do you want Karish for yourself? Why? He will never be the Duke of Westsea. It can't be done now."

She smiled again, and I could see she thought I had gone too far in my attempt to demonstrate her foolishness. "Shields never really learn about the world the rest of us live in," she said. "And why should you? You have important things to think about. All about how the world moves and how to keep everything stable. But Shields are known for being ignorant about how people move, and people can't be kept stable."

"Seriously, you're wasting your time. I don't know you. Why would I take your word over his?"

She pressed on with her prepared argument. "He is an accomplished lover, isn't he? So creative."

I rolled my eyes and pulled the bellpull. "Anyone would be able to guess that."

"He doesn't use his hands a great deal, though, does he? He seems to prefer his mouth."

That was true. It had, however, been equally true of other lovers I had had. Maybe that was just a male thing. "Mm."

"And that roll he does with his tongue."

Still didn't believe her. "What roll is that, precisely?"

"Perhaps he doesn't perform the same way with you."

"And perhaps we've reached the limit of what you're prepared to describe." She wasn't at all convincing. If Taro were to take up with someone, that someone wouldn't be the sort to show up in his bed naked for the purpose of making his life difficult. He had too much sense for that. And too much taste.

Really, I should start locking the door when I left the suite. "Do be comfortable," I told her, and when Lila came to our suite I ordered some coffee, settling in on one of the chairs in the sitting room to read a melodramatic novel.

I was curious to see how long she would wait in there. Maybe I hadn't been the original target. Perhaps she had really thought I would be in the library all day. Perhaps her original plan had been to have Taro walk in on her, and she would seduce him.

Either way, her plan had been very clumsily executed. Did she and the Dowager really think we were that stupid, that easily convinced of the outrageous?

So now the Dowager was working on separating us. Not just sundering our personal relationship. She wanted me gone, physically gone, and she was going to ludicrous lengths to accomplish that. Why? And why now?

In time, Simone appeared in the doorway to the bed-chamber. Dressed, thank Zaire. She had a bitter, twisted look on her pretty face. "You're a fool," she said.

"I'm not the one lying about naked in a stranger's bed," I pointed out.

"You don't understand our world. Shintaro's world."

"Your world never included Karish. He was excluded as a child." Oops, had she known that? I hated the thought of giving away Taro's secrets. "Most of his life has been spent as a Source." There, that covered me.

"And yet he has not completely left our world behind. You can hear it in his voice. See it in his mannerisms. He's still High Landed."

That was true. He still had a bit of the aristocratic accent, and he still sometimes moved as though he had a wooden rod tied up his back. "And if you ask him, he'll call himself a Source."

"And as a Source, he'll protect his own home. It's natural."

Just what did that have to do with trying to seduce him away from me?

Our door was thrown open. It was Taro. His eyes looked a little wild.

"What the hell are you doing here?" he roared at Simone.

And she went pale for a moment. Then she proved her gross stupidity by straightening her shoulders and saying, "I'm sorry, Taro. I know you didn't want her to find out like this."

I slapped my hand over my eyes. So stupid.

"What have you been telling her?" he demanded of her.

She took a step back. Taro could be a little frightening when he wanted to be.

"Nothing that I've believed," I said quickly. I didn't believe he would actually strike the woman, but he seemed to be quivering with rage, and it was alarming me.

"She sent you to where my Shield lives. Like a whore. You're a whore?"

Simone gasped and flushed and opened her mouth to speak, but Taro didn't let her.

"She thought that, what, I would take up with you just because you showed up? She really thought that would work?"

It did seem to me a rather weak plan. On the other hand, maybe there were men who would jump on that kind of opportunity without thinking. Maybe that was the kind of men the Dowager knew.

"You are irrelevant, do you hear me?" he ranted. "You could be the most beautiful person in the world. You could be the smartest person in the world. The best natured in the world. It doesn't matter what you are. It doesn't matter what Lee is. I will never want anything to do with you because you come from that woman. And now you come into my home, my very rooms, and try to interfere with my partner? What kind of parasite are you?"

He whirled around in place, tearing at his hair, his gaze moving about the room. He seemed to be looking for something. I tried to think of a way to calm him down. It would embarrass him later to have appeared so frantic in front of Simone.

"Why can't she leave me alone?" he demanded. "What is it going to take? Does one of us have to die before she'll leave me in peace?"

I felt my eyes widen as unease took root in my stomach. That was a dangerous thought for him to be having.

He abruptly left the room. I scrambled after him.

"I'm sick of it," he said. "Sick of it, sick of it. Water wiping away stone is what it is, scraping scraping scraping until there is nothing left."

He was heading swiftly down the stairs, continuing to talk as he went, servants stopping and staring as he passed.

"Taro, where are you going?"

He didn't answer me. "Black and rotting," he said. "Attacking pink flesh until there is nothing left but putrescence and stench and empty death." Down to the main floor and out the rear entrance.

"Taro, please talk to me."

"Pounding and pounding and pounding. Why won't she stop? She has to stop. I'll stop her."

That didn't sound good. "Please calm down. Please, Taro." I grabbed his arm but he easily pulled free. He was heading for the stables. "I don't think you should be riding now, Taro." What would I do if he insisted on riding? In this mood he was sure to be reckless and break his neck.

But we passed the stalls and entered the tack room at the back. Seeming to know exactly where to find what he was looking for, he grabbed up an axe.

Unease transformed into outright fear. "Taro!" He

wasn't going to kill his mother. He couldn't be that far gone to anger. Getting Simone to pull that little stunt was nowhere near the worst the Dowager had ever done.

I grabbed at the axe handle. "Put it down, Taro." He tried to pull the axe out of my hands, but I had been expecting that, my hands spaced wide on the handle, my weight balanced far back over my heels.

Taro twisted the axe end over end, wrenching it out of my hands. I fell on my behind on the floor. "Taro, please listen to me."

"Black," he said. "Nothing but blackness spreading everywhere and killing the roots."

"That doesn't mean you get to kill her."

I was relieved that, upon exiting the stable, he headed toward the manor rather than the dowager house. On the other hand, I liked the people of the manor much more than those of the dowager house. "Please give me the axe, Taro."

But no, he charged back toward the manor, constantly muttering in seething metaphor. He didn't run, so I could keep up with him, but he wouldn't listen to me, and he shielded the axe from my hands.

This didn't make sense. His reaction was so far out of proportion to what had happened. "You can't kill Simone, either."

Back in the manor, back up the stairs. Maids gasped as we passed. "Get Dane," I hissed at one.

"His Lordship isn't here."

"Then get Bailey!" Or some footman. Why wouldn't anyone stop him?

Ranting about poison and rotting and decay, he raged up the stairs to the third floor. I really feared he was going back to our suite, where I assumed Simone still was. But no, he passed it. I was relieved but baffled. What was he doing?

He threw open the doors to his old nursery. With a wordless cry, he swung the axe right at the wall. It sank

deep into the wood. "You know nothing!" he shouted,
yanking the axe free. "You are twisted!" Another swing
at the wall. "You are dark!" He smashed through a set of
shelves. "You are shallow and ignorant!" He swung at the
door itself, right at the hinges, and he kept swinging at
the hinges. "You are nothing to me! You have no power
over me! You have no rights to me! I will let you do nothing to me!" Once the door was wrenched from its fitting,
he started at the windowsills. "I will be free! You can't hold
me! I'm a Source and I'm free!" He swung the axe again
and again, at the windows, at the furniture and the walls and
the floor. The ceiling was spared only because he couldn't
reach it.

I jumped every time the axe struck wood. I watched
Taro, saw how no blow seemed to satisfy him. I could see
that the axe didn't sink deeply enough to suit him, watched
him wrench it free with a twist to do as much damage as
possible. Each strike seemed to fuel his anger instead of
easing it, and I worried how much worse it would get
when his frustration overcame him.

Splinters flew. Sweat soaked through Taro's shirt. His
shouting and screaming brought almost everyone in the
house. Including Bailey. None dared enter the room to try
to stop the destruction. We all crowded in the corridor by
the door.

"Is it not your place to soothe him?" Bailey asked.

Oddly enough, there had been no lessons on how to
deal with a Source when he'd gone berserk for little reason. I glared at Bailey. "You're welcome to try if you
think you can do better than I."

"You're not doing anything."

"He won't listen to me, and I'm not stepping close to a
swinging axe."

I didn't know how much time passed as Taro swung at
every surface in the room, shouting the whole time. It felt
like hours, and the shelves were reduced to useless chunks,
the walls and floors gouged full of holes, the insults he

shouted at his mother growing more and more obscure and incomprehensible. What would happen when Taro deemed the room damaged enough? Would he move on to something else?

But finally, the swings of the axe became slower and wider, the axe sinking less deep and sometimes bouncing right off the wood due to a poor angle. Taro was panting heavily, growing unable to shout. He was gleaming with sweat, and his hair was in disarray. He suddenly went from rage to peace, his shoulders slumping as he lowered the head of the axe to the floor and let it drop.

The following silence was suffocating.

What the hell were we going to tell Fiona and Dane?

I stepped into the room, slowly. Taro didn't look at me, his eyes on the axe. I realized he was whispering. I couldn't decipher what he said. More insults at his mother?

Not knowing if it would set him off again, I took his hand and squeezed it softly. He stopped whispering, and he looked at me for the first time since he'd started his rampage. I was surprised by how calm he looked, calmer than he'd been since we first arrived in Flown Raven. When I led him from the room, he followed meekly, silently.

What was the significance of what had happened? I hoped it didn't mean his mind had snapped. But what else could it mean? He'd destroyed that room. I understood that the room had been a great source of pain for him, but how did chopping it up help anything?

I took Taro back to our suite. Simone was gone. I ordered a bath for Taro. When the bath arrived, I helped him strip down. While he sat in the bath, I rinsed the sweat and flecks of wood from his skin and washed his hair. He was pliant and said nothing. I didn't speak, either. I had no idea what to say.

After his bath he went to bed, though it was still only the afternoon. He appeared to fall asleep immediately.

I sat in the sitting room and tried to figure out how worried I should be. It wasn't like Taro to explode like that, but then, he'd been unlike himself for weeks. It disturbed me that he had chosen to express himself with an axe, but maybe something this extreme would make him feel better. I wouldn't know until he woke.

I wondered how long it would take for everyone in the area to learn what had happened. Would they think he'd gone crazy? Or would they assume it was typical Source behavior?

He had scared the hell out of me. I really resented that. I might shout at him for that, once I was sure he was sane.

There was a brisk knock at the door, and I let in Fiona and Dane. I stifled the urge to tell them to keep their voices down, as Taro was sleeping. That might be considered being too presumptuous, under the circumstances.

"What the hell happened?" Fiona demanded.

I debated how much to tell her, and decided on as little as possible. "The Dowager has been harassing Taro since we arrived. Now her guest has gotten involved. He had enough."

"So he decided to purge his anger on my house? Will he go after the master bedroom next? After all, she used to sleep there."

"I'm really sorry about this. I know he will be, too, once he gets up."

"How often does he get into these rages?" Dane asked.

"I've never seen him like that."

"And what if next time he decides to swing an axe at a person?" said Fiona.

"He would never do that!" I protested, well aware I had been worried about that very thing.

"I wager this morning you would have said he would never destroy a room like that."

That was true. "Destroying a thing is leagues away

from destroying a person. Taro would never do anything like that."

"Are you sure?"

"Yes." I was now pretty sure I'd seen him at his worst.

Fiona sighed. "I suppose that will have to do," she said. "It's not like we use that room."

I loved practical people. And she gave me an idea. "You should get that young man to try that cleansing ritual again."

"Why?"

"It's just a feeling I have."

"Shields and their mysteries," Fiona commented sarcastically.

I resented that. I never tried to appear mysterious. "No. I just don't have a rational explanation. But I think it's worth a try."

After that, the most forgiving people I had ever met left Taro to sleep and me to think. In time I ate supper in our sitting room and then, after reading for a while, went to bed. Taro slept through it all and he was still in bed when I woke the next morning.

I was sipping on coffee when Fiona tapped on our door. "Want to go for a walk?" she asked.

"No, thank you. Taro's not awake yet. I want to be here when he rises."

"He's slept all this time?"

"Aye." I was starting to get worried, actually.

"Well, I thought you'd like to know that we brought Cavin in and he declared the room cleansed."

"That's excellent."

"So it appears Shintaro's rampage did some good."

"Strange, that violence can be cleansing." And offensive, really. Violence wasn't supposed to accomplish anything.

"Still, I'm not comfortable with what Taro did."

Neither was I. Taro wasn't a creature of violence and aggression. That wasn't his way, and I liked that about him. Having reacted that way once, was he more likely to react to frustration that way again? Just because he wouldn't physically hurt a person didn't mean he wouldn't be violent and disturbing.

Fiona left shortly thereafter, and then, finally, Taro woke. He shuffled from the bedroom, with his hair all rumpled, wearing his nightgown and looking adorable. "What time is it?" he asked.

"Late morning."

He looked at his hands, bending and straightening his fingers. "My hands hurt."

"That's from how you worked that axe yesterday."

He flushed, deep and full.

"What happened?" I was a little afraid to hear the answer, actually.

"I don't want to talk about it."

"You destroyed that room in front of everyone. You don't have a choice. I'd like to know what to tell people."

He rubbed the back of his neck. "I was angry. I had to get it out. That was all I could think to do."

"And did it work?"

He stared at the floor. "I feel looser. In a way I haven't for a long time."

That didn't assure me that it wouldn't happen again. "We're going to be here for at least a few years."

"I know."

"You're going to have to figure out how to deal with the Dowager."

"I know!"

All right, all right, I didn't want to start an argument and undo whatever good his rampage had done. "You know I would never believe anything the Dowager says, right? Nor any of her associates."

"Good."

Good. "So if you see any of them around, there is no need to assume the worst."

"Yes, yes."

He was acting like I was the one being unreasonable. I wasn't the one who'd gone crazy with an axe. I'd have to watch him, though I had no idea what I would do if he went crazy again.

Chapter Twenty-five

Taro was quiet and subdued through the morning, and he stayed close. I read while he stared out the window.

"Isn't Reid expecting you?" he asked eventually.

I stomped down on a spurt of irritation. "No," I said. "I've no reason to be in the library." I turned a page I hadn't finished reading.

"I've been very irrational recently," he said. "I'm sorry. It's like my mind has been clouded."

Well, that didn't sound good. "What do you mean?"

"No, not clouded. More like there are little wooden blocks stuck in my head, stopping my thoughts from flowing as they should, sometimes making them disappear altogether."

That had to be uncomfortable. "This place isn't good for you."

"I should be able to handle it better."

There was nothing I could say to that. Yes, he should

be able to handle it better, but as long as he recognized that, there was no reason for me to harp on it.

He stood suddenly. "Let's go see the Dowager."

"Really?" Did we have to? "Why?"

"I need to talk to her."

"That could be a good idea." Was he going to rake her over the coals for her stunt? That would be brilliant. As long as it didn't make him crazy again.

"So let's go."

"This sounds like something private. I shouldn't be there."

"I want you there."

That was that. I put my book aside with a sigh.

We were permitted into the dowager house by the handsome young man who served as her butler, and led into the larger waiting room I had been in the other day. As we waited, I noticed that Taro didn't seem as tense as he always was when it came to dealing with his mother. I was nervous enough for us both. I didn't know why I was always nervous around Taro's mother. She wasn't dangerous, just unpleasant.

She kept us waiting a good while, finally showing up looking freshly bathed. Simone wasn't with her, and that surprised me. I was expecting the Dowager to throw Simone into Taro's company whenever possible. Then again, perhaps Simone was too embarrassed from her stunt the day before to face Taro again so soon.

The Dowager looked perfect, elegantly dressed with every hair in place. Taro and I were windblown from our walk from the manor. I always felt so grubby around her.

Taro stood upon her entrance, as he would for anyone. "Good afternoon, Your Grace," he said with casual courtesy.

"I understand you put on quite a display for your household yesterday," was her response.

"Aye, I did." He didn't seem uncomfortable admitting it.

She seated herself with stiff precision. "Better things are expected of you."

"Lee seems to have forgiven me. And Fiona took the destruction of her room with great ease. They are the only people I have to worry about."

"You do not go far in life when your servants and neighbors don't fear and respect you."

And wasn't I glad not to have to work for her? Did her servants fear her? What did she do to them?

"I'm as far as I'm going to get," said Taro. "Certainly as far as I want to go. Or I will be once I am transferred away from here in a few years."

"You will never be transferred."

What would she know about it?

"It is the custom of the Triple S to transfer its Pairs every few years," Taro told her.

"The Triple S no longer has anything to do with you. The Emperor rules you now."

I'd already had this conversation with her the day before. Clearly, I hadn't made the slightest dent in her delusions. Was she going to bring up the separation of LeBarr and Taroque?

"Our only ruler is the Triple S," said Taro.

"The Emperor sent you here, did he not?"

"That doesn't mean he can keep us here."

"You will learn in time that the Emperor can do whatever he likes, but it will save you a great deal of aggravation if you accept the truth now."

"You don't speak the truth. You don't know the truth when you see it."

"I have no need to sit here and listen to any more abuse."

Abuse? She had the nerve to accuse him of abuse? After all the things she'd done and said to him during his whole life?

"You've made me listen to you often enough."

"I have never been anything other than correct."

"That's subject to interpretation. But it's in your best interest to listen to me now. It will save you a great deal of effort and time in the long run."

"How intriguing," she said, and she couldn't have sounded more bored.

"So I shall begin," he said. "That you bore me gives you no right to control me."

"It is the duty of every parent to guide her children."

"Not once those children are grown."

"The duty lapses only upon the death of one or the other."

"You tried to tell my brother what to do?"

That was an interesting question. From all reports, Taro's brother was a lush and a whore and pretty much useless. I was kind of interested in what the Dowager thought of her firstborn.

"The nature of the relationship between your brother and me is none of your concern."

"Which means no."

"You are in no position to know."

"That's true. Once I was at the Academy you lost whatever interest you ever had in me. There were no visits, no letters. It was only once my brother died that you found it worth your while to have any contact with me."

"Flown Raven was taken care of while your brother was alive."

I stared at her. So it was true. She didn't care the least about Taro while he was only a second child. And she had no problem admitting that. Bitch.

But Taro didn't seem to be upset by her coldness. "Flown Raven is taken care of now."

A flush came to the Dowager's face. I thought it might be prompted by anger. "That woman is not the legitimate titleholder."

"Of course she is. No laws were violated."

"I didn't say she wasn't the legal titleholder. There is a significant difference. Once your brother died, it was your duty to assume responsibility for Flown Raven. You obtained the code from me in bad faith and sent it to your cousin. That was not your right. Only the former titleholder can determine the next one."

"Then it wasn't your place, either. My brother certainly didn't choose me. You did. And you were never a titleholder."

Her eyes narrowed. "You made the decision in complete ignorance. You neglected to learn anything about Flown Raven before you gave it away." The flush was getting deeper.

"Because I already had responsibilities given to me by people who were actually willing to spend time shaping my character and preparing me for life outside of four walls."

"Your highest responsibility is to your family."

"My responsibilities are to Lee, to the Triple S, and to the people we protect. In that order."

The Dowager looked at me for the first time. "You may go."

"I don't think I will."

"This is my house."

"We won't be in it much longer," Taro told her. "I really haven't got much to say. You bore me, and I thank you for that, but you have no control over me. You have no influence over me. I don't value your opinion. Your priorities are so skewed that I can't possibly live up to them, and I don't care to. It will make me a person I don't respect, as I don't respect you."

The Dowager's head flung back as though she'd been struck. That was interesting. I would have wagered she didn't give a damn what Taro thought of her.

"I will not be in this house again, regardless of what summons you send. I have no control over whether you enter the manor, but I won't speak to you if you do. I certainly won't have anything to do with any woman you bring here in some twisted attempt to lure me from Lee.

That's disgusting and perverse. I won't believe anything you say, because whatever you say is—"

"That's enough!" the Dowager snapped. "You little fool. You don't know what you've done."

"So tell me what I've done."

"You have no idea how powerful Flown Raven is and you've let it pass from our hands, you idiot."

Oh, aye, she was furious. It was oddly satisfying to see her moved to such emotion.

"It doesn't matter how important Flown Raven is. I was never meant—" With a deep breath, he cut himself off. "It doesn't matter. I don't care. It's done and it won't be undone. I don't care what you want. I don't care what the Emperor wants or is willing to do. I am Source Shintaro Karish, and that's all I am. It is unfortunate that I can't have any immediate family, but you're poisonous, and I will no longer let you darken my days. It makes my life miserable, and we have too few years to let them rot under the influence of parasites like you."

"How melodramatic," she sneered.

"I'm a Source." He shrugged. "Melodrama is what we do. I'm not surprised you don't know that. I'm not the only one guilty of acting without knowing anything. But I've said what I've come to say. You are nothing to me. If there were some little ritual of separation, I would perform it. In the absence of that, I will bid you good day. I hope we never see each other again. Perhaps you'll travel again, go to one of your retreats, and that will settle your mood."

I stood and took his arm. "Have a good day," I said to be polite, but she didn't even glance at me.

"You are an ignorant fool," she hissed at her son.

We left her. I was satisfied with the encounter, largely because Taro had stayed so calm and loose. I had no confidence that the conversation had any impact on the Dowager. We might be finding more naked women in our bed.

However, if Taro could regard her proximity with equanimity, that was the most important accomplishment.

My breath was taken away by the strength of the wind that hit us when we left the dowager house. It whipped my hair right out of the ties, and Taro and I had to lean far forward to keep our footing. Walking was hard, hard work, and the way the trees bent with their branches careening about was highly alarming.

It was a relief to get back into the manor and push the door closed behind us. We were panting and sweating and looked like we had been put through some kind of physical trial. I was ready for a bath and a nap.

A maid rushing by us came to a sharp halt. "Sir, ma'am," she said in a breathless voice. "Her Ladyship has been looking for you."

"Why?" Taro asked. "What's happened?"

"It's His Lordship. He's out whaling."

"In this?" I asked.

And right then, we heard the warning notes from the Wind Watcher.

I didn't even want to imagine anyone on the water in that.

It took us a little time to track down Fiona. It appeared she was pacing the house in agitation. We finally ran her down in Stacin's room, flushed and a little wide-eyed.

"Shintaro!" She grabbed Taro's hands. "Why aren't you channeling? The wind is so strong. Why aren't you doing something?"

Taro was able to look frustrated and sympathetic at the same time. "I'm sorry, Fiona, but there's nothing I can do about this."

"This is what you do."

"No, it isn't. This isn't a natural disaster."

"Of course it is. Dane is out whaling. Wind this strong can kill people on the water."

"We can't channel this, Fiona."

"Then what good are you?"

An idea popped into my head. A really bad one. I grabbed Fiona's arm. "Where are the Guards?"

"They were out harassing the tenants. Hopefully they've been blown away."

"All right. There might be something I can do." I ran down to the library, Taro and Fiona following.

Reid was in the library, standing near a shuttered window, listening to the wind. He didn't appear to notice that we'd come in, which was not good. What if we'd been one of the Guards?

"Are there any spells in that book of yours that deal with controlling the wind?" I demanded with little real hope. I had to ask, though.

He blinked at me before striding to the table. From his pile of notes, he extracted a single sheet and held it out to me.

"You're kidding."

"It was one of the first spells in the book. It's hard to imagine, but perhaps the winds in this area have always been this strong. As Flown Raven was so important to the First Landed, they would have wanted to keep this area safe."

"Spells?" said Fiona. "You can perform spells?"

I would have preferred that she hadn't learned that, but there had been no getting around that once I'd decided to try my hand at settling the wind. "I've managed to make a few very simple spells work." I realized something. "Would there be anyone among your staff who could do this?"

"I have no idea. I don't know who can do what, whether they could do something like this, and I haven't got time to talk to them all. You're a Shield, and you can cast, and this is about the weather. You should be able to do this."

That wasn't actually a logical conclusion.

"Besides, getting one of the staff to do it may expose

them to the Guards," Taro pointed out. "We can claim we
did it through channeling."

I quickly read the paper. "I need four candles, fresh
mint, two hand fans, and cool water."

"I'll get everything," said Fiona, and she rushed out of
the room.

"Hand fans?" I said again.

I read the ritual. It had a short list of requirements,
thank Zaire. But it was the strange movement with the
fans that concerned me. I wasn't sure I understood the
movements correctly from what was written.

"It's like dancing," said Taro. He was reading over my
shoulder. "You're good at dancing."

"It's like no dancing I've ever done."

"I don't know. It might be like what you did during our
travels."

He was referring to the bastardization of bench dancing I'd had to do while we were exiled to Flatwell. I didn't
know that anything required by this spell was anything
like it. I feared this spell had to be seen to be learned.

I read through the ritual again and again, trying to
memorize it.

This was crazy.

Fiona returned with her hands full, dumping everything on the table.

"Where do the candles go?" Taro asked Reid, reaching
for them.

"I have to set up," I told him.

Fiona rubbed her hands together. "Shouldn't you get
started?"

"I need to know this before I do," I answered.

"Every moment he's out there is a moment he could be
killed."

"I can't help him if I can't do this correctly." Let me
read, woman.

I would have liked the chance to practice the spell a
few times, but three people were watching me read, Fiona

fidgeting all the while, and I couldn't concentrate as I should. Knowing that circumstances wouldn't change, and aware that Dane was in real danger, I put down the sheet sooner than I liked and picked up the candles.

I placed the candles on the floor in a large square. I placed the fans within the square. Then I picked up the candle Reid had been using, the mint and the water, and moved back within the square. I put the mint in my mouth and chewed it fifteen times before swallowing. "Sharpen my mind." I drank the glass of water. "Narrow my focus." I lit one of the four candles. "Winds of the north, bide by me." The second candle. "Winds of the south, bide by me." The next candle. "Winds of the east, bide by me." And the last. "Winds of the west, bide by me." I felt a strange clicking in my stomach, the strange jittering sensation, and a brushing feeling against my skin.

I picked up the fans and stood with one in each hand, down by my sides. I closed my eyes. "Bide by me, winds of all. Bide by me, winds of all. Bide by me, winds of all." The brushing against my skin grew stronger and wound around me. "I seek the wind to the west above the sea." The brushing against the right side of my body suddenly became a stronger force, nearly pushing the fan out of my hand.

The next step was to raise the fans and use them to shape the wind. But I couldn't raise my right hand. "Bide by me, winds of all," I ordered. The pressure on the right grew stronger. "Bide by me, winds of all!"

I couldn't raise my right hand. I could move my left, but that wasn't what I needed to do.

What was wrong? Had I missed a step? I imagined the paper in my hands again, going through each part of the ritual in my mind.

And the brushing and the pressure and the tingling disappeared. I had lost it all. "I have to start again," I said. "I need more mint and water."

But I had developed a crushing headache. And when I

tried the spell again, the brushing was lighter and I couldn't capture it with the fans. The third time I tried, nothing happened at all, and my headache was practically blinding me.

"I'm sorry, Fiona," I said to her. "I'm not able to do it."

She nodded rigidly. "Thank you for trying."

That was a horrible thing to hear. Gratitude for pathetic failure when someone's life might depend on success. I didn't know why I hadn't been able to do it. It had been simple. And it shouldn't have tired me so much. The other spells hadn't tired me at all.

It was frustrating. I'd been having little difficulty performing the variety of spells I'd chosen to practice in private, when it didn't matter. Now, the one time when someone had needed it, I had failed. That irritated me. I breathed deeply to stay calm as I collected the items off the floor. Why hadn't it worked?

Fiona left the library without another word, which made me feel worse. She remained secluded for the rest of the day.

We heard nothing of Dane before we went to bed that night.

I slept terribly. I woke up too early and, to avoid waking Taro, I moved to the sitting room and raised the shutter so I could stare out the window for a while.

What was I doing anyway, playing with spells? That wasn't what I was supposed to be doing. I was a Shield. All this fiddling about with rituals and poetic phrases wasn't for me.

And now there were two more people, Fiona and Reid, who knew that I was casting spells. I was sure Fiona would keep my secret, but would Reid? I had no idea. Certainly, he seemed a nice enough fellow, but not as discreet as one might like. After all, he'd shown me parts of the translated book before he'd shown Fiona. He might decide it would do no harm to tell some person, someone he trusted for no good reason, and that person might choose to tell someone else, and so on.

It might get back to the Emperor. Would he really have me flogged?

Or it might get back to the Triple S council. I didn't want that to happen, either. Whether the council believed casting was real or not wouldn't matter. They would think I was either a fool or something that needed to be contained. I really didn't want to receive any more attention from them.

Arms slid around my waist, and I smiled as I leaned back against Taro's chest. "You worry too much," he said in his rough morning voice. "And Fiona shouldn't have asked you to try that."

"She was worried. I don't blame her."

"And no one blames you for not being able to do what you're not trained to do."

"I think I forgot part of the ritual or something." And I'd been too disappointed to check. "If I'd remembered it correctly the first time, I might have been able to do something."

"They didn't give you enough time to learn the spell."

I knew that. Everything he said made sense. I still felt guilty about it.

He buried his nose in the hair behind my ear. "Stop thinking about it," he whispered, and he licked my ear.

I giggled.

Lila entered the room and curtsied. "Sir, madam, Her Ladyship wanted you to know His Lordship was killed at sea yesterday."

I put my hand over my mouth to cover the gasp. Taro tightened his grip on my waist. "How is Her Ladyship?" he asked.

"I couldn't say, sir."

I couldn't believe what I'd just heard. I pulled away from Taro and sat down. Dane couldn't be dead. I liked him.

"That's all, Lila," said Taro, and Lila left. He looked at me. "It's not your fault."

"I know." It wasn't my fault, but I could have saved him, perhaps, if I had been careful and done the spell right the first time. That was my failure, no matter what anyone said, and it was bitter.

Chapter Twenty-six

The wind picked up again. There were no warnings sounding from the Wind Watcher, but we could hear the wind itself causing the manor to creak, see branches torn off trees. It was bad enough that no one wanted to be out in it, and it felt to me like a constant reminder of Dane's death.

I couldn't believe he was dead. He had been alive just two days ago, large and smiling and kind. And what a stupid reason to die. Whaling wasn't something the Duke needed to be doing. Why had he been out there?

I should have been able to do something. I shouldn't have tried the spell. I should have used channeling. At least then I could do something. Even if the results had been unpredictable, it probably would have been enough to stop the wind.

I was driven to go to the library and get from Reid the sheet on which he had written the wind ritual. I read it over carefully. I saw, to my surprise, that I had performed the ritual correctly. "So why didn't it work?"

"Pardon?" Reid asked, looking up from his translations.

"Why didn't the ritual work?"

"Maybe you just don't have the power to make it work."

"I've been able to make other spells work." And hells, I shouldn't be admitting that out loud when there might be Guards creeping about.

"Perhaps those spells were easier."

Well, aye, they had been, but surely if I was able to perform one spell, I should have been able to perform another. "Can I have this copy of the ritual?"

"Why?"

"I want to try it again."

"This isn't the sort of thing you should be playing with."

"I'll be careful, but I want to try again."

"I'll need that back."

"I'll be sure to return it. Thank you."

Daris breezed in. She looked surprised and annoyed to see me. "Well, if it isn't our little Shield mouse," she drawled. "Creeping around listening to things not meant for her ears and interfering with things that are none of her business."

What had I done to deserve that? Well, what had I done that she knew about?

"You can go now," she said with a little wave of dismissal.

Although I had no reason to stay, her attitude annoyed me. "I am discussing something with Academic Reid."

"I'm sure the riveting details of when the road to Ursedon was built is fascinating to the two of you, but as a member of the family that hired the Academic, I have precedence. Leave now."

Really, she was annoying me, so much that I wanted to smack her. Which was a shocking reaction on my part. I was supposed to be calm in the face of trivial annoyances. And that, more than anything else, kept me from arguing further. "Thank you for your assistance, Academic." I gave Daris my brightest smile. "Have a wonderful day."

So I left the room, but I didn't go far. It was childish and rude of me, but I lingered by the door, out of sight of the occupants of the library. It was none of my business, true, but Fiona was going through a horrible time and she didn't need to be taking any abuse from her drunkard of a sister. If I could warn her of any upcoming problems, I would. It was my duty as her guest.

"What is this book about?" I heard Daris ask.

"I have not yet given Her Grace my report."

"You are to give that report to me first."

"With forgiveness, you are not the person who retained me."

"You do not seem to understand that I can bring you benefits or I can make your life very difficult."

"I have no doubt, but that is irrelevant. I have a duty to the Duchess, and I will not breach it."

I realized, belatedly, that I admired Reid, in a manner different from that which I had felt before I'd met him. He tended to blush easily, but he clearly had a spine. Daris struck me as the truly weak one. She resented Fiona for having the title and seemed to want nothing else. What had been her goal before Fiona had the duchy? Maybe she hadn't had any. Or had she craved Fiona's original title as well?

Huh. So this was the second time Daris had been ignored in favor of her younger sister. That had to sting.

Feeling assured that Reid could handle Daris, I stopped skulking about, eavesdropping in the hall. I returned to my suite, where Taro was playing with a deck of cards, his boredom evident in his slow, languid movements. "What do you think of Daris?" I asked him.

"She's a weak, useless parasite."

That kind of shocked me. "That's a little strong." Not that I really disagreed, but Taro was usually a bit more delicate.

"She does nothing."

"Most aristocrats could be accused of that."

"No, she does even less."

"Really?"

"So they say. She just drinks and sleeps around. So does Tarce, but he's harmless. He isn't trying to betray Fiona."

"I just overheard her trying to get information out of Reid. I don't know what she thinks that book has that will help her."

Taro snickered and then he sneered. "She's just trying to search out every angle."

"What do you mean?"

"She's rolling every die every which way to see what turns up."

"Meaning that Reid and the book are not the only avenues she's pursuing."

"Aye."

I crossed my arms. "How do you know that?"

He froze, briefly, in the act of turning over a card. "It's what I've heard."

If it hadn't been for that guilty little hesitation, I would have taken him at his word. "Really?"

"Aye."

"I think you have more immediate knowledge than that."

Taro just kept turning over cards.

That he wasn't denying it, that he wasn't frowning at me in confusion, told me I was on to something. "The less you say, the more I'll imagine."

"What's that supposed to mean?"

"I'll assume the worst." Really, I didn't even know what to assume. I just knew something was going on.

He scowled. "She said she was prepared to make it worth my while to reconsider abjuring the title," he finally admitted.

That wasn't so bad, I supposed, but it was kind of stupid. "What is it with these people? Surely she knows that's impossible."

"Apparently not."

"Do you think she's in league with your mother?"

He snickered. "No."

"Why was that a ridiculous thing to suggest?"

"Her Grace would have nothing to do with someone like her."

I didn't know about that. The Dowager associated with that Simone woman, housed her and encouraged her schemes, and Simone seemed no better than Daris.

"How would your getting the title back benefit her?"

He looked down at his cards and muttered something unintelligible.

"What?"

He heaved a big sigh and looked up at me, an expression of resignation on his face. "She offered to marry me."

I stared at him. "What?"

"You heard me."

She offered to marry him? Bitch! The nature of the relationship between Taro and me was obvious to everyone in the manor. How dared she try to interfere with that? "When did this start?"

"Pretty much when I got here."

I couldn't believe what I was hearing. "All of this hassle you've been giving me over Reid and you've been—you've been—" I didn't know how to put it. "You've been having meetings with Daris!"

"I have not!" he flared. "And it's not the same thing! I have no interest in Daris."

I just raised my eyebrows at him. How come that argument wasn't valid when I used it?

I didn't know if he could read my expression, or if he'd figured out on his own that his argument was lame, but he clearly felt compelled to add, "There's nothing appealing about Daris."

That, I thought, was pushing it too hard. "She's beautiful." If one liked that sort of look.

"She's an avaricious, small-minded inebriate." He looked at me in a challenge. "Reid is an academic."

"So it's inevitable that I'm going to sleep with him?" That was ridiculous. Sure, I liked smart people, but just because I met one didn't mean I was going to think Taro was somehow inadequate.

"I never said that," he protested.

"Why else have you been acting so strangely around him?"

He crossed his arms. "I haven't."

"You can't possibly believe that."

He said nothing.

I rolled my eyes. He wasn't going to admit he was wrong, and I knew I was right. There was no point in arguing further so I let it slide. I stared into air while Taro flipped over cards.

In time he asked, "What are you thinking?"

"I performed that wind ritual properly. It should have worked."

"Stop worrying about it."

He might as well have told me to stop breathing. "Dane died because I couldn't do it."

"That's not your fault."

"It's more my fault than anyone else's."

"It's no one's fault."

But I was the one with the opportunity to do something about it. And I'd failed. "I'm going to try it again."

"Why?"

"Why not?"

"I thought you didn't like playing around with that sort of thing."

I snapped my fingers, suddenly struck with a brilliant idea.

"This can't be good," said Taro.

"Reid has theorized that there might be a connection between Sources and Shields and magic."

"You're the one who keeps saying that what we do isn't magic."

"It's not, but that doesn't mean they can't work together."

"What are you talking about?"

When I'd attempted to manipulate the weather in the past, it had been through Taro, him channeling and me adjusting the currents through him. I couldn't control the elements as much as I felt I needed. When I tried the spell, I had the potential for control, but couldn't access the winds as I would have liked. So what would happen if I combined the two procedures?

It couldn't hurt to try.

Doing the spell while Shielding would be challenging but I was sure I could do it. "Will you channel for me so I can play with this?"

He shrugged. "Sure."

It helped that he had little to do, too.

I got the ingredients, the mint and the water and the candles and the fans. I locked the door. I chewed the mint and lit the candles and stood within them with the fans in my hands. "All right," I said to Taro, "please start channeling."

He opened himself to the forces. At the same time, while I was Shielding him, I went through the same steps of the spell I had before. I felt the same brushing against my skin I had felt before. It was stronger against my right than it had been before, but this time I could lift my right hand and shape the wind with my fans.

And suddenly, I was surrounded in fog. I hadn't expected that and it almost knocked away my concentration. Within the fog swirled tendrils of translucent blue. When I touched them with my fans, they shifted, and as they shifted, so did the wind rattling the shutters. "Bide by me, winds of all," I said, and with the fans held parallel to the floor, I crouched down and brought my fans lower and lower. There was pressure there, pushing against me, but I proved to be stronger. I was eventually able to lay the fans flat on the floor.

"Stop channeling," I said to Taro, and he did.

There was silence. The wind was gone.

"You did it." Taro sounded surprised. I guessed I couldn't blame him. After all, I hadn't been able to do it the last time. When it would have mattered.

Poor Fiona.

Was this why spells hadn't worked for the First Landed? Did one need to be part of a Pair to do it?

Of course, there were regulars who seemed able to perform spells. Maybe they could cast spells concerning the weather. Or maybe there was something about being a Shield or a Source that meant they had to have a partner when casting spells that affected the weather. But there were people who cast spells in High Scape, and if anyone had tried to adjust the horrific weather of the Harsh Summer, they hadn't appeared to be successful.

I didn't know. Didn't really care. I wouldn't be playing with the weather much. But my success gave me another idea. "I have to talk to Reid," I announced as I locked up the casting paraphernalia. Taro scowled. "It's important," I insisted, and I left before he could say anything, heading back to the library.

Reid, as I'd hoped, was still there.

"Can I take it you were successful?" he asked.

"Unbelievable, isn't it?"

"I wonder why it worked this time."

I wasn't going to tell him of Taro's involvement. Taro might not like it. "Maybe I was able to concentrate better because no one's life was at stake." Why hadn't I thought to work with Taro the first time? We always accomplished more when we worked together. "Are there any spells about calming earthquakes in that book?"

"They had spells for all natural disasters, from what I

can see. But what use would you have for something like that? You and Source Karish already know how to deal with those."

And I wanted him to keep believing that. "It behooves us to learn everything we can about such things."

"Behooves," he echoed, and I could see I hadn't fooled him at all. "Earthquakes, you say?"

"Aye."

"I'll make a copy for you."

"Thank you, Academic. I am most grateful."

Wouldn't it be marvelous if I'd found the solution to the difficulty we were having with channeling? Not that I wanted to stay in Flown Raven, but the idea of being driven out because of an inability to perform our tasks had a bitter taste I was eager to expel.

Chapter Twenty-seven

I jerked awake at the sound of a sharp thud, followed by footsteps running down the hall.

It was dark and cold and the wind was rattling the windows. Again.

"Come back here!" I heard Fiona shout.

A second set of footsteps thundered down the hall.

I scrambled out of bed, aware that Taro was doing the same. We raced to the door and out into the hall. But neither of us had thought to bring a candle and we couldn't see anything.

Tarce was smarter than Taro and I, coming out to the hall with a lit lantern, and we followed the footsteps and Fiona's shouts through the halls and down the stairs. In the dark I felt like we were going in circles, and I could hear other voices and footsteps. It was a chaotic chase, the candlelight bouncing against the wood paneling of the walls, and I thought the whole time that I would tumble down the stairs.

Someone started screaming. I didn't know who the hell

it was. I just wished they would shut up. They were add-
ing to the confusion.

Tarce, Taro and I, as well as Bailey and Frances, ended
up in the kitchen. A dangerous place to be in the dark. It
was so unfamiliar to me, and I knocked my hip against the
corner of one of the tables. That hurt.

Fiona was out the back door of the kitchen, and she
was still shouting. "I know who you are! I'll find you!"

"For Zaire's sake, Fiona!" Tarce snapped. "What's
going on?"

We heard nothing from Fiona, so the five of us traipsed
out into the grass, cold and wet against our bare feet. The
wind was fierce and bitter. The moonlight showed us
Fiona standing there in her nightgown, staring off into the
distance.

"Fiona!" Tarce barked.

Fiona turned around, her hair down and whipping
about in the wind, her nightgown plastered against her
legs and torso. "Did you see her?" she demanded.

"We didn't see anything," said Tarce.

"She attacked me in my room. I woke up and someone
was moving around beside me. She tried to kill me."

"Who was it?"

"I don't know. I couldn't see anything. Some woman."

Hell, nothing was going right for Fiona. It was just one
disaster after another. If I were her, I would be about ready
to give up.

I heard Taro's teeth chattering. It was freezing out there
in the wet wind.

"Come inside, Fi," said Tarce, reaching for her arm.

Fiona stepped out of reach. "She's out here."

"We won't be able to find her in the dark."

"We'll lose her."

"We've already lost her," said Tarce. "Come inside.
Let us take a look at you." He reached out and grabbed
her arm.

She hissed and yanked her arm back. "Don't!"

"Get inside, Fiona."

It wasn't until we were back in the kitchen with some more candles lit that we saw that the shadows on her sleeves were streaks of blood soaking through the white fabric. "You're bleeding!" Taro announced in shock.

"What the hell happened?" Tarce demanded.

"She had a knife," Fiona said, and her voice sounded calmer than it had earlier. That had to be a good sign. "She was trying to kill me. I got my arms up in time and tried to catch her, but I was tangled up in my bedclothes and she got away from me."

"And you didn't see anything?" Tarce asked. "Or hear anything?"

"Just that it was a smaller person, someone not able to overpower me. A woman, I think."

"I'm going to fetch the healer," said Tarce.

"Not in the middle of the night, Tarce," Fiona objected.

"Don't be stupid. You're bleeding. Go up to your room and get comfortable. Shintaro, Dunleavy, I'd appreciate it if you would stay with her to discourage any second attempts."

"Of course," said Taro.

"Bailey, I want you to check all the servants' quarters to see if anyone's missing."

"Yes, my lord."

"It isn't one of our people," Fiona protested.

"You don't know that, and we might as well cross off that possibility if we can."

"You realize that if it were one of the servants," I said, "they'd have had time to circle back to one of the other entrances and get back upstairs in time for Bailey to find them."

Tarce glared at me for pointing out the truth. There were times when the truth was unwelcome. Bailey left at a quick pace. Perhaps he would be able to catch someone getting back into bed. Tarce left, too, which left Taro and me to figure out what to do about Fiona.

"Let's get you back to your room," Taro said to Fiona.

"I'm not hiding in my room!" she snapped. "I'm finding the woman who did this!"

"Bailey's looking for her."

"None of our people would do this."

"If it's an outsider, we won't find her tonight."

I was thinking it would have to be a servant, or a servant would have to be involved, to know exactly where Fiona slept, but that was probably another truth no one wanted to hear.

"We will if we go from cottage to cottage and catch them in the act of bedding down," Fiona persisted.

"They've already bedded down by now, or they will have by the time we get there. Please, Fiona, be sensible. You're bleeding."

Fiona whirled on me. "Why can't you find her?" she demanded. "Use one of your spells."

"I haven't come across spells that find people. That's not what I do, Fiona."

"That's not what you do," she sneered. "You and Shintaro. He's just a Source and you're just a Shield and that's all anyone can ask of you. The rest of us don't have the luxury of being only one thing."

"Perhaps, but that doesn't change the fact that I can't use a spell to help you." And I wished I could. Fiona didn't deserve this.

"I'm going to have to insist, Fiona," said Taro. "If you faint down here, you'll have to be carried to your room. You don't want the servants to see that, do you?"

"I'm not going to faint," Fiona muttered.

"You don't want to risk it, do you? Blood loss can have unpredictable effects."

Either Fiona was convinced by Taro's argument or she was simply in too much physical discomfort to continue to debate the issue, but she allowed herself to be prodded into movement and escorted up to her room.

There was no screaming now, the silence broken only by the wailing of the wind. "I don't understand why all the servants aren't up and about," I said, "with all that racket."

"They don't want to risk catching the bad luck," Frances said in a hushed tone.

"Don't be foolish, Frances," Taro snapped. "I'm sure they merely wanted to avoid getting in the way. And I'm sure the healer will need some clean water. Please go fetch some."

Frances drew herself up to her full insignificant height. "I don't take orders from you."

"Frances," Fiona interjected in a soothing voice. "Please do as he asks."

Frances sniffed and glared before she left, muttering none too quietly about how some people just didn't know their place. I didn't know servants were allowed to do that sort of thing.

"Let me look at you," Taro said to Fiona.

"Do you know anything about healing knife wounds?" she demanded.

"No."

"Then you keep your eyes and your hands to yourself."

The thought of a knife sinking into her arms, the image of steel separating red flesh, made my stomach clench in disgust. Still, the way Fiona was moving and talking, it seemed the injuries were not severe. So there was no reason for Taro to be fiddling around in there.

"The room is clean," she whispered. "He promised the room was clean. This doesn't make sense."

"I don't understand," Taro confessed.

"Your room was bringing the bad luck," Fiona said in a loud voice, and she almost sounded as though she were accusing him of something. "Cleansing it was supposed to end it."

That was what she thought this was about? "This wasn't because of bad luck, Fiona."

"Of course it is. It's just another bead in the string with the fall and the cave and the wind and Dane."

"Dane was bad luck," I said. "But the rest of it is all because someone's been trying to kill you." I couldn't believe none of us had thought of that earlier. All those accidents, it was unrealistic to think they were just a series of unplanned mishaps.

"I don't think this is what Fiona needs to be hearing right now, Lee," Taro chided me.

"Of course she does. She needs to be prepared. Whoever is doing this has moved from trying to make her death look accidental to not giving a damn what things look like. That can't be good."

"Shut up!" Taro hissed.

"I'm cold," Fiona said, her voice suddenly sounding a little slurred.

"Let me rip the sleeves off your nightgown, Fiona, before the blood dries them to your arms."

"All right," Fiona said, still sounding slurred.

Taro carefully picked at the tears of her sleeve and ripped it up to the seam at her shoulder. There the tear ended, and after a few solid tugs Taro wasn't able to tear any further. He settled for making sure the various cuts were clear of all material.

I couldn't help myself. I had to take a look. It was difficult to tell in nothing more than dim candlelight, but the cuts weren't nearly as deep as I'd feared. I was sure they hurt like hell, though.

Frances returned with a jug of water and some towels over her arm. "Thank you, sir, ma'am, for staying with Her Grace. I shall look after her now."

"I will wait for Healer Browne to come," I said.

"Her Grace would be more comfortable with privacy," she argued.

"Lord Tarce asked us to remain until he returned, and so we shall." She wasn't going to drag us out by the arms and we all knew it.

So we waited. Fiona had gone silent and drowsy, speaking only to say she was cold. Frances had her lie out on a settee and covered her with a duvet, making sure her arms rested above it.

I was trying to figure who was attempting to kill Fiona. I couldn't see why anyone would, really. She was such a thoroughly decent person, I couldn't believe she had somehow earned anyone's murderous rage. True, I didn't know her well, and neither did Taro. I, in particular, was a terrible judge of character.

So, if she didn't garner such anger due to her actions or her personality, the next logical reason was her position. Someone thought they would benefit from her death, by having the title left open. And the first choice to come to mind for that motive was Taro's mother.

It made a sort of sense. She had been hinting that there was a possibility of removing Fiona from the title so that Taro, in her twisted reasoning, could claim it. She had tried to convince Taro to act out against Fiona. She had arranged for that stupid test that could have killed Fiona.

However, although hers was the first name to come to mind, I couldn't see her actually hiring someone—and someone would have to be hired; she wouldn't do it herself—to murder Fiona. It seemed too dirty for her. She seemed to take only the actions that could be cloaked in tradition or political maneuvering. Surely, if she had ordered the death of a person as important as the titleholder of Flown Raven, the Emperor would have to see even her properly punished.

Who else would benefit from the death of the titleholder?

Well, there were those among her people who probably thought they would. But it was a difficult thing for a person to bring themselves to kill one of the High Landed, no matter how much they hated or resented them. They would know they would get the harshest sanctions possible. Besides, it was unlikely that the tenants would know

Fiona's schedule and movements, or that they would be able to move about the manor unnoticed.

And really, why would a tenant murder a titleholder? They had no reason to believe the next titleholder would be any better for them.

Which brought me to Daris. She lived in the manor. She would know where Fiona was at all times and she could go wherever she wished. And she hadn't come out in the hall after all that racket.

Of course, if she were drunk, she might not have heard it. And she wouldn't benefit from Fiona's death. I had no doubt that Stacin had already been designated as Fiona's heir.

But then, Stacin was far too young to act as titleholder. Until he reached his majority, someone else would have to act as titleholder on his behalf. And that person, that trustee, would have complete control over Stacin, could mold him, could possibly raise him to be nothing more than a spineless face to hide the real power.

I'd never thought of that. That was a possibility Daris would consider. I had no idea whether Daris was capable of killing her sister or not.

Tarce and Browne finally arrived. Taro and I lingered outside Fiona's suite waiting to hear word of the extent of her injuries. I whispered to Taro my suspicions, even about his mother.

"I really doubt the Dowager is so crazy as to try murder, Lee," Taro said dryly.

"Then who do you think it is?"

"I have no idea. I can't see one of the tenants doing it. I can't see Daris having the wherewithal to do it."

"She's not drunk all the time. On the other hand, she might have had to be drunk to come up with something so stupid."

"It's probably someone we know nothing about."

"We have to do something."

"There's nothing we can do except keep our eyes

and ears open and tell Fiona of anything we think is strange."

Poor Fiona. Her husband dead, someone trying to kill her, unable to rely on her own family for support. Except Tarce, maybe, but he really didn't seem the most supportive of people, either.

In time, Browne left the suite, and she told us that while multiple cuts had been inflicted, most of them were shallow, and only two of them had required stitches. Tarce didn't come out, and it seemed there was nothing more Taro and I could do, so we went back to bed.

But I didn't sleep. I lay in bed, stared at the ceiling, and listened for footsteps. There was a would-be murderer in the manor. They were going to try again.

Chapter Twenty-eight

At sunrise, I could hear the wind wailing and the rain hitting the window. I wondered if there was something of a windy, rainy season in Flown Raven. I lay in bed and listened to the mournful noise and tried not to let it depress my mood. It wasn't a felicitous way to wake up.

It did, however, prompt me to rise and take some spell-casting supplies from the overmantel. I sat on the floor and put the ingredients in small bags to more easily pack into my purse. There had been a spell to stop earthquakes in the book Reid was studying. There were spells for each natural disaster, but given the nature of the events that were striking Flown Raven, I'd focused my attention on the spell for earthquakes. I couldn't easily carry all the supplies needed for all the spells.

I hadn't had a chance to practice the earthquake spell, of course, but I had memorized it. That was all I could do to prepare. That and assemble the ingredients needed for the spell. The next time we channeled, I would be ready.

Taro strode back into the bedroom from our sitting

room, still dressed in his nightgown. "Miserable place," he muttered, flinging himself into a chair. "Miserable weather and nothing to do."

"Well, you'll have to get used to it. We're stuck here for at least a few years."

"I don't want to get used to it."

That was particularly childish of him. I just looked at him without speaking.

He sighed. "What are you doing?"

"These are things I need for a spell to calm earthquakes. I told you about it."

"I don't like the idea of you using a spell to channel."

"I have to do something. I can't let things continue as they are."

"I don't like it. It's unnatural."

There were those who felt everything we did was unnatural. "It's either this or I'm telling the council we can't channel here."

"Whether I like it or not."

"Whether you like it or not. Our pride is not as important as our safety and the safety of everyone who lives here."

He offered up a bent smile. "I can't see you admitting that there is something you can't do."

"What's that supposed to mean?" There were lots of things I couldn't do. I knew that. "I can admit when I can't do something."

"Uh-huh." He sat down in front of me and rested one of my bare feet on his lap, rubbing my sole with his thumb. "I wonder if we were sent here because I chose Fiona as the titleholder."

"What would one have to do with the other?"

"I don't know. But the Dowager wanted me here as the titleholder, and the Emperor was agreeable to that, even though it would take breaking the law to accomplish. I made that impossible by choosing Fiona. Fiona refuses to do what the Dowager demands, refuses to do what the

Emperor orders. And the next time we turn around, we're sent here when Triple S policy says we shouldn't be. And the Dowager is telling me I could still have the title. Would she still be telling me that if I chose a titleholder more open to her influence?"

I shrugged, but I wondered if he didn't have a point. Maybe his mother merely wanted a puppet in the title. I didn't know why she thought Taro was likely to be that puppet, but I didn't really understand anything about the Dowager.

"And did the Emperor really tell her I could still have the title?" Taro went on. "Or is she just claiming he has?"

"There is no way for us to know."

"Except that he did send us here, and it wasn't to reward me for anything, no matter what he's said in that regard."

"But why would he want you here? Why would he even care?"

"Unless it's some kind of favor to the Dowager." He grimaced.

"What connection could there be between the two of them?"

"I shudder to think." And he actually shuddered.

"You're sending my mind to unwelcome places, Taro."

"Good. It can keep mine company."

"I don't want to try to figure out what your mother and the Emperor are up to." Largely because I thought it was a waste of time. I didn't know either of them well enough, and I didn't think Taro did, either. "It doesn't matter anyway. The Triple S doesn't like the idea of our being out here. It's only a matter of time before we're transferred."

He cocked an eyebrow. "You show enormous faith in the council."

Actually, I didn't know what to think of the council. Sometimes I thought that, of course, they would protect their interests, as they had done for centuries. At other times, I felt their power relied entirely on the respect of others, and if the Emperor felt no respect for them, they were helpless.

Taro had stopped rubbing my feet. I tapped his hand with my toes to remind him of what he was supposed to be doing. "It can't be good for them to have an Emperor who feels he can do what he likes with us," I said.

"I'd rather they didn't make us the example for some kind of struggle between the two of them. I want us to be forgotten."

"Even if it means we're left here for however long the Emperor wants us here?" I didn't want that. I didn't want to spend the rest of my life in Flown Raven. I didn't think it was good for Taro.

He frowned. "I don't know what would be best, to be honest."

This was ridiculous. We weren't supposed to matter to anyone beyond being just another Pair. And that was all we were, wasn't it? We were good at what we did, but so were other Pairs, and there was no reason for us to have any significance beyond the roles of Source and Shield. That we meant anything to people like the Dowager and the Emperor, that they were engaged in some kind of plan for us, was a ludicrous idea. "We're probably finding schemes in smoke," I said.

"You're probably right," he answered.

And neither of us really believed that.

Lila walked in with a large tray. "I have tea and coffee, sir, ma'am."

"Thank you, Lila," I said, pulling my foot from Taro's lap. I was feeling less embarrassed by being interrupted by her all the time. I was getting used to it, I supposed. "How is Her Grace this morning?"

"She appears hearty, ma'am." She curtsied and left.

Now, Fiona was someone with real problems. Someone was trying to kill her and there was no way of figuring out who. I couldn't imagine what that must feel like.

I felt Taro's protections fall. I put up my Shields as I jumped to my feet and pulled out my purse, dumping all the ingredients onto the bed.

This would be the test. Could I perform this spell while channeling? I'd done it once before, but then my eyes weren't filled with water and my mouth with salt.

I poured hanan powder, dark orange, on my left inner wrist. "Soil to obey me." I poured white icin powder on top, and rubbed it in. "Air to subdue soil." I opened a vial of whale oil and poured it on top. "Soothe the waters." I took out a red-bladed knife, procured from Browne. "I call to you all." I slid the knife lightly over my wrist, calling up the slightest trace of blood. "Bide by me." I picked up a pinch of soil and put it in the palm of my hand, curling my hand into a fist. "I hold the soil still. Soil trembles no more. Bide by me."

Something whirled in my stomach and flooded it into my mind. From there it rushed through me and into Taro.

I heard him gasp. "What the hell is that?" he demanded.

"Don't worry about it," I said, though I didn't know what I was talking about. Maybe it was something to worry about.

"Something is happening."

It was. I could feel it. The forces whipping through him slowed a little, and the pressure on my Shields lessened. So did the salt in my nose and throat and eyes. This enabled me to concentrate more thoroughly as I repeated the words of the spell.

The force from within me roared into unprecedented strength, flowing from me to Taro and then beyond. I could practically see it, watching it soaking into the soil, pressing hard into it. It felt strange, like my mind was being stretched beyond the limits of my skull. It was a little frightening.

But I felt no tremors.

It still took longer than I liked, but at no point did I fear I would lose control and fail Taro. I felt Taro manipulate the forces and for the first time in a long while, I didn't worry about how things would end.

And then everything stopped. Taro erected his own protections and I removed mine.

We stared at each other, gasping for breath. That had been weird. "I don't know that I like that," said Taro.

"If it keeps us and everyone else alive while we're here, I'm going to keep doing it. Maybe it will feel less strange in time." I was so relieved. I had found a way to make channeling in Flown Raven effective and bearable.

Taro was scowling.

"What's wrong?" I asked.

"Maybe you should be the Source," he muttered. "You don't need me for anything, do you?"

I stopped myself from sighing. "The spell doesn't seem to work without a Source."

"How kind of you to say so," he said bitterly.

Ah, the hell with patience. "Taro, I know it's hard for you to be here, but you can't wear it on your skin like this. You don't want to admit you're having trouble with channeling. You feel this ridiculous resentment for Reid. You—"

"It's not ridiculous!" he snapped.

Again, I just looked at him.

"He's so smart," he complained. "You have so much more to talk about with him than you do with me."

"I do enjoy talking with him. There's nothing wrong with that. Just because you and I love each other doesn't mean we have to be all things to each other."

His eyebrows rose. "You've never said you loved me."

I frowned. "I must have."

Looking amused, he shook his head.

"Oh. Well. I do. Love you."

"Be still my heart, you romantic, you."

A huge, groaning crack rent the air. I'd never heard anything like it, and it made the hair on the back of my neck stand up and sent a shiver up my back.

"What the hell was that?" Taro exclaimed. He went to the window, pushing at the wooden shutter. At first it resisted his efforts, and then it was flung up, letting in a blistery wet gale.

"Can you see anything?" I asked.

He backed away from the window. "Just a face full of rain." He reached out to pull the shutter closed, and he was half-drenched by the time he managed it.

"Rain and wind don't make that kind of noise."

Something made that kind of noise again as we quickly dressed. It was a horrible, frightening sound, and I found myself breathing faster in reaction to it. We left our suite in search of Fiona, trying first her suite, then the nursery, and then the sitting room. We finally found her in the kitchen, dressed in a slicker and boots, speaking in whispers with Bailey and Tarce, who were similarly dressed.

"We have to wait until we know it's stopped," was her greeting to us.

"What is it?" Taro asked her.

"It's the ridge. It's shifting or collapsing or something. Bailey, round up everyone and have them dressed for outside," Fiona ordered. "Tarce, go to every cottage in the village and bring every able-bodied person to the garden."

"There'll be objections to being out in this weather," said Tarce.

"Too damn bad. We need them to clean up the mess this could turn into."

"What do you think this might turn into?" I asked.

"I don't know!" she snapped.

I thought it a valid question. What was happening out there? Why did we need to do anything?

But apparently we needed slickers, and when Lila showed up, Taro asked her to find some for us.

The groaning sounds continued, joined by a horrible

grinding. It seemed like I could feel it, in the back of my teeth, and my mind developed images of the ridge tearing apart. Was that what was happening? Why? If it wasn't a natural disaster, what could be causing it?

"Isn't there something you can do about this?" Fiona hissed at Taro.

"No, damn it! I don't know what's causing this. For all I know, it's the result of one of the earthquakes that hit before we were posted here."

"It wouldn't take this long to happen."

"It's rock. It's heavy. Who knows how it reacts and how long it takes?"

"There are people who live on the other side of that ridge, Shintaro!"

"There is nothing I can do!"

Was there really not? He could move soil with amazing precision. The ridge was stone, which was a form of soil, wasn't it? Why couldn't he stop the ridge from doing whatever it was doing?

But I didn't want to ask that in front of Fiona. She didn't know about Taro's other talents. And I had to assume Taro had already considered whether he would be able to do anything or not. I was pretty sure he would be willing to reveal his secrets, if he had to, to help people, if he could. He had in the past.

I didn't know how long we stood and listened to the groaning of the ridge. It felt like an hour, at least, and all the servants were collected in the kitchen waiting for Fiona's next order. Even the Guards had shown up, dressed to help. I was surprised to see them, though I supposed I shouldn't have been. Just because I didn't like them didn't mean they weren't decent enough human beings.

There was a pounding on the kitchen door. Fiona yanked it open. I didn't recognize the woman standing out in the rain, but she wore a whaler's slicker. "There are people buried under the slides," she announced.

Fiona may have wanted to wait longer, to make sure

the ridge had actually settled before venturing out over it—I know I wanted to—but there was no sign of indecision about her expression as she nodded. "The healer shall choose who will assist her with the wounded. Everyone else follows me through the ridge. We don't stop until everyone's accounted for."

Everyone's accounted for. Not, until we save everyone.

We filed out into the rain. I heard Browne call out a handful of names. I wasn't among them, of course. We were joined by tenants as we moved through the gardens behind the house. There weren't as many as I expected, even taking out the children and those who had remained behind to watch them.

When we reached the ridge, we met our first obstacle. The pathway through the ridge was filled with jagged slabs of rock. There was no way through or around them.

"You climbed over that?" Fiona asked the whaler. The whaler nodded. "All right, everyone up and over."

"No!" one of the maids objected. "You can't ask that of us! We'll kill ourselves."

Fiona didn't even look at her. "Climb or find another position without a recommendation from me." And with those words, she began the ascent.

I shared the maid's unease. This was not a solid pile we were climbing. While the slabs were small enough that we were not scaling a sheer surface, it was not a settled pile of rocks, either. The surfaces shifted beneath our feet and every time they did, my heart jumped into my throat. While the pile didn't reach the top of the ridge, it was high enough that my legs were aching and my palms were raw by the time I reached the top, and the climb down the other side was just as strenuous as the scale up had been.

There were already people working on moving rocks, and the groups pointed out the areas of devastation. A huge portion of the ridge looked like it had been gouged out by some external force, the rock sliding down to the base and tearing away the work and residential structures with them. Already, injured people were being strapped to hastily structured stretchers for transport over the pile blocking the path. Getting them to Browne was going to be a hell of a job.

"Roshni," Tarce muttered, and he was running off toward the Wind Watcher's tower. I ran after him, my mind full of images of Radia's delicate form crushed under jagged rocks.

Running on uneven rock was difficult. The rain didn't help.

The tower had tumbled to pieces like a child's stack of blocks, the warning slab knocked clean over. Both such solid structures, it should have been impossible to damage them. Three people were already working on shifting the rock, using lengths of wood and long iron tools I didn't recognize.

"Give me that!" Tarce grabbed one of those iron tools from the woman who wielded it. "Roshni? Roshni!"

"We've been calling for her, milord," the woman said. "Haven't heard nothing yet."

"Does anyone know what floor she was on?" I asked.

"What does that matter?" Tarce snapped.

"It'll tell us where to dig."

"We've been digging at the base," the woman said. "That's been the deepest part."

"That's probably where she'd be at this time of day."

"She might have been in bed," I objected, but no one listened to me.

Tarce shoved the iron under a stone and pushed on it.

The woman left to get another iron rod, and I followed to get one of my own. They were long and heavy and difficult to manipulate in the rain. The iron bar wasn't designed to be a lever. Forcing it under a rock was a challenge, and I wasn't strong enough to shift any rock on my own. It took three of us to shift and push a single rock out of the way.

I felt the ridiculous urge to shout out at Radia, to tell

her we were getting to her. I couldn't imagine what it felt like to be buried under rock, possibly in agony, waiting for rescue. If she was even alive.

She'd better be alive. I didn't know how well I could balance the death of another person I knew and liked, so soon after Dane.

But it was grueling work, and I didn't have the stamina to toil at it for long. Others came to join us, and we worked in shifts. I was ashamed that everyone could work longer and with more vigor than I. I wouldn't have thought my life was so sedentary, but the insides of my fingers were sore from rubbing against the iron, and every muscle from my hands, arms and shoulders to the small of my back was screaming.

And it seemed we accomplished little for all of our efforts. That we couldn't even be sure we were digging in the right place added to my general anxiety. I wanted to call others to help us, to get us moving faster, but everywhere I looked, people were either digging in their own areas or getting the injured back over the ridge.

Had I somehow caused this, either by refusing to let Taro channel Flown Raven's events while we were still in High Scape, or by my meddling with a spell earlier that morning?

I attacked the next stone with renewed vigor.

In time, we seemed to have moved a substantial amount of stone. At least, I was recognizing wood and stone from the structure, rather than what had slid down from the ridge. Those items were smaller and more regularly shaped, and therefore more easily moved. It was encouraging, and we moved faster.

"Radia?" I called. I couldn't help it. I had been holding it in for hours. "Can you hear us?"

There was no answer.

More material was cleared away. The ceiling of the lower floor had collapsed in a relatively large piece and at something of a slant. An axe was brought in and Tarce tried to insist on wielding it himself, but he was tired and clumsy with it, and a whaler took it from him and turned the ceiling into kindling.

Radia was curled up in a corner that had partially withstood the onslaught. Her left leg was crushed under a rock, and she was unconscious. She didn't stir as the rock was removed from her leg. Tarce knelt beside her, putting his face close to hers. "She's breathing," he announced.

Oh, thank gods. Thank gods. That would have been so wrong.

I couldn't believe she had survived this. It seemed an impossible chance.

Of course, she still might not. Despite gentle attempts to rouse her, she didn't wake, and she remained unconscious as her leg was freed and she was strapped to a stretcher.

I expected Tarce to follow her back to the manor. He did not. After determining there had been no one else in the tower, Tarce ordered us to other groups, joining one himself. No one's day was over yet.

Chapter Twenty-nine

The rain finally stopped, which was one good thing to happen for us. Another was that the children had all been at the school in the village, so there were no small bodies to pull out of the rubble. But it was a grim, disheartening business finding the dead beneath the layers of rock. We found survivors as well, but those incidents decreased as time wore on, and our strength flagged.

I was so, so exhausted, and I didn't know if I was even doing any good. I left my group to drink some water from a cauldron that had been set up near the shore for that purpose. I drank down a couple of cupfuls in hands shaking and chapped from my labors.

Taro was able to sneak up beside me without my noticing, but I was too tired to jump when he said, "How are you doing?"

"I'm pretty useless right now."

"Aye, me, too. As is everyone else, from the looks of it."

"How do we know if we've got everyone?" I asked.

"What if people buried underneath have no one above-ground to say they're still missing?"

"We're not going to find everyone," Taro said.

"We have to."

"It's not possible. Look at this mess. We are not able to shift it all."

I glanced around and saw no one else close enough to hear us. Still, I whispered as I asked, "There's really nothing you can do?"

He just glared at me. I supposed that had to be answer enough.

I looked at the groups still working on the rocks, knowing I had to get back to them and wondering how I possibly could. My limbs felt like noodles, my back was a mass of knots, my clothes were soaked with sweat and rain, and my eyes were rolling in grit.

I saw a figure far along the shore, walking away from where the groups were working and toward the bend in the ridge. "Is that Lila?" She was carrying a shovel. As far as I knew, there was nothing to dig around the bend.

Taro turned. "Where is she going?"

"I don't know."

"Are there more rock slides around there?"

"Really don't know."

"Let's go check. It's out of view. If we didn't notice, maybe most others didn't, either. Our help might be needed."

I really didn't know if I'd be of any use to anyone, but a bit of a walk might give me enough of a break and loosen enough muscles to accomplish something when I went back to work. So I nodded and we started after Lila.

What a mess. Really. Fiona didn't need this. A disaster to join the string of incidents that the tenants felt she was responsible for. People had died, and grief easily turned to anger. I had no doubt there would be those who would blame Fiona for this as well.

What would they do, if they got angry enough? Were

there other challenges like the retesting that they could force Fiona to meet? Would they just leave? Could they leave?

Maybe it would be better if they did leave. Then new people could move in, people who didn't have preconceived notions of who should be the titleholder, people who could support Fiona in the manner she deserved.

We took the bend. There were no groups working on rocks beyond it. None that I saw. Of course, my attention was pretty thoroughly absorbed by the sight of Lila swinging a shovel at Fiona.

Fiona ducked and made a grab for the shovel, but missed. Lila swung again, aiming for Fiona's head.

Taro started running at them. I followed, but slowly, too tired for more than a light jog.

Fiona, I would have thought, should have been able to stop Lila, shovel or no. But Fiona was clearly exhausted, and Lila moved as though she were at full strength. I couldn't remember seeing her with any of the groups I'd worked with. That didn't mean she hadn't done any work, but she certainly looked like she was full of zeal.

And Fiona, rather desperately avoiding the swings of the shovel, stepped back into some loose rocks and fell flat on her back. Lila raised the shovel over her head, obviously planning to bring it down as hard as she could. But the angle implied she meant to use the flat of the shovel, not the edge, which was an interesting choice.

Taro tackled Lila when the shovel was an arm's length above Fiona's head. Fiona had been rolling away, but it looked doubtful she'd have been able to roll far enough fast enough. The shovel went flying and Taro and Lila landed on the rocky ground with an audible crunch.

Lila was on the bottom. That must have hurt. Yet immediately, she started screaming and struggling. She managed to push Taro off of her, but by that time I had reached them, and I jumped on her. I didn't aim for any kind of finesse. I just sat on her back.

With grimaces and groans, Fiona staggered to her feet. "You've been behind everything, all the accidents, haven't you?" she accused Lila.

Lila went still and silent.

My breath caught in my throat as images and ideas slotted into place. Lila, a servant, newly hired. She would know where Fiona was, what she was doing. She would be able to move about the manor, move about anywhere, without anyone questioning or even really noticing.

But why?

"Did you try to kill me in my room?"

No answer.

Fiona kicked the ground near Lila's face. "Tell me!"

Lila said nothing.

"You removed the rope from the cave. And I'll wager you cobbled the wind rock."

I remembered how insistent Lila had been that Fiona had to go out that day, regardless of the weather. "Answer her," I ordered.

Which I knew was stupid as soon as the words left my mouth. If she wasn't going to obey Fiona, she certainly wasn't going to obey me.

"Fine," Fiona spat. "You don't need to tell me. I know what I need to know. You tried to kill me today. I have two witnesses to it. That's all I need to find you guilty of attempted murder and have you executed."

Really? She could do that? For crimes committed against herself? Didn't they need someone who wasn't personally involved to make those kinds of decisions?

Fiona's threat finally got a reaction out of Lila. "You wouldn't dare," she smirked. "You and your cousin and his whore are the only ones who saw anything."

I blinked. I didn't think I'd ever been called that before.

"What were you playing at?" Taro demanded. "You were always so eager to tell me when Shield Mallorough was with Academic Reid. You kept walking in on us at times when any servant worth her bells would know not to interrupt. Was that part of some plan?"

Huh. It had never occurred to me that Lila's invasions of our suite at the most inopportune moments could have been deliberate. What would have been the point of it?

Lila didn't respond to that charge. She had a more serious one to justify. "You won't be enough to convince the people you have the right to kill me. They'll riot and you'll lose everything."

Fiona knelt down close to her head. "I don't care," she said in a low voice.

And I believed her. She would execute Lila, regardless of the consequences. Her resolution was chilling to witness.

Lila believed her, too, and she started squirming. I had gotten lax and was easily shoved off.

Taro opened up to channel, and almost before I knew it he had sunk Lila's arms, legs and part of her chest into the ground. Only her back and her head remained above the ground. It looked uncomfortable and I imagined it was a horrible position to be in.

Her eyes went impossibly wide, practically bulging in her face. Her skin grew pale. I could see her jerking against the ground, trying to free herself and failing.

And she was screaming. I didn't blame her. I'd descend into panic, too.

"Let me out!" she shrieked.

"No, I don't think so," Taro said mildly.

"I can't breathe!"

It sounded to me like she was breathing well enough, if she could make that much noise.

"Then tell us what we want to know."

"The Emperor will punish you!" she shouted.

"The Emperor doesn't give a damn about how I discipline murderous servants," said Fiona.

"I have the protection of the Emperor!"

What an odd, deluded little creature.

"Don't be a fool. The Emperor has little enough re-spect for titleholders. He's certainly not going to be con-cerned about a servant."

"Ask him yourself!"

"I'm not going to seek the Emperor's attention for a situation I can handle myself."

"If you kill me without contacting the Emperor, he will call you a traitor and kill you and take this land from your family. He's just looking for an excuse to do it."

That didn't make sense. If he wanted the land, why was he so eager for Taro to be the titleholder?

Of course, we didn't know that he did. That was just something the Dowager was saying.

Lila closed her eyes and squirmed, another attempt to free herself. When that didn't work, she screamed.

"You're not getting out until you tell us what we want to know," Fiona said coolly.

Lila continued to scream. I looked back up the shore, where, beyond the bend and out of sight, there were doz-ens of people working. Lila's screams didn't seem to bring anyone running.

We waited.

Lila eventually descended into mere gasps for breath.

"Tell me," said Fiona.

"He sent me," Lila said.

"Who sent you to do what?"

"The Emperor sent me. To kill you."

Shock had me sitting on the ground with a painful thud. The Emperor had sent someone to kill Fiona. My gods. How was that possible? What the hell was going on?

An Emperor trying to have a titleholder assassinated. He had no legal tools available for acting against Fiona. I had no doubt she was meeting every requirement de-manded by her role, and she hadn't yet spent any time at the Imperial court, so she couldn't have gotten herself in any trouble with any political games.

Lila had been trying to make Fiona's death look accidental, in the beginning. That was why the original attempts had been so clumsy and had fallen so short of the mark. The Emperor hadn't wanted anyone to know that Fiona had been murdered. But Fiona was strong in mind and body. She hadn't panicked when we'd been trapped in the cave, the wrong person, namely me, had been shoved out into the fog, and Fiona had survived being out in the wind, so Lila had moved on to more direct measures. Maybe that was why she'd been using the flat of the shovel. Maybe she thought a blow from a flat instrument would look less like murder, somehow.

"If you let me live, I won't tell the Emperor you're letting your tenants use spells," Lila said desperately. She looked at Taro. "I won't tell anyone you and your Shield are using spells. I saw you this morning. I haven't told the Guards, but I could."

What a unique strategy for pleading for your life. List all the reasons why someone would want you dead.

"Why were you interfering with Lee and me?" Taro demanded.

"He wanted me to poison your bond," she said. "He wanted the Shield gone."

As did the Dowager. "Why?"

"I don't know! I don't know! Let me out!"

And just like that, slabs and chunks of the ridge started tumbling down. Thundering groans filled the air.

"Get her out!" I shouted at Taro.

"Run!" he shouted back.

I thought we were far enough away to be out of danger. The crashing rock quickly proved me wrong, and Fiona, Taro and I had to run into the freezing water to avoid the damage.

Lila was screaming.

"Get her out!" I demanded.

I felt Taro's protections lower.

The rocks leapt onto Lila. They covered her completely. Her screams were cut off.

More and more slabs and rock piled on top of her. I cringed.

We waited. We had to, to make sure there was no more to slide.

"Think she's all right?" Fiona asked.

I winced. That was a stupid question. I didn't imagine Lila could have survived that. She had been completely exposed and unable to move.

A terrible way to die.

Could Taro have gotten her out?

I looked at him. He seemed shaken. But then, he had gotten used to sinking people into the ground without any consequences.

A few moments later, a handful of people ran around the bend in the ridge.

"Wait!" Fiona yelled. "Bring more spears! Lila is buried under there!"

Rods were brought over, and the rocks were attacked to dig out a woman I suspected was dead. That left me with a poisonous feeling in my stomach. Whatever she had done, no matter what her filthy schemes with the Emperor, she hadn't deserved to die like that.

Night was coming by the time Lila's body was uncovered. She was indeed dead, and if anyone thought it strange that she was more than half-buried in the dirt, they didn't say anything. All digging ceased after that. It was deemed too dangerous to continue searching. Climbing back over the ridge nearly killed me, it seemed, and when we got to the manor, Bailey had hot food and baths waiting for us.

I slept. I couldn't help sleeping. But I had horrible dreams about strangling Lila and my hands dripping with her blood.

Chapter Thirty

Two more days were spent digging people out of the rubble. By the third day, everyone we found was dead. It was demoralizing. People wanted to keep digging, but they couldn't afford to leave their work any longer.

The next morning, Fiona asked us to join her for breakfast in the sitting room. It was earlier than I liked, but of course we went. She had Stacin in her lap, and I found that heartbreaking. Would he have any memory of his father?

"I just wanted to thank you for all your help," said Fiona, her words slurred with weariness.

"It was merely part of our duty," Taro told her.

"I imagine there are Pairs who would think such labor beneath them."

"Perhaps, but they would be wrong," I said. "Has there been any word about Radia?"

Fiona smiled. "It looks like she will live, and keep the leg. Browne is wonderfully skilled. And dedicated. She has filled her cottage with the wounded and is seeing to them day and night. I've sent Avkas to give her any assistance she might need. He has gentle hands. And I've brought Roshni here so she can get some peace, but she might be up to visitors."

I would see her once Fiona dismissed us. "I'm curious. If something permanent had happened to Radia, who would have been your Wind Watcher?"

"We would have had to rely on someone who didn't have the talent for it, which would have been much less effective. One of the reasons I'm teasing Roshni about Tarce is that, as far as I know, no one has caught her eye. We need her to have some children so she passes down the talent."

Well, that had to be annoying. I was delighted that the ability to Shield was not genetic. While I would like to have children eventually, if it were possible, I didn't want anyone bothering me about it.

Reid walked in and seemed surprised to see us all. "Good morning, everyone." He poured himself some coffee.

"How does your translation go?" Fiona asked.

"I've just finished making a second copy," he said, sitting on the settee beside Fiona's. "I will keep one copy for myself, if that is acceptable. I'd like to show it to some of my colleagues. I can promise you they'll be discreet."

Fiona nodded.

"You should find the book interesting reading. And you might like to have Shield Mallorough look at it as well."

I had pretty much read the thing already, in dribs and drabs.

"The Guards have demanded a copy, too, have they not?"

"They have demanded it." Reid blew on his coffee. "I informed them that if they wanted a copy, they would have to apply to you. I've prepared documents you might want to give them if they do decide to ask you."

He'd created a false interpretation of the book. He was wily for an academic.

"So you're leaving us, then?" Fiona asked.

"I'll be leaving today. I hope to reach Rushed Caps within the week. I have a colleague who will be most eager to see this."

Discreet or not, I didn't think it was wise of Reid to be showing the book to anyone else, but Fiona didn't seem distressed, and hers was the opinion that mattered.

I glanced at Taro. He didn't seem to feel any reaction to Reid's departure. Good. So he shouldn't.

Hiroki rushed into the room. "My lady," he gasped. "The Guards have taken Healer Browne! They saw some of her healing tools and they claim they're for casting. They're going to flog her in the village square!"

Without a trial? Could they do that?

Fiona swore. "Get my horse, Hiroki," she ordered, and the young man ran out. "Frances!"

Fiona's personal maid walked into the room. Did she hover around her mistress at all hours to be readily available?

Fiona handed Stacin to Frances. "Tell Bailey to have all the strongest of the staff go to the village square as soon as they can." And then she ran from the room, too.

Taro and I followed her out the back of the house. A horse was in front of the stable, a groom in the process of tightening the cinch. Without a word Fiona mounted the horse and kicked it into a canter and then a gallop.

Taro and I didn't wait for permission or help. We chose two horses, threw their tack on, and were on their backs as quickly as possible.

It wasn't a long ride to the village, and we got there pretty much on Fiona's heels. Everyone was gathered in the square, shouting and booing. The village didn't have a flogging post, because they weren't barbarians. The Imperial Guards had commandeered a wagon and were trying to tie Browne to one of the wheels. This process was being hampered by the blacksmith and his two apprentices, who were pulling the Guards away and standing between Browne and the wheel. The First Lieutenant had a whip but didn't have the space to use it. No fists had flown and no swords had been drawn, but I had a feeling it wouldn't be long before they were.

"Stand aside!" Fiona shouted. "Stand aside! Stand aside!"

It took some time to get the people to pay attention to her, to get them moving out of the way. She slowly forced her horse forward.

The Imperial Guards noticed, of course. The First Lieutenant shouted something, but I couldn't hear it over the noise of the crowd.

I was thrilled that the tenants were protecting Browne. In High Scape, corporal punishment was a form of entertainment. I didn't know if I could bear to watch Browne being beaten. If she was going through it, the least I could do was bear witness, but I didn't think I had the fortitude for it.

Then Fiona was shouting, and I couldn't hear her, either.

This was getting ridiculous. "Will everyone shut the hell up?" I shouted.

The sudden silence was shocking and gratifying. Who knew I could do that? That had never worked at any other time in my life.

"This woman," the First Lieutenant announced, "has been found with books, purporting to instruct readers in the use of spells, and the tools used to attempt to carry out those spells. She is in flagrant violation of the law."

"Those are books and tools of healing," Fiona sneered. "I doubt you can appreciate the difference."

"It's interesting that you mention her ability to heal, Lady Westsea. She has a patient who should have lost her leg and possibly her life, and yet she has lost neither."

"And you're claiming Healer Browne cast a spell to accomplish this?" Fiona scoffed. "How very provincial of you."

The First Lieutenant flushed with anger. "Of course not."

"So you're saying Healer Browne pretended to cast a spell and that somehow caused the Wind Watcher to survive?"

"That doesn't make sense," the First Lieutenant snapped.

"You're quite right, and that leaves us with the only possible answer. Healer Browne is an effective healer and she doesn't use spells to do it."

"Don't attempt to twist things, Westsea." The First Lieutenant pulled a small book from beneath his belt. "This is a book of spells. She has fifteen others like it. That earns her—"

The blacksmith whipped the book out of the First Lieutenant's hands and passed it to another tenant. The book quickly disappeared into the crowd.

"Return that immediately," the First Lieutenant ordered, to no effect.

Fiona laughed. "I see no book of spells, First Lieutenant."

"You think this amusing?" he demanded, outraged.

Fiona's expression hardened. "I think you're ridiculous," she said. "Did you really think you could come here and flog people with no legal procedure?"

"We follow the Emperor's orders."

"Then the Emperor forgets himself, for not even his orders can supersede the law. These are my people, and I will not see them beaten on nothing more than your word. And if the Emperor has a problem with that, he can come here and tell me himself."

And then, to my surprise, everyone cheered. It was heartening, in a way, but it was also kind of disappointing. Had they really thought Fiona would let Browne be flogged by those interlopers?

"I think you've overstayed your welcome," Fiona said once she could be heard again. "You'll be escorted back to the manor, where you'll pick up your possessions, and then you'll be escorted off my land, and you can go back to the Emperor and tell him whatever the hell you want."

"You'll regret this," the First Lieutenant warned her.

"Perhaps, but not today, and tomorrow will have to take care of itself."

The blacksmith and his apprentices, along with Bailey and two footmen, escorted the Imperial Guards away. The miller was untying Browne from the wheel, and Fiona went to talk to her. I couldn't hear them from where I stood. "Fiona's going to pay for this," I said.

"Aye," said Taro. "But that will be in the future. I doubt she could have lived with herself if she had let Nab be flogged. From the sounds of it, Nab wouldn't have survived it."

"I agree, but she's walking a dangerous path. And she's all alone against him. When he chooses to, he'll squash her like a slug."

"Well, he's annoying the Triple S, too," Taro reminded me. "Maybe they can stand against him together."

Standing against the Emperor? Was that what we were saying? Were we insane? "So they can get squashed like two slugs."

"Don't borrow trouble."

He had a point there. And there was nothing I could do about any of it in any case.

Later that evening, the overmantel was emptied of its contents. The books were returned to the library. Fiona distributed the knives and the hairball and all the other items. I would have preferred to keep the books hidden in our suite, so I could read them unnoticed.

I wondered what the Guards were going to tell the Emperor about Taro and me. Did they suspect that I had used spells? Had Lila really told them nothing?

Was Lila even her real name?

I knew it was a waste of effort to worry about the future, but I couldn't help it. It seemed to me that Fiona was bent on aggravating the Emperor at every step. Sooner or later he would feel forced to stomp on her.

I liked her. I didn't want her harmed. There was just nothing I could do about it.

Chapter Thirty-one

To Shield Mallorough

As you have reported no difficulty in channeling, we have determined it is in our best interests to have your Pair remain in Flown Raven.

Good health to you,
Shield Kayan Lucitani
Secretary
Source and Shield Service

So few words to deliver such disappointing news. I didn't understand it. It was against Triple S policy. So what if we could channel? Barely. With the help of a spell. Which I couldn't tell them about. Why wouldn't they move us? If for no other reason but to show the Emperor who had control over the Triple S?

It was in the Triple S's best interest to have us stay in Flown Raven. What the hell did that mean?

Damn it, I'd been so sure they were going to move us.

It made perfect sense to move us. Transfer in a Pair who had no previous connections to the place, who didn't care about the Dowager Duchess, who wouldn't be a walking reminder of the family the tenants thought should be the titleholders, who would easily protect Flown Raven from natural disasters with no difficulties.

What was going on?

I sighed as I folded the letter into a tight little square. I really couldn't believe it.

We were staying in Flown Raven. For at least a few more years. In a place where the weather was always grim. In a place where we couldn't ignore the fact that the titleholder was barely hanging on to her authority. In a place where Taro's mother lived.

A slew of the servants had left, either frightened by the partial destruction of the ridge or infuriated that they'd been forced to dig through it looking for corpses. Some of the tenants had left for the same reason. It wasn't right. Fiona didn't deserve that.

I wouldn't have blamed her if she'd packed up her son and moved back to Centerfield, letting the estate fall into ruin. It wasn't as though she actually needed it to live well, with her own lands still earning money.

I would miss her if she left. She was one of the few sane people around.

I changed into a dark purple gown before going to the second-floor guest rooms. A quick knock on the door was answered with permission to enter. I stepped into the nicely appointed bedchamber that was housing Radia as she recuperated.

A maid I didn't know was collecting a meal tray. She curtsied before she left. I believed she was a new hire. I hoped she had nothing to do with the Emperor.

I sat in a chair drawn close to the bed. "How are you feeling?"

Radia, propped up on pillows, shrugged. "Only mildly uncomfortable. The healer has given me a serum that dulls the pain. It makes me thirsty, though, and leaves my mind smokey."

"Shall I get you something to drink?"

"No, no, I just had some water."

I would have liked to have had something useful to do, if only for a moment, to have had something to do with my hands. "How long will you need to be laid up?"

"Browne said nearly two months."

"That's a long time," I said with sympathy.

"I'm more worried about the fischen being sounded when needed."

That was the horn that was blown to warn the people of strong winds, and it, out of all her possessions, had survived the collapse of the tower. "Where is it?"

"In Lord Tarce's suite." She winced. "He has claimed responsibility for sounding it."

I grinned. "Has he, now?"

"He said it was the duty of the family to make sure the warnings were sounded while I was incapacitated."

"That makes sense."

"Aye, but Lord Tarce." She grimaced again.

"You don't think he'll do a good job?"

"I don't even know if he can get a note out of the horn, but no one else is available to do it. I can't even imagine why Lord Tarce volunteered."

"Do you not?" Of course she did. The girl wasn't stupid, after all. She just didn't want to talk about it. I didn't blame her, but I was sorely tempted to harass her about him, now that she couldn't run away.

"I regret that I won't be able to go to the funeral today," said Radia. "I believe Lady Westsea will need all the friendly support she can get."

The day was going to be pure hell for Fiona. The funeral was to commemorate both Dane's death and the deaths of those who had been killed by the rock slide. I had no doubt Fiona would have preferred a separate small ceremony just for Dane, but I didn't feel it was my place

to ask her why she wasn't having one. Holding the ceremony for everyone at once would mean Fiona would have
to show more concern for her tenants than for her own
loss, or someone would have something negative to say
about her. "I'm hoping the people who remained are the
ones who feel some loyalty toward her," I responded.

"They could merely be the ones too cowardly to leave
their homes."

"As long as they're prepared to support Fiona as they
should, I don't care what their motives are."

There was a knock on the door, and upon being bid to
enter, Taro stuck his head in the room. "Lee, they're starting to gather."

"Do you need anything before I go?" I asked Radia,
and she shook her head.

I joined Taro in the hallway, feeling a little uncomfortable in his presence as I had been for the past week. It still
upset me that he had failed to release Lila before the rocks
crushed her. I thought he'd had time to free her. And yet,
I wasn't sure I was right. He was the only one who could
bury people that way, after all.

He knew it still bothered me. He wasn't an idiot. But
we hadn't had an argument about it yet. I didn't know
what I could say that wasn't purely accusing him of deliberately killing her. I didn't believe that was what had happened. I was just so unsettled.

Despite the privacy Lila's absence had granted us, Taro
and I still hadn't slept together. Since Lila's death, we
hadn't laughed together, either. Taro was fairly formal
with me, and to be honest I appreciated that distance while
I tried to figure out how I felt about him.

We went out behind the manor. Fiona was already
there, as were many of the members of her staff, a handful
of tenants and almost every aristocrat in the area. Fiona
looked grim but well rested. I didn't know whether to talk
to her or not, so I settled on not. Noninterference was usually the better path of action.

The ceremony began. It required over twenty children to bring the personal tokens of the dead to the fire. The speeches about the dead took hours. And I could feel the anger in the crowd, see it in the glances sent Fiona's way, hear it in their clipped words.

Myself, I glared at the Dowager Duchess. She could have made this easier for Fiona. As a member of the original family of titleholders, she could have assured the tenants that nothing important would change when Fiona took the title, that they would be taken care of. Instead, she had helped poison their minds against Fiona.

Simone wasn't with her, or anywhere in the crowd. Maybe she had gone home. I wondered if that meant the Dowager had given up her plot to separate Taro and me.

The speeches wound down. After that, there would be eating and drinking. The drinking would include alcoholic beverages. Given the current mood of the people, I thought that was a bad idea.

But Fiona didn't dismiss everyone to the gardens. "I am the Duchess of Westsea," she announced. "I am the titleholder of this land, made so by tradition and law. Many of you have forgotten what that means. I have chosen this day and this time to remind you."

I expected whispers of resentment. There was silence.

"I, as titleholder, have responsibilities to you. I am to protect you from the incursions of others. I am to maintain law and order on my land and my waters. I am to provide aid and support during times of crisis. When the ridge fell, I did not hide in the manor and order others to risk their lives digging for survivors. I led them." That had a few people nodding. "I did not stand by and let Healer Browne be executed, but risked my position with the Emperor to protect her. This you must acknowledge." She paused, and while there were no shouts of agreement, I didn't hear much in the way of denial, either. "Your responsibilities to me include tithing, obeying the laws I establish, and loyalty. That many of you have failed in the latter, you must acknowledge." Some more mutters, but again, no outright denials. "I admit, most of that is my fault. I did not have you take an oath of fealty when I first came, thinking that an old-fashioned and unnecessary custom. I've come to realize my mistake. You need that ceremony, to remind you all what I am, and what you owe me. And so, we shall perform it now."

I had witnessed such a ceremony before. I found it demeaning, but I couldn't deny that something had to be done.

"You have chosen to remain here. Already you have proven yourself braver and more honorable than your brethren. But I still require your oath. Anyone who feels unable to give me their fealty will be out of their cottage within seven days."

That brought some protests, but Fiona merely stood there waiting for silence, and in a short while, she got it.

"The Dowager Duchess may be first," she announced.

My jaw dropped as my gaze snapped to the face of the Dowager Duchess. She looked stunned. I couldn't remember seeing her look so shocked before. It was hysterical.

"Don't be ridiculous," she snapped.

"You will show the others how it's done. From what I understand, my predecessor didn't hold the ceremony, either."

From what I knew of Taro's elder brother, he wasn't in Flown Raven long enough after receiving the title to perform any kind of ritual.

"I will not," said the Dowager in outrage, her usual frosty demeanor nowhere in sight.

"Then you will vacate the dowager house within seven days."

"You are required by law to maintain me in that house."

"I am required by law to maintain you, but not necessarily in that house. I can settle you elsewhere, somewhere far from here, where you will have no influence over others."

Send her away, woman. Her oath of loyalty would probably be worthless anyway.

"You wouldn't dare," said the Dowager.

"I most certainly would," said the Duchess.

"You certainly don't expect me to kneel."

The Duchess looked at Frances, who, apparently the only one to have been taken into her confidence about her plans for the day, took from a bag a small, rolled-up carpet and spread it on the ground before Fiona's feet.

Taro snickered.

We waited for a while in silence.

"If you're going to refuse," said the Duchess, "you might as well go to the dowager house and start packing now."

The Dowager glared at her, her expression sparking with hatred and resentment. She started walking toward the Duchess, and I suspected she was going to use this opportunity to smack the Duchess a good one across the face. I put the tips of my fingers against my lower lip, waiting for the inevitable blow.

The Dowager was very stiff as she lowered herself to her knees on the carpet before the Duchess. Gasps sounded out around me. I may have emitted one myself.

"I, the Dowager Duchess of Westsea," she said through her teeth, "offer to the Duchess of Westsea, and her heirs, my eternal loyalty and that of my heirs, the best of my holdings, and obedience to her laws."

"I, Lady Fiona Sterling Diane Keplar, Duchess of Westsea, accept the services of the Dowager Duchess and offer in turn my strength and my judgment." The Duchess knelt, grabbed up a handful of dirt, and held it before the Dowager. The Dowager raised her hand, palm up, and the Duchess deposited the dirt in it.

The Dowager immediately rose to her feet, brushing the dirt from her hands. She turned on her heel and headed back toward the dowager house.

"The next may proceed," the Duchess called, and more

than one person stepped forward to receive their clump of dirt.

As I watched person after person step forward, I had the sensation of something unsettled finding its place within me, stronger than the slight jittery feeling that was also present. The people who stepped forward to swear their loyalty all appeared sincere. I believed things would be much better in Flown Raven from then on.

What I did find interesting was that Fiona didn't require Taro or me to swear an oath. And so she shouldn't. We weren't supposed to swear oaths to titleholders. I supposed a part of me feared that the Emperor had set a precedent that others, even Fiona, might feel compelled to follow.

The Emperor and his damned oath. Lila had claimed that the Emperor had wanted Fiona killed and Taro alienated from me. The Dowager also wanted to separate Taro from me, and claimed that the Emperor still wanted Taro to hold the Westsea title. The Emperor continued to be interested in Taro. I couldn't see that changing. And that was going to be a problem.